He's not just the boss, he's the best there is!

Top-Notch Men!

Three heart-warming medical marvels from Melanie Milburne, Margaret McDonagh and Anne Fraser

Top-Notch Men!

MELANIE MILBURNE

MARGARET McDONAGH

ANNE FRASER

First published in Great Britain 2012
by Mills & Boon, an imprint of Harlequin (UK) Limited,
Eton House, 18-24 Paradise Road, Richmond, Surrey TW9 1SR

In Her Boss's Special Care, *A Doctor Worth Waiting For* and *Dr Campbell's Secret Son* were first published in Great Britain by Harlequin (UK) Limited.

ISBN: 978 0 263 89701 2
ebook ISBN: 978 1 408 97067 6

05-0912

Printed and bound in Spain
by Blackprint CPI, Barcelona

IN HER BOSS'S SPECIAL CARE

BY

MELANIE MILBURNE

Dear Reader,

One of the great privileges of being a writer is spending time with your beloved characters, talking to them, getting to know them, playing with them and then at the end of the book leaving them to get on with your own life. I guess it's a bit like being a grandparent—at the end of the day you hand the little darlings back!

How easy would it be for people like my hero Joel and his parents to walk away from what life has dished out to them? Such a dilemma was the premise for this novel and I couldn't think of a better heroine than Allegra Tallis, who showed such amazing compassion and hope against all odds.

However, outside of romantic literature not every story has a happy ending, and it is for this reason I dedicated this book to my three nephews and nieces, who daily deal with the human tragedy of what Joel Addison had to face.

My special thoughts and heartfelt love to all who have to do the same.

Melanie Milburne

Melanie Milburne says: "I am married to a surgeon, Steve, and have two gorgeous sons, Paul and Phil. I live in Hobart, Tasmania, where I enjoy an active life as a long-distance runner and a nationally ranked top ten Master's swimmer. I also have a Master's Degree in Education, but my children totally turned me off the idea of teaching! When not running or swimming I write, and when I'm not doing all of the above I'm reading. And if someone could invent a way for me to read during a four-kilometre swim I'd be even happier!"

To my nephews and niece Ben, Tommy, Peter and Katherine (Kathy) McNamara. You have all been through so much in your young lives and I am in awe of how you have coped. I love each of you very dearly and dedicate this book to you in acknowledgement of your struggles, your tragedies and your joys that I will always share with you, not with a glance of pity but with the steady gaze of compassion.

I would also like to give my heartfelt thanks and appreciation to the doctors and nursing staff of the Royal Hobart Hospital's Intensive Care Unit for their invaluable help in the research conducted for this novel, as well as Dee Nally from Salamanca Pharmacy for her advice. Thank you all!

CHAPTER ONE

'WHAT do you mean, he wants me to stop my research on the coma recovery assessment project?' Allegra Tallis asked the nursing sister on duty in Intensive Care. 'That's outrageous. The CEO gave me his full support, I've got ethics approval and I've got funding!'

Louise Banning gave her a sympathetic look. 'I know all that but Dr Addison is the new Director of ICTU and A and E now, and what he says goes.'

'Not if I can help it,' Allegra growled. 'I'm not giving up months of research to satisfy some control freak's demands to run a tight ship. Who does he think he is anyway? He might be the new director but if he thinks he can tell me what to—'

'Dr Tallis?' A deep male voice spoke from just behind her. 'We haven't had the opportunity to meet since I arrived. I'd like to speak to you in my office—now, if you don't mind.'

Allegra swung around to see a tall dark-haired man in his early thirties towering over her, the deep brown intensity of his eyes as they connected with hers making her throat move up and down involuntarily in a tiny swallow.

'Oh…Dr Addison. Well, I'm just seeing a patient right now…' she said.

His gaze hardened as one dark brow lifted in an arc of derision. 'Sister Banning is your patient, is she?'

Allegra tightened her mouth. 'No, of course not—I mean in the unit. I can see you in about five minutes.'

'Make if four,' he said. 'I've got a crammed schedule this morning.' He continued on this way, his starched white coat brushing against her arm as he went past.

Louise's brows rose expressively once he was out of their hearing. 'Not the best first meeting, I would say.'

'No.' Allegra frowned crossly. 'Well, I've been on night shift for the last week. I wasn't here for his welcome thingy.' She twisted her mouth and added, 'God, what a pompous idiot.'

'Yes, but a rather good-looking idiot, don't you think?'

She gave a little snort. 'If you have a thing for the tall, dark, brooding type.'

'You never know—he might improve on acquaintance,' Louise said. 'He's got a very good reputation. He's been head-hunted especially for the post so he can't be all that difficult to work with.'

'Yeah, well, I still think Dougal Brenton should have got the job,' Allegra said. 'He's been at Melbourne Memorial for years, and instead they bring in someone just because he's worked overseas in a war zone.'

Louise glanced at her watch. 'Could be this will be a war zone if you don't keep your appointment with him,' she said. 'I'll keep on eye on things here. You'd better go.'

'Thanks, I won't be long.'

Dr Joel Addison's office was in the middle of the multi-million-dollar newly built intensive care and trauma unit, providing the city of Melbourne with a state-of-the-art trauma and acute care centre—in fact, the largest in the country. With twenty-six ICU beds, a burns unit, a ten-bed trauma receiving area and two fully equipped operating rooms all in the same complex, it offered a breadth of care in one site that was second to none.

Allegra gave the director's door a quick hard knock and waited for the command to come in. When he gave it in a blunt one-word response, she opened the door to find him seated behind his desk with a large pile of paperwork spread out before him.

He rose as she came in, his height seeming all the more intimidating in the confines of his office.

He offered her a hand across his desk. 'We haven't met formally. I'm Joel Addison, the new director of ICTU and A and E.'

Allegra placed her hand in his briefly, her eyes skittering away from the chocolate-brown depths of his. 'Allegra Tallis.'

'Please, sit down, Dr Tallis,' he said. He waited until she was seated before resuming his own seat, his dark eyes steady on hers. 'You're an anaesthetist, I believe.'

'Yes. I'm on a twelve-month rotation in ICTU,' she answered, trying not to fidget like a naughty schoolgirl called into the headmaster's office. Her mouth felt suddenly dry and she would have loved to run her tongue over her lips to moisten them, but didn't dare do so with those dark, fathomless eyes seemingly watching her every movement.

A heavy silence pulsed for a moment or two. Allegra felt each thrumming second of it, wondering what he was thinking behind the screen of his darkly handsome features.

She hadn't had time to reapply her lipstick and her hair was falling from its clip at the back of her head. Heaven knew what her eyes looked like after a week of night duty. She'd barely been able to see out of them that morning when she'd dragged herself out of bed, but she knew there were shadows on top of shadows beneath them that no amount of cover-up could have concealed.

Her brief meeting with him in the corridor hadn't given her time to examine his face in any detail but now she could see how lean and chiselled his cleanly shaven jaw was. His skin was tanned, as if he spent outdoors whatever time he had away from the hospital. His hair was thick and dark with a hint of a wave running through it, and the way it was currently styled it looked as if his long fingers had been its most recent combing tool. His eyes were a deep brown, so dark she couldn't tell what size his pupils were as they seemed to be indistinguishable from his irises.

'I've heard some interesting things about you, Dr Tallis,' he said into the silence.

'Oh?'

He leaned back in his seat, his posture positively reeking of indolent superiority as his eyes held hers. 'Yes.'

She held his unwavering gaze with steely determination, not even allowing herself to blink. 'And?'

'I have some concerns about your research project. I find it hard to justify. I would appreciate your explanation of its scientific merit. As far as I can see, it would be more appropriate at a mind and body expo than in an ICU unit.'

Allegra straightened her spine, her green eyes flashing with fury at his condescending attitude. 'I've had full ethics approval for my coma recovery assessment project,' she informed him. 'And I have a research grant from the hospital.'

'The ethics is not what I take issue with, Dr Tallis, it's the scientific merit, unfortunately, in my opinion, spelt out by the first letters of the project name. As far as I can see, the research committee seemed swayed by factors other than scientific validity.'

She shifted in her seat again. 'I don't exactly know what you're getting at, but if you read the proposal…' It hit her then, the acronym he had made of her project. CRAP. She inwardly seethed but she was loath to allow him the credit of making a joke out of something she took very seriously.

His cool little smile already suggested to her his inbuilt cynicism. She'd seen scepticism before, but somehow Dr Joel Addison took it to a whole new level. She silently fumed at his attitude, wishing yet again that Dougal Brenton had been given the job of new director.

'I have read it—several times. How long have you been at Melbourne Memorial?' he said.

'I did my training here,' she answered.

'So you haven't worked anywhere else?'

It was amazing how someone who had worked overseas always had to hold it over the heads of those who hadn't, Allegra thought resentfully. She'd seen it time and time again. Even registrars, who, after a short stint in the UK or even in a developing country, came back with a superior attitude, as if Australia was a backwater wasteland with limited training experiences.

'No,' she said with more than a hint of sarcasm. 'I haven't as yet had that wonderful privilege.'

He ignored her comment to ask, 'What is the gist of this project—in one sentence?'

Allegra forced her shoulders to relax, wanting to come across as coolly efficient and in control. 'I'm examining the effect on coma recovery of different methods of sensory contact, using a BIS monitor as a key detector of effect,' she said.

'Sensory contact…' He lifted one dark brow in query. 'Such as?'

She gave him a very direct look, mentally preparing herself for his reaction, a reaction she had seen far too many times to hope that this time would be any different. 'Reiki therapy, massage therapy, music therapy and aromatherapy.'

'So…' The leather of his chair creaked as he leaned back even further, his expression unmistakably mocking. 'It sounds to me that if ever I'm feeling a little tense in the shoulders, I should head right on down to ICTU, feign a coma in one of the incredibly expensive beds and hope for a quick massage from you. Is that right, Dr Tallis?'

Allegra felt her anger rising to an almost intolerable level. 'I believe that human touch is an important part of a patient's recovery, comatose or not,' she said through tight lips.

'Important—I doubt it,' he returned. 'What ICU specialises in is ensuring good oxygenation and blood pressure maintenance—if brain injury is not too severe, recovery will occur. As far as I can see, these alternative therapies are marginal at best, maybe counter-productive at worst. There is no scientific evidence that they are effective, and attempts to prove their unlikely effectiveness are unaffordable in this unit.'

'That's not true. Reiki therapy has been shown to increase local circulation and—'

'Dr Tallis.' The little mocking smile was still in place. 'Increasing the circulation by touching someone's arm is not the same as increasing cerebral blood flow. And these smells and so-called natural aromas, your oils or whatever—what if someone suffers an allergic reaction to them?'

'I've done a literature review on—'

'I've seen the "literature review", as you call it, hardly peer-reviewed journals—more like the latest women's magazines.'

'That's so totally unfair!'

'Look, Dr Tallis, you've spent—what is it now?—six years at medical school and a further four years studying anaesthesia. It's called medical science. That's what we practise here, and it's damn expensive. Leave the quackery to the quacks and let's get on with the job of saving lives. That is what you have been trained to do and that is your primary responsibility while you are working in ICTU.'

'Patrick Naylor, the CEO, has given me his approval,' she put in with a tilt of her chin.

He held her defiant gaze for an infinitesimal pause, before asking, 'Is it true that you and he are an item?'

Allegra felt hot colour rush up into her face. How had he found out about her one dinner with Patrick? How had *anyone* found out about it? One date did not constitute a relationship as far as she was concerned and, besides, Patrick was still getting over a nasty separation. She had agreed to have dinner with him more because she had felt sorry for him than any degree of attraction on her part. It had been her first date in eighteen months and certainly no one's business but her own.

'I hardly see that my private life is any concern of yours,' she said with a heated glare.

'No, indeed, but if it interferes with how ICTU is run then

it becomes of great concern to me. I'm here to put ICTU at Melbourne Memorial on the map as best practice for trauma reception and acutely ill patients, and I will not tolerate either my reputation or that of this hospital with the introduction of alternative "medicine" practices that do not have a scientific leg to stand on. We've a got a big enough workload with conventional medical care.'

Allegra got stiffly to her feet. 'The work I'm doing on my project does not interfere with my regular workload. I do most of it in my spare time.'

He rose to his feet, his superior height immediately casting a shadow over her. 'I'm going to give you a month to get whatever results you can, but then I'm reviewing it. And let me tell you, if there are any complaints about the methods you are using then I'll pull the plug on your study there and then. This is a new unit and every professional and political eye is focused on it to make sure the hefty amount of public money that's been allocated to it has been spent wisely. And my reputation is riding on it as well. I don't want the press to get wind of trauma patients having their tarot cards read as part of their recovery program in ICTU.'

Allegra had never felt so incensed in her life. Her hands were clenched by her sides so she didn't give in to the temptation to slap that supercilious smirk off his face. She didn't trust herself to speak even if she could have located her voice; it seemed to be trapped somewhere in the middle of her throat where a choking nut of anger was firmly lodged.

'Good day, Dr Tallis,' he said, moving past his desk to open the door for her. 'I'm sure you've got patients to see. I don't want to keep you from them any longer.'

She strode past him with her head high, her mouth tight and her eyes sparking with ire.

'Oh, and one more thing,' he said, just as she'd brushed past.

She stopped and turned around to face him, her expression visibly taut with rage. 'Yes?'

His eyes twinkled with something that looked suspiciously like amusement as he took in her flushed features. 'If you don't mind me saying so, for someone who is so into alternative relaxation therapies, you seem a little tense. Have you thought about booking in for a massage yourself?'

'Why?' she asked with a curl of her lip. 'Are you offering your services?'

He suddenly smiled, revealing perfectly even white teeth. 'I'm not sure in this case that my touch would have the desired effect.'

'Not unless I was completely comatose,' she clipped back, and stalked out.

CHAPTER TWO

'HOW did your meeting with the director go?' Louise asked later that morning.

'Grr…' Allegra answered with a fiery look. 'Every time I think of that man I want to punch something.'

'That doesn't sound like you,' Louise remarked. 'You're always the one telling the rest of us how to chill out and relax. Is he really going to put a stop to your study?'

'He's giving me a month to prove that it's worthy of "medical science"—his version of science anyway,' Allegra answered. 'But how can I do anything in a month? It all depends on what patients come in. We haven't had a coma patient since poor Alice Greeson, three weeks ago, and she didn't recover.' She blew out a sigh of frustration. 'I have to change his mind. I really want to do this study, Louise—it's important to me.'

The hospital intercom suddenly blared out in a tinny voice, 'Code Blue, Surgical Ward,' repeating it several times.

'Got to go, Louise,' Allegra said, heading for the lift. 'I'm on the crash team this morning.'

The surgical ward was on the sixth floor, but when Allegra got to the bank of lifts none of them seemed to be moving. She shifted from foot to foot impatiently, before turning and heading for the fire exit. She started running up the stairs two at a time, glad she'd resumed her fitness programme now that Christmas had passed.

When she arrived on the ward the curtains were drawn around one of the beds in room two, the crash trolley, two nurses and the intern already doing cardiac massage on the patient.

'What's the story?' she asked, as she pushed aside the curtains.

'Sixty-five-year-old male, two days post right hemicolectomy,' the intern answered. 'The nurses were getting him out of bed for a wash and he collapsed. Looks like a PE, maybe an infarct.'

'Is the floor anaesthetist on the way?' Allegra asked.

'He might not be coming,' one of the nurses answered. 'There's some sort of complicated case going on in Theatre that's tied up a lot of staff.'

'I'll intubate him,' Allegra said, moving to the head of the bed and picking up the sucker from the emergency trolley. 'You'll need to help me,' she said to the nurse on her left.

'But I'm just out of grad school,' the young and rather nervous-looking nurse said. 'I'm not sure what I'm doing. I've never been to an arrest before.'

'Just do what I say, you'll be fine. Turn on wall suction,' she said, as she suctioned the patient's mouth and reapplied the oxygen mask. Allegra picked an endotracheal tube and checked the laryngoscope battery. 'OK,' she said to the intern who was bagging the patient between cardiac compressions from the surgical ward nurse, 'I'll tube now. Put on cricoid pressure, will you?'

The intern stepped aside and applied cricoid pressure while Allegra removed the mask from the bag and oxygen. She rapidly intubated the patient and connected the oxygen, handing the bag back to the intern to continue ventilation while she secured the tube. The medical registrar, Peter Newton, had by now arrived and was looking at the ECG trace.

'He's got a rhythm,' he said. 'Looks like VT. We'll need to cardiovert. I'll do it.' He took the paddles from the defibrillator and dialled up 100, applied the paddles to the patient's chest and called, 'Clear.' All staff removed their hands from the patient while the intern continued to ventilate. With a jerk the patient's back arched and then fell back as the current was applied.

'He's in sinus rhythm,' Allegra noted, looking at the monitor. 'What drugs do you want up?' she asked the registrar.

'He's had an infarct is my guess. There's a few VEBs. I'll start a lignocaine infusion, but we need to get him round to ICTU and keep him well oxygenated. I'll contact my boss and bring him round to ICTU for a consult.'

'You look as if you could do with a bit of oxygen yourself,' Allegra said, taking in Peter's flushed features. 'Are you OK?'

He gave her sheepish look. 'The lifts were busy. I had to run up two flights of stairs. I guess I'm not as fit as I thought.'

'Lucky you,' she said as she moved aside for the trolley men who had come to do the transfer. 'I had to run up six.' She gave him a smile and added, 'Go and have a glass of water. I'm going back to ICTU anyway so I'll hand the patient over.'

Allegra accompanied the patient, Gareth Fisher, to ICTU and had not long informed the surgeon, Bruce Crickton, of his patient's condition when the ICTU registrar Danielle Capper approached.

'Dr Tallis, can you help me on bed five?' she asked. 'It's Mr Munsfield, the Whipple procedure. He was extubated yesterday and was doing OK, but his sats have gone down in the last hour and he's on 60 per cent oxygen. He's become febrile and has abdo pain.'

'Sure.' Allegra began walking with Danielle to the far end of ICTU, where bed five was situated. 'Have you had any bloods done?'

'They should be on the fax now in the office. I'll grab them and see you there,' Danielle said.

Allegra reached bed five and after greeting Fiona Clark, the nurse in charge of beds four and five, took a look at the patient, who was pale, slightly cyanosed and very breathless. His sats monitor showed 80 per cent, BP 100 and pulse 110.

'Deep breaths, Mr Munsfield,' Fiona instructed the patient. 'I've just given you some IV morphine for the pain.'

'What was the last temperature, Fiona?' Allegra asked.

'Thirty-nine. It's been up all morning,' Fiona answered.

'Where's the pain, Mr Munsfield?' Allegra addressed the patient gently.

'In...my stomach, and in my back...' he gasped and puffed. 'In the middle of my back...like a knife...'

Danielle arrived with the printouts, accompanied by Joel Addison, who had been collecting pathology reports from the printer. 'Hb is 80, white cell count 25 with neutrophilia, and his amylase and lipase are through the roof, Dr Tallis,' he said, looking intently through the sheath of figures before he met her eyes briefly. 'What do you feel is the problem?'

'Looks like we've got pancreatitis, maybe pancreatic sepsis. Could have an anastomotic leak,' Allegra said.

'I agree. We should also consider an anastomotic leak as the precipitating problem,' he suggested.

'Danielle, get the surgeon down here now. We need an urgent surgical review, and get X-ray up here, too—we need a chest X-ray. Those sats are worse. My guess is adult respiratory distress syndrome.'

'ARDS is almost certain, Dr Tallis. We'll need to intubate pretty much straight away but it's your call,' Joel said, giving her an unreadable look.

Allegra explained to the patient that there was a problem in his abdomen and that it was affecting his lungs, making it hard for him to breathe. She explained the procedure of intubation to him before instructing Fiona to obtain drugs and airway equipment.

'His Hb has dropped too, Dr Tallis,' Joel said, when she'd turned back from the patient. 'There are a couple of cross-matched units left over from surgery.' He turned to address Danielle. 'Can you retrieve those from the blood fridge while I help Dr Tallis here?'

After pre-oxygenating as much as possible, Allegra got Joel to inject 10mg suxamethonium and 10mg diazepam and applied a mask and bag.

'He's hard to inflate. His lungs are stiff with pulmonary

oedema,' she said. 'I'll have to intubate him—he's too hard to keep bagging. Hand me the laryngoscope and tube, Dr Addison.'

Allegra introduced the laryngoscope and attempted intubation but the patient had only been extubated forty-eight hours before and the larynx was red and swollen. To make matters worse, he had a short, bullish neck. She couldn't see the cords and reverted to bag and mask, but could hardly keep a seal on the face with the mask because the insufflation pressure needed was so high.

She muttered a curse under her breath, conscious of Joel watching her every move. 'I'll have to try again. We're in real trouble here.'

'I can see that, but you're the most skilled here at airway management,' Joel said calmly. 'Just tell me how you want me to assist.'

Allegra threw him a quick grateful glance and tried the laryngoscope again but still could not intubate the patient. Mr Munsfield's sats were now 70 per cent and he was looking deeply cyanosed.

'We need to get an airway, Dr Tallis. He's badly hypoxic and throwing off VEBs,' Joel said.

'I can't get a tube in,' she said, her brow beading with perspiration. 'I'll have to do a surgical airway. Open the tray, Dr Addison, stat.'

Joel opened the surgical airway pack on the top of the trolley. Allegra put on sterile gloves and made a transverse incision over the cricothyroid membrane with a disposable scalpel. Taking a pair of artery forceps, she widened the hole, and passed in a cuffed tracheostomy tube and inflated the cuff, then connected the tube to the oxygen bag. The chest rose and fell with each pump on the bag, though the insufflation pressure was high.

Allegra flicked her gaze to the sats monitor, which showed the patient's sats coming up into the 90s. She connected the ventilator and set the dials to cope with the high pressure and poor oxygen exchange.

'Well done, Dr Tallis,' Joel said, briefly placing a hand on her shoulder to steady her. 'That was a top-notch surgical airway under pressure. Things look back under control here. I'll leave you to fill Harry in—he's just arrived.'

He moved off towards the A and E area before Allegra could thank him for his help. She frowned as he went through the swing doors, her feelings towards him undergoing a confusing change which she couldn't quite explain.

The surgical registrar arrived with the consultant, Harry Upton, and was briefed by Allegra.

'He needs to be opened, I agree. The pancreatic anastomosis has probably leaked, and on top of that he's got pancreatitis. Thanks for salvaging the situation, Allegra.'

Danielle filled Harry in on the rest of the patient's details before he turned back to speak to Allegra. 'You look like you could do with a break.'

Allegra blew a wisp of damp hair off her face. 'I'm off for a break right now. It's been one of those mornings.'

'So you've finally met our new director,' Harry said with a twinkle in his eyes. 'I didn't see you at his welcome function last week.'

'I was on nights,' she explained, her mouth tightening a fraction.

Harry grinned at her sour expression. 'So what gives, Allegra? You don't like his…er…aura?'

She gave him a mock reproving look. 'Don't you start, Harry. He totally rubbished my project as if it was a load of pseudoscience. "Can't afford alternative therapies in his science-based unit", I think was how he put it.'

'Yeah, well, I guess he's under a lot of pressure to make this place work,' he said. 'There's a lot of cash been poured into it, and there are a few irate unit directors who think they should have got the funds instead. If it doesn't shape up fast, his head will roll.' He grimaced as his pager went off. 'I'm due in Theatre. I'll see you around. Good work on Mr

Munsfield, by the way. You and Joel Addison make quite an impressive team.'

She gave him another mock reproving glance but a small smile softened it. 'Thanks, Harry.'

Allegra was using the staff restroom to freshen up when Kellie Wilton, one of her colleagues, came in.

'I was hoping I'd run into you,' Kellie said as she washed her hands at the basin. 'I heard about your meeting with Dr Addison.'

Allegra frowned as she twisted her light brown hair back into its clip. 'The hospital grapevine is running rampant again, I see,' she said, turning to look at her friend. 'Who told you about it?'

'Louise mentioned it at morning tea,' Kellie said, leaning back against the basin. 'It certainly sounds as if you got off on the wrong foot. What's his problem with your project? I thought Patrick Naylor was touting it as a unique study.'

'He did, but apparently Dr Addison is under the impression that *his* decisions bear more weight than those of the chief executive officer. I hate men with overblown egos and closed minds.'

'How is your relationship going with Patrick, by the way?'

Allegra put her hands on her hips and gave her friend a frustrated grimace. 'Listen, Kellie, I had dinner with him—once. It wasn't even in a posh restaurant and I ended up paying because his credit card wouldn't swipe. We had pizza and a bottle of awful red wine, which I was still paying for with a headache the next morning. He spent the whole time complaining about his soon-to-be-ex-wife. Hardly what I'd call a date.'

'Yeah, I'd heard his separation had hit him hard,' Kellie reflected. 'You do need to get out more, Allegra, with some fresh talent. Have you ever thought about using a dating service? My sister did and got a real honey.'

'I don't believe what I'm hearing, Kellie. What do you think—I'm desperate or something?' Allegra gaped at her. 'I can find my own dates without the help of a computer, thanks very much.'

'One bad dinner in two years is not a good track record,' Kellie pointed out.

'Eighteen months,' Allegra corrected her swiftly.

'Look, Allegra, you're twenty-eight years old. We've known each other a while now, and as far as I can tell the only fun you've had lately is sharing tubs of chocolate-chip ice cream with me while watching soppy movies at my place.'

Allegra sucked in her stomach and groaned. 'Don't remind me. It's taken me four weeks to get my jeans to do up again after the last time.'

Kellie smiled. 'Some of us are going to go out for drinks this evening after work. Why don't you join us?'

'Where are you going?'

'Just down to the pub on Elgin Street. It won't be a late night. You're not on call, are you?'

Allegra shook her head in relief. 'No, thank God.'

'So will you come?' Kellie urged. 'You never know, you might pick up.'

'What? A cold sore or a strep throat?'

Kellie laughed. 'You *are* a sad case, Allegra. You've been hanging around unconscious people way too long.'

'Maybe,' Allegra said with a wry smile. 'But they don't break your hearts and they're not unfaithful.'

Kellie's expression softened. 'And they don't always live, no matter how hard you try.' She placed a gentle hand on her friend's arm. 'Alice Greeson didn't have a chance, Allegra. You did your best.'

'I know…' Her shoulders slumped a little. 'But telling the family is always so hard. She was just twenty-one. I thought she was responding…'

'She was brain dead, Allegra,' Kellie said. 'It was hopeless right from the start. You did what you could but the brain injury she sustained in that car accident was beyond anything medical science could repair.'

Allegra gave a long sigh. 'I know, but I guess I was hoping

for a miracle. They happen occasionally, I just so wanted one for Alice and her family.'

'You'll get your miracle one day,' Kellie said. 'We all do. It's what keeps us going. Why else would we work the hours we do if there were no miracles?'

Allegra smiled. 'You're right. Thanks, Kel. What time did you say drinks are on?'

'Just come when you've finished your shift. The place will be rocking by the time you get there so come no matter what time you finish. You need some chill-out time.'

'You sound like my mother.'

'Yes, well, mothers often know best, although I'm not sure mine would approve of the date I have lined up for the weekend.'

'Don't tell me you're doing that internet dating thing, like your sister?'

Kellie grinned. 'Why not? Look at her, six months on and she's married and pregnant to a gorgeous guy. It could happen to any of us.'

Allegra rolled her eyes. 'My mother would have a coronary if I told her I was dating someone I'd met on-line. My father would be even worse. They'd be doing a personality inventory and an astrology and numerology profile on the guy, and checking out his background with a private investigator. I think I'll have to do it the old-fashioned way, you know, boy meets girl, that sort of thing.'

'That sort of thing usually ends in divorce,' Kellie pointed out. 'Physical attraction is one thing but finding someone you can relate to is the stuff that really counts. You need to be friends first, lovers second.'

'Yeah…I guess you're right, but with the sort of hours I work, how am I going to find the time to make friends with anyone halfway decent? Most men expect you to sleep with them on the second or third date these days. They're not interested in friendship, they're interested in getting laid as soon as they can.'

'That's why the dating service is so useful,' Kellie said. 'It cuts corners for you by weeding out the weirdos and the ones who have no interests in common with you. Think about it. I can get Jessica to do a preliminary printout for you to show you how it works.'

'I'll think about it,' Allegra said, as she shouldered open the door. 'I'll see you tonight.'

The door swung shut behind her but halfway along the corridor she came face to face with Patrick.

'Hello, gorgeous,' he said, planting a moist kiss to her mouth before she could turn her head away in time.

'Patrick…I…' She tried to push herself away but his hands were heavy on her shoulders.

'Have dinner with me tonight?' he asked, his tone pleading.

She opened her mouth to respond when just past his right shoulder she caught sight of Joel, coming out of one of the smaller meeting rooms used for conferencing with the relatives of patients. His dark eyes were cynical and there was a hint of something that looked very much like a smirk at the corners of his mouth.

'Sorry, Patrick, but I promised Kellie I'd join some of the others for drinks later this evening,' she said. 'Maybe some other time.'

'I'll hold you to it,' he said, and, pressing another quick kiss to her mouth before she could avoid it, went on his way in the opposite direction.

Joel stepped away from the doorjamb he'd been leaning against and walked towards her, his eyes very dark as they held hers. 'Dr Tallis, no doubt you will disagree with me on principle, but perhaps it might be prudent to refrain from fraternising with members of staff in the corridors of the unit. I wouldn't want any of our patients' relatives to think that you're acting unprofessionally.'

'I wasn't acting unprofessionally, I was just—'

'Dr Tallis.' His low deep tone brooked no resistance as he pointed to the room he had left a short time ago. 'In that conference room are the parents of a young man who was admitted to ICTU a short time ago. He fell from a building site and has suspected spinal injuries. I do not think that they need to see right now two members of staff going for it in the corridor.'

She glared at him in affront. 'We were not going for—' But she cut herself short when out of the corner of her eye she saw the conference-room door open down the corridor. She watched in silence as a middle-aged couple came out with the head neurosurgeon, Anthony Pardle, in attendance, their faces ravaged by the emotion they were going through on hearing of the extent of their son's injuries.

As much as Allegra wanted the last word, she knew it would be pointless. Joel had yet again stripped her of her professional dignity, and the last thing she wanted was for anyone else to witness it. She didn't understand why he had to be so obstructive. He had been so helpful with Mr Munsfield earlier, but now it looked as if the momentary truce was at an end.

She waited until the patient's parents and Anthony Pardle had passed before lowering her gaze and briefly apologising, even though the words felt like acid in her throat. 'I'm sorry. It won't happen again, Dr Addison.'

'Fine.'

Allegra felt the silent magnetic pull of his dark brown gaze, her breath stalling somewhere in the middle of her chest as their eyes locked. The silence was so thick she felt as if it was going to choke her. Her heart began to thump a little irregularly as his gaze slipped to her mouth for a nanosecond before returning to her wide green eyes.

'Fine…' he said again, running a hand through the thickness of his hair in a manner that appeared to Allegra to be slightly agitated. 'I'll…er…let you get back to work.'

She watched as he turned and walked with long purposeful strides up the length of the corridor, before disappearing from sight through the swing doors at the end.

She blew out a little uneven breath and gave herself a mental shake.

Don't even think about it, she scolded herself sternly. Dr Joel Addison was definitely in the 'too hard' basket. And for the sake of her heart he had better stay there.

CHAPTER THREE

THE pub was noisy and crowded by the time Allegra made her way there, but she wove her way through the clots of people to the table where some of the other Melbourne Memorial staff were sitting, chatting volubly over their drinks.

Kellie waved to her as she approached. 'Come and sit here, Allegra.' She made room for her on the booth seat. 'What will you have to drink?'

'I'd better start with something soft,' she said. 'After five nights of on-call my head for alcohol gets a little wonky. I'll have a lemon, lime and bitters, but you sit down—I'll get it. Do you want a top-up?'

'Thanks. Vodka and orange,' Kellie said.

Allegra made her way to the bar, saying a quick hello to two of the surgical registrars who'd been on call with her the last week. After a short exchange with them she carried the drinks back to the table where Kellie was and sat down with a sigh of relief marking the end of a stressful day.

'How's your coma study going, Allegra?' Margaret Hoffman, an anaesthetic registrar, asked.

Allegra exchanged a quick glance with Kellie before responding. 'The new director doesn't think it's scientific enough for his exacting standards. He's giving me a month to prove it's worthwhile.'

'Oh?' Margaret looked surprised. 'But it's all been approved and your work on the Greeson girl was worthwhile, I thought.'

'The Greeson girl died,' Allegra said with a despondent sigh.

'I know, but what you might not have realised at the time was how much it meant to her parents, having you there. I saw the way they drew comfort from you massaging their daughter's legs and arms, touching her like a real person, instead of someone who'd been written off as a vegetable. You gave them a lot of comfort in a tragic situation, Allegra. Even if the study achieves nothing for the patient, it sure as hell gives the relatives comfort—shows that the staff are treating their loved one with dignity, like a real person.'

'She's right, Allegra,' Kellie said. 'That's what's missing from medicine these days. The staff are all run off their feet, no one has time any more for simple things, like holding a patient's hand or listening to their worries or giving them a soothing back rub.'

'I guess you're right. But if I'm going to show anything from the study, I'm going to need the support of the director,' Allegra said, reaching for her drink. 'He seems against it on principle, and we haven't exactly had the best start to a working relationship.'

'I thought he was lovely when I met him at the welcome function,' Margaret said with a twinkle in her eye, 'and good-looking, too, which of course always helps.'

'I wouldn't care if he looked like the hunchback of Notre Dame as long as he lets me do my project—it's really important to me,' Allegra growled.

'Ah, but your involvement with Patrick Naylor gives you the trump card, surely,' Margaret said. 'I say, why not aim for the top if you can.'

Allegra frowned as she put down her drink. 'I'm not involved with Patrick. Not in any way. Who on earth starts these rumours?'

It was Margaret's turn to frown. 'But I heard him tell everyone in the doctors' room the other day how you had dinner together. He's really into you, Allegra. He made that very clear.'

'He's still officially married, for God's sake,' Allegra said. 'Besides, I'm not the slightest bit attracted to him.'

'Well, someone's definitely got their lines crossed,' Margaret said, as she leaned back in her seat. 'The way Patrick tells it, it sounds as if you are the reason his marriage split up in the first place.'

'No!' Allegra gasped. 'That's not true! I only went out with him as he seemed so down. It was more of a goodwill gesture. I was worried about him. He told me his wife had left him and he started to cry. I'm hopeless when men do that, it really gets to me. I just can't help going into rescue mode.'

'Uh-oh,' Kellie said, glancing towards the bar. 'Don't look now but guess who just walked in?'

Allegra groaned and put her head in her hands. 'Please, don't let it be Patrick Naylor. I just couldn't bear it.'

'It's not Patrick.'

Allegra lifted her head out of her hands and swivelled in her chair to see Joel looking straight at her. She turned back to her drink, her face feeling hot all of a sudden.

'Guess who's blushing,' Kellie teased, and, leaning closer, whispered, 'Go on, admit it, Allegra, he's hot. Look at those biceps—he must be lifting bulldozers in the gym.'

'Shut up—he'll hear you,' she muttered hoarsely.

'He's coming over,' Kellie said. 'Hello, Dr Addison. There's a spare seat over here opposite Allegra.'

Allegra stifled a groan and sent her friend a blistering glare.

'Thanks,' Joel said, taking the seat facing Allegra. 'Can I get anyone a fresh drink?'

'I'm fine, thanks,' Margaret said with a friendly smile.

'Me, too,' Kellie said. Giving Margaret a surreptitious nudge, she got to her feet. 'We're calling it a night anyway. We're on early, aren't we, Margi?'

'Are we? Oh, yes…silly me.' Margaret grinned sheepishly and wriggled out of the booth. 'See you later.'

Allegra would have sent another scorching glare her friend's way but Joel's dark gaze had already searched for and located hers.

'What about you, Dr Tallis?' he asked, once the girls had left. 'What's your poison?'

'I'm only drinking soft this evening,' she said, her eyes falling away from his.

'On call?'

'No.'

A small silence tightened the air.

'I hope I didn't frighten your friends away,' he said after a moment. 'They seemed in a hurry to leave once I arrived.'

Her eyes came back to his, her expression taut with resentment. 'They were trying to set us up. Surely you could see that?'

He frowned in puzzlement. 'Set us up? What do you mean?'

She resisted the urge to roll her eyes. What planet had he just come down from?

'Set up as in matchmake,' she explained with a disapproving grimace. 'Kellie does it all the time. It drives me nuts.'

Joel took a leisurely sip of his lime and soda as he studied her expression. She had a wry twist to her mouth, as if the thought of being connected to him in any way was impossible.

'I take it she doesn't approve of your relationship with the CEO?' he inserted into the silence.

'I am *not* having a relationship with the CEO.' She bit out each word with determination.

'So that little tableau I witnessed earlier today was an aberration of some sort?'

'Patrick and I are friends…sort of…' she said. 'He's going through a particularly acrimonious separation. I found myself lending an ear one day and now it seems the hospital is rife with the rumours of us being involved. Nothing could be further from the truth.'

'Hospitals are like that. Members of staff have only to stop and talk in the corridor and everyone thinks something's going on,' he commented. 'But perhaps you should be straight with him. He seems to think you're his for the taking.'

Allegra frowned. 'I know…but I don't know how to avoid hurting his feelings.'

Joel finished his drink. 'He'll get over it. Tell him you're involved with someone else.'

'Yeah, right, like who?' she said, with another rueful twist to her mouth. 'I work thirteen-hour shifts. I don't even have time to do my own laundry and shopping, let alone find a date.'

'I know what you mean,' he said with a wry smile. 'I haven't had a date in a year and a half. My mother is threatening to register me on an internet dating service.'

Allegra stared at him.

'What's wrong?' he asked. 'What did I say?'

She gave her head a little shake and picked up her almost empty glass for something to do to occupy her hands. 'Nothing… It's just that Kellie was suggesting I do the same.'

'When you think about it, it sounds good in theory.'

She scrunched up her face in scepticism. 'You think so?'

'Yeah.' He leaned back in his seat, one arm lying casually along the back of the booth. 'It cuts the chaff from the wheat, if you know what I mean.'

Allegra couldn't stop a bubble of laughter escaping her lips. '*Chaff and wheat?* Is that how guys these days refer to women?'

He gave her an answering smile. 'I guess it's not the best metaphor, but I thought sheep and goats would probably be worse.'

'You could be right,' she said, still smiling.

Joel ran his eyes over her features, taking in the light brown slightly wavy hair that seemed to be protesting about being restrained at the back of her head with a clip of some sort; loose tendrils were falling out around her small ears, and one long strand was over one of her rainforest green eyes. He watched as she tucked it behind her ear with her small slim fingers, her nails short but neat. Her face was faintly shadowed with residual tiredness but he knew if he looked in a mirror right now, his would look very much the same. Her mouth was soft and full, and her skin creamy white, as if she hadn't seen much of Melbourne's hot summer.

She looked like she worked hard and he felt a little uncomfortable with how he had spoken to her earlier. She had a good reputation among the staff, everyone spoke highly of her dedication to patients, but he couldn't help feeling her project had all the potential to provoke criticism and crackpot commentary as the new ICTU was evaluated by those who had backed its funding and those who had lost out on their own funding as a result. From what he'd heard so far, her study was time-consuming, had little theoretical basis and it would be hard to show results. And he of all people knew how important results were. His parents' situation was living proof of how the wrong results could change everything—for ever.

'So…' Allegra said, moistening her lips as she searched for something to fill the silence. 'How are you enjoying things so far at Melbourne Memorial?'

'It's a great facility,' he answered, 'the first of its kind in Australia. Having Trauma Reception on the same floor as ICU means that ICU staff are at close hand to be involved with trauma management. It's a very innovative concept, even for a level-3 trauma centre.'

'Yes, it makes a lot of sense. Less handing over of patients from one group to another, involvement of ICU staff right from the start of resus, and less movement of patients, too,' Allegra agreed. 'Wheeling patients twenty metres straight into ICU, instead of the old arrangement of up two floors and the opposite end of the hospital is a huge plus in itself.'

'And having the two fully equipped operating theatres in Trauma Reception is real cutting edge,' Joel said, 'although some of the surgeons and theatre staff I've spoken to haven't been too keen on it, actually. They don't like splitting the staff and equipment between the main theatre and us.'

'It can be disorientating, working in an unfamiliar theatre,' Allegra pointed out, in the surgeons' defense.

He held her gaze for a moment. 'There are some good people here. But it's a high-pressure job and I'm very conscious of being the new broom, so to speak.'

'You really like your metaphors, don't you?'

His smile was crooked. 'I do, don't I?'

Allegra found the friendly, more approachable side to him totally refreshing and wondered if he was trying to make up for the bad start they'd had. Without the stark backdrop of the hospital and without his white coat and tie, he looked like any other good-looking guy in his early to mid-thirties. His face was marked by fatigue but, looking around the bar, most of the hospital staff who were still here looked much the same. It came with the job. Chronic tiredness was a given, especially in ICU, where the shifts were long and the work intense.

'I heard you've been working overseas,' she said, toying with the straw in her empty glass.

Joel's eyes went to her hands before returning to her face. 'Would you like another drink?'

'Um…why not?' she said, deciding she was starting to enjoy herself for the first time in ages. 'Vodka and lime.'

'Coming up,' he said, and got up to get their drinks.

He came back and, placing her drink in front of her, took his seat opposite. 'Yes, I was overseas for a while.' He returned to her earlier question, his expression clouding a fraction.

'Where were you stationed?'

'In the Middle East.'

'That would have been tough, I imagine.'

He took a sip of his drink before answering. 'Yeah, it was.'

Allegra could sense he didn't want to talk about it in any detail and wondered if he'd been involved in any of the skirmishes that had seen countless people injured or maimed for life.

She took another sip of her drink and changed the subject. 'Are you a Melbourne boy?'

'Yep, born and bred. What about you?'

'I'm a bit of a crossbreed, I'm afraid,' she said. 'My father is originally from Sydney and my mother is a Melbourne girl. They both live here now but not together. I've spent equal amounts of time with them over the years.'

'They're divorced?'

'They never married in the first place,' she said. 'But they're the best of friends. They never went down that blame-game route. They're what you might call…progressive.'

'Progressive?'

'They have a sort of open relationship. They don't live together but whenever my mum needs a partner for some function or other, she takes my dad, and vice versa.' She gave him a little embarrassed glance and added, 'I wouldn't be surprised if they still occasionally sleep together.'

'You're right,' he said. 'That's pretty progressive.'

'What about you?' she asked, picking up her glass. 'Are your parents still together?'

'Yes, for something like thirty-five years.'

'Do you have any brothers or sisters?'

His eyes moved away from hers as he reached for his glass, absently running the tips of two of his fingers through the beads of condensation around the sides. 'I have a twin brother.'

There was something about his tone that alerted Allegra to an undercurrent of emotion. His expression was now shuttered, as if he regretted allowing the conversation to drift into such personal territory.

'Are you identical?' she ventured.

'Yes and no.'

Allegra frowned at his noncommittal answer but before she could think of a response to it he met her eyes and asked, 'What do your parents do for a living?'

'My father's a psychologist, who specialises in dream therapy, and my mother is a Tai Chi and yoga instructor.'

His eyebrows rose slightly. 'No wonder you have a tendency towards the other-worldly.'

'I would hardly call what I do *that,*' she protested, with a reproving glance.

'So what exactly is it you do?' he asked, settling back into his seat once more.

'You'll only rubbish it so what would be the point?'

'I promise to listen without comment,' he said. 'Look, right now we're just two overworked, tired people in a bar, chatting over a drink, OK?'

She let out a tiny sigh after a moment's hesitation. 'All right.' She took a little breath and briefly explained her theory of how human sensory touch could strongly trigger memories that might be integral to stimulating consciousness in a comatose patient. 'There is evidence that skin sensation is wired up as our most primitive memory system, plugging more directly into primitive brain areas. If you think about your dreams, and record them after you wake up, the sensations you were experiencing just before you woke up are nearly always touch-related sensations. So—in this study, I encourage the relatives, particularly those who are most intimately involved with the patient, to touch them in predetermined ways. I teach them how to massage and touch their loved one in ways we think will trigger strong memories.'

Joel remained silent as she talked passionately about some of the trials she'd done, including one involving a post-heart-surgery coma patient.

'It was striking,' she said. 'The relatives were advised to consider turning off his life support. There was virtually no sign of brain activity. But then his wife told me their daughter was flying back from Canada to say goodbye to him. She hadn't seen him in fifteen years. When she arrived I got her to touch him on his eyebrows, nose and lips and talk to him just like she did when she was a child and he used to put her to bed with this little routine. His eyes opened, he looked directly at his daughter's eyes for about thirty seconds, and then a few minutes later died peacefully.'

'So he didn't recover.'

Allegra tried not to be put off by the inherent cynicism in his tone. 'No, but that's not the point. He woke up in time to say goodbye. He recognised his daughter's touch—some powerful memory was triggered that induced momentary consciousness.'

'There's no way of testing that scientifically,' he pointed out.

'I realise it's just one case, and there was no measurement of brain activity being done on him. But that's the whole point of my study now—to get some measurements of these effects. And other triggers, too. Some of the other therapies I use involve other body memories, such as smell and sound. Haven't you ever heard a piece of music and found it took you back to a time that was significant to you? Music stirs emotions, so do certain aromas. And emotional memories are the most powerful, centred in the amygdala of the brain. The so-called healing properties of essential oils such as neroli, Roman chamomile, frankincense, bergamot, clary sage may have more to do with how they neurologically trigger emotional memory.'

'Yes, but none of these are controlled substances—they could have contaminants. There are cases where clary sage used topically by pregnant women were associated with birth defects. Peppermint oil can trigger epilepsy. My concern is that you are introducing therapies into a high-tech area that have never been through any approval or evaluation process. If there was even the suggestion of some adverse reaction, we'd be crucified.'

'I'm following strict guidelines—they've been approved by the ethics and research committees. My goal is to make a substantial breakthrough in coma recovery. I don't want to be stopped by closed-minded bureaucracy.'

'I suppose by that comment you're referring to me.'

'Well, you've hardly been encouraging,' she said with a hint of pique.

'It's not my job to win a popularity contest. I have to run this new and very expensive department according to the guidelines laid down in my contract. And it boils down to, one, dollars and cents, keeping within the budget. And, two, best practice, with significant benefits from the expense of the new layout. I can't be seen to be dabbling in pseudoscience with hard fought-over hospital money.'

'So you still think it's a worthless enterprise to touch a person who is ill or dying, or in a coma, do you?' she asked, unable to remove the stringency from her tone. 'For relatives and friends to spend hours by their bedside, holding their hand, stroking them and telling them how much they love them?'

He frowned at her censure. 'No, of course not. It's just that ICTU is cluttered enough as it is. It's not the place or the right time to bring in alternative therapists and their potions and sounds. And think of the increased risk of infection if people came and went all the time without proper regulation.'

'I don't often introduce other therapists,' she said. 'I do most of the work myself.'

'So you've got a degree in quackery as well as medicine, have you? What a busy little bee you have been over the last few years.'

Allegra got to her feet in one stiff movement, her expression tight with anger. 'You know something, Dr Addison? It's just as well you weren't recruited for a popularity contest because if it was up to me, you wouldn't have got past the first round of selection criteria.'

'And what criteria would they be, I wonder?' he asked, with a little curl of his lip. 'Perhaps my aura isn't giving off the right vibes or maybe my office doesn't have the right Feng Shui. Perhaps you should make an appointment with me to rearrange it for me.'

She pressed her hands on the table and leaned across so the other people close by couldn't hear, her green eyes flashing with anger. 'The only things I'd like to rearrange are your attitude and personality, and if there wasn't a law against it, I'd like to apply some touch therapy to your face as well—in the form of a very hard slap.'

His dark eyes glittered as they held hers. 'Go right ahead, sweetheart, and see how quickly you get fired from the department.'

'You can't fire me,' she spat back defiantly. 'Patrick Naylor does the hiring and firing.'

He got to his feet, his sudden increase in height making her shrink back in intimidation. 'I can assure you, Dr Tallis, that it would take just one word from me and the CEO will tear up your contract and your project into a thousand pieces,' he said, and with one last glowering look brushed past her and left.

CHAPTER FOUR

'SO HOW was your little drink last night with the director?' Louise asked in the female staff change room the next morning.

Allegra scowled as she thrust her handbag into her locker and turned the key with a savage twist of her hand. 'I'm going to kill Kellie Wilton and Margaret Hoffman.'

'So he didn't invite you back to his place for coffee, then?'

'No, he did not. He threatened to have me fired, that's what he did.'

'Fired! Can he do that?' Louise asked. 'I thought the CEO was the only one who could hire or fire?'

'I'm beginning to think Joel Addison could do anything if he put his mind to it.'

'It's tough, being at the top, Allegra,' Louise pointed out reasonably. 'There's been a lot of opposition about the refurbishment being so innovative and all. Dr Addison is probably being overly cautious, which is perfectly understandable. You know the fuss the surgeons made about the new trauma theatre locations. If this unit doesn't produce results and come in on budget, Dr Addison's the one who will take the rap.'

'I know all that,' Allegra said, pocketing her locker key and turning to face Louise. 'You know, for a while there last night I was starting to see a glimpse of a nice sort of man. He was chatty and seemed interested in what I had to say.'

'So what happened?'

She gave a frustrated up-and-down movement of her shoulders. 'Who knows? He just seems to really have it in for anyone a little to the left of what he believes is scientific. It's as if it's a personal agenda or something.'

'Maybe someone in the past gave him a lousy massage,' Louise said with a little grin.

Allegra rolled her eyes. 'The only thing he wants massaged is his ego, but I for one am not going to do it.'

'Have you told him your personal reasons for being so committed to your project?'

Allegra blew out a breath and leaned back against the lockers with a noisy rattle. 'No… If I did, it would only make things worse. He'd only say I was looking through an emotional lens instead of a scientific one.'

'But it might help him understand why it's so important to you if you tell him what happened to your friend in med school,' Louise said gently.

Allegra pushed herself away from the lockers as her beeper sounded. 'Look, I've put what happened to Julie behind me. I can't allow myself to dwell on it. It won't change anything. But I owe it to her memory to stop it happening again and, so help me, God, Dr Addison had better not try and stop me.'

She made her way quickly to the trauma centre sandwiched between the ambulance bay and the main ICTU. Two trauma bays were in operation when she arrived, ambulance personnel, including two crews of Heli Flight Retrieval Paramedics intermingling with the A and E medical and nursing staff.

'What's going on?' Allegra asked Alex Beswin, the A and E senior staffer, as she reached the scene of flurried activity.

'Hi, Allegra. Two people brought in from the Victorian Alps after a single vehicle accident. Seems their car went off the side of the road and ended up in the river. A car travelling behind stopped and the driver managed to get the mother and the kid in the car free, but both were unconscious and spent a bit of time in the cold water until the rescue team arrived to haul them out. The kid is still unconscious and still hypothermic and bradycardic. The mother has been rewarmed, but she has head injuries, a flail chest and blunt abdo trauma. We need your help on the boy—he was tubed at the scene but the airway's not great and he'll need to go up to CT soon. Joel Addison is heading the team getting the mother under control—she's going to CT now. They'll both need ICTU after we've finished here.'

'Right,' Allegra said, heading for bay one, where the small child was contained.

Tony Ringer, one of the A and E staff consultants, who was directing the care there, looked up in obvious relief when Allegra appeared at the foot of the bed.

'Allegra, listen—this tube's in too far, it's too small and there are anterior neck injuries from the air bag. We need to change it but I'd be grateful if you would do it. I'll help.'

Allegra moved to the head of the bed and, taking the airway bag and checking the tube and connectors, she listened to the chest with her stethoscope. 'Yes, you're right, Tony. The left side's not inflating, the tube is too small and probably down the right main bronchus. We'll change it for a six point five but we need to be ready for a surgical airway if his larynx is oedematous. I'll change the tube over an introducer to maintain access.'

Tony took over bagging the child while Allegra, with the help of one of the nursing staff, arranged all the equipment she needed, setting it out for easy access.

'Right, Tony, let's do it,' Allegra said, taking a breath to steady herself.

She took a long flexible plastic introducer and, after disconnecting the endotracheal tube from the bag, passed the introducer into the ETT and the right main bronchus. She then deflated the ETT cuff and pulled the tube out of the airway and over the introducer. She rapidly passed a cuffed 6.5 ETT back over the introducer and into the trachea with not much difficulty, positioning the tube this time in the trachea so that both lungs would be inflated, and blew up the cuff. She checked the insufflation of both lungs with her stethoscope and, satisfied that the tube was in the correct position, secured it with tape.

'Good job, Allegra,' Tony said. 'It's a godsend, having someone with increased airway skills for this sort of situation.'

'Thanks, Tony. I guess that's a benefit of the anaesthetic rotation through ICTU.'

'True,' Tony replied. 'Listen, this kid's still hypothermic. We're running in warmed intraperitoneal saline now, and as soon as his temperature is up we'll need to get him next door for a head CT. Can you manage the airway for his transfer and then settle him into ICTU for us? I want to look over the second team treating the mother. And word's just through that the husband and father has just been located. He's on his way in.'

'What's the boy's name?' Allegra asked.

'Tommy Lowe,' Tony answered. 'I don't know his age, his father was too distressed to talk. What do you think?'

Allegra looked at the tiny body on the bed with tubes running out of him, her stomach clenching in distress that someone so young had had to suffer so much. 'I reckon he's about six or seven.'

'Too young for this sort of caper,' Tony said, stripping off his gloves and tossing them in the bin.

'Tell me about it,' Allegra said. Stripping off her own gloves, she reached out with a gentle hand and touched the little boy on his arm, her fingers soft and warm on his cold pale limb.

Joel was in ICTU, finishing setting the mother up on a ventilator, when Allegra brought the little boy Tommy round from CT.

'CT on the mother shows some contusion, but no intracranial haemorrhage,' he said, glancing at her briefly, his expression coolly professional, showing no trace of his anger of the night before. 'She's got a flail chest on the right and underlying contusion. She had an intercostal tube put in before they transferred her. I've just had to retape the connectors, otherwise that's OK. Her abdo CT shows a liver contusion, but no free blood, so the surgeons are treating it expectantly at this stage. She'll have another CT tomorrow. Her bloods were pretty normal, the Hb down as expected. But there was one unexpected finding, about which we'll have to inform the police.'

'What's that?' she asked, as she supervised the transfer of Tommy from the trolley to the ICTU bed.

'Her blood alcohol is through the roof—point one. No wonder she ran off the road.'

'That's unbelievable!' Allegra said. 'How could a mother drive along a winding mountainous road with a child in the car, having drunk herself stupid?'

'I'm sending off a drug test as well,' he said with a grim set to his mouth. 'I have a bad gut feeling about this scenario. Something else is going on, maybe suicide—actually, a murder-suicide.'

Allegra felt a cold shiver of unease pass through her as she looked at the woman hooked up to the ventilator. What circumstances in her life would cause her to take that drastic step?

'What about the boy?' Joel asked. 'Any results from the CT?'

'No detectable macro brain injury. He could have general minor contusion, maybe slight cerebral oedema. His core temp's up to 37 now. No other major injuries. We ran the scanner over his neck, chest and abdo—all clear,' Allegra reported.

Danielle Capper appeared. 'Dr Addison? Dr Tallis? Mrs Lowe's husband is here. Perhaps you should speak to him before he comes in. He's very agitated. I've made him a cup of tea and he's in conference room two.'

Joel helped Allegra set Tommy up on the ventilator then while Allegra set up the IV lines with the nursing staff, Joel removed the intraperitoneal catheter, which had been used to rewarm the patient, stripped off his gloves and exchanged a quick glance with Allegra. 'We'd better talk to the father together.'

'Right,' she agreed, mentally bracing herself. How would the father of the little boy cope with hearing his wife had been driving under the influence, let alone if what Joel suspected was true—that she'd done so deliberately in an attempt to kill herself and her child?

Joel opened the conference-room door to find a man in his mid to late thirties pacing the floor, his face haggard, his clothes looking as if he'd just thrown them on haphazardly. His tie was hanging loosely and his shirt buttons were done up crookedly.

'I want to see my son! Where is he?'

'Mr Lowe, I'm Dr Joel Addison and this Dr Allegra Tallis. Your son is in ICTU—we've just stabilised him.'

'And my wife?' Mr Lowe asked, his hands tightening by his sides.

'She's also in the unit,' Joel said. 'Both she and your son are being ventilated with a machine to help with breathing. They both have head injuries. We're not sure yet about how severe those injuries are. The neurosurgical team is coming down now, and will almost certainly want to do a minor procedure on each to insert a pressure monitor. We'll have a lot better idea when that's in, and also with a period of observation.'

'She was drinking, wasn't she?' Mr Lowe said through clenched teeth. He swung away and turned with his back to them and looked out of the window, which overlooked the hospital garden.

'I know this has been a terrible shock for you, Mr Lowe,' Allegra said gently, 'but if you're up to it now, can we ask you a few questions to help us with planning management before we take you in to see them?'

He turned around and with a heavy sigh took the nearest chair and collapsed into it, his head going to his hands.

Joel waited until Allegra was seated before he took the other chair. 'Mr Lowe, your wife had a blood alcohol level of point one—that's double the legal limit for driving. Was she taking any medication that you were aware of?'

Mr Lowe lifted his head out of his hands and looked at Joel through red-rimmed eyes. 'She's been on antidepressants for six months.' His eyes shifted away to look down at his hands.

'And drinking on and off for a few weeks. But I never thought she'd do something like this…'

'You think she crashed the car deliberately?' Allegra asked.

Keith Lowe looked at her with a grim expression tightening his mouth. 'We've been having some…trouble…in the relationship. I was trying to work things out with her. I suggested counselling, but she wouldn't hear of it. This supposed disaster of a holiday in the mountains was my idea to try and patch things up. She was against it, of course…but she eventually agreed to come. I had some business in town to see to so she and Tommy drove up first. I was to join them later.' He rubbed at his jaw and added, 'If I'd suspected this was what was going through her head, I would never have allowed her to go…'

'Has she ever shown suicidal tendencies before?' Joel asked.

'No, not really, just troughs of depression. She'd sit around the house and do nothing…for weeks at a time and then snap out of it.' He ran a hand through his coarse, wiry hair. 'It's been a living hell, I can tell you. But I had to stick it out…if for nothing else than for Tommy's sake.'

'Yes, of course,' Joel said. 'Would you like to see them now?'

'Yes…' The man's eyes moistened. 'I want to see that Tommy's alive…' He choked back a sob and Allegra silently handed him the box of tissues from one of the side tables.

'Try not to be put off by the tubes and machinery—it's all support equipment to keep things stabilised while we watch for improvement. I know how terrifying it all looks. He's young and strong—I know having his father by his side will help him.'

Keith blew his nose and wiped at his eyes before turning to Joel. 'I'd rather not see my wife right now, if you don't mind. Not after…this….'

Joel got to his feet and placed a reassuring hand on the man's shoulder. 'We understand. She's in the next cubicle but I'll make sure the curtain is pulled across between them. We can move them apart if you can't cope.'

Mr Lowe appeared to think about it for a moment.

'No…no…you don't have to do that. I guess Tommy would want her near… I'll manage.'

'There are staff in constant attendance in ICTU,' Allegra said. 'You can ring and talk to the one looking after Tommy at any time.'

'How badly injured is my…wife?' he asked after a tiny pause.

Joel answered. 'Well, apart from a head injury, which is why she's unconscious at present, she has broken ribs, some bruising of a lung and bruising of her liver. She has a plastic drain in the chest to keep the lungs inflated. The liver injury seems stable, it probably won't need any surgery. And she has bruising around both upper arms, maybe where someone grabbed her to pull her out of the car, and in the middle of her back, maybe from prolonged pressure on the spine board during the transfer. She's deeply unconscious,' Joel said. 'It will be a few hours before we can get all the test results back.'

Mr Lowe's eyes shifted again. 'Is…?' He cleared his throat and continued, 'Is she expected to live?'

'She's in a serious condition but she's stable. We're giving her maximal supportive therapy. I think there's a fair chance for recovery,' Joel said.

Allegra stood to one side a few minutes later as Keith stood by his son's bed. She could see the up-and-down movement of his throat as he swallowed the rising emotion, and her chest felt uncomfortably tight at what he must be going through. How many times had she seen scenes just like this? Too many to recall, but this had to be one of the most tragic. Car accidents were horrific enough, without a suicide or murder motive attached.

'You can talk to him, Mr Lowe,' she said. 'Touch him and speak to him as much as you like.'

Keith Lowe kept his eyes trained on his little son. 'But he can't hear me, can he?'

'He is unconscious but that doesn't necessarily mean his brain won't register the sound of a very familiar voice. Your touch, too, is part of that memory process.'

Keith reached out a hand and placed it tentatively on his son's leg. He opened his mouth to speak but closed it again. Removing his hand from the boy's leg, he moved away from the bed, his expression tortured as he faced Allegra. 'I can't do this… I need to get some…air… I'm sorry… I can't cope with seeing him like this…'

'It's all right, Mr Lowe,' Allegra said softly.

His eyes spouted tears as he ground out bitterly. 'How can you possibly understand? That is my son lying there because that bitch behind that curtain put him there. If anyone deserves to die, it's her, not him. He's only seven years old, for God's sake!'

'Mr Lowe, I think it would be best if—'

'Excuse me.' Keith brushed past Allegra roughly and left the unit, ripping off the white protective surgical gown all visitors were required to wear in ICTU and tossing it roughly in the vague direction of the laundry bin.

'Dr Tallis?'

Allegra let out a little sigh and turned to face Joel, who had been attending to another patient nearby. 'Yes?'

'I'd like a word with you if you're free,' he said, 'in my office. No hurry. Just come when you get a spare moment.'

'I'm free now.'

'Good,' he said, moving past to shoulder open the swing doors. 'I'll have some coffee sent up.'

Louise sent Allegra a musing glance once the doors had closed on Joel's exit. 'Coffee or an olive branch, I wonder?'

Allegra rolled her lips together for a moment, her eyes on the small child lying so lifeless on the bed, only the hiss and groan of the ventilator breaking the silence.

'Allegra?' Louise gave her a little prod. 'Are you OK?'

She blinked and, giving her head a little shake, gave Louise a crooked smile. 'Sorry, I was miles away. Did you say something?'

'Nothing important,' Louise answered. 'But you'd better go and have that coffee with the director. You look like you need it.'

'Yes…' she said, and made her way out of ICTU to Joel's office a few doors down the corridor, a tiny frown taking up residence on her forehead.

CHAPTER FIVE

'COME in,' Joel called at Allegra's knock a short time later.

She came in and found him taking two cups of coffee off a tray, the fragrant aroma instantly teasing her nostrils.

'Quite a day,' he said, handing her a cup. 'Do you take milk or sugar?'

She shook her head. 'No, straight up is fine.'

Joel waited until she sat down before he took his chair behind his desk. His dark chocolate gaze connected with hers, the edge of his mouth tilted slightly. 'I suppose you're wondering why I've asked you to see me after what occurred between us last night.'

Allegra felt her colour rise but there was nothing she could do to stop it. 'As you said during the course of that…er…unfortunate conversation, we were two tired, overworked people, having a drink.'

There was a surprising level of warmth in his gaze as it held hers. 'Yes, that's true, but I still thought I should apologise, for being so…' He seemed to be hunting for a suitable word so she supplied it for him.

'Overbearing?'

He gave a soft chuckle of laughter, the sound of it sending a river of tiny feathery sensations down Allegra's spine. His eyes crinkled at the corners and his whole face softened, the tension and guardedness she was so used to seeing there now completely gone.

'I've been described as a lot of things in the past but "overbearing" is a first,' he said.

She arched one of her brows sceptically. 'Really? I'm surprised.'

His smile faded a little and he put down his cup. 'Look, Allegra, I know we haven't had a great start to our working relationship but I wanted to apologise for my part in last night's…er…unfortunate conversation, as you called it. I have no intention of speaking to Patrick Naylor about you. From what I've seen, you are a very competent anaesthetist with a high level of compassion for patients.'

'Thank you…'

'However, I did want to advise you about your handling of Keith Lowe.'

Allegra felt herself stiffen. 'Oh?'

'He's still in shock over what's happened. Also, I don't think he's the touchy-feely sort. A lot of men aren't. I was watching from bed four. He seemed very stiff and uncomfortable at touching the child.'

She frowned at him. 'So what are you saying?'

'I think it would be wise to go slowly with him in regard to your coma recovery plan. Somehow Keith Lowe doesn't strike me as a man who would be comfortable singing lullabies to his kid, no matter what the circumstances.'

'I wasn't thinking along the lines of lullabies, but I do think it's important Mr Lowe speaks to his son at the very least.'

'True. I agree. But the man's trying to come to terms with the as yet unanswered question of whether or not his wife tried to do herself in and take the child with her. To make matters worse, Kate is one bed away. He's edgy and very uncomfortable.'

'You think we should move her—maybe to one of the isolation rooms?'

Joel drummed his fingers on the desk for a moment. 'It's a

thought…but, no, I think the transfer might be interpreted the wrong way. The father's already agreed Tommy might benefit from having his mother nearby.'

'Even though she tried to kill him?'

His eyes came back to hers. 'We don't know that. It could have been an accident.'

'You mean, straight driving under the influence?' she said. 'Driving with point one alcohol in the blood is hardly responsible behaviour for anyone, let alone a mother with a small child in the car.'

'Look, I know I brought up the suspicions in the first place, but it's probably wise not to make any judgements until we have more facts.'

'But Mr Lowe said she had a history of depression and he immediately assumed she'd been drinking, as if it was a regular occurrence.'

'Lots of people suffer periods of depression without trying to take their own or other's lives,' he pointed out.

'So why did you order a drug test? You must be more than a little suspicious.'

He let out a sigh and ran his hand through his hair. 'I just thought it best to make sure either way.' He glanced at his watch. 'The results should be in now.'

'What do you think they'll show?'

'One would assume she's been taking her antidepressant, so that will show up—but at what level? And any other drugs—sedatives, tranquillisers. Maybe she took a cocktail of things.' He reached for the telephone and dialled the pathology department.

Allegra sipped her coffee and listened as he discussed the results with the lab.

'That high, huh? Both of them?' He raised his brows at Allegra. 'Yeah, I guess so. Right, thanks for speeding it through. The police will want a copy. I'll get them to contact you themselves—they may have their own questions.'

He put the phone down and sent Allegra a grave look. 'Mrs

Lowe was on a cocktail of three drugs. Paroxetine at five times the maximum therapeutic level, diazepam at a high level and traces of codeine.'

'So she was really serious about doing it properly,' she said, starting to chew at her bottom lip.

'Looks more like it now.'

Allegra's frown increased. 'That's three drugs. You said "both of them". What exactly did you mean by that?'

'I wasn't referring to the number of drugs. I had the lab examine the boy's blood as well. It now seems that he had detectable diazepam as well, but not as high as hers.'

'What! She sedated the boy first?' she gasped in shock.

'That's what it looks like. Hard to believe someone would do such a thing, but it's not the first time a parent has taken things to such extremes.'

'It's just so awful to think that if that car hadn't been behind them they would have died for sure…' she said, staring down at her hands.

'Maybe it was meant to happen this way.'

She looked up at that. 'What? Don't tell me the incredibly scientific Dr Joel Addison actually believes in something as metaphysical as destiny?'

He leaned back in his chair and studied her for a lengthy moment before asking, 'What have you got planned for the rest of the evening?'

She gave him a startled look. 'Planned?'

'After you finish work,' he said. 'What have you got planned?'

'Um…well, nothing really. I should do some washing, I guess. My machine broke down and my shifts have made it impossible for me to be there for the technician, but I can tell you the thought of sitting in a hot laundromat isn't too appealing.'

His smile relaxed his features again. 'So if I offered to take you out to dinner I might be in for a chance at you accepting, given the competition being so poor?'

Allegra felt her stomach do a funny little flip-flop. 'You're asking *me* to dinner?'

'You sound surprised.'

'I am.'

'Don't you get dinner invitations very often?'

She gave him a rueful look. 'Only from recently separated men who do nothing but whinge about their soon-to-be-ex-wives the whole time.'

'Well, I can assure I'm not married or separated or involved with anyone at present, much to my mother's ongoing disappointment.'

'You could always try internet dating,' she suggested with a tiny wry smile.

'I thought I might try this way first,' he said, and pushing out his chair got to his feet. 'That's if the laundromat isn't a better offer.'

Allegra stood up as well, wondering why her legs felt so wobbly and strange all of a sudden. 'It's close…but I suppose as long as you don't offer me pizza and cheap red wine, you're a marginally better prospect than the laundromat.'

'Marginally, eh?' He smiled as he held the door open for her. 'I'll pick you up at eight or is that too early?'

'No, but I haven't even given you my address.'

'Good point.' He reached for a pen and paper and she rattled off her street and apartment block number and watched as he wrote it down in a strong forceful script which she knew her mother would have a field day interpreting.

'See you tonight, then,' he said, pocketing the note.

'Yes… Thanks for the coffee.'

'You're welcome.'

She felt the pull of his gaze for several long seconds before she dragged hers away to walk through the door and down the corridor on legs that still felt as if someone had taken out the bones, just leaving the marrow…

* * *

Allegra checked on Tommy Lowe before she left for the evening. The neurosurgeons were planning insertion of intracranial pressure monitors on both him and his mother that night in the ICTU theatre. Susie, the ICU nurse looking after Tommy, reported all his obs stable, and the same for Kate, who she was also temporarily attending whilst Chloe, Kate's nurse, was out at tea.

'Poor little chap,' Susie said. 'How could a mother do that to an innocent child?'

Allegra wrote up the notes and handed the nurse the chart. 'It seems unbelievable, doesn't it? Mind you, it's still speculation so far, so better not to spread rumours we might regret later.'

'I hate the thought of even going near her,' Susie confessed. 'I can't wait for Chloe to come back from her break.'

'We've got to treat Mrs Lowe like any other patient in ICTU, Susie—we're health professionals, not judges,' Allegra reminded her sternly.

'I know, but what the poor father is being put through…he's a complete wreck,' Susie said. 'And you could hardly blame him for being so angry.'

'Has he been back in?'

'Yes, just a few minutes ago. He didn't stay long. I had to get him a glass of water and a couple of paracetamol almost as soon as he laid eyes on Tommy. I don't think he can handle the sight of his little boy so badly injured. He probably blames himself for not seeing it coming.'

'Yes, I guess you're right,' Allegra agreed with a heavy sigh. 'Suicide always creates such a lot of guilt. You always wonder if you could have done something to prevent it.'

Susie gave her a thoughtful look. 'That sounds to me like the voice of experience. Someone close to you?'

Allegra was privately impressed by the nurse's percipience but didn't know her well enough to share what had happened to her friend Julie during their first year at medical school. She'd only shared it with Louise because Louise's brother had made a suicide attempt a couple of years previously after a relationship break-up. He had recovered, however, and was now in a happy relationship and had dealt with the issues that had led to his attempt on his life.

Allegra's experience with her friend had been a harrowing time and she still had nightmares about it. She still tortured herself over all the signs she'd missed, all the opportunities she could have taken to prevent a tragedy that she knew would haunt her for the rest of her life.

'No…' she answered, straightening the bed clothes over the child. 'But you sort of get to know this stuff from working in a place like this.'

'Yeah, tell me about it,' Susie said. 'You see it all and then have to go home and sleep.'

'Sleep…' Allegra forced a wry smile to her lips. 'Now, there's something that'd be incredibly tempting.'

'Not as tempting as coffee with the new boss,' Susie said with a little twinkle.

Allegra frowned. 'Don't you nurses have anything better to do than gossip all the time? It was just coffee, all right? It doesn't mean a thing.'

'What about Patrick Naylor?'

'What about him?' she snapped back irritably.

'He's not going to be too happy about you fraternising with the director when he had first call.'

'For pity's sake, how often do I have to tell everyone that I am *not* involved with Patrick Naylor?'

'I guess the only way to do that is by making it obvious you're dating someone else,' Susie suggested.

'Yeah—well, maybe I will do just that,' Allegra said, and giving the nurse one last little hardened glare turned on her heel and left.

CHAPTER SIX

JOEL adjusted his tie for the third time and rocked back on his heels as he waited for Allegra to answer her apartment intercom. It had been so long since he'd been on a proper date he'd almost forgotten how to go about it. Not that this was a proper date. Not really. It was dinner with a colleague.

A get-to-know-you-better dinner.

Nothing else.

'Hello?'

'Hi, Allegra, it's me, Joel. Shall I wait for you down here?'

'No, come on up. I'm not quite ready,' she said a little breathlessly.

He made his way to the fifth floor via the lift but before he could raise his hand to knock on her door she opened it and ushered him in.

'Sorry,' she said, stooping to pick an earring off the floor and inserting it in her ear lobe. 'I got held up in traffic. I won't be a minute. Have a seat. Would you like a drink or something?'

'No, I'm fine.'

She gave him a nervous little smile and disappeared into a room that he assumed was her bedroom. He heard a couple of stiff curses as she dropped something and he smiled to himself. Maybe he wasn't the only one who was a little out of practice when it came to dating.

She came out a short time later dressed in a simple black dress with heels that, in spite of their lethal-looking height, still only brought her up to his shoulder. She was wearing subtle make-up, the smoky eye-shadow highlighting her green eyes and sooty dark lashes. Her lips were lightly coated with a pink-tinged gloss and her shoulder-length light brown hair was loose about her shoulders, falling in soft waves that made his fingers itch to reach out and see if it was really as silky as it looked. He had to stuff his hands in his trouser pockets to stop himself from giving in to the temptation.

'I'm sorry to keep you waiting,' she said as she reached for her evening bag on the sofa, sending a soft waft of her light perfume his way. 'I'm not usually so disorganised.'

'It's been a hectic day,' he said. 'I had to rush at the last minute as well.'

Allegra followed him out to his car. 'Do you live close to the hospital?' she asked, once they were on their way.

'I'm just renting a place in South Yarra at the moment,' he answered. 'I'm still trying to work out what sort of place I want to buy.'

'You mean an apartment or a house?'

'Yes. Both have their advantages but with the hours I work it doesn't make sense to rush in and buy a house with a big garden when I haven't even got the time to sit in it, much less maintain it.'

'That's what gardeners are for,' she said. 'I'm even thinking about getting some help in to water my pot plants. I just don't seem to have the time.'

He glanced across at her and smiled. 'You could always get plastic ones.'

'Now, that would really send my mother into a tailspin,' she answered with a dancing gleam in her eyes. 'Fake plants are not good for positive energy flow.'

He turned back to the traffic, a small smile tugging at the corners of his mouth. 'You know something? I'm beginning to suspect you're not quite as alternative as you make out, Allegra Tallis.'

'And you're not quite the overbearing ogre you want everyone to think you are, are you, Joel Addison?'

His warm brown eyes held hers for a moment before shifting away to concentrate on locating a parking spot. 'I guess you'll just have to wait and see.'

The restaurant he'd booked was in Toorak Road and after they were shown to their table and left with menus and the wine list, Allegra felt herself begin to relax a little. She sank into the comfortable chair and examined the menu.

Phew! Not a pizza in sight.

'What's that little smile for?' Joel asked.

She met his gaze across the table. 'I was just checking for pizzas.'

He handed her the wine list. 'Maybe you should choose the red wine. I don't want to be accused of picking a cheap one.'

'You don't strike me as the cheap red wine type,' she said, handing it back to him.

He gave her a teasing look. 'You can tell that from my aura?'

She pursed her mouth at him but ended up releasing it on a reluctant smile. 'I hope you're not trying to pick a fight with me, Dr Addison.'

'Not tonight,' he said. 'We're just too overworked, tired people having dinner, OK?'

'Now who's reading auras?' she asked. 'And here I was, positive I'd managed to conceal the shadows underneath my eyes.'

'I don't know anything about auras but I can tell you work hard, harder than most.'

'Now, I *am* really going to ask for a refund on that eye cream,' she said with a rueful grimace.

He smiled at her but just then the waiter approached to take their drinks order and to advise them on the daily specials.

Allegra studied Joel covertly as he asked the waiter about

the menu, the low, deep timbre of his voice and gentle respectful manner as he listened to the young man telling her more about him as a person than anything else she'd seen so far. She inwardly cringed as she recalled her date with Patrick, who'd practically abused the young inexperienced waitress for not bringing the garlic bread out on time.

After the waiter returned with their wine and took their order for meals, Joel sat back in his seat and surveyed her features in silence for a moment or two.

'So what made you choose coma recovery as a project?' he finally asked.

Allegra met his dark gaze guardedly. 'Is this what this dinner is about—me having to justify my project to you all over again? If that's the case, I might as well leave now and save the chef the hassle of cooking a meal I won't be able to eat.'

'No, I'm just interested in what motivated you to choose that particular study over any number of other topics you could have chosen instead. There are a lot of people who would feel it's unlikely to produce anything of scientific significance.'

'It's pretty clear which camp you'd be in.'

'Come on, Allegra,' he reasoned. 'Everything in our profession is data-driven now—if you can't measure it, it probably doesn't exist. Anecdotes and expert opinion are no longer good enough.'

She sent him a hardened glare. 'Can we talk about something else?'

'OK, but there are two deeply comatose patients in ICTU right now but I don't want you to do anything that would draw unnecessary attention to the unit at this time.'

'What do you mean by that?' she asked with rising anger. 'What do you think I'm going to do? Cast a spell or something?'

'I just want you to tread very carefully. I'm just concerned that if Mr Lowe's son dies, you could be an easy target to blame.'

'*Me?* What about his wife? She's the one who drove the car!'

'I know, but you know how people are when they're under a lot of stress. The whole spectrum of emotion gets played out in ICU. The very best and worst of human behaviour comes out. In my opinion, Keith Lowe is a litigation time bomb waiting to go off.'

Allegra couldn't help agreeing with him, although it pained her to admit it. 'He does seem the type, I guess,' she said, lowering her gaze a fraction.

'I'm not trying to sabotage your project, Allegra, nothing like that. If anything, I would actually be delighted if you were able to deliver some measurable and repeatable results. But is this the right time to do it, the right case to start with?'

She raised her eyes back to his. 'Are you expressly forbidding me to do anything or just asking me to be discreet?'

He held her gaze for a lengthy period. 'I said I'd give you a month and I'll stick by that. But if you're going to use this case, I want you to keep a low profile. Things are much more tense than usual because of the question mark hanging over Kate Lowe. One press leak and public emotion will be running high. The notion of a mother trying to kill her own child in her own suicide attempt is bizarre—the press would play it from every angle for all it's worth, every day either of them survives. And if, on top of that, they got wind that they were being used in a research project, especially using not-strictly-medical methods, they'd have a field day—none of us might survive it.'

'I understand,' she said. 'But I'd still like to try with the little boy. I'll ask the father for his permission, of course.'

He held her direct look for a moment. 'Fine, but all I'm saying is that emotion runs high when children are involved. Just keep that in mind.'

Allegra thought back to her earlier conversation with Susie but decided against mentioning it. The nursing staff were well used to dealing with all sorts of people and could be relied on to remain professional at all times.

After a short pause she released a heartfelt sigh. 'I often wonder how they get on—you know, once they leave ICU. We patch them up and send them on their way, but we get very little long-term feedback. Don't you wonder how they manage to adjust, especially the ones with permanent disability?'

Joel examined the contents of his wineglass, a shadow of something coming and going in his dark eyes. 'I try not to think about it too much.'

She looked at him, her expression softening. 'But you do, don't you?'

He gave her a twisted, humourless smile. 'Well, it's part of the job, isn't it? You go home exhausted after long shifts, then you can't sleep, worrying you could have done more.'

'I know… It's a wonder we don't all end up on stress leave.'

'It's why doctors' marriages have a higher than average failure rate,' he said, reaching for his wine and taking a sip.

The waiter arrived with their meals and once he'd left, Allegra said into the little silence that had fallen, 'You never told me what your parents do for a living.'

Joel put his glass back on the table before answering. 'My father is a teacher and my mother hasn't worked outside the home since my brother and I were born.'

'That must have been nice for you and your brother,' she said, 'having a full-time mum at home.'

'It certainly had its advantages.' He reached for his cutlery and asked, 'What about your early childhood? Did your mother choose to work or stay at home?'

'My mother wasn't the stay-at-home type. My father did a lot of the child care in the early days, but I seem to remember a few child-care centres along the way.'

'But you had a happy childhood?'

'Of course. My parents were a bit "out there" at times, but I can't remember ever being unhappy. Even when they went their separate ways, they did it so wonderfully well that I was the envy of all my friends for having such trendy, cool parents.'

Joel looked at her in silent envy. His childhood had been marked with tragedy, a tragedy relentless and ongoing. The last time he'd visited, just two days ago, his mother had aged and visibly shrunk even further, and his father's face had become a mask of pain from their situation, each line more deeply etched, each shadow a darker curtain.

Allegra became aware of his silence and wondered if she was boring him. 'I'm sorry…' She pushed her glass out of her reach. 'I tend to talk too much about myself when I drink wine.'

He gave her a lopsided smile. 'Truth serum?'

'Next I'll be telling you all my innermost secrets.'

'You seem to be pretty much an open book to me. You wear your heart on your sleeve, which is unusual in a medico. It usually gets hammered out of you at medical school.'

She lowered her gaze to the small flickering candle on the table, a small frown bringing her finely arched brows together for a moment. 'Well I must have been absent that day at medical school.'

'What happened?'

Allegra brought her eyes back to his, surprised yet again at the warmth she could see reflected there. 'I lost my best friend during second year.'

'An accident?'

She shook her head. 'Suicide.'

'I'm sorry. That must have been a tough time.'

'It was… I blamed myself for not seeing the signs.'

'Most people who know a suicide victim suffer the same guilt. Look at Mr Lowe today. I'm sure that's why he's unable to cope. He probably thinks it's his fault.'

'Yes…but in Julie's case I should have known. I was her best friend. We'd shared everything since the first day we met during orientation week at university.'

'You can't always read people's minds,' he pointed out.

'My mother would totally disagree with you,' she said, trying to lighten the conversation. She gave him a little smile and added, 'She insists she can infallibly detect what people are thinking just by looking deeply into their eyes.'

'Oh, really?' He didn't bother disguising his scepticism but this time it was tempered with a smile. 'And have you perhaps inherited this little gift?'

'I don't know. I haven't really put it to the test.' She leaned forward to look into his eyes. 'Let me see now… Hmm—you definitely have sleep on your mind. I can see you haven't had a decent night's sleep in weeks if not months.'

'Not bad,' he said. 'There might be something in this after all.'

She leaned closer to peer even more, her hair falling forward to brush the back of his hand where it rested on the table near his glass in a soft-as-air caress that sent a charge of electricity straight to his groin as her greener-than-green gaze meshed with his.

'What do you see in my eyes now?' he asked, his voice sounding a little rough around the edges.

Allegra looked deeply into his darker-than-night eyes, an unexpected pulse of desire beginning to beat a steady tattoo low and deep in her body. Her chest felt as if it had shrunk to half its size, the air she tried to breathe into her lungs catching on its way down. She moistened her lips, her skin lifting in awareness in a way that had never happened to her before. Her breasts felt full and heavy, her nipples puckering beneath her black lace bra as she felt the searing burn of his dark gaze as it held hers.

She sat back in her chair and tucked her hair behind her ear as she gave a little self-conscious laugh. 'I've definitely had way too much wine to drink.'

'The eyes are supposed to be the window to the soul,' he said as he signalled to the waiter for the bill. 'But what if you don't have one?'

'Everyone has a soul,' she protested.

He gave her one of his cynical smiles. 'Don't go looking for one in me, Allegra, for you won't find one. It died a long time ago.'

Allegra followed him out of the restaurant a short time later, her heart contracting painfully at the thought of what he had seen and experienced out in the field to have hardened him in such a way. She'd seen shadows of pain in his eyes that she knew no amount of sleep would ever erase. And she knew if he'd looked deeply into her own he would have found the very same shadows lurking there…

CHAPTER SEVEN

'THANK you for dinner,' Allegra said once he'd walked her to the door of her apartment block. 'I had a good time. It was a nice restaurant. Not a pizza in sight.'

'Aren't you going to ask me in for coffee?'

'I was going to but I wasn't sure if you would take it the wrong way.'

'I take it the same way you do—black.'

She gave him a quelling look. 'I meant…well, you know what I meant.'

He smiled at her flustered expression and before he could stop himself lifted a finger to her cheek, trailing his knuckle over the creamy curve where a spot of heightened colour had pooled.

Allegra ran her tongue over her lips in a nervous gesture. 'I'd better go in. It's getting late and I'm on early and…' She stopped when she saw the dark glitter in his eyes as they caught and held hers, her stomach hollowing in anticipation.

His head came down slowly, his warm breath brushing over her lips before he placed his mouth on hers in a soft, hardly touching kiss.

She looked up at him, her heart increasing its pace as he ran his tongue over his lips as if tasting her sweetness.

'I probably shouldn't have done that,' he said.

She swallowed the restriction in her throat and croaked, 'Why?'

'Because now I know what it feels like, I want to do it again.'

'Oh…'

'It could cause all sorts of problems,' he said, taking her by the shoulders and bringing her one tiny step closer, her breasts brushing against his chest.

'You think so?' she asked, leaning into his hardness instinctively.

'I know so.'

'Too bad…'

He held her gaze for several pulsing seconds. 'The gossip would be unbearable.'

'Totally…'

'And then there's the problem of shifts.'

'Yes…' She moistened her lips again. 'That's always a downside.'

'And then there's the issue of your place or mine.'

'Tricky.'

He smiled and tipped up her chin. 'You are one hell of a temptation, Allegra Tallis, but I'm going to be the strong one here and step back before we drift into dangerous territory.'

'OK…' She swallowed again as she felt the hard ridge of his growing erection against her. 'That would be wise, I guess.'

'Very wise.'

A full thirty seconds passed.

'So…so why aren't you doing it?' she asked.

'Doing what?'

'Stepping back,' she said. 'You said you were going to be the strong one and step back.'

'You're right,' he said, his gaze dipping to her mouth. 'Now would be a good time.'

'A very good time…'

Her stomach did a complete somersault as his hands slid down the length of her bare arms to encircle her wrists.

'Why don't we do it on the count of three?' he suggested, after another heart-stopping pause.

Allegra's fingers curled around the length and strength of his. 'Right…let's do that. On the count of three.' She took a breath and began the countdown, 'One…'

'Two…' he said, and released her wrists to place his hands on her hips.

Another deep throb of silence passed. Allegra knew it was her turn to say the last number but somehow she couldn't get the one word past the trembling shield of her lips. Her gaze locked with his as the time beat on, his hands on her hips feeling like a slow burn as his heat passed from his body to hers.

'Aren't you going to say it?' he asked, his breath caressing the surface of her mouth as his head came inexorably closer.

'I was getting to it…'

She felt the imprint of his lazy smile on her lips before he gradually increased the pressure, each slow drugging movement of his mouth on hers sending her senses into overload. The sexual charge of his tongue probing for entry made her legs buckle with instant uncontrollable need and she pressed herself against him, relishing in the feel of his body's instant reaction to hers. She wasn't without experience but never had she felt the energy and force of such fierce attraction before. It was like her body had been storing up its need for this moment when his mouth scorched its timeless message on hers.

Her tongue played with his boldly, each movement inciting her desire to a higher level, moving even further out of her control. Her mind swam with images of how they would be together, his strong leanly muscled body pinning her beneath him.

A passing car's headlights brought her back to earth with a shaft of exposing light that she knew would do her no credit with her overly conservative neighbours.

She eased her mouth away from his and said somewhat breathlessly, 'Th-three.'

Joel's hands moved from her hips, his wry smile sending another wave of longing through her. 'There, I knew you could do it.'

'It was a tough call but I guess someone has to do it.'

'Yes,' he said, brushing the curve of her cheek once more. 'Someone does.'

'So…' She tried to sound casually unaffected, as if she kissed handsome, full-blooded men on her doorstep all the time. 'I guess I'll see you at work tomorrow.'

'Yes, I guess you will.'

''Night…'

'Goodnight, Allegra. I really enjoyed this evening. You're surprisingly good company.'

'Better than an internet date?'

'Way better,' he said, staring again at her mouth.

'Um…this is the bit where you go down those steps and get in your car and drive home,' she said, pointing to where his car was. 'Do you think you can manage that?'

'I'm working myself up to it.'

She couldn't help laughing. 'You have definitely graduated with honours from the school of irresistible charm.'

He bent his head and pressed a soft kiss to the side of her mouth. 'So have you, Dr Tallis.' He gave her cheek one last gentle flick with his finger and stepped away, walking with long strides towards his car.

'Have a good sleep,' she called out, as he got in his car.

He turned his head to lock gazes with her. 'Are you joking?'

'No…not really…'

He lifted his hand in a wave and with a deep throaty roar of the engine drove off and disappeared around the corner.

Joel hadn't expected to sleep but when the phone rang beside his bed at three a.m. he realised he'd been in a deep dreamless slumber that took some effort on his part to come out of. He reached blindly for the phone and answered it groggily, 'Joel Addison.'

'Dr Addison, it's Brian Willis, I'm on night shift for the unit. We've got one hell of a problem here. I thought I should tell you about it now instead of when you come in the morning.'

Joel rubbed his face and sat up. 'What problem? What's going on?'

'It's Mrs Lowe,' Brian said. 'Her ventilator has been tampered with and she had a respiratory arrest.'

'What?' Joel leapt off the bed, his pulse accelerating. 'What the hell do you mean, her ventilator was interfered with? Interfered with by whom? Is she all right?'

'She's fine, Dr Addison. It's all back under control here, but the nursing staff are very shaken. Judy Newlands was looking after her and raised the alarm. If she wasn't as organised and level-headed as she is, it could have been a total disaster,' Brian said. 'Someone had switched off the ventilator alarms and switched oxygen and nitrous oxide inputs to the ventilator—she was breathing a 50-50 mix of nitrous and air.'

'That's impossible, Brian, the connectors are different. You can't screw an oxygen supply to a nitrous inlet, or vice versa.'

'I know that, but that's not how they did it. They cut the tubing and used clip-on joiners to switch the tubing. Nitrous comes out of the wall, and halfway along the tubing it changes into the oxygen tubing input of the ventilator. And the opposite for the oxygen supply.'

'This is serious, Brian. I'll be there in fifteen minutes. Have hospital security and the police been notified?'

'The place is crawling with them right now, Dr Addison, and somehow the press has been informed. There are at least two newspapers here already and security tells me there's a TV news van setting up a satellite dish out the front.'

Joel let out one sharp expletive. 'I'll be there as soon as I can.'

A group of journalists approached Joel as soon as he headed for the front doors of the unit. 'Dr Addison? You're the new director of Melbourne Memorial's innovative new ICTU. Do you have any comments on Kate or Tommy Lowe's condition? Has this incident or accident in the unit involved either of them?' one of them fired at him.

'I'm sorry but I am not at liberty to discuss patient details with anyone other than close family members,' he said, and made to brush past.

'Dr Addison, there are rumours that Kate Lowe tried to kill herself and her son, and there are rumours that an attempt was made on her life in the early hours of this morning in your unit. Do you believe there is a major weakness in security in the new unit? Could anyone just walk in and interfere with patients?'

'Is the public safe in your unit, Dr Addison?' another journalist persisted.

'Please, get out of my way,' Joel said, swiping his pass key to enter the building.

He located Brian Willis and almost frog-marched him into his office. Once there, the door shutting behind them with a snap, he asked Brian to fill him in on events of the night in detail.

'Whoever did this didn't realise about all the other separate alarms,' Brian said. 'The first thing to go off was the alarm on the pulse oximeter. Then the heartrate alarm went off at the desk. We were a bit short on staff, and had a one-to-three nursing ratio for about fifteen minutes down that end of the unit. Judy had gone to mix an antibiotic dose for Tommy, I was in the office. Judy heard the first alarm and came back in. The ventilator seemed to be working fine, she saw the alarms were off and switched them back on, and of course they all started sounding off. Oxygen sats had dropped to 70 per cent, so Judy just disconnected Mrs Lowe from the ventilator and hand-bagged her. Her obs came back to normal. She then reset all the ventilator settings and reconnected her, but within a minute all the alarms went off again.

We decided the ventilator was faulty. We bagged her while one of the unused machines was brought across by Chris Farmer, the orderly. We set her up on it on its bottle supply and it worked fine, so we disconnected the wall supply, moved out the old one, moved in the new one, connected the wall supply to the new one, then all the alarms went off on the new one. We knew the wall supply must have been OK because it's driving every other ventilator in the unit. It's just didn't add up. Then Chris found the connectors and switched-over tubing—one loop of it, with the connectors, was concealed under the equipment trolley in the corner of the cubicle.'

'This is not just sabotage, Brian, this is attempted murder,' Joel said.

'I agree. The police think so, too. They're interviewing Judy and Chris now. I gave a statement a while ago. They want to talk to you at some point.'

'Were there any relatives in the unit?'

'There were people coming and going earlier in the night, up till pretty late actually,' Brian answered. 'You know what it's like in here sometimes, we allow relatives as much contact as possible. That boy that came in the other day—you know, the spinal injury? His parents have barely left his bedside. I think his sister and girlfriend have been in, too, but it's impossible to keep track of everybody in a unit as big as this.'

Joel ran a distracted hand through his hair. 'I know…it's hard to tell people to stay away when it could be the last time they see the patient.' His hand fell to his side. 'Has Mrs Lowe's husband been informed?'

'Yes.'

'What was his reaction?'

'Apparently pretty cold and dismissive about it,' Brian said. 'Quite frankly, I don't think he'd care if someone pulled the plug on his wife.'

Joel frowned. 'Was he in the unit at any time during the night?'

'I'm not sure, I'd have to check with the nursing staff. Do you think he did this?'

'It'd be a pretty stupid thing to do under the circumstances,' Joel said. 'The finger of blame would point straight at him.'

'Yeah, I guess you're right. But he must be extremely cheesed off about it all the same. The kid isn't doing so well. Mr Lowe will probably lose it if his son doesn't recover or if he's left permanently brain-damaged.'

'Let's hope it doesn't turn out to be permanent,' Joel said, at the same time as his phone rang.

'I'll leave you to it,' Brian said and made his way out.

'Joel, it's Patrick Naylor here,' said the voice on the phone. 'What the hell is going on in the unit? I just had a call from Switchboard that the press and the police are crawling all over the place.'

'There's been an incident in ICTU with a patient,' Joel explained, pinching the bridge of his nose with two fingers to release the tension he could feel building behind his eyes. 'It's under control now but the press will expect a statement from one of us—if it's me, I want you to clear it before I make it. You'd better come in and I'll fill you in with the details.'

'For God's sake, man, it's four a.m.!' the CEO said. 'Can't it wait until morning? I normally don't get in till eight-thirty.'

Joel dropped his hand and rolled his eyes, actively forcing himself to remain polite. 'If that's what you'd prefer.'

'Good. I'll see you in my office at eight-thirty. And get Security to get rid of the press. I don't want to be harassed by journalists getting from my car to the lifts.'

'Fine, but if it's going to be eight-thirty I can't be held responsible for whatever unenlightened speculation appears on the front of the Melbourne papers,' Joel said, but the CEO had already hung up.

CHAPTER EIGHT

'DID you hear what happened last night in ICTU?' Margaret Hoffman, the anaesthetic registrar, said the next morning as she came into the main operating theatre change room where Allegra was changing for the first case on Harry Upton's long list.

'No, I came straight up here. I'm doing my round later. What happened?'

'Someone tried to kill Kate Lowe.'

'What?' Allegra's eyes went wide. 'How?'

'They tampered with the ventilator, cut and switched nitrous and oxygen gas lines into her ventilator.'

'That's incredible! Have they caught the person responsible?'

'No, but I bet it was the father,' Margaret said.

'It could have been anyone,' Allegra said, not sure why she was springing to Keith Lowe's defence. 'It might have even been a member of staff.'

Margaret frowned as she tightened the waist ties on her scrub trousers. 'But if it was a staff member, they would have known how the alarm system worked and circumvented it. That woman would be dead by now and I know a few people who would be glad of it.'

'Come on, Margaret, that's a bit harsh, isn't it? The police haven't even established whether it was an attempted murder-suicide.'

Margaret handed her the newspaper from inside her locker. 'Haven't you read this morning's paper?'

Allegra unfolded it and looked down at the front-page story, her stomach sinking in alarm. There was a fairly recent picture of Kate and Tommy and below, the stark black headlines couldn't have been more condemning of the mother's motives.

'She's as guilty as all get-out,' Margaret said. 'Look at her. She looks the type, all dowdy and depressed. The inside story is the husband asked for a divorce and it sent her crazy. She didn't want to give up custody of the little boy so decided to take matters into her own hands.'

Allegra refolded the paper and handed it back. 'She's still entitled to a fair trial.'

'Yeah, right, where she gets some hot-shot lawyer to get her to plead temporary insanity and she gets off scot-free,' Margaret said in a scathing tone. 'What's fair about that? How does that help that poor little kid hooked up on that ventilator?'

'What would help both Tommy and his mother would be the staff getting on with their job of taking care of their recovery instead of gossiping and speculating about them,' Allegra said.

'Surely you don't think she's innocent, do you?' Margaret asked. 'How can she be when she was high on drugs and drink? She was driving the car, remember, no one else.'

'I know…' Allegra sighed as she stepped out of her skirt. 'But I just can't get my head around the idea of someone trying to kill their own child, not unless they were actually not in their right mind.'

'I feel sorry for the husband,' Margaret said. 'It said in the paper how he'd done everything he could to try and save the marriage.'

Allegra frowned as she tied her hair with a bandana. 'And yet the paper said he asked for a divorce.'

'Well, everyone has their limits,' Margaret said. 'Maybe he'd finally had enough and found someone else. That's the trend, isn't it? Trade in the old wife for an updated version?'

Allegra turned to face her, a contemplative expression beginning to settle on her features. 'Or get *rid* of the old wife.'

Margaret's mouth dropped open. 'But how would he have done it? When it happened he was in Melbourne. He's got an iron-clad alibi.' She folded her arms across her chest and added, 'Now who is doing the speculating?'

'You're right,' Allegra said with a rueful twist to her mouth. 'We'd better leave this stuff to the professionals while we get on with what we're trained to do. Is Harry here yet? I want to get on with the list so I can do some preliminary work on Tommy and his mother.'

'So you've managed to convince the new director, have you?'

'I wouldn't go as far as using the word "convince",' Allegra said. 'He has a lot of reservations. And this latest drama is not going to help things. Everyone will be as edgy as all get-out around there. But unless Kate or Tommy wake up, we're never going to know what happened—the truth might never come out. Maybe a murderer will walk free. As I see it, my project is now doubly important.'

'But what if the truth is she did try to kill her son and herself? How is the little boy going to cope with that?'

Allegra sighed as she reached for her theatre clogs. 'How does anyone cope with the truth? It hurts for a while but somehow you have to pick yourself up and get on with life. Kids are amazingly resilient and incredibly forgiving.'

'I can tell you one thing for free—if that woman was my mother, I would never forgive her,' Margaret said with feeling. 'That kid is likely to be brain-damaged for the rest of his life. That's beyond forgiveness, if you ask me.'

'No one is beyond forgiveness, Margaret. There isn't a person alive who hasn't made a mistake some time during their lives. We don't know the circumstances of Kate Lowe's life, or at least not firsthand. She might have felt completely different on another day. That's the hardest part of it to comprehend. What loomed so large in her life might have been dealt with totally differently, given a few hours either way. And as for Tommy, well, at this stage we don't know the extent of his brain injury,' Allegra reminded her. 'For all we know, he could make a complete and full recovery.'

Margaret gave her a sceptical look as she shouldered open the change-room door. 'You really do believe in miracles, don't you?'

'We have to sometimes, Margaret,' she said. 'Science can't fix some things, and it can't tell us our values. If we haven't got values, we may as well go downstairs and turn off the ventilator now.'

'God, I hope it doesn't ever come to turning off Tommy's ventilator.' Margaret grimaced. 'Especially not so soon after Alice Greeson.'

'It won't come to that, Margaret,' Allegra said with determination. 'I'm going to do everything in my power to make sure of it.'

Allegra had not long finished Harry's list, which had run overtime due to a complication with a patient, when she received a call from the CEO, insisting on an immediate meeting with him in his office. 'But I have to get down to ICTU,' she said, hoping to put him off.

'Why?' Patrick's tone became resentful. 'So you can have a little rendezvous with the new director? I heard about your cosy little dinner last night.'

Allegra felt her hackles rising. 'Look, Patrick, I'm sorry but I'm not interested in a relationship with you. What I do in my spare time is my business. I'm sorry to be so blunt, but that's the way it is.'

There was a tense little silence.

'It's all right, I understand, but can't we just meet as friends?' Patrick asked, his tone now sounding more than a little emotional. 'You've been wonderful to me lately, that's why I supported your project so strenuously, apart from the fact that I do think it has merit. I felt I owed it to you for being such a good friend to me when I most needed it. Meet for a drink tonight at the Elgin Street bar at seven-thirty. That's all I'm asking. Please, Allegra.'

Allegra suppressed a sigh of resignation. Patrick was right. He had gone out on a limb for her and she owed him her friendship at the very least. 'All right, just one drink. But as friends, nothing else,' she relented.

'That's fine,' Patrick said. 'But I still thought I should warn you about getting involved with the new director. You'll only get hurt.'

She felt her tension increase slightly. There was a hint of something in the CEO's tone that made her blood feel a little cold in her veins. 'What are you saying, Patrick?' she asked.

'Look, I know he's a damn good intensivist but I can tell you right now he only asked you out last night to keep you away from the unit. He doesn't want you messing with the Lowe boy.'

'Come on, Patrick, that's an outright lie,' she said, but the black, long-legged spider of doubt was already crawling insidiously across her mind as she recalled Joel's totally-out-of-the-blue dinner invitation. They had barely been seated at the table when he'd brought up the topic of her study and the dangers of involving Kate and Tommy Lowe in it.

'Go and ask him,' Patrick challenged her. 'He won't deny it. He doesn't want you to interfere with how the unit is being run. The press attention has been damaging enough. They're making the unit sound as if anyone can walk in on any patient in there. And if they get to hear of you waving crystals or scented candles about, we'll be a laughing stock.'

'But you said—'

'I know what I said and I still stand by it. I do think your project has potential but I'm afraid I'm with Joel Addison on this particular case. There's just too much at stake. Just keep that in mind if he asks you out again. He could be operating under false pretences.'

'Don't worry, I will,' she said, and after a quick goodbye stuffed the phone back in her pocket.

* * *

Joel was returning to his office after the X-ray review meeting in the radiology department when he encountered Allegra stalking up the corridor towards him, her face looking like a brewing storm.

'Just the person I was hoping to run into,' he said with a smile. 'Got time for a quick coffee in my office?'

Allegra gritted her teeth. 'Why? So you can keep me out of the unit and away from my project for a little longer?'

He frowned at her tone. 'What's that supposed to mean?'

'Surely you don't need me to spell out your own despicable motives for you.'

'I haven't the faintest idea of what you're talking about.'

She gave him a glowering look. 'Why did you ask me out for dinner last night?'

He met her glittering green gaze head on. 'Why does any man ask a beautiful woman out for a meal?'

Allegra had to force herself not to be mollified by his compliment and injected even more venom into her tone. 'If you were any other man, I would have answered that you wanted to get to know me, but I am well aware of your real reasons for taking me out.'

'All right,' he said with a crooked smile. 'I admit it. I had an ulterior motive.'

There was a three-beat pause.

'Well,' she said with a dark frown, 'aren't you going to come clean?'

He took her by the hand before she could stop him and pulled her into a storeroom off the corridor and closed the door. She opened her mouth to rail at him but his mouth came swooping down and covered hers with a hot drugging kiss that left her breathless and totally disorientated in the dark, suddenly intimate confines of the small room. His body was pressed so tightly against hers she could feel the small buttons on his shirt through the thin cotton of her top and his belt buckle against her stomach. She had trouble containing her reaction to him. It seemed to come from deep inside, out of reach of her brain, which insisted she remove herself from his embrace.

He lifted his mouth from hers and flicked on the light switch near her left shoulder, his dark eyes smouldering with desire as he held her gaze.

'You had no right to do that,' she said, wishing her voice had sounded a little more strident and infuriated, instead of breathless and weak.

'You asked me to explain my motives. I thought it best to demonstrate them instead.'

'What you just demonstrated is your incredible gall. You only asked me out last night to lure me away from the unit so don't bother denying it.'

'I'm not going to deny it.'

She glared at him furiously. 'How dare you pretend to be attracted to me? That is so low.'

'I'm not pretending anything, Allegra.'

'I don't believe you,' she tossed back. 'You've been against me from the start. I should have guessed you were up to something when you dropped that dinner invitation into the conversation so unexpectedly.'

'I admit it was a little spontaneous but—'

'Spontaneous?' She felt like stamping her foot in fury. 'You deliberately lured me away from the unit.'

'I asked you out to dinner, for God's sake.' His voice began to tighten in anger. 'Is there a law against that these days? What is it with you? I asked you out because I'm attracted to you and I want to get to know you, but if you're not interested, fine. Maybe I'll take my chances with that internet dating thing after all.'

'I hope you end up with a psychopathic crackpot,' she returned bitterly.

'Yeah, well, it wouldn't be the first time,' he said, and, brushing past her, clicked the door shut behind him.

* * *

ICTU was quieter than normal due to the high level of security. Relatives of patients were being asked to limit their visits and to submit to a bag search, and the staff also had to comply with security measures—bag and locker searches, and a permanent security guard in the unit.

Kate had now been moved into one of the isolation rooms and was under police guard. Tommy was still showing no signs of waking, and the nurse on duty for him, Bethany Gladstone, relayed the neurosurgical plan for a repeat brain CT and an EEG.

'Has the father been in today?' Allegra asked.

'He's been in and out,' Bethany said. 'He should be back any time. He was going to have a bite to eat.'

Allegra looked at the unconscious child on the bed and wondered how anyone could think of food when their only child was hovering precariously between life and death.

'He's a bit of a detached sort of bloke, don't you think?' Bethany said. 'The father, I mean.'

'Why do you say that?'

The nurse gave a little shrug. 'I don't know… He just doesn't seem to be all that keen on hanging around here.'

'It's tough on parents,' Allegra said. 'They don't always cope with the emotions of it all. It doesn't get much worse than this—the thought of losing your only child.'

'Yeah, I guess so,' Bethany said. 'What's your plan with him?'

'Tommy, you mean?'

Bethany nodded.

Allegra looked at the little boy for a moment. 'I'd like to speak to the father about Tommy's history. The things he loves—books, movies, that sort of thing. I want to feel as if I know him in order to find ways to get through to him.'

'His father doesn't seem the type who knows his son all that well. Some dads are very hands on, sitting and talking to their kids, holding their hands, stroking them and so on. I don't think Mr Lowe has touched his son once the whole time I've been on duty.'

'Not all fathers are the same,' Allegra said. 'Besides, you

know how some people can't cope with illness and the prospect of death. They come in here and totally freak out when they see all the machines, while others react with calm.'

'Yeah, well, I think Mr Lowe needs to take lessons on fatherhood from Jonathon Sprent's father. Ever since that young man has been in here with that spinal injury his dad has hardly left the bedside, neither has his mum. That's what I call perfect parenting.'

'How is he doing? I haven't had much to do with his case.'

'Anthony Pardle did a spinal decompression and things are looking a little more hopeful—he's had a tingling sensation in his legs.'

'That's good. Even after all this training and time, I still can't bear the thought of a young man of nineteen confined to a wheelchair for the rest of his life,' Allegra said.

'I know,' Bethany sighed. 'He's had some time off the ventilator and coped pretty well. There's talk of moving him to the high-dependency unit in a couple of days.'

'It's nice to hear of something positive happening around here,' she said, looking at Tommy again.

'So you want me to let you know when Mr Lowe gets back?' Bethany asked.

'That would be great, thanks,' Allegra said, turning around to face her again. 'I'll be in the ICTU office, catching up on paperwork.'

A short time later Allegra looked up to see Keith Lowe outside the glassed-in office in ICTU. She got to her feet and with a reassuring smile led him to a private corner so she could speak to him.

'How are you doing, Mr Lowe?'

'I'm fine, but I want to know what's happening with my son,' he said rather impatiently. 'I've got a business to run and all this waiting about is not helping.'

Allegra had to fight down her instinctive reaction to his callous dismissal of his son's condition in preference to his career. 'Tommy is doing as well as can be expected at this stage,' she said.

'Look, Dr…er, Tallis,' he said, peering at her name badge. 'I want my son out of here, and fast. Don't get me wrong. My business can wait, but I can't juggle the two like this for too much longer. Is there anything I can do to help my son regain consciousness?'

'Yes, there is, actually,' she said, hope lifting like a suddenly inflated balloon in her chest. 'I need you to tell me some of Tommy's favourite things at present, such as music, stories he likes to hear or read, movies or DVDs he likes to watch, activities.'

'That's easy,' Keith said. 'Tommy has been totally obsessed with the Harry Potter stories. Whenever I get the chance, I read him his favourite passages. I bought him the first DVD and he's watched it countless times. He can even recite the dialogue practically verbatim.'

'Brilliant!' Allegra said. 'Would you have any objection to me setting up a portable DVD player near him to see if it triggers brain activity?'

He frowned at her. 'You think playing a DVD will make him regain consciousness?'

'I'm not making any promises but the human brain is complicated. Sometimes neural activity can stop for functional reasons when there is no physical damage. Tommy's brain CT looks normal. CTs are not perfect—there could be widespread scattered damage that doesn't show up on CT and could be enough to be severe brain damage. But the normal CT could alternatively give us hope. It is possible that there are functional blocks to Tommy's brain activity. It might be feasible to kick-start his conscious processes. The five senses—touch, smell, taste, sight and hearing—if we could find some powerful stimuli through one or two of these that trigger potent memories—that could trigger consciousness. Perhaps listening to his favourite movie will trigger something in Tommy's subconscious and he will start to wake up. There's no guarantee, and not a lot of research in this area—but with someone like Tommy it's worth trialling the technique.'

'If you think there's a chance…' Keith didn't sound particularly optimistic but Allegra refused to be daunted. She'd already passed the biggest hurdle: parental permission.

'I'll organise everything,' she said. 'I have a portable DVD player and I even have my own copy of the movie. Is there anything else you can think of that Tommy particularly likes? Songs he always listens to, favourite foods?'

Keith wrinkled his nose in scepticism. 'What, are you going to wave chicken nuggets and chips under his nose to see if he responds?'

'Is that his favourite food?'

The set of his shoulders seemed to go down a notch as he let out a deep sigh. 'So often I'd come home and…Kate would have no dinner prepared.' He looked at her and continued, 'Don't misunderstand me. I'm not really the where's-my-dinner type, but Tommy's a little kid—he needs regular meals. My wife wasn't good at doing that stuff and because of the pressures of my job I'm away a lot. I can't remember the last time she actually cooked a real meal—one that didn't come out of a packet with instructions to heat and serve.'

'It's not easy, being a mother,' Allegra felt compelled to put in, given her own shortcomings when it came to preparing gourmet meals. 'There's so much to do and so little time to do it, especially with a small child underfoot.'

'I know…' He gave her a vestige of a smile but there was no humour in it. 'Have you got kids?'

'Er…no…'

'It all changes once you do, you know,' he said. 'You have such ideals, but when reality hits they come crashing down.'

'This is a hard time for you, Mr Lowe. But I think we can work together to try to get Tommy to wake up, if it's at all possible. You love him and even though you might not think he is aware of your presence here, it's definitely possible that in some way he is conscious of it. He's just not quite able to wake up.'

'When will he be able to?'

She touched him gently on the arm. 'I hope he will wake up when we touch on what's most important to him. It could be the movie. Maybe it could be your voice or your touch. If we can just find the trigger that will get him to respond.'

'Have you done this sort of thing before?' he asked. 'You know…woken someone from a deep coma?'

Allegra pushed Alice Greeson's broken body from her mind and tried to concentrate on the rare successes she'd had so far. 'I have had some success, yes.'

'What about my wife?' he asked, his tone becoming harsh. 'Are you going to try and coax her awake as well?'

'I would like Kate to regain consciousness so we could at the very least establish what actually happened and why,' she said.

His eyes became like chips of cold blue ice. 'What happened was she wanted to take Tommy away from me permanently.'

'So there's absolutely no doubt in your mind that Kate tried to take her own life and that of Tommy?'

'Of course there's no doubt. It's what the police suspected from the start. She tried to commit suicide and kill Tommy to get back at me for asking for a divorce.'

'When did you ask her for a divorce?' Allegra asked, watching him closely.

He gave a shrug, his eyes falling away from hers. 'I don't know…a couple of days ago.'

'What was her immediate reaction to your request?'

'She wasn't too happy about it, obviously.'

'Did she say or do anything then to make you suspect she would take things this far?'

His eyes came back to hers, his expression growing impatient. 'Look, Dr Tallis, I have no idea what was going on in my wife's mind. Quite frankly, I haven't for years. I just wanted to end the marriage as soon as possible. I gave it my best shot but I decided it was time to leave.'

'Did you discuss custodial arrangements with Kate when you asked for a divorce?'

'I might have. I don't really remember. Now, if you'll excuse me, I have to get back to the office. I have a meeting and I'm already twenty minutes late as it is.'

Allegra watched him walk out briskly, as if he couldn't wait to get out of the building. He didn't even pause by his son's bed on the way past.

'What did I tell you?' Bethany said, joining her once more. 'Cold and clinical.'

'He certainly is,' Allegra agreed. 'But at least he's given me the go-ahead to work with Tommy. I was worried he might dismiss it right out of hand, but he was surprisingly agreeable.'

'I don't suppose he wants you to work on his wife,' Bethany said cynically.

'No, but that doesn't mean I can't.' Allegra looked towards the isolation room where Kate was being monitored, a tiny frown bringing her brows together. 'Has anyone been in to see her yet?'

'No one at all. I guess she either doesn't have any relatives or if she does, they're all too angry with her to visit—not that you could blame them after what she tried to do.'

'Surely there must be someone close to her, a friend or sister or cousin, if not her parents. She can't possibly be all alone in the world. Someone must care about her.'

'Doesn't look like it,' Bethany said, 'Unless the husband has deliberately not told them.'

'It's been in the papers though…'

'Not everyone reads the paper every day,' Bethany said.

'True, but news has a habit of travelling anyhow so you'd think someone would have at least called to ask after her by now.'

'I guess you're right,' Bethany said. 'And when you think about it, Tommy hasn't had too many visitors either.'

'Has anyone apart from his father been in?'

'Mr Lowe's sister, Tommy's aunt, has come in a couple of times.'

'What was she like?'

Bethany screwed up her face. 'Exactly like her brother, cold and distant. She was dressed to the nines—you know the type, the cloying perfume and the coiffed hair and designer gear and heavy jewellery. She barely sat by Tommy's bed for more than a minute or two before leaving.'

'Does Tommy have grandparents?'

'I heard one of the nurses ask Mr Lowe that earlier,' Bethany said. 'He made no mention of Kate's parents but he said his were travelling somewhere interstate and couldn't be contacted.'

Allegra's frown increased. 'Which probably means he doesn't want them to be contacted. I wonder why?'

'Beats me,' Bethany said. Changing the subject, she asked, 'What are you going to do with Tommy?'

'His father said he loves Harry Potter movies. I'd like to set one up playing next to his bed—it might trigger memories, stir some neurological activity. It's part of the coma recovery protocol, using familiar auditory stimuli as triggers.'

'What are you going to play it on? This place is pretty cluttered as it is.'

'I've got a portable DVD player and stereo earpieces,' Allegra said as she reached for a piece of equipment. 'I'll set it up on the side shelf out of the way. Also, I want to put on a BIS monitor to record any sort of cerebral activity. This strip sticks on his forehead, and the lead plugs into the monitor. This one's got an eight-hour recorder. I'll set it going now, and take a baseline record. In an hour, can you plug in the earpieces and start the DVD? When it's finished, just take out the earpieces. Leave the BIS going till I come in later tonight, OK?'

'Sure' said Bethany. 'Got that. What time will you be back in?'

'About eight-thirty tonight, I think. I've just got one social engagement, and then I'll come in and collect the stuff and go home.'

'I didn't know you even had a home,' Bethany said with a wry grin. 'You seem to spend most of your time here.'

Allegra sent her a rolled eyed look as she left. 'Don't remind me.'

CHAPTER NINE

ALLEGRA had not long completed the pre-admission clinic for Harry Upton's list for the following week when her mobile phone buzzed with an incoming text. She looked down at it and saw it was from Tony Ringer, the night duty intensivist, informing her that Joel was in the high-dependency unit with Harry Upton, assessing the patient who'd had the complication after surgery that morning and that Joel needed anaesthetic information urgently.

Allegra remembered the case well. Gaile Donovan was a forty-eight-year-old woman with ovarian cancer that had invaded the pelvic wall and sigmoid colon. Harry had helped the gynaecologist with the pelvic exploration. The gynaecologist had been keen to get the tumour out but after five litres of blood loss, the normally calm-under-pressure Harry had broken out in a sweat trying to control the bleeding and had insisted they pull the plug before the patient expired on the table. They had packed the pelvis and temporarily closed the abdomen, with the intention of a second-look laparotomy the next day.

When Allegra arrived in HDU, she could hear Harry and Joel discussing the plan of action.

'The patient's BP has hit the floor, Harry,' Joel said. 'She's obviously bleeding again—you have no choice but to operate again now.'

'It was a nightmare the first time around,' Harry said. 'I think an angiogram and embolisation would be a better choice for controlling the bleeding.'

'Listen, Harry,' Joel said. 'She's pouring blood and wouldn't survive the trip to X-Ray, let alone a couple of hours on the X-ray table, having films done. The blood loss has got to be stopped or at least slowed a hell of a lot first. Maybe embolisation, then.'

'Damn it! I wish I'd never become involved in this case,' Harry grumbled. 'I could see it was trouble as soon as we opened.'

'Use the theatre here,' Joel suggested. 'It's on site, it's staffed and it's got angiography capability. Why don't you talk to Radiology now so they come in and set up in case you want to do on-table embolisation?' He turned as he saw Allegra, his expression visibly hardening. 'I thought Tony called for the anaesthetist on duty.'

'I'm the one he called, but if you'd prefer someone else, fine—go ahead,' she said with a flash of her green eyes.

He shifted his mouth in what was clearly reluctant resignation and turned back to Harry. 'Dr Tallis can anaesthetise for you. I've got to get a new central line in quickly to catch up with volume.'

'Right.' Harry nodded in agreement and with a quick grimace in Allegra's direction headed towards Radiology and the ICTU theatre.

Once Harry had left, Joel turned to fill Allegra in on the patient's condition. 'Mrs Donovan's MAP's 50, pulse 160, sats 80—not good. I've got a norad infusion up and fresh blood pouring in, but she needs surgical control of the bleeding. I'm replacing your central line from this morning—it seems to be kinked or compressed somewhere and I just can't get enough volume through it. Harry's using the theatre here.'

Allegra had to force aside her personal issues with him to maintain professional calm. 'I'll head down now and set up. Will you bring her down?'

'Yes, in about ten minutes. How much blood altogether did she have in Theatre this morning? I haven't had time to familiarise myself with the anaesthetic charts here—it would take me ten minutes to add it all up.'

'Yes, they are confusing. Fifteen units of packed cells and four units of whole blood. She also had four packs of albumin volume expander and three fresh-frozen plasmas. How many have you crossed-matched now?'

'Twenty packed cells—that's the current hospital supply of B at the moment. Red Cross are bleeding call-ins tonight to replenish supplies,' he answered.

'Good. I'd better get going,' Allegra said, and left the unit.

Joel turned back to the patient, his brow tightening with tension as he called on all his intensive care skills to work to salvage the rapidly developing disaster in front of him.

Gaile Donovan had two young teenage daughters and a loving husband waiting anxiously in the waiting room for news of their loved one's condition. Gaile's cancer diagnosis had been bad enough, but to suffer this complication during surgery added an element of potential tragedy that would be very hard to announce to the family if things didn't go well.

With the help of Danielle and the nursing staff, he replaced Allegra's previously inserted central line over a guide-wire and ensured it was running rapidly.

'Danielle, increase the noradrenaline infusion to three now, please, to help maintain blood pressure. I'm starting a vasopressin infusion to reduce venous pressure in the pelvis,' Joel instructed.

'Dr Addison, she's bleeding from every puncture site,' Danielle observed with growing alarm.

Despite massive transfusion, it was clear to Joel that coagulopathy was developing, and his inner tension went up another notch. Gaile's young daughters' faces swam before his eyes and his stomach clenched uncomfortably at the thought of having to face them with the worst news in the world.

'Unless we get this blood loss stopped now, no amount of intensive care is going to help her,' he said. Turning to the nurse at his side, he instructed, 'Get me four packs of FFP and I'll call the blood bank myself to retrieve ten packs of platelets.'

The ICTU nurse left to retrieve the packs of fresh-frozen plasma, which were stored in the ICTU blood fridge, as Joel reached for the nearest telephone.

A few minutes later a courier came in with the thawed platelets and Joel stabilised the patient to the point where she could be transferred to the operating theatre for a further attempt at pelvic packing and possible embolisation.

In Theatre, Allegra had set up the anesthetic machine, arterial line and monitoring equipment, and Harry and the scrub team were already scrubbed and waiting.

'She's extremely unstable, Dr Tallis—I'm just keeping up with fluids and she's coagulopathic. She's on norad at three and a vasopressin infusion. I've got FFP and platelets running and we're onto unit ten of fresh B blood, with ten left to go. Blood bank is scouring for more,' Joel said as the patient was transferred to the operating table.

Allegra gave him a worried look. 'I've really got my hands full here. Once we open up, her BP is going to hit the floor again.'

'I know that. I'll stay here and help with fluid and coag management while you manage the anesthesia,' he offered.

'That's a first,' Harry said, as the scrub nurse handed him scissors to open the previous incision. 'You don't often see an intensivist in Theatre.'

'That's the whole point of this new unit,' Joel said, as he assisted Allegra to attach the arterial line and monitor. 'Overlap of skills to break down the rigid barriers between specialties.'

While Allegra concentrated on anesthesia, Joel juggled fluid input, coagulation factors, consultation with the haematologists and blood bank, and provided general support to Allegra during the procedure. After rapid prepping and draping of the abdomen, Harry opened the previous incision to be greeted by welling up of venous blood from the pelvis.

'Her blood pressure's 60, Dr Addison,' Allegra said with concern, as she pumped in blood through two lines.

'Harry, we're not winning up this end. Can you control anything down there?' Joel asked over the drapes.

'I'm doing my best, guys, but there's no one bleeding point,' Harry rasped back, beads of sweat appearing on his brow above his mask.

Harry rapidly removed the old packs and repacked the pelvis, this time using multiple thumbtack-shaped staples to pin down every obvious bleeding vein to the pelvic walls before compressing with packs. In addition he ligated both internal iliac arteries. Although a drastic step, the bleeding finally slowed then stopped with repacking the pelvis.

'I can see clotting. You must have improved her coag profile significantly,' Harry said with obvious relief in his eyes as they connected briefly with Joel and Allegra's.

'She's just about used up the entire supply of platelets and FFP. I think she'll run into ARDS after all of this,' Joel said.

'Her ventilation pressures are up, she's got pulmonary oedema—she's already in respiratory distress. I appreciate your help in Theatre, Dr Addison, but I'll be fine in here now. I'm sure you've got other concerns in the unit apart from this one patient,' Allegra said with brisk formality.

Joel gave her an indecipherable look before shifting his gaze towards the surgeon. 'See you later, Harry. Good luck with the rest of the procedure.'

'Yeah, thanks, Joel. I think I like this cross-over idea, ICU, anaesthesia and Theatre all in one for this sort of case. I just hope this poor lady makes it. She's put up one hell of a fight so far.'

'It's not over till it's over,' Joel said as he shed his theatre overgear and dropped it into the bins as he went. 'I'll speak to the relatives if you want me to, and then I'll do a quick change-over round with Tony Ringer before I leave.'

'No, don't worry, Joel, I'll see them. It's my responsibility,' Harry replied.

Joel nodded and left the theatre.

Harry looked at Allegra once Joel had left. 'I know I've said it before, but you two work well as a team,' he remarked. 'Are the rumours true, then?'

Allegra gave him a quelling look. 'I thought it was only the nursing staff who indulged in such a useless pastime as gossip.'

'In spite of your little formal act just then, anyone can see you and he have something going on.'

'Yes—an argument,' she said.

'He's a nice chap,' Harry said, as the nurse handed him another pack. 'I've worked under a lot of directors in the past but I can tell Joel Addison is switched on.'

'He's highly skilled, yes,' Allegra agreed, not quite able to disguise a little scowl.

Harry gave her another quick glance before he positioned another pack in the patient's abdomen. 'Are you still worried he's going to stop your project?'

'He's not keen on me working with the Lowe boy, especially now.'

'That's to be expected, I guess,' Harry said. 'God, it was a shock to think someone could waltz in and interfere with equipment like that on the mother. Have the police got any idea of who did it?'

'Not that I know of.'

'What about the father?' Harry asked. 'He's certainly got a motive, I would think.'

'He's also got an alibi,' Allegra pointed out.

Harry gave a grunt as he began to close the abdomen. 'How very convenient for him.'

'I don't think he did it,' she said, hoping her gut feeling was right.

'Not personally, but perhaps he had someone do it for him,' Harry said.

Allegra frowned as she checked the anaesthetic monitors. The same thought had crossed her own mind. Had Keith organised someone to get rid of his wife? It was clear he hated her for what she'd done to their son and if Tommy's injuries proved to be permanent, how much more would he want to avenge his son's life?

'What if he was the one who drugged her up and sent her off in that car in the first place?' Harry said into the silence.

Allegra swung back to look at him. 'With his own son sitting in the back seat? Come on, Harry. Keith might not win the husband-of-the-year award, but he loves his son. Besides, he wants me to do what I can to get Tommy to wake from his coma. If he was involved in any way with his wife's accident, I hardly think he'd want a seven-year-old witness on hand to testify against him.'

'Yeah, I guess you're right,' Harry said. 'But it pays to look at it from all angles.'

'That's what the police are for. There's already been too much gossip and innuendo as it is.'

'Speaking of gossip, Patrick Naylor was crowing about you and him having a drink later this evening,' he said as he finished closing the wound.

Allegra let out a frustrated breath as she began to reverse the anaesthetic. 'I'm only having a drink with him because he's been supportive of my project, although he's wavering on it in the Lowe boy case. It seems he's joined the Addison camp.'

Harry removed his mask and stripped off his gloves. 'There was a lot of opposition to your project, as you know. It was good of Patrick to stand by you, no matter what his motives.'

'What's your opinion, Harry?' she asked. 'Were you for or against my study?'

'Look, Allegra, you know I'm not one for reading auras or any of that stuff, but what you did with the Greeson girl was beyond what anyone else in the unit could offer. Her parents drew a lot of comfort from how you handled things. Even if your study goes on to prove nothing of scientific value, who's to say it's not worthwhile? Everyone wants results these days but sometimes we have to settle for what is. You helped two devastated parents cope with the worst tragedy imaginable, and you did it by maintaining their daughter's dignity right to the very end. So, yes, I was for your study, and still am.'

She gave him a grateful smile. 'Thanks, Harry.'

He winked at her. 'You remind me of my eldest daughter, Amelia. She wants to take on the world, and heaven help anyone who gets in her way.'

'The only person in my way is Joel Addison,' she said, with another downturn of her mouth.

'He's not in your way, Allegra,' Harry said. 'He's just trying to make sure the unit brings in the results everyone is expecting. I know you would have preferred Dougal Brenton but personally I think Joel Addison is streets ahead. He's had experience in a war-torn country and he's got a clear, calm head under pressure. He's innovative and focused, which is exactly what this hospital needs in its ICTU director right now.'

'I know all that but he has such a bias against me,' she said. 'I don't know how to get through to him.'

'I don't think you need to worry about getting his attention, Allegra,' he said with a grin. 'It seems obvious to me that you've certainly got that.'

She gave him a speaking glance. 'I've got his attention, but for all the wrong reasons.'

'I don't know about that. He's a reasonable enough man. If you can produce results, I think he'll come round.'

'I need more time to produce the sort of results he requires,' she said. 'It can take some patients weeks, if not months to regain consciousness. He's given me a month, but it's not long enough to do what I want to do.'

'Just do what you can in the time you have. You've got a

chance with the Lowe kid—he's young and his brain damage may not be as bad as first expected. I've seen kids like him on ventilators for weeks and then suddenly they're up and running about as if nothing had happened.'

'I hope that's how it will be for Tommy,' she said. 'He's just seven years old.'

Harry gave her a probing look. 'You're not getting too emotionally involved in this, are you, Allegra? I know you had a rough time with the Greeson girl but we all have to move on. They're our patients and we do what we can, but it's not our fault if we can't pull a miracle out of the hat every time.'

'No, I'm fine,' she said, wondering if it was true. 'I just want to give this my best shot. I know there's potential in this study. I can sense it.'

'You have to show it, not sense it,' he reminded her, with scientific pragmatism.

'I know that, Harry. I'm well aware of the parameters I have to work within. I just think there are ways we're not utilising that could help patients regain consciousness. Everything seems to be economically rationalised these days—if there's no EEG activity after X days and Y dollars of ICU support, pull the plug. But with a different theoretical approach and some time and effort, I believe we could start a paradigm shift in the management of post-traumatic coma.'

'I hope to God you're right, Allegra,' he said, as he removed his surgical gown. 'I hate it when ventilators are switched off on live bodies. It doesn't matter how many CT scans and EEGs, I still can't help feeling there might have been…' He didn't need to complete the sentence.

'I know,' she said with a heartfelt sigh. '"Brain dead" is a cold, hard term. I realise we can't keep people alive indefinitely on a ventilator when there's clearly no hope. I just want to make absolutely sure there *is* no hope, that we're covering every aspect, not giving up before every option is explored.'

'I know it's a well-worn adage, but I really do believe that where there's life there's hope. Joel was right when he said earlier that it's not over until it's over. Even Gaile Donovan here—sick as she is—still has a slim chance of making it.'

Allegra looked down at the pallid features of the patient under her care. 'I certainly hope so, Harry.'

He gave her a weary glance as he helped move the patient from the operating table to the ICTU bed. 'I'm going out to speak to the husband and daughters now. I wish I could promise them more but I'm not a miracle-worker.'

'She's alive, Harry,' Allegra said. 'That's all that matters right now. That's all they'll want to hear.'

'I know, but for how long?' he asked as she wheeled the patient past him out of Theatre.

Allegra didn't answer. She didn't like Gaile Donovan's chances either, but to voice them seemed to be inviting the worst. She'd already had enough of the worst. What she needed now was a miracle and she was going to go looking for it, no matter what Joel Addison said to the contrary.

CHAPTER TEN

PATRICK Naylor was sitting in the bar, waiting for her, when Allegra finally arrived, the two empty glasses in front of him suggesting he'd been there for quite a while.

'I'm sorry I'm late but I had to go back to Theatre,' she said as she sat down opposite him.

'I wasn't worried…not really,' he said, giving her a quick on-off smile before his eyes moved away from hers as he stared into the empty glass in front of him, his shoulders suddenly slumping. 'I just needed to see a friendly face.'

'Is everything all right, Patrick?' Allegra asked.

He gradually brought his gaze back to hers, the moisture shining there indicating he was having trouble keeping his emotions at bay. 'My wife is pregnant to her lover,' he said. 'I found out about it this morning.'

'I'm so sorry. That must be awful for you.'

He wiped at his eyes with the back of his hand. 'The irony is it was me who kept putting off having a family. I guess that's why she went looking elsewhere.'

She reached for his hand and gave it a gentle squeeze. 'Is there anything I can do?'

He shook his head and covered her hand with his. 'No, there's nothing anyone can do. I have to deal with it myself.' He released a little sigh and continued, 'I've booked in to see a counsellor. I think it's time I did some work on myself.'

'That's very brave of you,' she said softly.

He removed his hand from hers. 'I'm sorry I've been so full on lately. I thought if I threw myself into a new relationship I wouldn't feel so bad about it all.'

'I understand.'

He gave her a twisted, somewhat grim smile. 'I wanted to make my wife jealous. I thought if she saw you hanging on my arm she'd change her mind and come back, but that's not going to happen now. It's over.'

'I'm glad you explained it to me.'

'There's something else…' He pushed his empty glass out of his reach before his eyes returned to hers. 'Joel Addison didn't ask you out for the reasons I said. He is concerned about some issues pertaining to your project, especially since the Lowe incident, but I was just jealous and wanted to cause trouble.'

'Oh…'

'It was pathetic, I know, and I'm ashamed of myself. I hope I haven't made things difficult for you. I know you have to work pretty closely with him.'

'I'm sure we'll sort it out…' Allegra said, already mentally rehearsing an apology as she recalled her heated interaction with Joel earlier.

Patrick got to his feet and, leaning down, placed a quick peck on her cheek before straightening. 'Thanks for listening, Allegra. See you around some time.'

'Be kind to yourself, Patrick. These things take time. Bye.'

Joel wrote up the last of his notes before leaning back in his chair with a tired sigh. He rubbed his face, grimacing at the sound of his palm on his unshaven jaw. His conversation with Anthony Pardle about Tommy Lowe hadn't been encouraging. There didn't seem to be much hope but Joel had wanted to make sure he wasn't allowing his personal feelings get in the way. He had rearranged the shifts so the more experienced nurses were looking after the little boy and he had restricted visitors so that noise and disruption was at a minimum.

He'd even spent some time with the little boy after Anthony had left, sitting by his bed, talking to him, telling him some of the stuff he used to do as a kid.

'I had a bike, a red one with blue stripes,' he'd said, holding the boy's small hand in his. 'I thought I was pretty cool, riding up and down the street while my brother watched on the sidelines.'

A nurse had come past and he waited until she'd moved on before continuing in a low, urgent tone, 'Come on, Tommy, you have to do your best, mate, to wake up. No half-measures, got that?' He gave the little hand in his a gentle squeeze. 'I'm counting on you to pull out of this. You have to do it, for yourself, not just for your parents and Dr Tallis. You have to do it for yourself.'

'How's Tommy doing?' Allegra asked Bethany, when she returned to ICTU before heading home for the night.

The nurse handed her the BIS readouts. 'No sign of any brain activity, I'm afraid.'

Allegra fought against her disappointment as she read the printout.

'The movie finished a while ago,' Bethany said. 'Do you want me to rerun it?'

'Yes—it can't hurt to give it another go,' she said, still hoping for a miracle.

'Anthony Pardle came in a little while ago,' Bethany informed her. 'I overheard him talking to Dr Addison about Tommy.'

'What did he say?'

'He doesn't think there's much hope of Tommy recovering.'

Allegra refused to be put off. 'You know what neurosurgeons are like—they see the worst so they always imagine the worst.'

'Maybe, but Dr Addison seemed to be in agreement with him,' Bethany said. 'He agreed with Mr Pardle that Mr Lowe should be informed of the possibility of withdrawing life support from his son.'

Allegra felt her stomach drop in alarm. *'So soon?'*

'Brain dead is brain dead, Allegra,' Bethany said. 'An hour, a day, a week or a month won't make Tommy's brain repair itself.'

'But it's only been a couple of days!' she argued. 'We normally give patients a week or ten days before making that sort of decision. Besides, he's a child. Studies have shown that children sometimes do recover from severe head trauma after prolonged support.'

'I know, but Dr Addison and Mr Pardle have the final say, in consultation with the father, when they think the time is right,' Bethany reminded her. 'The sad thing is the mother is starting to show signs of regaining consciousness. It doesn't seem fair that she gets another chance at life when her son doesn't.'

'What's been happening with Kate Lowe?'

'They've withdrawn the barbiturates, as we have with Tommy, but while in Tommy's case nothing has happened, Kate has shown signs of spontaneous breathing and she opened her eyes once.'

'And her BIS monitor scores?'

'There are definite signs of brain activity,' Bethany said. 'But not in Tommy's.'

Allegra compressed her lips together as she looked at the small child being kept alive, his tiny limbs seeming to be even smaller than the day before. 'Come on, Tommy,' she pleaded softly. 'Wake up, honey. I know you can do it.'

Bethany gave Allegra a surreptitious nudge. 'Here comes Tommy's father and his aunt.'

'Dr Tallis,' Keith greeted her. 'I'd like you to meet my sister, Serena Fairbright.'

'Hello,' Allegra said, offering her hand to the glamorous woman accompanying Tommy's father.

Serena's hand brushed Allegra's briefly. 'How is my little nephew?'

'He's doing as well as can be expected,' Allegra answered.

'How did you go with the movie?' Keith asked.

'We're playing it again now.'

'So he hasn't responded?' Keith asked.

'No, but I'd like your permission to try a couple of other things,' Allegra said. 'Firstly I would like to try a particular massage therapy to see if he responds.'

'Massage?' Serena gave a sceptical frown. 'How is that going to repair his head injury?'

'Children are very touch-sensitive,' Allegra explained. 'Young children in particular are used to being touched by their mother and father in loving ways, such as helping them dress each morning, doing their hair for them or cuddling them.'

'Look, Dr Tallis, I'm not a new-age sort of man, as you've probably already guessed,' Keith confessed. 'I was brought up by strict parents who only ever touched me with a strap or a belt in their hands. I find it hard to express physical affection. I've never really kissed or cuddled Tommy, or at least not since he was about a year old.'

'I know this is painful for you to answer, but did his mother have any particular physical routine that you can recall that Tommy might respond to?' Allegra asked.

He gave her a shamefaced look. 'I was always on at Kate for being too soft on the boy,' he said. 'She was always touching him, kissing him or playing with his hair. I was frightened she would make a sissy out of him.'

'A lot of men feel that way, but let me assure you nothing could be further from the truth,' Allegra said. 'Touch is essential in a child's life. Why not sit with Tommy now and tell him you're here? And if you feel up to it, touch him in any way that makes you feel comfortable.'

'We haven't got long,' Serena said, with an impatient glance at her diamond-encrusted watch.

'If you think it would help…' Keith said, although he looked as doubtful as his sister.

Allegra left them in privacy to return to the office, where she made a few notes, but she'd hardly finished a sentence or two when she saw Keith and his sister leave the unit once more.

'What did I tell you?' Bethany said poking her head around the glass partition. 'She's exactly the same as him—cold as a frozen fish.'

'Yes, well, with that sort of background, what else could you expect?' Allegra said as she toyed with her pen. 'I can't believe how cruel some parents can be. It's no wonder Mr Lowe didn't want Tommy's grandparents to be contacted.'

'I guess you're right,' Bethany said. 'Well, I'm off now that Chloe's back. I did an extra couple of hours to cover for her. Dr Addison is insisting only the senior staff look after Tommy.'

Allegra looked up at that. 'Oh?'

'Yes, he may not be too keen on your project, but he's certainly doing his best to help Tommy before he makes his final decision. I saw him sitting with him earlier. He was talking to him and stroking his hand. If you ask me, he was a whole lot better at it than the kid's own father.'

'Thanks for helping with Tommy,' Allegra said after a tiny pause. 'I'm going to head off home.'

'No hot date tonight?'

'I have a date with a good book and a glass of Pinot noir,' she answered. 'That's about as hot as it gets in my life right now.'

'You could always throw a vindaloo curry in there somewhere to turn up the heat a bit,' Bethany suggested with a smile.

'What a great idea,' Allegra said, as she dragged herself to her feet. 'The last thing I want to do is cook. Take-away, here I come.'

The Indian restaurant not far from her apartment had a small waiting area for customers waiting for their take-out orders. Allegra sank gratefully into a vinyl chair once she'd placed her order and picked up a magazine that was at least two years out of date, flicking through it absently.

Once her number was called she collected her meal and made her way out to the street, but had only gone a few paces when she saw a very familiar figure heading her way.

Joel looked down at the container in her hand. 'Great minds think alike, it seems,' he said. 'What did you get?'

'Beef vindaloo.'

'Enough for two?'

'No.'

'Pity,' he said. 'I guess I'll have to go and order my own.'

She pursed her lips for a moment. 'I suppose I could make it stretch, but only if you've got a decent bottle of wine.'

He gave her a smile that melted her instantly. 'I'll go and get one from the bottle shop and meet you back at your place. Is there anything else you need?'

Only my head read, she thought as she returned his smile with a tentative one of her own. 'No, the wine will be fine.'

Allegra answered the door a short time later and he held out the bottle for her to inspect. 'Mmm…' She peered at the label. 'Last Hope Ridge, a '98 Merlot. Not a bad vintage. You have good taste.'

'In some things,' he said, looking down at the soft curve of her mouth.

Allegra felt her senses spring to attention at the smouldering heat in his dark gaze as it returned to hers, her skin feeling tight and overly sensitive, as if preparing itself for his touch.

'So I take it internet dating didn't work out?' she said, surprised her voice sounded so normal when her breathing was all over the place.

'I was seriously thinking about it,' he said, stepping closer. 'But I wasn't sure if you'd cast a spell on me earlier today so that I would end up with some wacko woman intent on having her wicked way with me.'

'I do not cast spells,' she said, trying to sound cross and indignant, but it didn't quite work, with him smiling at her so disarmingly.

'Yes, you do,' he said, tugging her closer, his hands on her hips. 'You're doing it right now.'

'That's totally ridiculous,' she gasped as his lower body came into contact with hers. 'I wouldn't know the first thing about magic…and all that…stuff…' She swallowed as he brought his head down, his warm breath caressing the surface of her lips.

'What about this stuff?' he asked, as his mouth brushed hers.

'That's not magic…' she breathed into his mouth.

'What is it, then?' he asked, his warm breath mingling with hers.

'It's…madness…' she said, kissing him back softly, her lips clinging to his. 'Total madness…'

'It's not madness,' he growled as he pulled her even closer. 'It's desire.'

'Lust,' she corrected him. 'It's good old-fashioned lust. It will go away if we ignore it.'

'How do you suggest we ignore it?' he asked, nibbling gently at the soft underside of her neck.

'Um…we could try some other activity…' She shivered all over as the tip of his tongue briefly entered her ear.

'What did you have in mind?' He grazed her top lip with the masculine and totally irresistible rasp of his tongue. 'Scrabble?'

'I cheat at Scrabble,' she said, sagging against him as he found her bottom lip and stroked it with his tongue, back and forth until her lip began to swell with need. 'I make up words and I always win.'

'I'd never let you get away with it,' he warned softly, as his mouth hovered over hers.

'No one's beaten me yet.' Her breath mingled intimately with his, making her stomach feel hollow.

'I like the sound of being the first to conquer you,' he said, pressing his mouth to hers in a scorching, probing kiss that left her totally breathless. Her arms wound around his neck as she rose on tiptoe to get even closer to him, her fingers delving into the thick black pelt of his hair, her body soft against his hardness, her legs feeling unsteady and trembling with desire.

He lifted his mouth from hers after endless minutes, his dark eyes alight with rampant need as they locked on hers. 'We should eat before this gets out of hand. We've both had a long day and we're not thinking with our heads here.'

'You're right,' she said, unwinding her arms from his neck and stepping back from him. 'Besides, I need to get an apology out of the way.'

'What do you need to apologise for?'

'Patrick told me you had only asked me out to keep me away from the unit. I was angry with you for exploiting me without checking to see if what he'd said was actually right.'

'I see.'

'He apologised for it earlier this evening. He's going through a rough time in his personal life.'

'And here I was thinking it was my kisses that finally convinced you of my motives,' he said, with a wry twist to his mouth.

'Your kisses are definitely very convincing,' she admitted, lowering her eyes from the steadiness of his. 'But…but aren't we rushing things a bit?'

'What do you mean?'

She raised her eyes back to encounter his unwavering dark brown gaze. 'We may be attracted to each other physically, but we're poles apart professionally. You have issues with my study and I have issues over your decision to withdraw life support on Tommy Lowe. This is never going to work between us.'

'Come on, Allegra.' His tone became impatient. 'You know the routine with head injuries. Once the patient is declared brain dead by the neurosurgeon we have no choice but to advise the relatives to consider withdrawing life support. It's not fair to the patient or the relatives to let them hang in limbo for no gain.'

'Tommy is a young child,' she countered. 'Numerous studies have demonstrated the possibility of recovery after more prolonged support in children.'

'Yes, but exactly what sort of recovery are we talking about?'

'A full recovery, of course.'

He let out a short rough expletive. 'You really are off with the fairies, aren't you? Damn it, Allegra, you know there are degrees of recovery in these sorts of cases. Tommy could end up permanently disabled, either physically or intellectually or, God help him, both. He'd be totally dependent on his father or his mother if she survives. What sort of life is that for any of them?'

'He'd be alive, that's all that matters to a parent,' she argued.

'Is it?' he asked, his eyes glittering with some indefinable pent-up emotion she couldn't quite recognise.

'Of course it is! Losing a child is the most devastating thing that can happen to a parent. The grief is total and all-consuming.'

'So is the grief of being totally responsible for a child who will never grow up, either physically or mentally,' he said, grasping her by the upper arms, his fingers biting into her tender flesh. 'Have you thought about that any time in your fairy-dust study? Have you ever interviewed the relatives of a child who didn't get your magical full recovery? Have you asked them what it's like to have to change their adult child's nappy several times a day, to spoon food and drink into them while most of it dribbles down their chin? Have you asked them what it's like to lie awake at night, listening to their child uttering screams and cries that no physical comfort or words will ever ease? Have you asked them what it's like for the rest of the family, their marriage, and all their other relationships? *Have you?*'

She shrank back from the vitriol in his tone. 'I—I... No I haven't, but I—'

He dropped his hands from her so suddenly she almost stumbled backwards. 'You don't know what you're doing, Allegra. I could see that from the first moment I looked at your study. You can't keep people alive indefinitely without weighing the costs.'

'Neither can you play God,' she said. 'You can't possibly think it's reasonable to wander through ICU and switch off ventilators, without giving the relatives adequate time to make that decision if it's called for.'

'Tommy Lowe will be given the same time frame every other patient in his condition is given. But once ten days is up, if there is still no brain activity his father will be informed of his choices. We can keep that child alive for months, but while he's soaking up valuable resources, three or four other children will die for want of organ donation that Tommy's brain-dead body could provide. Why don't you go and visit some of them in the children's ward? Have a talk to the parents sitting there hour after hour, with the clock on the wall ticking away their child's last chance at a normal life.'

Allegra knew his argument was reasonable; she was well aware of the lifesaving transplants that offered hope when all else had failed. It was, after all, sometimes the only comfort in losing a loved one to know that some part of them lived on, giving precious life to some other person who then could go on to live a normal life. Julie's parents had made the very same difficult decision when their daughter's ventilator had finally been switched off. But Allegra had always thought Julie had deserved more time. It gnawed at her constantly. She couldn't help feeling her friend's parents had been pressured into their final decision.

'I understand what you're saying, but I still think your bias against me is colouring your judgement,' she said. 'All I'm asking is for some extra time to work with Tommy.'

'You've got a week,' he said, moving past her to the door. 'Ten days at the most, and then Anthony Pardle and I will have to organise a meeting with the father.'

She swung around to look at him. 'You don't have to leave—I thought we were having dinner?'

He gave her one hard look and opened the door. 'Maybe some other time. I seem to have lost my appetite.'

She frowned as he closed the door, the sound of his footsteps gradually fading before she turned and leaned back against the door, her shoulders slumping despondently against the hard surface. 'Help me to prove him wrong, Tommy,' she said out loud, the words bouncing eerily off the stony silence of the walls.

CHAPTER ELEVEN

ALLEGRA arrived in ICTU the following morning well before her shift officially began, and painstakingly looked through the printouts on Tommy's BIS monitor. There had been no change, which was dispiriting enough, but with the deadline Joel had now attached to the case, the sense of urgency seemed all the more gut-wrenching. She had hardly slept for thinking about the little boy's life, how he would look in five, ten years' time if he survived. Would he retain the slight build of his mother, or during adolescence develop the shorter and thicker set of his father? Would he do well at school? What sort of sense of humour would he have?

And what about his aunt? Was Tommy close to her? Did he understand at his young age the difficulties of his father's relationship with his own parents, Tommy's grandparents? Did he see much of his mother's parents and if not, why not?

There were so many unanswerable questions that she was finding difficult enough—how much worse would it be being the parent and never having those questions answered? She had seen that level of devastating grief on the faces of Julie's parents all those years ago and more recently on the faces of Robyn and Jeff Greeson as their precious daughter's chest had moved up and down for the very last time. Allegra had seen the pain flash across their faces as they'd come to terms with the fact that they would never know what their daughter would have looked like on her wedding day, never know what sort of man she would have fallen in love with. Every birthday, Christmas or special anniversary would no longer be a cause for celebration but a reminder of their unrelenting pain.

Statistics showed most couples didn't survive the loss of a child and it was easy to see why. The burden of grief was like a sharp, invisible knife that progressively severed the ties of even the closest couple with cruelly isolating dissection. Allegra had felt it herself all the way through medical school and beyond. She'd felt as if she'd been walled inside a see-through barrier that no one could penetrate. She'd been cut away from the rest of her peers by the experience of her closest friend's suicide, and her guilt and sense of inadequacy had been intensified by that ongoing isolation.

Allegra looked up from Tommy's notes to see Judy, the nurse in charge of Kate Lowe's room, approach. Judy had been the one who had been on duty when Kate Lowe's ventilator had been sabotaged two nights previously.

'Dr Tallis? You're in early this morning. I was just going to call you at home,' Judy said. 'I thought you might be interested in Mrs Lowe's current condition.'

'How is she?' Allegra asked.

'She's extubated, and drifting in and out of lucidity,' Judy informed her.

'Has she said anything at any time during her conscious times?'

'She's said Tommy's name several times and the nurse who covered for me over my break said she asked for Tommy's aunt once or twice. She hasn't said anything for several hours now but I thought you might be interested.'

'I am—very. How are you coping with all this?' she asked. 'Is this your first time taking care of a patient with a police guard present?'

'Here, it is, but at the previous hospital I worked at in Sydney I had to nurse a prisoner who had been injured in a cell brawl.

But after what happened the other night, I'm glad someone is keeping watch. I still can't believe we almost lost her.'

Allegra leaned back in her chair and looked at the nurse intently. 'So you don't think she deserves to die for what she tried to do to her son?'

The nurse looked shocked. 'Of course not! I'm a mother myself. I've had some rough times, I can tell you, especially after my husband left me when my daughter was only three weeks old. I know what it's like to feel overwhelmed and depressed. There were numerous times when I seriously considered ending it all. I think if more women were honest about it, you'd find most would confess to having experienced the same feelings at times. I was lucky, I had a mother who saw the desperate state I was in and stepped in and took over until I got myself back on my feet. Others, like Kate Lowe, obviously don't have that supportive network. I feel sorry for her. No one has even called to ask after her, which shows how lonely and isolated she must have been at the time.'

'Yes, that does seem a little unusual,' Allegra put in. 'Even the most hardened criminals have relatives who love them and call and ask to see them.'

'Yes, that's true…' Judy gave her a pensive look. 'But the funny thing was during that time when I wanted to end it all I had systematically cut myself off from all of my friends. It's the irony of depression, I suppose. The one time in your life you need the loving support of people around to help, you actively push them away. I know I did it, often cruelly at times. A couple of my friends never quite forgave me for it. Maybe Kate over time has pushed everyone away, including her parents. Family feuds are all too common these days. Some people never speak to each other again. It's such a terrible shame.'

'I guess you're right…' Allegra said, as she got to her feet. She touched the nurse briefly on the arm and added sincerely, 'The world needs more people like you, Judy.'

Judy gave her a shy smile. 'I was just thinking that about

you, Dr Tallis. I've been meaning to tell you how much I admired you for fighting for the opportunity to do this study. If I had taken the drastic step Kate Lowe did—and let me tell you I was close to it—I would have wanted someone like you to give me another chance.'

'We all deserve a second chance, Judy,' Allegra said. 'But unfortunately there's someone out there or even here in the hospital who doesn't think the same as you and I. They wanted Kate Lowe to die and if it hadn't been for you, she very well could have done so.'

'I hope the police find out who did it soon,' Judy said. 'It doesn't look good for the unit or the new director, does it?'

'No.' Allegra let out a little sigh as she thought of the immense pressure Joel was under. She had been too quick to judge him without considering how difficult things had been for him, newly appointed and with so many people's expectations burdening him. Every time she saw him he looked even more exhausted. No wonder he had been so short with her the night before. He wanted results and he wanted them quickly. And yet, in spite of his misgivings, he had ensured Tommy received only the best attention and care.

'I'm off home now,' Judy said, interrupting her reverie.

'Lucky you,' Allegra said, wincing as she looked up at the clock on the wall. 'I've only got thirteen and a half hours to go.'

The police officer guarding Kate Lowe's room looked up as Allegra came in after the mandatory security check. Allegra introduced herself and explained briefly about her study before she came over to the patient's bed and looked down at the young woman lying there. Without the hiss and groan of the ventilator, the room seemed extraordinarily quiet. The monitoring equipment still attached to Kate made her seem small and vulnerable, not unlike her little son further along the unit.

'Kate, my name is Allegra Tallis,' Allegra said, as she took one of the woman's hands in hers and stroked it gently.

'I'm a doctor, an anaesthetist, and I've been looking after your son, Tommy.'

Kate's eyelids fluttered for a moment, as if the mention of her son's name had stirred her from her unconscious state. Allegra waited for several moments before continuing in a soft, soothing voice, 'He's doing OK. I've been playing his favourite movie for him.'

Kate's mouth moved and a breathless, almost inaudible sound came out. 'Tommy…'

'Tommy is doing as well as can be expected, Kate,' Allegra reassured her, hoping that by saying the words it would someone make it true.

'Serena…' Kate's lips moved again but then she groaned and slipped back into unconsciousness.

Allegra stroked the woman's thin hands, using the massage technique she had been taught, separating each finger, stretching them gently, lengthening the tendons to release built-up pressure. She turned over Kate's hand palm upwards and froze when she saw a series of tiny, nick-like, whitened scars on the underside of the wrist. She reached for Kate's other arm and found the same bizarre pattern carved on the other wrist.

'She's a fruit cake,' Ruth Tilley, the nurse assigned to the isolation room, muttered under her breath, but even so it was more than obvious that the police officer had heard every word.

Allegra frowned as she turned to face the nurse. 'Please, keep your personal opinions to yourself. If you feel uncomfortable nursing this patient, I suggest you ask to be transferred.'

The nurse gave an insolent sniff and moved to check the monitors, making a note of Kate's BP, pulse and sats. 'I know how to do my job, no matter how horrible the patient is. Anyway, I've nursed much worse than her.'

'I would prefer you to speak appropriately and professionally at all times in this room,' Allegra insisted. 'Kate Lowe is unconscious but may well be able to hear everything you say.'

'I don't care if she does,' Ruth said. 'She's tried to do herself in numerous times. If she recovers, she'll only do it again. I've seen it all before. These sorts of people are nothing but trouble for their families. They put them through hell, keeping everyone on tenterhooks, wondering when the next attempt is going to happen and whether it will be successful.'

Allegra tightened her mouth as she saw the look the police officer gave the nurse, as if he was in silent agreement.

'Excuse me,' she said as she brushed past to leave. 'I have other patients to see.'

Once outside Kate's room Allegra expelled a frustrated breath, her hands clenching at her sides to keep control. She walked towards the office of ICTU where Louise was sitting, looking over the night shift notes.

'Uh-oh,' Louise said as she looked up. 'I don't like the look of your aura right now. I can practically see sparks of anger zapping off the top of your head. Has the dishy director got under your skin again?'

'Surprising as it may seem, no. It's not Joel this time—it's one of the nurses.'

'So we're on first-name terms, are we?' Louise asked with a playful smile.

Allegra ignored her friend's teasing look. 'I want Ruth Tilley removed from Kate Lowe's room immediately.'

Louise frowned. 'But why? Ruth is one of the most experienced ICTU nurses we have here.'

'I don't care how experienced she is, I don't like her attitude,' Allegra said. 'Has Joel Addison arrived yet?'

Louise's frown deepened. 'You're going to ask him to move her?'

'No,' she said, as she straightened her spine. 'I'm not going to ask him—I'm going to *tell* him.'

'I think he's headed down to Gaile Donovan's room. He's waiting for Harry Upton,' Louise said. 'The husband's been there all night. Joel came in early to discuss her treatment options with Harry.'

* * *

Joel looked up from Gaile Donovan's notes as Allegra entered the small private room where the patient was being closely monitored. 'Have you seen Harry come in yet?' he asked, without so much as offering a simple greeting.

'Good morning to you, too, Dr Addison,' Allegra said with an arch look.

He frowned and resumed looking at the notes. 'Sorry,' he said a little gruffly. 'I hadn't noticed it was even morning. I came in before the sun was up.'

Allegra felt annoyed with herself for being so petty when it was clear Joel had bigger concerns on his mind, such as the patient lying between them. But before she could offer an apology, Harry Upton came in.

'Morning, Allegra, Joel. How were things overnight with Gaile Donovan?'

'She's been stable, Harry,' Joel answered. 'Certainly no more bleeding, but Allegra was right about the ARDS. We did a chest X-ray this morning and there is a virtual white-out of most of both lung fields.'

Allegra checked the ventilator readings and reported, 'Her ventilation pressures are high and she's needing 40 per cent oxygen.'

'What about coagulopathy?' Harry asked. 'At some stage in the next 48 hours I'm going to have to remove the pelvic packs. How are we placed timing-wise?'

'She's stable at the moment and we've got her on broad-spectrum antibiotic cover,' Joel said. 'My advice would be to leave things alone the full 48 hours. Coags are better than they were, but PT is still prolonged and her platelets are low. We can work at improving those and hope her chest improves, before subjecting her to the potential of another hypovolaemic insult.' He turned his gaze towards Allegra. 'Do you agree, Allegra?'

'Yes.' Allegra was momentarily taken aback by the dark shadows beneath his eyes. He looked like she felt—tired, defeated, and a little out of his depth. It made him seem less of an enemy and she felt something that had been previously hard and closed off inside her begin to soften a little. She suddenly became aware of both Harry's and Joel's expectant gazes trained on her. 'Um…yes, I would prefer not to have to re-anaesthetise her until we see how the lung function pans out.'

Joel shifted his gaze and checked the obs with the attending nurse, Jayne Stephens. He listened to Gaile's chest but there was very little in terms of air entry, and a lot of crackles and crepitations. He knew Gaile was in for a rough ride but he had seen such patients recover with adequate ICU support—the key was to avoid sepsis and maintain organ support and brain oxygenation.

'We should go and have a chat with her husband,' he suggested, once he'd finished his checks. 'He's been here all night. I sent him out to the conference room a few minutes ago to stretch his legs.'

Harry's beeper went off and he grimaced as he looked at the screen. 'Sorry, guys, I've got a surgical tutorial with the trainees and I'm already ten minutes late. You know what these young folk are like—if we don't turn up on the dot they think we've cancelled and go off and have a latte instead.'

Joel smiled at the older surgeon. 'Can't say I blame them. I could do with a double-strength latte myself right now.' He turned to Allegra once Harry had left, his easy smile replaced by a little frown. 'Do you want to come with me to talk to Neil Donovan or is a coffee more preferable?'

'I was coming to see you anyway about another matter,' she said. 'After we've spoken with Mr Donovan, perhaps you could fit me into your busy schedule.'

He gave her an unreadable look as he held the door for her. 'I'll see what I can do.'

They moved from the unit past the security guard to the conference room along the corridor, where Neil Donovan was sitting with his head in his hands. He looked up as they came in, the dread on his face clawing at Allegra's already overstretched emotions.

'How are you holding up?' Joel asked.

'I'm just hoping she's going to be OK,' Neil said, his eyes red and weary beyond description. 'The girls and I just couldn't go on if…' His voice trailed off and Allegra swallowed against the lump in her throat.

'She's been stable overnight, Neil,' Joel informed him, closing the small distance to place a reassuring hand on his shoulder. 'That's positive. She's getting the best talent this hospital has.'

'I know…' Neil said, not bothering to disguise the track of tears moving down his unshaven cheeks. 'I just hope it's enough. I'm not a religious man but I've been praying all night for a miracle.'

Joel glanced briefly in Allegra's direction. 'Miracles are hard to arrange, Neil. Maybe they happen—certainly some people believe in them. Try to hold onto hope. There's still a decent chance she can pull through. We'll explore every feasible option.'

'Can I go back to her now?' Neil asked.

'Of course you can.' Joel smiled warmly. 'Who's looking after the girls for you?'

'I left them with my mother, although they weren't too happy about it,' Neil said.

'If they want to be here with their mother, that's where they should be,' Joel said. 'If there's anything you want any of us to do, just let us know.'

'Thank you, Dr Addison. You, too, Dr Tallis,' he said. 'I don't know how you doctors deal with this stuff day in and day out. It must really get to you after a while.'

'We're trained to cope with it,' Joel said. 'Mind you, it's totally different when you're on the other side. I haven't as yet been a patient myself, but I've had plenty of practice at being a patient's relative. It's a tough call. You're doing a great job, Neil. Your ongoing support is just what your wife needs right now.'

Neil Donovan gave them both a tired smile and, thanking them again, left to be with his wife back in the unit.

'He's certainly a very different kettle of fish to our friend

Mr Lowe,' Allegra couldn't help commenting as the door closed on his exit.

Joel turned and looked down at her, his nostrils instinctively flaring so he could take in more of her light perfume. It reminded him of freshly cut spring flowers warmed by the sun, heady and evocative without being too overpowering. He wanted to haul her into his arms and kiss her deeply so he could carry the sweet tantalising taste of her throughout the long, arduous day ahead. His groin tightened at the thought of slipping his tongue inside her mouth to curl around hers, the palms of his hands sliding under her clothes to cover her breasts to feel their softness crowned with her hardened nipples.

With a gargantuan effort he forced the images of their bodies locked in passion from his mind and asked, 'What did you want to see me about?'

'I want you to remove Ruth Tilley from Kate Lowe's room,' she said implacably. 'In fact, not just Kate's room but ICTU altogether.'

His brow wrinkled as he brought the senior nurse's features to mind, mentally reminding himself of her impressive capabilities. He'd seen her manage a trauma patient with multiple injuries almost single-handedly the previous week when several multi-trauma patients had arrived simultaneously and the medical staff had been stretched beyond the limits. She had saved a young man's life and surely didn't deserve the indignity of being dismissed from the unit without a very good reason.

'Why? Have you some sort of issue with her?'

'Yes, I do, actually. She's got the wrong attitude.'

His features hardened. 'According to who?'

Allegra could feel his intransigence like an impenetrable wall being built brick by brick between them. She drew herself up to her full height and bit out, 'According to me.'

'Let me guess.' His mouth quirked a fraction. 'Her aura is off centre, is it?'

Allegra had had enough. 'Don't you dare make fun of me, Addison. If anyone's aura is askew, it's yours.'

He looked down at her flashing green eyes and his smile tilted even further. 'Are you threatening me, Dr Tallis?'

She held his taunting brown gaze for several heart-chugging seconds, the atmosphere tightening around them to snapping point. The air was thick with it. She couldn't even breathe properly. Her chest felt restricted, her head light as if not enough oxygen was getting through to her brain. Deep and low in her belly a throbbing pulse had begun a tattoo that triggered a silky liquid response between her thighs, which she suddenly realised with a jolt of awareness were way too close to his. Their hard muscled presence alerted her too late to the hot sexual current charging between their bodies, a current that she had tried desperately to ignore because of what she knew it signified.

She tried to step back but both of his hands countered it by coming down on her hips and with one short hard tug bringing her up against him.

'Who's going to throw the first punch, Allegra?' he asked, staring at her mouth as if mesmerised. 'Or should we kiss and make up instead?'

She moistened her lips nervously, her heart leaping in her chest as he brought his head down, her breath consumed by the greedy hunger of his mouth as it captured hers.

CHAPTER TWELVE

HIS kiss was a searing reminder of her escalating feelings for him, feelings she had never expected to feel for anyone, or at least not at this level of intensity. She wasn't cynical enough to discount the prospect of ever falling in love, but never had she expected to do so in such a short space of time. She had not been in love with anyone before, although she had slept with previous boyfriends, more because of their expectations than anything she'd felt herself. But somehow Joel Addison, the one man who stood in the way of what she wanted to achieve, had stolen her heart without her being able to do anything to prevent it. She hadn't even seen it coming. It had crept up on her with every look he'd sent her way, every word he'd spoken and with every nuance of his face as she'd watched him deal sensitively with patients and relatives and staff.

She wasn't fool enough to imagine he had similar feelings for her. She knew enough about male hormones to recognise full-on lust when she saw it. Every determined stroke of his tongue against hers reminded her of how his body would feel inside the silky cocoon of hers. No rational argument was going to be enough to fight this overwhelming attraction that had crackled constantly between them almost from the first moment they'd met.

She returned his kiss with the same fire as his, her tongue

dancing with his, her small teeth nipping at his bottom lip in response to the similar tantalising treatment by his. It was a primitive sort of exchange, at times bordering on the edge of pain, as if they were both trying to find each other's boundaries.

Allegra imagined he would be a demanding but totally enthralling lover. She could feel it in his hands as they ruthlessly tugged her shirt out of her skirt, his warm palms possessing the aching weight of her breasts until her stomach caved in with out-of-control desire.

Her fingers curled into the thickness of his hair as she struggled to control her reaction to him. She was within a second of begging him to take her then and there when he dragged himself away to look down at her with glittering eyes, a dull flush of colour beneath the tan of his face.

'Maybe I should have let you punch me instead,' he said with a rueful smile that melted her almost as much as his kisses had done. 'It might have been less complicated.'

She tidied her clothes as best as she could, trying her best to sound casual even while her stomach was still crawling with desire. 'I don't believe in violence,' she said. 'I would never have hit you.'

'That's very reassuring. For a moment there I thought I was going to have to make an emergency appointment with my orthodontist.'

She gave him a shame-faced look from beneath her lashes as she tucked in her blouse with unsteady hands. 'I'm sorry. I didn't have a good night's sleep and Ruth Tilley's attitude towards Kate Lowe this morning upset me. I took it out on you.'

'You can take it out on me any time you like if you choose the same *modus operandi,*' he said. 'In fact, how about we have dinner tonight and we can pick another fight? Is it your turn to choose or mine?'

'I think it might be your turn,' she said, unable to affect a reproving look in time and smiling at him instead.

He gave her an answering smile and brushed her cheek with

the back of his hand. 'Let's keep this out of the corridors, OK? I don't want to have to deal with the speculation right now. There are other pressing matters I have to concentrate on, but that's not to say that during out of working hours we can come to some arrangement that is mutually satisfying.'

She lowered her gaze. 'I understand…'

He tipped up her chin and looked deeply into her eyes. 'I'm not sure you do, Allegra Tallis. I don't think you have a clue about what I'm thinking right now.'

'You don't think I can read your mind?'

His eyes became like dark, unfathomable pools as he held her gaze. 'It's been a long time since I've been in a relationship, for a variety of reasons which I won't go into now. Suffice it to say you don't know me very well. I don't want you to think I'm someone I'm not.'

'We all have baggage,' she said, trying to read his expression, but it was as if a mask had come down over his face, effectively shutting her out.

'Maybe, but being involved with me involves sacrifices most women don't have the fortitude to take. Believe me, I know it from experience.'

'Has someone hurt you in the past?' she asked softly.

'I'm not the broken-hearted sort,' he said. 'I'm just aware of my own limitations in what I can offer another person in an intimate relationship.'

'You're a nice man, a decent gorgeous man…' She gave him a spontaneous hug, leaning her cheek against his chest where she could feel his heart beating. 'I'm willing to take the chance.'

He put her from him with a gentleness that was girded with firmness, his eyes meeting hers once more. 'We'll see.'

Allegra looked up at him, the shadows in his eyes worrying her. She eased herself away, feeling embarrassed and far too exposed. 'I'm sorry… If you're not interested, just say so. I can handle it.'

'I don't suppose there's any hope of me denying my attraction to you with any efficacy,' he said. 'After all, you have the physical evidence which has been to date both repeatable and provable.'

She smiled crookedly in spite of her inner pain. 'Ever the scientist, aren't you?'

He pulled her close for one last kiss. 'You'd better believe it, baby.'

'I believe it but I still think there's room for the grey areas that science overlooks.'

'I've never said science has all the answers, Allegra. I just don't want you to inadvertently bring disrepute on the unit, especially not now when every calculating eye is on it.'

'You make it sound as if I'm a complete amateur who has no clue what she is doing.'

'*Do* you know what you're doing?'

She frowned at him. 'Of course I do. I want what is best for both the patient and their loved ones.'

'But what if the patient and loved ones have totally different needs, what then?'

'Surely they would want the same things?' she said. 'Life is not a dress rehearsal. This is it. We get one chance at it. Life is precious in all its forms.'

She felt his sigh as if it had happened in her own chest, even though he was now at least half a metre away from her.

'There's a part of me that admires your commitment to what you believe in,' he said heavily. 'But another part—the realistic part—wants to shake you into the real world and show you that what you're searching for doesn't exist.'

'Miracles, you mean?'

'Miracles, fairy dust, aromatherapy—the tools of your moonlighting trade,' he said. 'They just don't bring about the results people are desperate for, and I hate the thought of anyone being fooled into believing they can. It's unspeakably cruel to offer hope when there is none. Lives get destroyed, hanging on the thin thread of a hope that just doesn't exist.'

'I'm not fooling anyone.'

He gave her one of his arched-brow expressions as he opened the door to leave. 'Only yourself, and maybe in the end that is the worst sort of deception of all.'

Allegra sank to the nearest chair as the door closed. She *had* to prove him wrong, but how?

Tommy Lowe was still in the same comatose state when Allegra finished in Theatre to check on him later that day. His BIS monitor scores showed no brain activity and to make matters worse, his temperature had crept up to 38.5.

Keith Lowe came in while she was massaging Tommy's feet, using acupressure to release tension in his little body.

'What are you doing?' Keith gave her a suspicious look, his whole demeanour seeming on edge as he hovered at the side of his son's bed.

'I'm using touch therapy to connect with Tommy,' she explained. 'Children usually have very ticklish feet. It's a way of ramping up the level of sensory input.'

'None of this is working, is it?' Keith said after a long, tense moment.

Allegra stilled her massaging movements to look at him. 'We don't know that yet. We need more time.'

He gave her a defeated look, before shifting his gaze to the monitors and machines that were keeping his son alive. 'If I can't have Tommy back as he was, I don't want him back at all.'

Allegra stared at him in shock. 'You surely can't mean that?'

He met her eyes briefly. 'You don't understand,' he said. 'There's life and there's life.' He rubbed a hand over his face and continued in a tone that sounded empty and defeated. 'I told you yesterday about my family background. My parents were not the emotional, nurturing sort.'

'A lot of parents of your generation weren't,' she offered.

He gave her a brief glance and, shifting his gaze, continued in the same flat, emotionless tone. 'They would have been except for the fact that I had an older sister who was the biggest disappointment of my parents' life. They took their disappointment out on me. If I let them, they would still be doing it.'

Allegra sat very still, a sudden chill travelling down the length of her spine. 'What happened?'

'My older sister had a severe form of autism,' he said, looking down at his hands. 'She was diagnosed far too late to do anything to help her. It ruined my parents' lives, so in a way I can't really blame them for how they reacted to me. I guess it was a combination of guilt and frustration, which they could hardly take out on her so they chose me instead.'

'I'm so sorry. It must have been very difficult for you.'

'Yes…yes, it was…'

'What about your other sister, Serena?' she asked gently. 'Were your parents hard on her as well?'

He met her eyes for a moment before turning away. 'Yes…yes, it was difficult…for both of us.' He released a heavy breath and went on, 'I simply can't bear the thought of my son having a major disability of any sort. Not after what I've been through. I'd would rather he died now.'

'What eventually happened to your older sister?'

'She died of pneumonia at the age of sixteen,' he said. 'I can still see the relief on my parents' faces. I can't help thinking they paid the doctor not to treat her appropriately.'

Allegra felt an upswell of emotion fill her chest until she could hardly breathe with comfort. 'Tommy might not have any form of brain damage at all,' she said, dredging up the last of her hope to convince herself, even as she wanted to convince Tommy's father.

Keith turned to look at her. 'It's a risk I can't afford to take. Not after what I've been through with my sister and my parents. I personally witnessed the damage of what a needy child can do.' He looked down at his hands once more. 'I'm in a new relationship. My…partner would never cope with Tommy if he was…damaged in any way.'

'Don't rush into this,' Allegra pleaded. 'Tommy is a child with his whole life ahead of him.'

'But what sort of life are we talking about?'

Allegra tried not to be put off by the similarity to Joel's words the night before. 'Tommy could make a full recovery. I really believe that,' she said, mentally crossing her fingers.

'That's not what the neurosurgeon intimated,' he said.

'Mr Pardle is a brilliant neurosurgeon, but over the course of his long career he has seen too much to be able to offer hope in cases like this. He's lost children of Tommy's age and condition before and, believe me, it takes its toll, but that's not to say Tommy can't prove everyone wrong.'

Keith got to his feet, his movements slow and tired as if he'd reached the very end of his tether. 'I don't really care what happens with my wife but I want my son to die with dignity. I don't want him to suffer for months on end. I would like his life to count for something.' He scraped a hand through his hair, which did nothing to bring any sort of order to its already haphazard arrangement on his head before he continued, 'Tommy and I discussed this once not that long ago. When the time comes, I want his organs to be donated to give life to others. It's what he would have wanted.'

'You don't have to decide anything like that at this stage,' she said. 'There's still a chance he will wake up.'

'It's a slim chance, though, isn't it?' he asked, for once meeting her gaze directly.

She rolled her lips together, searching for a moment for the right words to say to offer him hope. 'It's slim but not impossible.'

'You're the only one who thinks it's possible. Everyone else I've spoken to has given me a thin slice of hope tempered with the reality of a life blighted by impairment.'

'It might not be anything like that…'

'I can't take the risk,' he said, 'For Tommy's sake.' He looked down at the small frail figure lying connected to the numerous machines hissing and groaning and pumping in the background, each one keeping the child's life suspended in an indefinable place that had no real future and a past that was all too short.

Seven years.

It had taken Allegra longer to get her qualifications.

'I may not be a great father, according to the rules of the current times, but one thing I know for certain is that Tommy wouldn't want to live half a life,' Keith said. 'I would be an even worse father to stand by and let his life be reduced to that.'

'Please, give me some time with him,' she begged. 'No matter what the other specialists say, please, don't give up until I've exhausted every possible avenue. Please, Mr Lowe…Keith… He's your son, your only child. Surely you owe him this one last chance at life?'

Tears sprang into Keith's eyes and he brushed at them impatiently, clearly embarrassed by this momentary lapse. 'I'm not sure I can do this… It's too risky…'

'What about your sister?' she asked. 'Would she be willing to help me? I can't always do this on my own, I often have to rely on relatives to pitch in.'

His eyes shifted away again. 'I'm not sure my sister is the right person…'

'But your wife asked for her several times during the night,' Allegra informed him.

He looked across at her, surprise evident in his expression. 'Are you sure?'

'Yes, I heard it from one of the nurses and then I heard it myself when I was in her room. She definitely said your sister's name as well as Tommy's. Are they particularly close?'

His eyes fell away from hers. 'I'm afraid Kate hasn't let anyone close to her for years…'

'Depression is a distressing condition for the sufferer and all those in close contact,' Allegra said, recalling her conversation with Judy earlier. 'But perhaps Kate has remembered your sister's past kindness. It happens in cases like this. The most insignificant act of charity can be imprinted on the brain in such a way that when the chips are down, the one person who has stood by is remembered.'

'My wife is not close to anyone,' he said. 'She had a falling-out with her family well before we were married. Her parents haven't even met Tommy. They live in Western Australia. The last we heard it was Fremantle, but they could very well have moved by now. Kate has a sister somewhere…last time I heard she was living in a remote part of a developing country. She's a missionary, but as far as Christian charity goes, it apparently doesn't stretch as far as this.'

'Is there any way of contacting Kate's parents and sister?'

His eyes were cold and distant as they met hers. 'Why would I bother? In many ways they are the reason Kate and I came unstuck. When I married her I thought I could help her overcome her past, but in time I realised it was beyond me. Kate suffered some sort of abuse as a child, she has never said exactly what, but her frequent episodes of depression seem to indicate it was serious.'

So you bailed out when things got tough? Allegra was too professional to say the words out loud, although she dearly longed to, but Keith must have sensed something for he said without apology, 'I have met someone else. She is everything my wife is not. She is confident, assured, going somewhere and determined. She is an extrovert and meets my needs in a way Kate has never done.' He paused, almost guiltily. 'Look, Dr Tallis, I've spent close to ten years propping my wife up with every means available. She's been in and out of clinics and I can no longer carry on supporting her. I want a life of my own without the burden of a partner who is bordering on the psychotic most of the time.'

'But what about your son?'

His eyes fell away from hers again. 'My son is not likely to survive…I know that. I guess I've known it from the first moment. I'm simply doing my best to prepare myself for the inevitable.'

'So you're giving up, just like that?'

'You would do the same if you were in my situation,' he said. 'Most people would.'

'That's not true,' she protested. 'Just because you think something is too tough to face doesn't mean others don't have the courage to face what life dishes up.'

'Maybe life hasn't dished up something you have been thrown by, but you just wait until it does. You might think differently then.'

'Tommy deserves a life,' she said. 'At this moment you are the person who holds that life in your hands. Don't throw it away because of the fear of the unknown. Mr Pardle's and Dr Addison's opinions need to be taken into account, but you have the final say. Please, don't forget that. Don't let their pessimism sway you. They have seen brain damage in all its forms and to a lesser degree so have I, but I have also seen lost opportunities, lives cut short that might have been rehabilitated if given a chance.'

'I can't play Russian roulette with my son's life,' he said. 'I have personally seen the damage of an extremely needy child, how it erodes the very essence of a person's life. I know this is probably a shocking statement for you to hear, but let me tell you there are worse things than the death of a child. Much, much worse.'

Allegra watched as he moved away from his son's bedside, barely sparing a glance at the tiny body on the bed as he twitched aside the curtains and left.

CHAPTER THIRTEEN

ALLEGRA was in the office in ICTU, hunting through the phone book for Serena Fairbright's phone number, when Joel came in.

'Are we still on for tonight?' he asked, his glance going to the f section of the phone book open in front of her. 'Who are you looking for?'

'Tommy's aunt,' she said, running her index finger down the seemingly endless list. 'I wonder what her husband's name is. It would make this a whole lot easier.'

'She might be divorced,' he suggested, looking over her shoulder, his aftershave, in spite of a full day at work, still lingering on him, instantly stirring her senses into overdrive. She disguised her reaction by peering even closer at the fine print, but it became blurred and unreadable.

'Why didn't you ask Keith Lowe for her number when he was in?' he asked. 'I just saw him a few moments ago in the car park, not to speak to, but if he was just here you could have saved yourself the trouble of trawling the phone book, especially if you don't know which suburb the woman lives in.'

She blew out a tiny frustrated breath as she leaned back in her chair. 'Mr Lowe's not the most co-operative person. He doesn't think his sister is going to be much help, but Kate Lowe has said Serena's name several times now, almost as many times as she's said Tommy's.' She closed the phone book in defeat. 'She must have an unlisted number.'

'What did you have in mind for her to do?'

Allegra hunted his face for any sign of ridicule but she was pleasantly surprised by the absence of any such thing. Instead, she saw concern in his dark brown eyes as they held hers.

'I'm not sure…' she confessed, gnawing at her bottom lip for a moment. 'I thought I'd just ask her to come in and sit by Kate's bed and talk to her, you know, like any good friend would do.'

'You're assuming they are good friends,' he said, yet again demonstrating his penchant for solid testable evidence.

'They must have some sort of relationship,' Allegra pointed out. 'She's Kate's sister-in-law and therefore Tommy's aunt. She's visited him at least three times.'

'But not Kate.'

'No…'

'Family relationships can be tricky, especially after what happened in this case. Have you met this woman—the aunt?'

'A couple of times.'

'And?'

'Well, for one thing, you can definitely see they came from the same nest. Mr Lowe told me a little of their background. It was quite tragic so I guess that's why he comes across as so emotionally distant. She's just as bad. Affection was in short supply in their childhood. God knows how they survived it.'

Joel perched on the edge of the desk, his long thighs close to her chest where she sat in the chair. 'What happened?'

She met his eyes. 'He had a sister with autism, a severe form apparently, the eventual diagnosis too late to help. The parents weren't able to cope and took it out on Keith—his sister Serena, too, I suppose—but I get the feeling he copped the brunt of it for some reason.'

Joel's gaze shifted from hers as he looked at the closed phone book in front of her. 'That's tough. No wonder he's so uncomfortable with illness and hospitals. It must bring back some pretty distressing memories.'

'Yes…' She pushed back her chair and stood up and stretched, visibly wincing as a muscle protested in her back.

He sent her a teasing look. 'Maybe I should cancel dinner and book you in for a massage instead. But, then, I seem to recall you telling me you would need to be comatose to allow me to do it, or words to that effect.'

She gave him a playful poke in the ribs. 'If I don't get something to eat and drink in the next hour, I *am* going to be comatose, and it would take a whole lot more than a massage to wake me.'

'Ah, but you haven't yet experienced the magic of my touch,' he said. 'Or at least not on the whole of your body.'

Her eyes met his and she felt a sensation pass through her that felt like a surge of electricity at the thought of his hands moving all over her already tingling flesh. She could well imagine his touch would do more than wake her from a deeply unconscious state. In some ways she felt he had already done so. For years she had avoided the emotional intensity of an intimate relationship and yet his very first kiss had brought her to full and vibrant life.

'Come on,' he said, as he began to lead her out of the office. 'We'd better get out of here before someone needs us. I've had a fifteen-hour day as it is.'

'Only fifteen?' She glanced up at him playfully. 'What are you doing, slowing down or something?'

He grinned as he waited for her to pass him in the unit doorway. 'You're a fine one to talk, young lady. I will have to think of a way to make you forget about work for a while. Good food, good wine and something else.'

'A good movie?'

He tapped her on the end of her uptilted nose, his dark eyes smouldering with promise. 'You'll just have to wait and see.'

The restaurant Joel had booked was in the Southgate complex, a strip of shops, bars and restaurants along the Yarra River, interspersed with hotels, galleries and the world-renowned Crown Casino situated at the far southern end. The Italian restaurant he'd chosen was exclusive and intimate, and they were soon led to a table overlooking the river where the late evening summer sunshine was shimmering on the surface of the notoriously murky-looking water.

Joel caught her looking down at the river and smiled. 'It's not exactly tempting in terms of taking a dip, is it?'

She returned his smile. 'I've been in many times. I was a rower for my school team. Many times on frosty mornings I rowed up and down further along from here.'

'I'm impressed,' he said, leaning back as the waiter handed him a menu and the wine list. 'Do you still row?'

'On the rare occasions my nagging conscience compels me to go to the gym. I do the token thing with the rowing machine, feeling a fool for breaking out in a sweat after three minutes.'

He gave a soft chuckle of laughter. 'I know the feeling. I haven't been near a gym for ages.'

'How do you keep so…so pumped?' she asked.

'Pumped?'

'You know…' She gave him a little embarrassed glance, trying not to let her gaze linger too long on the broad muscles of his shoulders clearly visible through his shirt. 'You've got a well-defined body. You must do something to keep it in shape.'

'I run a bit, I also push a few weights around the house, more to move them out of the way when I haul the vacuum cleaner around.'

Allegra couldn't hold back a gurgle of amusement. 'There must be thousands of homes out there with unused gym equipment gathering dust and cobwebs. I hired a treadmill once but in the end I used it as a clothes horse. I really missed it when the contract ran out.'

His mouth softened in a smile, his eyes warm as they meshed with hers. 'What do you think about the hospital installing a gym for the staff?' he asked.

Her hand stalled as she reached for her water glass. 'Wow, you really are an ideas man, aren't you?'

'Seriously, though, Allegra,' he said, leaning his forearms on the table, 'what do you think? Would you, for instance, use it if it was available?'

She thought about it for a moment. 'I guess it would be better having it on site rather than going home exhausted from work and trying to summon up the energy to go out again to a local gym.'

'And it would encourage a community atmosphere among the staff,' he said. 'I know it's not an original idea—there are other hospitals with gyms—but I thought it would be a way of building a better social network. I get the feeling there are warring factions all over the place at Melbourne Memorial.'

'Yes, that's true, but only because, like every other public hospital, everyone is overworked and stressed. The new development came at a high price for other specialties.'

'I am very much aware of that, and that's why I want to do everything within my power to make this work.'

'Even if it means I don't get to achieve the goals of my project?'

He lifted his eyes from the menu he'd been looking at to connect with hers. 'Let's not fight tonight, Allegra. I'm tired and so are you. We'd end up saying things we don't mean and ruining what could prove to be a really nice evening.'

'I know, but I can't help feeling the pressure of time running out. I want more time to work with Tommy Lowe.'

His eyes clashed with hers. 'Is that why you agreed to come out with me, to try and convince me to change my mind?'

Allegra didn't like the accusing edge to his tone. 'Is it so much to ask? He's a small child. What are a few more weeks? Surely you can allow me that to work a little longer with him?'

Joel put down the menu as if the thought of food was suddenly nauseating. 'Drop it, Allegra. I don't wish to discuss work this evening.'

Something about the implacability of his expression made

her back down. It wasn't something she was used to doing, but she recognised the pressure they had both been under and, like him, wanted to enjoy the evening for what it was. Heaven knew, they both deserved a break. It had been a hell of a week so far and wasn't over yet.

'All right,' she said, picking up her menu and burying her nose in it.

Joel stole a glance at her, inwardly grimacing at the way her eyes were doing their best to avoid his. He knew how passionate she was about the Lowe boy and privately he admired and loved her for it. He'd seen the same passion so many times, and yet from his personal experience he couldn't quite allow her free rein. He knew the other side and it wasn't pretty. He admired her for believing in miracles, he had believed in them himself once. So, too, had his parents until the brutal blow of reality had laid its heavy weight on their shoulders. He felt the crushing burden of it even now. He imagined his parents just kilometres away, locked in a prison of suffering that had no key to freedom.

'Guess what?' Allegra said, jolting him out of his tortured reverie. 'They have pizza on the menu.'

He gave her a twisted smile. 'No kidding?'

She showed him the place on her menu. 'See. Pizza. I know it's in garlic or herb bread form, but pizza is pizza.'

'Let's have a look at the wine list,' he said, reaching for it and giving it a quick perusal. 'I think we should have the most expensive one to compensate.'

'But I feel like pizza bread tonight,' she said. 'Would you mind?'

He rolled his eyes. 'I wish there was a manual issued with every woman, just like a car, so a guy has a chance to figure out how to work her out.'

'I'm not that complicated,' she defended herself, with a little smile.

'Yes, you are.'

'No more than you.'

'What makes you say that?' he asked, pretending an avid interest in the wine list.

'You have an atmosphere of pain around you.'

He didn't bother lifting his head from the wine list. 'So we're back to reading auras, are we?'

'I have never said at any point that I was into reading auras,' she said. 'I don't even know what exactly what the word means. But I do know that every person sends off body language and I am very familiar with reading those signals.'

'So what does my body language reveal to you apart from an atmosphere of pain, which could simply mean I have a headache or a stomach upset?'

'Are you unwell?'

He raised his eyes to hers. 'I'm a doctor, for God's sake. Do you think I wouldn't be able to tell if I was sick or not?'

'Doctors make terrible self-diagnosticians and even worse patients,' she pointed out rationally. 'We all kid ourselves that illness can't happen to us. We develop a sense of invulnerability. Then we overlook the most obvious signs in ourselves when disease does occur, and try to just carry on while everyone around us is telling we look grey and sickly.'

'I can assure you I am very well at present. I am, however, tired and have a tendency for tension headaches from time to time, but apart from that I enjoy robust health, so there goes your body language theory.'

'I could give you a massage to ease the tension in your neck,' she offered.

His dark eyes connected with hers. 'Only if you promise to work your way down to where the real tension is building every minute I sit looking at you.'

Allegra felt the full force of his sexual invitation, as if he had reached right across the table and touched her where she most wanted to be touched. A shiver of anticipation ran the length of her spine, lingering among the fine hairs at the back of her neck until she could barely sit still in her seat. She was incredibly conscious of his long muscled thighs just centimetres from her own. And she knew if she so much as stretched her legs, she would encounter them. The temptation to do so was almost overwhelming.

'Is a relationship between us advisable?' she asked, more out of a need to fill the suddenly throbbing silence than any real need to know. She already knew the answer. It was asking for trouble to get involved with a man who held so much of himself aloof. Her mother would be appalled. Her father would immediately try and diagnose some sort of personality disorder, no doubt warning her about becoming involved with a man who seemed to have 'Keep Away' invisibly printed on his forehead.

'Probably not, but we can keep it private,' he said. 'At least for the time being.'

'Great,' she said with heavy sarcasm. 'I finally find a man I admire and respect, and he wants me to keep our relationship quiet. Some girls have all the luck.'

He reached for her hand across the table, linking his long fingers with hers. 'Listen, Allegra. You're a beautiful person. I'm seriously attracted to you, probably more attracted to you than I have been to anyone in the last decade. But I can't make you promises that this will last for ever. I'm not planning to head down the marriage-and-kids track. I think you need to know that from the outset. If you want an affair with me, I am more than willing to commit to that for however long it works for us, but as to a house in the suburbs and a couple of kids and a car pool routine—forget it. It's just not me.'

Allegra felt as if someone had ripped her heart from her chest. She felt empty and hollow inside, bleeding and raw, torn apart with the pain of making a choice that she knew would only cause her more suffering in the end.

In spite of her parents' open relationship, the one thing she had longed for all her life had been a wedding with all the regalia. It was practically every girl's dream to be a princess for a day, and she was no different. She wanted kids, two at least, and a dog, maybe even a cat, one of those big fluffy ones that left long hairs on the couch. She wanted runny noses and sleepless nights; she wanted her own Tommy, a little boy with the world in front of him. She wanted a princess, just like Alice Greeson had been for her parents. She wanted it all. And most of all she wanted Joel Addison—but he came with conditions, conditions she wasn't sure she could cope with.

'This is a tough decision to make.' She tried her best to sound light-hearted, even as her very bones ached and creaked with disappointment.

'I would have thought someone with your sort of progressive background would have jumped at the chance of a no-strings affair,' he said.

'Yeah, well, strange as it may seem, my parents' example has had a sort of reverse psychology effect. I can think of nothing better than settling down with someone, building a life and family with them and working for common goals, just like your parents have. You said they've been married for close to thirty-five years. Doesn't that prove that long-term relationships do sometimes work?'

Joel was relieved with the waiter arrived to take their order. It saved him having to tell Allegra his parents had lived in misery for the majority of that time, linked together by tragedy. He gave the waiter his order after Allegra gave hers and deftly changed the subject, inwardly sighing with relief when she spoke animatedly of a movie she'd seen recently. Fortunately it was one he'd seen as well, which meant he could continue to steer the subject away from his personal life—that had to remain private for as long as he could keep it that way.

CHAPTER FOURTEEN

AFTER their meal was over they took a leisurely walk along the waterfront, stopping to listen to a particularly entertaining busker who was playing a banjo with great enthusiasm and mediocre skill. The night was still warm but a light breeze had taken the sting out of the February heat and the pitch out of the banjo. Allegra found it a slightly strange but delightful experience, walking hand in hand with Joel, their footsteps in time, although she was very much aware he'd shortened his long stride to accommodate her shorter one.

They hadn't spoken much during the rest of their dinner together. Allegra had sensed that she had stepped a little too close in remarking on the pain she felt surrounded him. She imagined it had something to do with his time in the Middle East. One of her former colleagues, who now worked in Brisbane, had spent six months in a war-torn town and had suffered post-traumatic stress pretty much indefinitely afterwards. Even the mention of the country was enough to stimulate painful memories.

Joel hadn't returned to the subject of their relationship either, and she hadn't pressed him on it, somehow sensing he was keen to take things one day at a time. She knew that was more or less the pattern of modern relationships these days. The term used to describe such arrangements was a crude one, but essentially boiled down to having a no-strings sexual partner on call whenever you wanted company. It wasn't what she wanted but she did want Joel, and if that was the only way to have him then she would settle for that and try to be content with it.

'I should get you home,' Joel said, once they had walked back the way they had come. 'It's getting late and we've both been up for far too many hours.'

'Yes, I guess you're right. Are you on early tomorrow?'

He glanced at his watch. 'It already is tomorrow.'

Allegra looked at her own watch and groaned. 'How could it possibly be one a.m.? Last time I checked it was nine-thirty.'

He linked his arm through hers and led her towards the rear of the boardwalk where his car was parked. 'You know what they say—time seems to fly when you're having fun.'

'Did you have fun tonight?' she asked, looking up at him.

He held her gaze for a long moment. 'Yes.'

She slipped into his car and breathed in the scent of leather and his aftershave, wondering if he would take their relationship to the next level tonight. Her body came alive at the thought of being possessed by him, all her nerves leaping inside her skin, the blood in her veins beginning to pump with increasing fervour.

Joel walked her to her door and when she asked him to come in for coffee she knew the only thing that was going to be boiling was the passion she could see reflected in his eyes as they locked down on hers as the door closed after they'd entered her apartment.

'This is the part when you say "Thanks for a lovely evening" and send me on my way,' he said, looking down at her mouth.

'OK… I'll give it a shot,' she said, moistening her lips. 'Thanks for a lovely evening. There, how did I do?'

He pulled her closer until their bodies were touching all the way down. 'That was good. Now this is the part where I give you a goodnight kiss.'

'Sounds good,' she said, watching in mesmerised fascination as his mouth came down and covered hers. It was a very soft brushing of lips, stirring every single sensitive nerve of her mouth into a wanton craving for more.

He lifted his head and stared down into her eyes. 'How was that?'

'Not bad. So what happens now?'

'Well, theoretically I should get my butt out of here within the next four or five seconds, otherwise I suspect the sleep we both need is going to be temporarily postponed.'

Allegra stood silently before him, her body pressed against his as she mentally counted the seconds, one million and one, one million and two, one million and three, one million and four, one million and…

Joel's head came back down and a deep groan escaped from his mouth just as it connected with hers again, this time in a searing kiss of out-of-control desire, his arms wrapping around her tightly. His tongue entering her mouth set off a fiery explosion of need throughout her body.

Somehow through a series of stumbles and furniture-knocking on the way, they made it to her bedroom, falling in a tangle of limbs on her bed. His weight on her was a blessed burden, their clothes a barrier that was soon dispensed with in hurried, almost frenzied movements of hands and fingers. Hands dealt with buttons and zips, shoes thudded to the floor, along with the softer landing of clothing being tossed aside in order to gain access to naked skin.

Allegra had never felt so swept away by desire before. She'd had two lovers previously but she could not recall ever feeling this incredible wave of longing with either of them. It made her feel as if her whole body was collapsing with it, the hollow emptiness that longed to be filled gnawing at her like a savage hunger she'd never experienced before. She had no control over it. Her body ached from head to toe with the need to feel Joel inside her. She didn't care that they hardly knew each other, she didn't care that he was the one person in the way of her achieving her goal with her project—all that mattered right now was his touch, the heat of his mouth, the raspy sexiness of his tongue and his hardened arousal probing her in its quest for the liquid warm sheath of her body.

His mouth found her naked breast and sucked on it hard. She arched her back in pleasure as his tongue rolled over her engorged nipple, the feel of his moist heat almost too much for her to bear. She whimpered in rapture as he moved to her other breast, one of his hands splayed over her flat abdomen, his long fingers reaching for the short, neatly cropped curls that housed her femininity.

'Oh, my *God…*' she gasped as she tried to hold back, but there was no way of stopping the storm of feeling that crashed over her as he continued his caressing movements against her. She felt herself lift off and soar, floating for a moment before tumbling down in a splintering of sensation that felt as if the skin of her scalp was lifting with the sheer ecstasy of it all.

'You are so very responsive,' he said against her mouth.

'Not usually…' She tried to get her breathing under some measure of control. She stretched like a languorous cat who had over-indulged on the richest cream.

'You're not getting sleepy on me, are you?' he asked, tipping up her chin to look deeply into her passion-slaked eyes.

'No,' she said, smiling as she traced a fingertip over his upper lip. 'It's your turn, I believe.'

'Only if you've got a condom handy,' he said with a rueful grimace. 'I've somehow got out of the habit of carrying them.'

Her eyes went wide and her chest slammed with panic. 'You've been having unsafe sex?'

He shook his head. 'I've been celibate for eighteen months. Not by choice, more by circumstance.'

'Well, thank God for friends like Kellie Wilton,' she said, as she rolled towards her bedside table and opened the top drawer. She took out a packet of condoms and dangled them in front of him. 'What do you think?'

He took one from the pack, his dark eyes alight with purpose. 'I think you're right—it's my turn.'

Allegra sighed raggedly as he possessed her, his body rocking with building momentum, taking hers along with it in a rush of feeling that gave her no choice but to respond. He carried her along on the tide of pleasure she could hear in each of his deep, rumbling groans. She felt the delicious pause that signalled he was hovering precariously on the edge, his whole body tensing momentarily before he fell forward with a thrusting plunge into paradise, his raw groan of release triggering a wave of pleasure through her as his body jerked urgently against hers until, finally spent, he went limp in her arms in a way she found touchingly vulnerable and trusting—again, a new experience for her.

'How many condoms did your friend give you?' Joel asked, after they had come back to earth a few moments later.

Allegra propped herself up on her elbows and gave him a sultry smile. 'Enough to wear out the average man.'

His dark eyes flickered with unmistakable desire as he pressed her back down on the bed. 'Perhaps I should have warned you earlier—I'm not the average man.'

Allegra smiled as he settled himself between her thighs. 'I knew that.'

'Was it my aura that gave me away?' he asked with a teasing smile. When she smiled up at him he felt himself go over the edge with a plummet of feeling that made him forget about everything but the mind-blowing experience of being with a woman he was rapidly falling in love with.

That in itself was a first—allowing himself to feel an emotion so deep and consuming that it threatened the high wall of resistance he had constructed around himself for most of his life. Allegra Tallis with her way-out ideas but deeply caring nature had, almost from the moment he had met her, been systematically demolishing his barriers, brick by brick, until if he wasn't careful she would finally see him for who he really was.

He had nothing to offer her.

What woman would commit to his responsibilities once his parents could no longer cope? They were heading inexorably that way as each day passed. The brief phone conversation he'd had with his mother the previous day had confirmed yet again that time was running out. He had sensed the desperation in her voice and yet again the craggy fingers of guilt had clawed and scraped at his insides.

Allegra deserved much more than he could give her. Her life would become burdened as his had become when fate had chosen its victim, leaving Joel with the crushing weight of survivor guilt that would never go away, no matter how hard he tried to ignore it or rationalise it away. Even thousands of kilometres had done nothing to separate him from it.

Allegra wriggled back up to snuggle close and a clamp tightened around his heart. He placed his arms around her and held her close, one of his hands going to the back of her head, his fingers stroking through the silky strands of her hair.

There was so much he wanted to say but the words were locked in his throat. The irony wasn't lost on him.

After all, wasn't Jared, his identical twin, exactly the same?

CHAPTER FIFTEEN

ALLEGRA woke to the sensation of Joel's mouth pressing a soft kiss to the naked skin of her shoulder. She dragged herself upright, her eyes adjusting to the light from the struggling sunshine at war with some storm clouds that looked very much as if they were going to win in the end.

'I've got to leave,' he said, regret in his tone as he looked down at her.

'What time is it?' She peered at the clock by her bedside but her eyes were sticky and blurry from lack of sleep.

'Five-thirty. I've got to get back to my house and shower and be back at the hospital in time for the intensive care and anaesthetic registrar tutorial.'

'You work too hard.'

He dropped a swift kiss to her soft bow of her mouth. 'So do you. See you at the unit.'

'Joel?'

He turned at her bedroom door to look back at her, his heart squeezing at how adorable she looked all mussed from sleep and sex, her mouth swollen from his kisses and the fragrance of their intimacy lingering in the air between them, linking them in a way he'd never felt before.

He hid his reaction behind an emotionally distant one-word response. 'Yes?'

'I enjoyed last night. I know you're not ready for a long-term commitment but I just want you to know that I really enjoy your company.'

He allowed his guard to slip a fraction as a smile softened his features. 'I enjoyed it, too. But I wonder how long it will be before the whole of Melbourne Memorial is in on our secret relationship?'

'Is that going to be a problem for you?'

'No, but it's going to be a problem for you when I have to review your project.'

Allegra stared at him, wondering what to make of his comment. Had last night meant nothing to him? Would he still—in spite of their relationship—put an end to her study?

'I just want some more time,' she said. 'Surely you owe me that?'

His expression hardened. 'The first thing you should get straight in your head, Allegra, is that it is always a fatal error to sleep with the enemy.'

'What are you saying, Joel?' she asked. 'That you're my enemy? That what occurred between us last night meant absolutely nothing to you?'

'What I'm saying is that if you think by offering your body as a means to sway me into your way of thinking, you have definitely deluded yourself. My assessment still stands. The decisions I have to make in ICTU have nothing to do with whatever relationship we conduct outside work hours. If I feel it's appropriate to pull the plug on your study or advise either Keith Lowe or whoever else happens to have a relative classified as brain dead, I will make those decisions on professional grounds and stand by them, irrespective of what happens between us privately.'

'Then perhaps it will make things a whole lot less complicated if we put an end to this right now,' she said. 'I can't see the point in having a relationship with someone who is so determined to play God.'

'Fine,' he said. 'I guess I'll have to clock last night up as a one-night stand—my first, in fact. You should feel honoured.'

She clutched the pillow with white-knuckled force to stop herself throwing it at him. 'I don't feel honoured. I feel disgusted.'

'So I guess this is the part where I leave and say thanks for the memories?' he said, unable to remove the mockery from his tone.

She threw off the covers and, wrapping the sheet around herself, stomped over to him and wrenched open her bedroom door, her green gaze glittering up at him with rage. 'No, this is the part where I tell you to go to hell and that I never want to see you again.'

'Which, of course, would work if not for the fact that we still have to work together,' he said in the same mocking tone.

'I don't think that is going to be a problem for too much longer,' she threatened. 'Because if you put a stop to my project, I swear I will resign the very next day.'

'There are plenty of other anaesthetists who will gladly take your place,' he said, knowing it was lie and that no one could ever reproduce her particular mix of skills. What she brought to the unit and indeed to Theatre was clearly going to be hard to replace, but his pride would not allow him to admit it.

'Then go and find one who will work the hours I do and care for people everyone else has given up on,' she threw back, tears spouting from her eyes. She scrubbed at her eyes but it was too late—he'd seen them.

He took a step towards her but she held him off with a raised hand. 'Get out. I mean it, Addison. Get out or I'll call the police and have you physically removed.'

He held her challenging glare for a tense moment before he turned on his heel and left. It was better this way, he consoled himself on his way out to his car. Better to put an end to it now before the hurt became more permanent. But as he drove away the ache inside felt as if it had lodged itself in a place that wasn't going to be so easy to remove.

Maybe it was already too late.

* * *

Joel had finished his tutorial and the morning ICTU round when his pager beeped. He unclipped it from his belt and read the message. *Drowning: due in TRU 10 minutes.*

He took a breath to prepare himself. The trauma reception unit, with the intensivists involved as early as possible in the management of incoming trauma, was one of the main advantages of the unit. He'd always maintained that hospital management should be involved in clinical decisions and not become isolated from patients. He had seen the all-too-familiar pattern of decision-making by managers who had lost touch with the real issues of patient care. That's why he had put himself on the standard roster of duty for intensivists and today he happened to be the floor co-ordinator for the whole complex.

He finished the medical entry in the last patient's notes and made his way to Trauma Reception.

As he arrived, an ambulance was backing into the ambulance bay and the TRU consultant, Rod Banks, and his registrar, Justin Denby, were busy setting up bay one with the help of nursing staff.

'Dr Addison,' Rod greeted him quickly. 'The patient's just arrived.'

'Do we have any preliminary details?' Joel asked after he'd replied to the greeting with one of his own.

'A guy in his mid-thirties found floating face down in a swimming pool in Toorak. Apparently has a head injury, unconscious, intubated. That's about it until the ambulance crew fills us in.'

'You'll supervise the resus, then, Rod? I'll lend a hand with Justin,' Joel said.

'I don't mind,' Rod said, 'but why don't you take this one? Justin and I were up half of last night at the resident's dinner—we've both feeling a bit seedy.'

'OK, it looks like we're on, then,' Joel said, as the ambulance crew wheeled in a pallid man, head bandaged, his neck in a cervical collar, intubated and being ventilated by one of the crew.

'Justin, you take over ventilation,' Joel directed. 'Rod, can you supervise the transfer to the trauma bed, check the line and get in another IV, and get off bloods for pathology?'

He turned his attention to the attending nursing staff, issuing directions on removing the patient's overalls and inserting a nasogastric tube. As the nurses cut away the patient's clothing, Joel noticed the logo on the right-hand breast pocket, which seemed to suggest the man was some type of pool maintenance technician. Presumably he had met with some sort of accident, perhaps falling into a pool he was servicing.

He turned to address the ambulance crew. 'Any details on this patient?'

The senior paramedic spoke first. 'We were called by the neighbour next door. She claims she heard some sort of argument going on but she was busy with one of her young kids so didn't go out to investigate. A short time later she came out and looked over the fence and saw this guy face down in the pool. She called out to another neighbour on the other side who was mowing his lawn. He hauled the patient out of the pool while she ran back and phoned the emergency services. When we got there the patient had sputtering respirations, obviously lungs still full of water and a stream of blood from the back of his head. I intubated him and sucked out his lungs as best as I could, put on a hard cervical collar and bandaged his head to control the bleeding. My guess is he's got a fractured skull.'

'What's with the police?' Joel asked, nodding his head to where two officers were standing across the corridor.

'I called them,' the senior paramedic said. 'It's now our standard protocol if there is a potentially fatal trauma. They seemed a bit agitated at the scene. The extent of the head injury doesn't sit well with where he was found.'

Joel made a mental note to confer with the police once he had stabilised the patient.

'Second line's in,' Rod said. 'And the nasogastric's returned about a litre of bile-tinged pool water. This guy didn't go down without a fight. To swallow all that water you'd have to be conscious for a fair while.'

'It doesn't look like an accident,' Joel said. 'The police are interested and the ambos suspect a fractured skull. Can we reassess the primary survey? Then I want a look at that skull and do the secondary survey.'

Joel replaced his gloves with a clean pair and, adjusting his splash-guard goggles, removed the head bandage from the patient. What he saw was clearly not the result of an accidental poolside slip or fall. The back and the side of the skull were crushed, there was bony crepitus, and obvious cerebrospinal fluid leakage from one ear, as well as renewed bleeding once the pressure from the bandage was removed.

'Hell, what's happened to this guy?' he said, in shock at the extent of injury.

Rod inspected the site and grimaced. 'Doesn't look like a trip on slippery tiles, does it?'

Joel gave him a grim glance before he ensured the head bandage was adequately reapplied. 'No, it does not.' He swivelled to address the nurse. 'Get Neurosurgery on the phone. We need an immediate CAT scan to establish the extent of injury.'

Once the nurse had left to do as he'd instructed, Joel turned back to Rod. 'Let's run through the secondary survey, then I'd better have a word with the police.'

'He's not going to make it, is he?' Rod asked.

'If he does, he might not like what's left of his life,' Joel said, performing a detailed head-to-toe examination of the now stabilised patient. Stripping off his gloves and protective gear, he then made his way over to where the police were waiting to speak to him.

After receiving a brief description of the patient's injuries, the officer in charge of the investigation said, 'We'd like to follow up on this. You said you've ordered blood tests, I assume you have included a drug screen?'

'Yes, it's standard procedure,' Joel said. 'Do you guys have any personal details on this man? His name or relatives who need to be informed of his condition?'

'His name is Terry Fowler,' the second officer informed him. 'He's well known to us, if you know what I mean.'

Joel screwed up his mouth for a moment as he took this in. 'He's got some sort of record?'

'As long as your arm,' the older officer said. 'Looks like someone meant business. He wasn't meant to survive, going by what we saw at the scene.'

'So it's an attempted murder investigation?' Joel queried.

'We're treating it that way for the moment, yes. We're following up on a couple of other leads,' the officer said. 'We'll keep you informed of anything relevant. We've organised a guard. We'll try and keep it quiet. This place has had its share of publicity lately.'

'Have you progressed any further in your enquiries into the attempt on Kate Lowe's life?'

The officers exchanged a brief glance before the senior officer turned back to Joel. 'We've now gone through hours of security tapes filmed on the night in question. The image is not as clear as we'd like, but a man with features remarkably similar to Terry Fowler's was captured on tape entering the hospital during the time frame the attempt on Mrs Lowe's life was made.'

Joel frowned, his brain reeling with possible motives. 'Have you any idea what his connection to Kate Lowe would be?'

'Not as yet but, as we said, we have a few leads we're following up. In the meantime, if you think of anything that might be in any way significant, please contact us.' The officer handed Joel a card. 'And it goes without saying that if Mrs Lowe regains full consciousness, we'd like to be informed immediately.'

'Of course,' Joel said.

'How is the little boy doing?' the younger officer asked. 'I have a son the same age.'

'I've been an intensivist too long to offer hope when there isn't any,' Joel said. 'He's showing no signs of brain activity, which means a decision will have to made soon as to what to do next.'

'How's the father taking things?'

'He's doing his best to resign himself for the worst,' Joel said.

'I'm sure his mistress is offering the best comfort she can under the circumstances,' the junior officer said, receiving a quick reproving frown from his superior.

'Yes, well, that's his business, I suppose,' Joel said. 'His sister has been in a few times, or so I'm told.'

'His sister?' The senior officer's frown deepened.

'Yes, I can't quite recall her name…' Joel wrinkled his brow as he tried to recall the name Allegra had been searching for last night before they'd gone for dinner. 'It started with F—Fair-something, I think.'

'Serena Fairbright,' the officer said.

'Yes, that's it. Fairbright.'

'Thank you, Dr Addison,' the officer said. 'We'd better let you get back to your work.'

Joel stood for a while after the police had driven away, a small frown drawing his brows together.

'Dr Addison?' Rod Banks approached. 'I've just had news about the head-injury guy. He had an arrest in CT—they'd just got him off the scanner. I don't think there was much Mr Pardle could have done, there was major brain damage under the fractures.'

Joel blew out a breath as he turned to go back inside. 'It's probably just as well.'

'Don't let Allegra Tallis hear you say that,' Rod said, more than a little wryly. 'She's in with little Tommy Lowe right now. Apparently the BIS monitor started showing brain activity last night. Allegra whizzed through here and filled me in on the news some time ago—she's busy arranging a repeat EEG.'

Joel stared at him, hope lifting for a moment then crashing back down in his chest. 'What sort of BIS activity did she mention?'

'Not much apparently, but enough to justify another few extra days of monitoring, she thinks,' Rod answered.

'Has the father been told?'

'According to Allegra, he's on his way in.' Rod hesitated for a moment before adding, 'Sorry we couldn't salvage the Fowler chap. I guess his number was up.'

Joel gave the young man a world-weary glance. 'Believe me, he wouldn't have wanted it any other way.'

CHAPTER SIXTEEN

ALLEGRA had not thought when she'd arrived for work that morning that the ache she had felt in her heart could have been eased in any way, but when she had looked at Tommy's overnight BIS monitor scores her hopes had soared in spite of her fractured relationship with Joel.

Kellie, the medical registrar, went through them with Allegra. 'See there, that's definite cerebral activity—at one point it's as high as eight. It's small but there's been nothing prior to that, and the activity has continued at a lower level since then.'

Allegra knew an eight was not an indication of full recovery, far from it, but it meant Tommy had an intact cerebral cortex, and that was the basis for recovery of consciousness.

'Can I see his obs chart for last night?' she requested.

'Sure, here is the chart from midnight the previous night,' Kellie said, as she passed across a large sheet with manually entered graphs.

'Look at this, Kellie—at around the same time as the first BIS response, there is a rapid rise in pulse and BP. Like a stress response,' Allegra observed.

'I'd not noticed that.'

'Did Tommy have any visitors last night?' Allegra asked. 'His father or aunt?'

'I don't really know. As far as I've heard, it was fairly quiet.

I've only just started my shift. I could check with the nurses. Why, do you think something precipitated this?'

Allegra frowned as she looked back at the printouts. 'It's hard to tell. Nothing I've done so far has stirred him and yet here we have an eight seemingly out of the blue.'

'Yeah, well, you and I know an eight isn't exactly an indication that a rocket scientist is still residing inside that little head,' Kellie said.

Allegra flicked a quick glance in her friend's direction. 'No, but it means he deserves more time.'

'Have you told Joel Addison about this latest development?'

Allegra carefully avoided her friend's eyes. 'No, not yet, but no doubt he will soon hear of it and dismiss it as insignificant.'

'Yes, but the father will be pleased surely? He has the final say.'

'The father gave up hope days ago,' Allegra said. 'He's terrified of being left with a permanently disabled child.'

'I can't say I blame him,' Kellie said. 'Have you ever thought about what sort of life some of our patients go on to live once we patch them up and send them on their way?'

'I had the very same conversation with Joel Addison the other night,' Allegra said. 'But then I think of Alice Greeson's parents, who would have been grateful to have taken their daughter home in whatever state she was in. They would have nursed her lovingly for the rest of her life.'

'But what happens when they get too old to do the care?' Kellie asked. 'It falls on the siblings or other relatives, and that's hardly fair. They have their own lives to live.'

Allegra sighed as she thought about it. 'Yes…I can see it's not exactly a black-and-white issue, but I want to do my best in this case. I feel I owe it to Tommy. His mother is clearly mentally ill. Have you seen the self-mutilation scars on her wrists?'

Kellie nodded. 'Sad, isn't it? I wonder what her story is?'

'Probably abuse of some sort in her childhood,' Allegra said. 'The husband intimated as much. He has also had his fair share apparently, his sister, too.'

'They're very close, aren't they?'

Allegra swung her chair around. 'Who, Serena and Kate?'

'No, Keith and his sister.'

'What do you mean, close?'

Kellie gave a little shrug. 'I don't know…it's just an impression I got. You know that date I had organised with the internet dating agency? Well, we met for drinks and then went to that new swanky restaurant on St Kilda Beach. I saw Keith and his sister at a nearby table. I don't think they recognised me. Besides, they hardly even once looked my way. At first I was a bit surprised that a brother and sister would…you know…act that way. It seemed a little weird, sort of creepy.'

'Weird? In what way?' Allegra could feel a strange chill being to pass over her.

'Well…' Kellie dangled her leg from her position where she was perched on the desk beside Allegra. 'I have three brothers and let me tell you as much I love each of them dearly I would never let any of them hold my hands for ages across a restaurant table, and I certainly would never let them kiss me full on the mouth.' She gave a little grimace.

Allegra stared at her friend for so long without speaking that Kellie gave her a little nudge with her foot. 'Hey, what did I say?'

Allegra got to her feet, the office chair she'd been sitting on rolling backwards to bump against the filing cabinet. 'Excuse me, Kel. I have to see Joel Addison for a minute. Page me if anything else happens with Tommy.'

Kellie turned to watch her leave the unit. 'That girl really needs to get out more,' she said to herself, before sliding off the desk and answering the phone that had just started to ring.

Joel was just coming out of his office when he saw Allegra heading his way. He straightened to his full height, mentally preparing himself for yet another showdown, but to his surprise as she got closer he could see no trace of anger on her beautiful face, but worry instead.

'Can I see you for a minute?' she asked.

'Sure.' He reopened his office door and waited for her to precede him, her perfume filling his nostrils as she moved past. 'What can I do for you?'

'Well, for a start let me assure you this is not one of those morning-after-the-night-before scenes,' she said turning to face him, her slim hands twisting in front of her. 'Neither am I going to apologise and beg you to reconsider our relationship. As far as I'm concerned, you and I are not going to work. It was a moment of madness to even make an attempt.'

'I agree,' he returned coolly.

Allegra fought down the disappointment his response triggered. Couldn't he have at least shown a little remorse for his part in last night? He had offered her nothing but an affair, and it had hurt her terribly to be considered a temporary option. She knew she deserved better than that and he did, too, but for some reason he wasn't interested in even giving it a chance.

'I heard about the BIS monitor scores on the Lowe boy,' he said into the little silence. 'What was the reading?'

Allegra dearly wished she could tell him fifteen, but there was no point lying when he could just as easily verify the results for himself. 'It was an eight for a brief period last night, and a few low-level traces since,' she said. 'His pulse and blood pressure went up for about twenty minutes around the same time.'

'Can you account for it in any of the things you've been doing with him? I heard you were playing his favourite movie repeatedly. Do you think that had something to do with it?'

'I don't know…' She undid her hands to tuck a strand of her hair behind her ear that had slipped from its restraining clip. 'Kellie Wilton, the medical registrar, is checking with the night staff to see if anyone noticed anything.'

'Did he have any visitors during the night?'

'I'm not sure. I'm waiting for the father to come in to ask him. He doesn't usually come in at night, or at least not for very long.'

'I expect he is too busy with his mistress,' Joel said, echoing the cynical opinion of the police officer he'd spoken to earlier.

'Yes…I suppose you could be right…' She worried her bottom lip for a moment before she went on, 'Joel, have you ever met Keith Lowe's sister?'

'No. Why?'

'I have a funny feeling about her,' she said.

'We're not talking auras here, are we?'

Allegra looked up at him but for once there was no sign of mockery on his face. 'Kellie saw Keith and his sister having dinner in a restaurant a couple of nights ago,' she said. 'She saw them holding hands and kissing in a way that suggested they have a slightly unusual relationship for two people who claim to be siblings.'

Joel listened as intently as he could, his brain shooting off in all directions when Allegra tapped into some of his own lurking suspicions. His conversation with the police had stirred up questions that he would very much like some answers to.

'Each family has its own code of affection.' He did his best to go down the logically sequential route. 'Hugs, kisses, that sort of thing vary between family groups, even between individuals within the one family.'

'Yes, I know that, but remember I told you about Keith Lowe's background? How he had been brought up in an overly strict, punitive way? He spoke openly of the difficulty he had showing affection, and yet Kellie swore she saw him holding his sister's hands for ages and kissing her on the mouth. That doesn't add up, to my way of thinking. Besides, I know you don't give much credence to my reading of body language, but I can't help feeling something is not quite right with those two. I understand how having a relative in ICTU is traumatic and makes people act in unpredictable ways, but Serena Fairbright doesn't seem at all attached to Tommy. She barely spends more than a minute or two by his bedside. She hasn't even brought a special toy or anything to him. I know men sometimes overlook those sorts of things, but women are usually good at that. Look at Jonathon Sprent. He may be a fully grown adult but his mum and his sister brought in his childhood teddy bear and a fluffy one-eared rabbit and propped them by his bedside on the very first day he came in.'

'But you said the abusive background of Keith Lowe and his sister made them wary of showing emotion. It seems reasonable to assume that toys and other sentimental tokens of childhood would not feature highly in their scheme of things.'

'I guess you're right…' Her shoulders sagged. 'I just can't help feeling as if something's wrong here and we're not seeing it.'

'Has Kate Lowe had any other episodes of lucidity?' he asked.

'Yes, but that's what's so confusing. She says Tommy's name and then Serena's soon after. If the family is not close in the normal sense, why would Kate be calling for her son and sister-in-law and not her husband?'

Joel frowned as he took in what she was saying. 'I can see what you mean…it doesn't make a lot of sense. But, then, the marriage was in trouble so it could be that Kate confided in Keith's sister about the difficulties she was having.'

'I find that hard to believe, especially since Keith insisted his wife has no close friends. Not only that, you know as well as I do that blood is thicker than water. Why would Serena side with Kate, the woman who had made her brother turn to another woman in desperation?'

Joel's dark gaze locked with hers. 'But what if Serena is not really Keith's sister?'

Allegra stared at him as the penny dropped with a clang inside her head. 'Oh, my God! *She's* his mistress! No wonder she has no affection for Tommy. I can't believe I didn't figure that out first. It's so obvious when you think about it. They don't really resemble each other in looks, although I know that's not unusual—many siblings don't. I just assumed like everyone else that she was his sister. He introduced her as that, I suppose because he was uncomfortable bringing his mistress in to the unit where his wife's and son's lives were hanging in the balance.'

'What if Serena was the one who tried to get rid of Kate?' he said, confirming Allegra's escalating suspicions.

'You mean with the ventilator?' She frowned as she let the possibility sink in. 'But that was a feat of complicated engineering. Serena doesn't strike me as someone with the sort of mechanical skills to cut and join hoses. For a start she has nails practically longer than chopsticks. I can't imagine her using pliers and pipe joiners.'

'No, but what if she got someone else to do it for her? Someone who did have the necessary skills.'

'Who? I mean… Think about it, Joel. How many people could you ask to do something like that without it coming back to bite you? You'd have to pay them a heap of money and hope they kept quiet. It would be an incredible risk to take.'

'Not if you got rid of them permanently.'

Allegra felt a cold shiver pass through her at his words. 'You mean…*murder* them?'

He gave her a grave nod. 'We had a guy come into TRU this morning. The police were very interested in the case. I've been thinking about it ever since.'

'The drowning with the head injury?' she asked. 'I heard something about it. What, they think it wasn't an accident?'

'The head injury he sustained suggested he was bashed with a heavy object, a crowbar or something like that. He may not have fallen into that pool by accident. Someone wanted him to die then and there, but a neighbour heard something and hauled him out. He died before Anthony could get him to Theatre, not that any operation was going to repair his pulp of a brain.'

'But what has this got to do with the Lowes?'

'Nothing maybe, but, as I said, it got me thinking. The guy who died had a criminal record. One could assume he'd be exactly the type to accept a contract, for the right price. Maybe if what we suspect is true, and Serena is not, in fact, Keith's sister but his mistress, she would have a very good motive to get rid of Kate.'

'Maybe…but I still don't understand why Kate would be calling for Serena, the woman her own husband's having an affair with.'

'It happens all the time, Allegra,' he said. 'A mate of mine found out his best friend had been sleeping with his wife for months. He didn't suspect a thing. They played golf together every weekend, had a beer or two once or twice a week after work, but he never once suspected anything was going on.'

'But aren't you clutching at straws? Anyone could have tampered with Kate's ventilator, or at least someone with a bit of inside knowledge. You said it yourself: emotions run high when a child is involved. That's why I asked you to remove Ruth Tilley from the unit.'

'Ruth Tilley has gone on stress leave as of this morning,' he said. 'I don't for a moment suspect her of tampering with Kate's equipment, but the press attention and the police presence has taken its toll on her. It's taking its toll on all of us.'

'I know what you mean,' she said, rubbing her hands up and down her arms. 'I can't believe this place has turned into such a circus. Working in ICTU is stressful enough, without the pressure of a murder inquiry and constant security checks going on in the background.'

'Tell me something I don't already know,' he said, pinching the bridge of his nose, his eyes squeezing shut momentarily.

Allegra looked at him, her earlier anger melting at the obvious stress he was under. His eyes were tired, probably more bloodshot than hers, and his body looked tense, as if he hadn't allowed himself to relax in days, maybe weeks or even months.

She stepped forward and touched him on the arm. 'Joel…sit down and let me massage your neck and shoulders. It won't take long and it will make all the difference, believe me.'

He opened his eyes and met her concerned gaze. 'It's just a tension headache. I get them all the time. I'll take a couple of paracetamol in a minute. Besides, I'm sure you have better things to do right now.'

She smiled and with one firm hand pushed him down into his chair. 'Close your eyes and think of something pleasant. Let yourself relax for ten minutes while I work some magic on those tight muscles of yours.'

Joel settled into the seat but the only pleasurable thing he could think of was how it had felt to have her in his arms the night before, her body writhing beneath his, pleasuring him in an act that he had felt akin to worship. He hadn't been able to remove the images from his mind, no matter how hard he tried. He had pushed her away, just as he had pushed away every other person who had tried to come close, but she was a little more determined than most, a little more—no, a *lot* more—irresistible than most, and it felt good to let his guard down just for a few minutes.

He rolled his head forward as she worked on his tight shoulders through the cotton of his shirt, but he ached to feel her soft warm fingers on his flesh. As if she had read his mind, she moved her hands to the front of his chest and released and removed his tie before undoing each of his shirt buttons, one by one. He did nothing to stop her. He couldn't. The desire to feel her hands on him was so overpowering it was like a fever in his blood.

Finally his shirt was off and her hands were working on his neck and shoulders in rhythmic soothing movements that relaxed those muscles but set up immediate tension in others. He could feel the deep throb of desire spring to life in his groin but he did his best to ignore it, although it took a huge effort. Her fingers increased their pressure, unlocking the tight golfball-sized knots bunched beneath his skin until he finally felt the tension behind his eyes gradually begin to ease.

'How do you feel?' she asked a few minutes later as she handed him his shirt.

He gave her a grateful glance as he shrugged himself back into his shirt. 'That really helped—thanks.'

'You should have more regular massage. People still think it's a luxury treatment that you have once a year when you're on holidays, but it's much more therapeutic if you have it regularly.'

'Yeah, well, time is always an issue,' he said, reaching for his tie.

She watched as he knotted it and positioned it around his throat, adjusting it into place. It was still slightly skew when he'd finished so she stepped forward and centred it.

Joel looked down at her standing so close, her breasts almost touching his chest, one of her hands flat on his chest, the other still on the knot of his tie.

'Allegra…' His voice came out raspy and rough as his hand moved up to cover hers.

'I should get back to work…' she said softly, her eyes feeling as if they were being lured into the deep dark depths of his.

'Yes…yes, you should…' he said, as one of his hands went to the small of her back and brought her forward until she was touching him thigh to thigh.

Her lips were soft and yielding beneath the hard pressure of his, her breath warm and sweet as it filled his mouth and curled around his tongue as he plunged into her moistness. The rush of desire rose in his blood like a rushing tide, as her body instinctively searched for the heat and possession of his.

The mobile phone on his belt brought him back to earth with a shrill reminder of his responsibilities and the lives that depended on him. But when he released Allegra with a wry apologetic grimace and answered it, it wasn't a life that needed saving from within the hospital at all.

It was a life much closer to home…

CHAPTER SEVENTEEN

'HOW is he doing?' Joel asked the cardiologist in the cardiac unit.

'Your father's had a small inferior myocardial infarct,' Tim Lockerby informed him. 'I want to keep him in for a few days on a streptokinase infusion, and get angiography organised.'

Joel thanked him and moved to the cubicle where his father lay hooked up to an ECG and pulse oximeter, an IV line and oxygen mask.

As if he sensed his son's presence, Garry Addison opened his eyes and removed his oxygen mask. 'Sorry about this, son. I hate to be causing all this fuss.'

Joel took his father's hand in his and gave it a warm affectionate squeeze, fighting back emotion. 'You silly old goat,' he said gruffly. 'You're not causing any fuss. You'll be on your feet again in a few days.'

His father's eyes shifted to the blue cotton open-weave blanket covering him from the waist down. 'Your mother will need some help. I hate to put this on you but—'

'Don't worry.' Joel's grip on his father's hand tightened reassuringly. 'I'll sort something out with Jared. We all knew it would come to this some time.'

'It will break your mother's heart…'

The irony of his father's words weren't lost on Joel. 'At this point in time it's your heart we have to concentrate on. I'll sort out things with Mum, don't worry. I'll take a couple of days off to organise things.'

'But you've only just started this job,' his father protested. 'We've been so worried about the stress you've been under. You look worn out.'

'Well, you're not looking so great yourself, Dad,' Joel joked. 'I'm fine. In fact, not fifteen minutes ago I had a workplace massage. See how well I'm taking care of myself these days?'

'About time, too,' his father grumbled. 'I hope it was done by a pretty woman. It's been far too long since you've had the touch of a woman to take your mind off work and…home…'

'She wasn't pretty,' Joel said, as his patted his father's leg, 'she was gorgeous.'

'So you're dating her?'

He gave his father a mock reproving look. 'Thirty-four-year-old men should never discuss their private lives with their parents, you know that—it could cause heart strain.'

Garry gave him a weary smile. 'Thirty-four-year-old men shouldn't do a lot of things, but sometimes life doesn't hand you the cards you want.'

'How is Jared handling this?' Joel asked after a tiny pause.

'You know Jared. He doesn't make anything easy…'

Joel gave his father another gentle pat. 'Just concentrate on getting well. I'll deal with Jared and Mum. Leave it to me.'

Allegra rushed up to Joel as he was leaving the hospital. 'Joel, how is your father? Is there anything I can do?'

Joel looked down at her, his chest tightening at what might have been if circumstances had been different. 'No, but thanks anyway. He's had a myocardial infarct and needs angiography. I'm taking a couple of days off to sort some domestic stuff out. My mother needs some help. It will take me a day or two to organise it.'

'What about your twin brother?' she asked. 'Can't he help?'

His eyes shifted from hers as he thrust his hand in his trouser pocket for his car keys. 'My brother is totally useless and has been for most of his life.' He rattled his keys impatiently and she stepped back so he could leave.

She watched him drive off, the squeal of his tyres as they hit the tarmac of the road making her wince. It didn't seem fair that he had to shoulder his father's illness without the support of his brother. What were families for anyway, if not to pull together when things got tough? She didn't have a brother or sister but she knew for certain that if she did, they would be close and supportive because her parents would have done everything in their power to ensure it.

Her pager beeped and she looked down at the message, her heart leaping in hope. It was from Kellie, telling her Kate had just regained consciousness.

Kellie was waiting just outside Kate's cubicle when she arrived. 'She's finally awake. She just opened her eyes and asked for Tommy, clear as a bell. The police want to interview her but I thought you should assess her first before they barrage her with questions. They're waiting over there.' She pointed to two tall detectives lingering near the office.

Allegra opened the door to the isolation room where Kate was being managed, and smiled as she approached her bed. Kate still looked terribly fragile, especially as her bruises from the accident had now turned into a kaleidoscope of colour.

'Hello, Kate, my name is Allegra Tallis,' she said, repeating almost verbatim her previous introduction when she'd first visited Kate while she'd been unconscious. 'I'm an anaesthetist on rotation in ICTU. I've been looking after your son.'

'I want to see him,' Kate said, becoming agitated, tears rolling down her cheeks. 'The other doctor and the nurse keep telling me he's all right, but I need to see him to make sure.'

'That can easily be arranged,' Allegra said. 'He's in the unit, further down. He's still unconscious but I'm hopeful he will wake up soon.'

Kate choked on a sob. 'What happened to us? Why are Tommy and I in hospital?'

Allegra's heart sank at the woman's distressed questions. 'You had a car accident a few days ago, Kate. Do you remember anything at all about it?'

Kate screwed up her face as she tried to recollect, but it was becoming clear she had no memory at all of that day. She shook her head, wincing at the pain it triggered. 'No…it's blank…. I remember we were at the chalet…Tommy and me…'

'What about Keith? Was he there?'

Kate tried to concentrate, but it looked as if she was having trouble with the details. 'I can't remember. He might have been. I think that was the plan… Tommy and I to drive up first and settle in and Keith was going to join us…' She looked at Allegra, her eyes immeasurably sad. 'We've been having some…trouble… My husband wants a divorce. I was upset… I know I'm not a good wife…I get bouts of depression. I don't blame him for wanting to leave me. But Tommy, it would hurt him so much. I thought…if we could just sort things out…'

'So you don't remember why you got in the car with Tommy?'

'No… No, I can't remember.'

'Kate, I know this is going to be difficult for you, but the police want to speak to you about that day.'

'Police! Why the police?' Kate looked frightened. 'Did I do something wrong? Was the accident my fault? Oh, God! Did someone else die? Did I kill someone? Is that why there was a police guard here when I woke up?'

Allegra stroked the woman's hands soothingly. 'No, no one else was hurt, apart from you and Tommy. It was a single-vehicle accident. Your car went off the road into the river. A car travelling behind you saw it happen. He was the one who rescued you and Tommy.'

Kate's distress was obvious. 'Tommy could have died… My precious baby could have died…'

'But he didn't, Kate. He's alive, I'll arrange for your bed to be wheeled to his cubicle.'

Allegra went to where the police were waiting. 'She's still very fragile and has amnesia. It's not a good idea to press her too hard. If she regains her memory, and in cases like this some people never do, she will be able to cope better with a more intensive interview.'

'Does she know someone tried to turn off her ventilator?' the detective sergeant asked.

'I didn't think it wise to mention it,' Allegra said. 'She has enough to deal with at the moment.'

'We'll be maintaining our close watch over her, especially now she is conscious.'

'I don't believe she tried to commit suicide,' Allegra felt compelled to say. 'But I do believe someone wanted her dead.'

'Murder-suicides make people angry, especially when young children are victims,' the detective said. 'But in this case I'm inclined to agree with you.'

'Oh, really?' She gave him a surprised look. 'Have you uncovered something in your investigation?'

'Dr Addison, your colleague, ran a drug test on a patient that was brought in earlier this morning.'

'Terry Fowler, the head injury-drowning victim?'

'That's the one,' he said. 'As you know, he subsequently died from his head injury, but the pathology report showed up a cocktail of drugs in his system.'

'I haven't seen the report but can you recall exactly what the drugs were?'

'An antidepressant and a sedative,' he replied, checking his notebook. 'I'm not sure of the actual amounts but paroxetine, codeine and diazepam were definitely present.'

Allegra was getting so used to chills running up and down her spine now that she hardly noticed this one as it occurred. 'That's interesting. That's exactly the same cocktail of drugs found in Kate Lowe's blood.'

The detective frowned. 'I'll have the records correlated immediately. There might be some link between Fowler and Mrs Lowe. I'll get our people onto it straight away.'

Allegra went back to Kate's cubicle and immediately organised for her to be transferred to Tommy's bedside. The police guard accompanied them but he kept at a discreet distance.

Kate's face crumpled when she saw her little boy lying hooked up to the ventilator and monitors, his little chest rising and falling mechanically.

Allegra touched her on the arm. 'Don't let the machines upset you. You were on exactly the same ones and here you are awake and getting better by the minute.'

'But what if he doesn't get better?' Kate turned her agonised face to Allegra. 'Brain injury is serious in anyone, more so in a child. What if he's…permanently damaged?'

Allegra tried to offer the best possible hope. 'We are still not sure how severe his head injury is. We've run some tests, which at this stage are inconclusive.'

'This is all my fault…' Kate said brokenly.

'No, that's not true,' Allegra insisted. 'You didn't do anything to deliberately harm Tommy.'

'If only I could remember…' Kate began pulling at her hair as if it was in the way of her memory.

Allegra looked in horror at the clump of hair that came away from the woman's head. 'Kate, please, don't torture yourself like this. Tommy needs you to be strong right now.' She took Kate's hands in hers and began to massage them. 'I need you to help me get through to Tommy. I know you can't remember anything about the day of the accident, but can you tell me about Tommy's favourite things? His father told me he loves the Harry Potter movies and books and I've had the DVDs running almost constantly, but what about something else? Can you think of anything that he loves more than anything in the world?'

Kate's face brightened with a glimmer of hope. 'He has a teddy bear. He's had him since he was a baby. It's got a little key in the back that when you wind it up it plays "London Bridge is Falling Down." He never goes anywhere without it. He sleeps with it every night.'

'Have you any idea where is the bear now?'

'I don't know… We took it to the chalet but if we left in the car it might have been with us…'

And lying at the bottom of the river, Allegra thought with a sinking feeling. 'I'll chase it up with the police and SES,' she said. 'They usually remove all personal items and return them to the owners.'

'Dr Tallis,' Kate appealed to her with her big soulful hazel eyes. 'I read of a case not that long ago of a girl in a coma. She was declared brain dead and the machines that were keeping her alive were switched off. That won't happen to Tommy, will it?'

Allegra had never felt so out of her depth in her life. 'Kate.' She took the woman's hands in hers once more. 'I promise you that I will do everything in my power to prevent that happening.'

'I don't care if it turns out that he's…damaged,' Kate said. 'I just want him alive. He's my son…my only baby. I will look after him, no matter what. That's what being a mother is all about. He's all I live for.'

Allegra stood back as the orderlies helped to transfer Kate back to her room. Once she was settled, Allegra left to call the SES team that had retrieved Kate's vehicle. As luck would have it, they had found the teddy bear and the man she spoke to was planning to come to Melbourne for a social event and promised to deliver it personally to the hospital.

The next call Allegra made was to Joel, but she got his answering service on both his home number and his mobile. She left a brief message but as the hours dragged by she ached to see him in person, partly for her own reasons but also to talk about the developments the police had discussed with her.

By sheer chance she ran into Tim Lockerby from the cardiac unit who she knew was looking after Joel's father.

'Tim? Do you happen to know Joel Addison's parents' home address? I need to see him about something and he's not answering either of his phones.'

'It will be on Mr Addison's file. I'll get the ward clerk to give it to you. I heard you've been dating Joel.'

She frowned. 'Who told you that?'

'His father did,' Tim answered, with a glinting smile. 'He was right chuffed about it. Said it was the first time in years his son had been so taken with a woman.'

'I can't imagine Joel Addison announcing to all and sundry that I was the woman of his dreams,' she said with a cynical twist of her mouth.

'He didn't,' Tim said. 'His father figured it out for himself, as did the rest of the staff in CCU. As soon as Joel mentioned he'd had a workplace massage by a gorgeous woman, it was easy to do the numbers and come up with you.'

'He said I was gorgeous?' She gaped at him incredulously.

'Don't you have mirrors at your place?' Tim teased. 'If I wasn't already married to a beautiful woman, I'd be requesting a workplace massage myself. Joel is a great guy, Allegra. You deserve to have a social life. You work too hard as it is.'

'I know. It's getting to me, believe me,' she said with a rueful look.

'Take care of yourself,' he said. 'You've had a tough time recently. Don't go working yourself into a breakdown.'

'I'm fine, Tim, but thanks for being concerned. I'll just get that address and another fourteen-hour day will be over.'

Tim grinned. 'And another will appear tomorrow morning.'

'Don't remind me,' she growled, and made her way to the ward clerk's desk.

The drive out to Box Hill was interrupted by heavy traffic due to roadworks. The heat of the evening was stifling in spite of her car's air-conditioning. She pulled up in front of a modest single-storey house in a quiet leafy street, turned off the engine and took a minute to look around at the house Joel had spent his childhood in.

She wasn't sure what she'd been expecting but somehow she couldn't help thinking the slightly run-down appearance of the house and garden didn't sit all that well with Joel's position as a highly qualified doctor. But then she remembered his car. It, too, was modest, nothing like some of the flashy sports cars that littered the hospital car park.

She made her way up the concrete path, glancing down at the ramp that led to the front door. She pressed the bell and after a short wait the door opened and a small woman with salt-and-pepper hair and a tired face looked up at her with a tentative smile. 'Hello? Can I help you?'

'Mrs Addison?' Allegra offered her hand. 'I'm Allegra Tallis, a doctor at Melbourne Memorial.'

The woman's face seemed to almost collapse in dread. 'This isn't about Garry, is it?' she asked. 'He's all right, isn't he? I'm just on my way to visit him. Don't tell me something's gone wrong before I could get there to be with him.'

'No, nothing like that. Mr Addison is doing very well. I was talking to his cardiologist not long ago,' Allegra quickly reassured her. 'I'm here to see your son, actually.'

The relief on Joel's mother's face completely transformed her features. She placed a thin hand on her chest as if to settle the flutter of her heart. 'Oh, thank God. You had me worried there for a moment. But I'm afraid Joel's not here right now. He's out with his brother, but I'm sure they won't be too long. They went to the park but should be back soon. You can wait here or, if you like, you could go and meet them there. I have to dash. I haven't had a chance to take my husband's toiletries in to him yet.'

'A walk in the park sounds wonderful,' Allegra said, feeling uncomfortable about waiting in Joel's family home alone.

'It's just at the end of the street,' Mrs Addison said. 'It was nice meeting you. I hope you'll come again when things aren't so…so stressful.'

'I'd like that,' Allegra said with complete sincerity. She felt a warmth coming off Joel's mother that somehow reminded her of her own mother.

The pavement was hot under her feet as she walked to where the park was situated. She could see a group of teenage boys kicking a football about and secretly admired their energy in the cloying heaviness of the humidity that suggested a storm was imminent. Perspiration was already plastering her thin cotton blouse to her back and the tops of her thighs were sticking together uncomfortably.

She followed the path for a bit longer until she saw the unmistakable figure of Joel in the distance. He was pushing a wheelchair, and as he came closer she could see the identical image of him sitting slumped in the chair.

She stood stock still as if suddenly frozen, shock widening her eyes as Joel stopped in front of her. She gave herself a rough mental shake and, shifting her gaze to his level, reached out a hand to Joel's brother.

'Hi, you must be Jared,' she said with a smile. 'I'm Allegra.'

'He can't hear you,' Joel said.

She looked up at Joel in astonishment at his curt, emotionless tone. She turned back to Jared and greeted him again, using sign language, but it was clear he had no understanding. He looked at her, his head wobbling as he tried to focus on her face, a smile momentarily appearing on his mouth.

Allegra bent down and took Jared's limp hand in hers and gave it a gentle squeeze. 'Hi, Jared. I'm sorry you can't hear me, but it's nice to meet you.'

Joel looked down at her squatting in front of his brother, his heart feeling as if it had someone had just put it in a vice. This was another first—no woman had ever greeted his twin as a real person before. This was usually the part where they would shrink back in horror, making some hastily murmured embarrassed comment about having something pressing to go to.

He would never see them again.

No one had ever bent down to Jared's level and looked deeply into the eyes that were like his own and smiled at his brother with respect and compassion instead of pity.

'He can't understand a word you say,' he said. 'He's intellectually disabled. He's in a permanent vegetative state.'

Allegra straightened to meet Joel's eyes. 'That doesn't mean he doesn't deserve respect.'

'He shouldn't be alive.'

She stared at him, open-mouthed. 'How can you say that? He's your brother! Your twin brother!'

'He's ruined my parents' lives. My father wouldn't be in hospital right now if it wasn't for Jared. I know it's not his fault, but every day of their life and mine has been tainted with the pain and grief of looking after him twenty-four hours a day.'

She applied the brake on the wheelchair and, taking Joel's arm, led him a short distance from his brother. 'Life is precious, Joel. Your limbs were wrapped around Jared's in your mother's womb for nine months. How can you possibly wish he wasn't alive?'

'Don't misunderstand me, Allegra. I love my brother but it doesn't change the fact that it's no picnic being responsible for him. I've lived with it all my life, knowing that sooner or later the responsibility was going to be handed to me when it became too much for my parents.'

Allegra stared at the moisture glistening in his eyes, her heart aching for what he must have suffered as a child, seeing his brother, the image of him, locked in a body and mind that was surely one of the worst of all human tragedies—permanent and totally devastating disability.

She stepped forward and placed her hand on Joel's arm. 'Why don't you go and have a long walk or have a coffee somewhere while I take over with Jared? It seems like you could do with a break. You've had so much to deal with, you look exhausted.'

'You'll never be able to manage him. None of your fairy-dust theories are going to work, no matter how hard you try.'

'Please, Joel,' she insisted, trying not to be put off by his hardened tone, recognising how he must hate showing his vulnerability in such a raw way. 'Give me the keys to the house and I'll sit with your brother for a couple of hours.'

He handed her the keys, turned on his heel and walked away without a backward glance. She watched him for a moment or two before Jared began to rock back and forth in his chair in frustration.

'Sorry about that, Jared,' she said, bending down to release the brake before straightening to run her fingers through his thick dark hair that so reminded her of Joel's. 'Your brother needs a break.'

Jared rocked again, one of his hands flying upwards to hit her in a glancing blow on her cheek. She couldn't escape it in time and knew it would give her a spectacular bruise, but as she wheeled his chair back along the path, she reminded herself it was nothing compared to what Joel had done to her heart.

CHAPTER EIGHTEEN

ALLEGRA had seriously underestimated the level of care Joel's brother required. No sooner had she entered the house than he began to wail in distress, his arms flailing about until she had to make a conscious effort to duck out of their way. She considered lifting him out of his chair but while he had nothing of the muscled bulk of Joel, he was still at least twice her weight.

She made him a cool drink and after a few attempts, which involved a change of bib, she managed to get some into his mouth. His gulping swallows tore at her heart, his eyes rolling about as he tried to grasp at her with his twisted hands.

She hunted through the refrigerator for some semblance of a meal, and chatted to him all the while as she made an omelette with softly steamed vegetables, presuming his brain damage made it difficult for him to chew normal food.

She was right, for even though she had prepared a mushy meal, most of it ended up on his chest or on the floor. She reassured herself that his hunger must have been satisfied because he seemed to be content for a while, sitting in his chair, looking at her with vacant eyes.

'I'm in love with your brother,' she said into the silence. 'I think you should know that.'

'Meeting you has answered so many of my questions,' she went on. 'He is terrified of someone ending up with what you have to deal with. I can see that now. This isn't easy for you, is it, Jared? It's not easy for your parents and Joel. I have been so focused on my own goals I haven't considered the other side.' She let out a little sigh and continued, 'I have this little boy in ICTU. His scans show he's brain dead. I guess that's a term that your family is pretty familiar with, although clearly your brain still functions in some areas but not enough to give you the sort of life you deserve. Tommy is a little boy of seven. I guess I hadn't ever considered he could end up living the life you are now forced to live. But your parents love you, so does your brother, otherwise he wouldn't have given up so much to be here with you so your mum could visit your dad.'

Jared's head drooped to one side. Allegra sighed as she got wearily to her feet and turned his chair to look for his bedroom.

If feeding him had been one of her biggest challenges, preparing him for bed surpassed it in spades. He was totally incontinent, which meant she had to deal with the change of a soiled nappy while he protested, his contorted limbs flying about until she was close to tears.

Finally she did what had to be done and dragged him towards the mattress on the floor that was his bed. He fought her for a while but she turned him over onto his stomach and began to massage his tight legs, working her way up from his feet until she got to his lower back. His breathing became relaxed and he gradually drifted off to sleep.

She covered him with a light cotton sheet and sat back on her heels and began to cry, softly and brokenly, her heart breaking for what Joel and his parents had endured for so long.

Joel found her there a short time later, her face pink, her eyes red and swollen as she turned to face him.

He gestured for her to leave the room in case his brother woke up and she followed him with dogged steps, her shoulders at an all-time low.

He took her in his arms, burying his head in her fragrant hair as she sobbed against him.

'I'm so sorry…' she choked. 'I had no idea…'

'Most people don't.'

'I can understand why you're so against my project…'

He hugged her close. 'I wish it could work, Allegra. I would give anything for my brother to have even a fraction of the life I have. I feel guilty that it's him, not me. I've carried that all of my life.'

She eased herself away from him to look up at him. 'What happened?'

'Bacterial meningitis. I was born first. Jared's delivery was delayed. By the time he was born, meningitis had taken hold and fried his brain.' He gave her a rueful grimace. 'If he had been first, I would have been the person you would have spent the last couple of hours with, spoon-feeding.'

Allegra felt his pain as if it were her own. 'I would still have done it, and gladly.'

He smiled down at her, although it was tinged with sadness. 'You know something? I think you are the very first person I have ever felt I could have a relationship with. When you took Jared for the last couple of hours I suddenly realised how much I care for you. But I'm what is known as a package deal. My parents will not be able to cope with Jared's care for much longer. There are limited spaces in care homes for people with his level of disability. There are issues to face.'

'But if we face them together, the burden won't be so heavy. I love you, Joel. I think you know that. I would do anything to help you deal with Jared if it means I can be a part of your life.'

'But there is still an unresolved issue between us.'

Allegra knew what was coming and it was now nowhere near as clear-cut as it had been a few short hours ago. 'Kate Lowe regained consciousness earlier today,' she said. 'She remembers nothing of the accident but she is prepared to have Tommy in whatever state he is.'

'She sounds just like my mother. My parents were advised

to let Jared go but Mum wouldn't hear of it. They've both had to deal with that decision ever since.'

'So that's why you are so against coma recovery. You don't want to risk the same situation happening.'

'Can you blame me?'

She saw no point in defending her position. 'No, I can see how you've come to the decisions you have. I would have probably done the same. But I had a friend in medical school—I mentioned her to you previously. She had a break-up with a boyfriend and took an overdose. It was an impulsive knee-jerk reaction. On another day she would never have done it, I know it. She was on a ventilator for ten days and her parents were advised to withdraw life support. I had a feeling it had more to do with the organ donor waiting list at the time than Julie's needs.'

'If she was declared brain dead, there was no point stretching out the agony.'

'There's a part of me that realises that—the scientifically trained part of me. However, another part of me believes in second chances. Julie deserved a second chance, as does Tommy.'

'Even if he ends up like my brother?'

That was one question she was unable to answer. 'It's a risk. Some parents are prepared to take it, others not.'

'Well, I for one can tell you I wish my parents had never taken it, and if you asked them they would answer the same. Don't get me wrong—my parents love my brother, they always have. I am constantly amazed by their continued devotion, but the reality is he should never have been resuscitated. Some lives are just not worth living.'

'I know this is the worst possible time to ask you this, but will you, please, let me work with Tommy a little longer?'

'You can work with him if you are prepared to accept the responsibility of him turning out like Jared. Can you deal with that?'

'I'm hoping it won't come to that. Now that his mother has regained consciousness, I think there's a chance we can touch Tommy's subconscious in a way his father couldn't.'

'Even though Kate did her best to take her life and that of her son?'

'She didn't attempt suicide,' Allegra said. 'I'm absolutely certain of it. Even the police agree with me.'

'Has there been some new development in the investigation?'

'Yes. You know the drug test you ordered on the guy with the head injury? He had a cocktail of drugs in his system—exactly the same cocktail that was found in Kate's blood.'

Joel frowned as he took Allegra's words in. He had been mulling over the possible connections between the Lowe case and Terry Fowler, but so far hadn't come up with anything. But if the same cocktail of drugs had been in Fowler's blood as Kate's then there had to be someone who was connected in some way to both of them.

'Do you happen to know where Serena Fairbright lives?' he asked.

Allegra shook her head. 'No, but we can always get the police to find out.'

Joel unclipped his mobile from his belt and switched it on.

'No wonder you didn't return my calls,' she said, glancing at his phone as it booted up.

'I wanted to forget about the hospital for a while,' he explained. 'I had other pressing matters on my mind.'

Allegra listened as he called a friend in the police force, who gave him the information he was after within a few minutes. He hung up and met her gaze. 'Guess whose pool Terry Fowler services regularly?' he asked.

It was, after all, surprisingly easy to come up with the answer. 'Serena Fairbright's?'

He gave her a grim nod. 'The police are on their way to interview her now. She is, as we suspected, not Keith Lowe's sister but his mistress.'

'If only Tommy would wake up,' she said. 'Kate remembers nothing of that day, but if Tommy regained consciousness we might get all the puzzles pieces on the table.'

Joel met her eyes, his expression offering no promise. 'He might never wake up, Allegra. You need to prepare yourself and his parents for that possibility.'

'Kate will never agree to turn off his ventilator, no matter what her husband says.'

'Ultimately the court would have to make the final decision on that.'

'I hope it won't come to that.'

'It might,' he warned. 'This could go on for months.'

'I know, but I'm still hoping for a miracle.'

He shook his head at her but for once there was no trace of mockery in his expression. 'I think that's why I've fallen in love with you,' he said. 'That in itself is a miracle. I've never been in love with anyone before.'

She smiled up at him, her eyes shining with hope and joy. 'Neither have I,' she said, and lifted her mouth to kiss his.

CHAPTER NINETEEN

'ALLEGRA.' Kellie rushed towards her as soon as she arrived at the unit the next morning. 'You have to come and see this!'

'What?'

'It's amazing,' Kellie said. 'Tommy's score's gone up to the maximum.'

'Fifteen?' Allegra gasped.

Kellie nodded excitedly. 'The SES guy you called me about dropped in the teddy bear. He was a little the worse for wear but he seems to have done the job.'

'The teddy bear or the SES guy?' Allegra asked as she matched strides with her friend as they made their way to Tommy's cubicle.

Kellie gave her a sheepish look. 'The SES guy was totally gorgeous. We're meeting up this evening and, yes, he was a little worn, but the teddy bear came in a close second.'

Allegra smiled. 'Has Tommy woken up yet?'

'No, but I reckon if you bring in his mum, he won't take long to do so. Shall I get the orderlies onto it?'

'Yes, you do that. Has Keith been in?'

Kellie shook her head. 'He hasn't been in since Kate woke up. I still can't help feeling he has something to do with all this. The police were looking for him, too.'

Allegra entered Tommy's cubicle and was deeply moved by

the actions of the attending nurse who was rewinding the teddy bear as if she had done it many times before. She set it by Tommy's head and stepped back, only then noticing Allegra watching her.

She gave Allegra a little smile of embarrassment. 'I have a daughter the same age.'

'Don't apologise,' Allegra said. 'Kids are kids, no matter who they belong to.'

'He's a darling little thing,' Lucy Piermont said. 'So small, but fighting all the way.'

Allegra felt a rush of warmth towards the nurse and wanted to hug her for her show of support for the little boy that just about everyone had given up on. She had to control her urge to cry. Ever since she had spent the evening with Joel and his twin, she had been feeling incredibly emotional. She couldn't stop thinking about Joel and how he had suffered the guilt of being the healthy twin.

'Hi, Tommy,' she said, to force her thoughts away from such painful territory. 'I've arranged for your mum to come in. She's on her way.'

Tommy suddenly opened his eyes and began to fight against the ventilator. His eyes were wide with panic until he twisted his head and saw his teddy bear next to his head. His struggle lessened and his eyes lost their terrified glaze as the music of his infancy calmed him, as it had no doubt done countless times in the past. His eyelids fluttered closed, his chest rising and falling in time with the ventilator, but Allegra knew the major fight had been won.

She vainly tried to swallow back the rising lump of emotion in her throat but it was beyond controlling. She sat, her tears rolling down unheeded as Tommy's mother was wheeled in.

'Oh, my God!' Kate cried as she saw Allegra's face. 'Is he…dead?'

Allegra stumbled to her feet and wrapped her arms around Kate's frail shoulders. 'No,' she sobbed. 'He's alive. He's alive.'

'You mean he's not brain dead?'

'No.' Allegra lifted herself away, scrubbing at her face, still choking back sobs. 'No one who opens their eyes like that can possibly be declared brain dead. We did it, Kate. You did it. You brought your son back from the brink.'

'No.' Kate was openly crying now. 'You did it by not giving up. My son might have been lying on a cold slab in a morgue by now if it hadn't been for you. I owe you so much.'

'Neither of us did it,' Allegra said, looking at the teddy bear propped beside Tommy's head, still playing its song. 'That's the little guy we have to thank.'

A few hours later Tommy was able to breathe without the ventilator and he gradually filled in the memory blanks his mother hadn't been able to fill.

Serena had arrived at the chalet and introduced herself as a neighbour. His mother, out of politeness, had offered her a drink and he recalled Serena had asked for vodka and orange juice, which she helped his mother prepare. Tommy had sipped at a glass of orange juice Serena had poured for him, but he'd felt uncomfortable with her presence. He left the room for a short time, only to come back when he heard a vicious argument erupting between his mother and Serena. His mother had grasped at Tommy and hurriedly bundled him in the car, and she'd seemed very agitated. He could remember that a few minutes into the journey his mother had seemed unable to control the vehicle. Thankfully he couldn't recall the exact moment they had gone over the edge, but he was in no doubt that his mother had been frightened of the other woman and had wanted to put as much distance between them as possible.

The police interviewed Tommy and a short time later sought out Joel and Allegra to fill them in on the rest of what they had discovered in their investigation.

'Terry Fowler was the pool maintenance guy Mrs Fairbright used occasionally,' the detective in charge of the investigation informed them. 'She offered him a contract on Mrs Lowe's life after she herself was unable to successfully bring about Kate's death via the accident. She had slipped a cocktail of drugs into Kate's drink as well as a triple shot of vodka. Her intention was to get rid of the wife and child. She paid him to sabotage the ventilator that was keeping Mrs Lowe alive.'

'Was Keith Lowe involved in any of this?' Joel asked.

The detective shook his head. 'We've taken a statement from him and his alibi stands up. He appears totally devastated by the news of his mistress's actions. We've charged Mrs Fairbright with murder in the first degree for the death of Mr Fowler. She confessed she drugged him, using the same drugs she'd used in Kate and Tommy Lowe's drinks when she'd gone to the chalet. She also confessed to hitting him from behind with a crowbar and pushing him into the pool. She also faces further charges of attempted murder for her actions in regard to Kate and Tommy.'

'Why did she make an attempt on Mr Fowler's life in her own back yard?' Allegra asked. 'Surely she knew it would point the finger of blame at her.'

'When news got out Kate Lowe was beginning to regain consciousness, Mrs Fairbright panicked. Terry Fowler began to put the pressure on her for more money to keep quiet, and she became desperate.'

'It all seems so unbelievable…' Allegra said, rubbing her arms as if warding off a chill.

Joel stepped closer and, placing an arm around her shoulders, pulled her into his warmth. 'Thank you, Detective Lacey, for filling us in.'

'No problem,' he said with a smile. He shifted his gaze to Allegra and added, 'You did an amazing job with the little boy. It was a stroke of genius, getting his teddy bear to him. Who knows what would have happened if he hadn't woken up?'

Allegra was too choked up to answer but Joel spoke for her, his words making her heart swell until it felt as if it was taking up all the space in her chest. 'She's a wonderful doctor who cares very deeply for patients, no matter what potential they are left with. I have learned a lot by working alongside her and this hospital will go down in the history books as one of the most innovative in the country, not because of me, as I had hoped and planned, but because of a young woman who believes in miracles.'

The detective smiled. 'Someone has to believe in miracles,' he said. 'How else would doctors or cops survive the stress and strain of what we have to face every day?' He shook both their hands and, wishing them well, left a short time later.

Joel turned Allegra in his arms, his eyes warm and melting as he looked down at her. 'You know, I'm really getting into this miracle thing myself.'

She smiled up at him. 'What do you mean?'

'My mother has never quite given up hope that I would one day find someone so perfect for me that it would make me rethink my decision to stay single and unattached all my life. She's been praying for a miracle and now she's finally got it.'

Allegra felt as if her chest was going to burst as she waited for him to continue. His smile lit his eyes and his body, where it was pressed against hers, told her more than words ever could, but she needed to hear them all the same.

'Allegra Tallis,' he said in a gruff, unashamedly emotional voice, 'will you do me the honour of being my wife? I love you and want nothing more than to spend the rest of my life with you. I want you to have my children, two at least, and maybe we could have a dog, one of those with big muddy paws. What do you say?'

She smiled up at him, her green eyes dancing and shining with joy. 'I'm surprised you even felt the need to ask me that. I would have thought my aura had well and truly given me away.'

He grinned as he brought his mouth down close to hers. 'No,' he said. 'It was this.' And his lips covered hers in a kiss that sealed their love for ever.

A DOCTOR WORTH WAITING FOR

BY

MARGARET McDONAGH

Dear Reader,

From my first childhood visit I fell in love with Scotland and her people, and the rural south-west is especially beautiful. I am also intrigued by the dynamics of small communities, and the special people who provide dedicated health care in these areas, developing a broad interest in their patients and wider families. So I was determined to write books within this setting.

A Doctor Worth Waiting For tells the story of Dr Conor Anderson, irreverent, caring and drop-dead gorgeous, and Dr Kate Fisher, a woman guarding secrets and inner pain.

Coming to work in sleepy Glentown-on-Firth, Kate has not counted on meeting someone like Conor. Can the breath-taking landscape, close-knit community and Conor's care combine to help Kate face her past? Conor and Kate are very special to me, and I hope you will enjoy their book. Look out for mentions of Kyle Sinclair and Alexandra Patterson—I hope to tell their story very soon!

Happy reading,

Margaret McDonagh

Margaret McDonagh says of herself: "I began losing myself in the magical world of books from a very young age, and I always knew that I had to write, pursuing the dream for over twenty years, often with cussed stubbornness in the face of rejection letters! Despite having numerous romance novellas, short stories and serials published, the news that my first 'proper book' had been accepted by Mills & Boon for their Medical Romance™ line brought indescribable joy! Having a passion for learning makes researching an involving pleasure, and I love developing new characters, getting to know them, setting them challenges to overcome. The hardest part is saying goodbye to them, because they become so real to me. And I always fall in love with my heroes! Writing and reading books, keeping in touch with friends, watching sport and meeting the demands of my four-legged companions keeps me well occupied. I hope you enjoy reading this book as much as I loved writing it."

You can contact Margaret at http://margaretmcdonagh.bravehost.com

With thanks to Gwen Baxter, Michael Quigley,
Lucy Hadley of the Forestry Commission,
Scottish Ambulance Service and
Galloway Mountain Rescue for
generous research advice.
And to Gill, Gwen, Wolfie, The Grumpies
and my Guardian Angels, without whom
I would cease to function.

CHAPTER ONE

'HAVE you heard the news? Did Fred reach you?'

'I have and he did.' Dr Conor Anderson smiled at Aileen Nichol, their first-rate practice manager, whose question greeted him as he arrived at the surgery on Tuesday morning. 'I was out hillwalking with Kyle Sinclair,' he continued, referring to his best friend, a fellow GP who worked out of the Rigtownbrae practice some miles away. Arriving home late, he had found a message from his partner, Fred Murdoch. 'I gather our new locum has arrived early.'

Aileen nodded with customary vigour, her dark red curls bobbing. 'Yesterday.'

Kate Fisher had been recommended by Fred's old friend, Professor James Fielding-Smythe, a renowned London-based surgeon. Rather than the traditional interview, her CV had been faxed through and Fred had spoken with her and James at length by telephone. There was no doubt Kate's qualifications and references were impressive but Conor was intrigued by the gaps. He had not noticed them at first, they were well hidden—intentionally or not he had yet to discover—but there were unexplained breaks between recent employment dates. Why? And why did Kate, highly qualified and used to a busy London practice, want to locum in rural south-west Scotland? She would have her pick of jobs.

Fred was anxious to give Kate a chance and, despite his reservations, Conor had backed his older partner's judgement. The niggling feeling remained that Fred knew more than he'd let on, which increased Conor's curiosity. But he trusted Fred. And Fred trusted James, whose endorsement of Kate was glowing. Why one of Europe's top orthopaedic specialists should involve himself in the career moves of a young GP was another puzzle Conor had yet to solve.

'What's Kate like?' he asked, propping his medical bag on top of the reception counter.

'She's a lovely lassie, but…' The expression in Aileen's grey eyes turned thoughtful as she paused and his attention sharpened. 'I don't know how to explain it, Conor. She's guarded. I sensed…something.' She shrugged and frowned at him. 'Fred's protective of her.'

That had been his impression, too. Fred had been cagey on the phone, giving scant information about the new doctor. 'Do you know why, Aileen?'

'No. He took her to lunch before house calls. I introduced her to the others, then took her upstairs to the flat. Kate seemed nervous at the interest in her, uneasy answering questions about herself.'

'It's daunting meeting a group of strangers, especially a nosy lot like you!' Conor teased, although Kate's reaction was interesting.

Aileen swatted his arm in affectionate reprimand. 'Get away with you.'

'Any reason why Kate arrived earlier than arranged?'

'She knew her predecessor left last week and suspected we'd be pleased for her to start,' the older woman explained.

'That sounds reasonable. We can certainly use the help. Let's hope she continues to be as conscientious.'

'I can't imagine Kate being unreliable,' Aileen commented, setting out his tray of patient notes for morning surgery.

Conor hoped not. Would the city girl find herself a fish out of water in sleepy but beautiful Glentown-on-Firth? The secrecy surrounding Kate, the gaps in her CV and Aileen's impressions sparked his curiosity.

'With Fred at the care trust meeting, we decided Kate should sit in on my consultations and house calls,' he informed Aileen, picking up his medical bag and wedging the tray of notes under his arm.

'I doubt you'll find that a hardship.' Aileen smiled, her eyes mischievous.

'Yeah?' Conor raised a speculative eyebrow. 'If Kate's as good a doctor as we've been led to believe, I'll be happy. Will you let me know when she comes in, please?'

'She's here.'

Aileen's pronouncement had him turning back in surprise. 'She is? Where?'

'She's waiting for you in the private sitting room. I thought it would be quieter for you to introduce yourselves there than in the bustle of the staffroom.'

'Thanks, Aileen.' Grateful for her thoughtfulness, his smile was warm. 'I'll go and collect her. Give us a few moments to get acquainted before sending anyone through.'

'Of course. Buzz when you're ready. I'll update Jenny,' she added, as the young receptionist arrived for work. As he went to move away, Aileen rested her hand on his arm. 'Conor, be careful with Kate.'

As he headed through the rambling old building to his consulting room, Aileen's words preyed on his mind. What was it about Kate that inspired concern in people? The professor, Fred…now Aileen. Soon he could form his own opinion. A ripple of anticipation shivered down his spine, catching him unawares. Leaving his things in his room, he headed along the corridor, pausing at the staffroom to say good morning before continuing to the cosy sitting room they used for various situations from breaking bad news to distressed patients to providing a quiet space should a member of staff need privacy.

He paused at the doorway, his appreciative gaze locked on the sole occupant of the room. The woman was stunning. He had been intrigued to meet Kate Fisher but had never imagined that his first sight of her would send his senses whirling and set his heart thudding. Tense, she stood by the window, her arms folded across her chest, even white teeth worrying the sensual curve of her lower lip. His breath caught. Glossy brown hair, the colour of polished walnut, fell to her shoulders in a satiny curtain. Her face was captivating, her smooth complexion olive-toned, the bare minimum of make-up enhancing her natural beauty. She had perfect cheekbones, slightly slanting eyes, straight nose and that sensual, irresistible mouth with luscious, dusky-rose lips he found himself longing to taste.

She looked younger than her thirty-two years. Above average height, she was dressed in a charcoal-grey trouser suit that hinted at the deliciously curvy figure beneath. Red-hot desire slammed inside him. He shook his head to clear the fog that hazed his brain, shocked by his instinctive response to this woman.

Walking towards her, he saw a pallor underlying her skin, making him wonder if she had been ill, and then he met her gaze and all other thoughts faded. She had the saddest eyes he had ever seen. Dark brown, fringed with long lashes, they were soulful, full of hurt and loss. There was pain here, some terrible inner torment she was struggling to conceal or avoid, and in that moment he determined he was going to discover what was troubling her and do something about it. The urge to hold her, comfort her, protect her was as overwhelming as the fresh wave of desire that coursed through him, more intense than anything he had ever experienced.

Kate stared in shock at the man who entered the room, taken aback by his striking good looks, the dark blond hair, short at the back and sides but thick and wayward on top, falling in unruly fashion across his forehead. In his mid-thirties, around six feet tall, his athletic frame was dressed in the kind of leg-hugging jeans that ought to be illegal and a long-sleeved white T-shirt that suggested at the leanly muscled definition of his chest, arms and shoulders. Smooth-shaven, his jaw was masculine without being heavy, his cheeks lean, his nose in perfect proportion to his other features, and his mouth, curved now in a small but sinful smile, was temptingly kissable. He was the most gorgeous, intensely sexy man she had ever seen. Startled, her gaze clashed with his, the warmth and obvious interest in his riveting green eyes enough to suck every scrap of air from her lungs.

'Hello, Kate.' The husky, gently accented voice was impossibly intimate, wrapping around her, ensnaring her. She battled the instinctive urge to back away as he breached the gap between them, his body close enough that she could scent his earthy male aroma. 'I'm Conor Anderson.'

'You are?'

Unable to mask her surprise, cursing her inane reply, Kate could do nothing but stare, swallowing against the lump lodging in her throat as she assessed his casual clothes, his heart-stopping appeal. He didn't look like any doctor she had ever seen. Oh, hell! Coming here was meant to be safe. But there was nothing safe about this man, or the way her blood was singing in her veins as an unwanted curl of desire knotted her insides. No! She didn't want this. She had come here to sort out her professional life, not complicate things further. She didn't need the warning bells clanging in her brain to know that Conor Anderson was someone to steer clear of. The comments of the staff the previous afternoon had alerted her...Conor was a womaniser and a serial heart-breaker.

Conor has quite a reputation across the county.

You won't have worked with anyone like our Conor before!

You're going to love him, Kate. Everyone loves Conor. Especially the women!

And he loves them—providing they don't expect too much or try to hold him.

The trail of disappointed women left in his wake will testify he's a perpetual bachelor.

It doesn't stop them making a play for him, though. Men like Conor don't come along very often. He's enough to make many a woman think it worth the risk of breaking her heart.

The laughing remarks flashed through her mind and she recalled the brief asides Fred Murdoch had made during their telephone conversations before she had accepted the locum position. Fred had joked about Conor not yet settling down and always finding himself the centre of attention. Female attention. She should have given more credence to her uneasiness at those words at the time but she had been too nervous about the job to pay proper attention to her early-warning system. Ignoring that flicker of unease had been a mistake. Now, as she assessed Conor, she was paying the price for her lapse. He looked more like someone from a bad girl's erotic dream than a professional doctor, she decided with unease and disapproval. Focusing back on his face, she discovered him studying her, amusement shining in those green eyes.

'Welcome to Glentown-on-Firth.'

'Thank you.'

He held out his hand but the last thing she wanted was to touch him, scared what might happen if she did. Had James Fielding-Smythe had done this on purpose? He had been evasive about Conor Anderson when persuading her to take this post, focusing on the older, unthreatening Fred Murdoch and sidestepping her queries about the younger partner. But the prof would know how this full-of-himself doctor with a womanising reputation would affect her and she had made another miscalculation by allowing James to distract her attention. Conor made her think of Darren, pain and humiliation. Things that were two years in the past, pushed to the back of her mind by the far worse events that had happened since then to challenge her. But she remembered. And it was not a place she planned to revisit, no matter how outwardly appealing the man and how strong the temptation.

The unwanted frisson of awareness that rippled through her when she forced herself to complete the handshake, as politeness dictated, was worse than she'd anticipated. His fingers curled around hers, firm and warm, holding her longer than convention demanded, his touch sending a lightning bolt of sensation shooting up her arm and searing along her nerve endings with the force of a million watts. She knew Conor felt it too because his eyes darkened and his lips parted, mirroring her own involuntary response. Alarmed, she snatched her hand free, unable to meet that intense green gaze, stepping back, desperate to put space between them. But the distance did nothing to lessen his impact. She could feel his touch, scent his earthy fragrance, an inappropriate flare of arousal burning inside her. The knowledge that she would have to spend time with him while she learned her way around the area filled her with dismay. She needed to keep as far from him as possible. Conor Anderson was dangerous.

'We're pleased you chose to join us, Kate.' The warm intimacy of his voice sent a fresh shiver down her spine. 'What made you decide to come to Scotland?'

'The job was highly recommended,' she explained, tensing as she worried what other questions he might have.

'Your qualifications are impressive—we're lucky to have you.'

She didn't know about that. At the professor's instigation, she had reworked her CV, hoping neither GP partner would notice that the information was not one hundred per cent comprehensive. She had tried to disguise any gaps but had deliberately omitted mention of her additional surgical skills and the advanced trauma life support course. Neither had she mentioned the work she had done this past year. The last thing she wanted was to explain where she had been and why she had given it up. It was in the past and she planned it would stay that way. There was no need for anyone to know. It had no bearing on the present—except in her own head, feeding her doubts and bringing her nightmares.

'There won't be much call for your expertise in tropical medicine here.' Kate smothered a groan at Conor's remark, realising she had concentrated on searching for surgical references and had forgotten to remove the tropical diseases and hygiene diploma. 'An interesting line of study.'

'The opportunity was there and it was another string to my bow.'

Kate's heart sank. Conor had obviously considered her CV with more care than Fred had. Hoping Conor would be satisfied, having no wish to impart further information, she flicked him a glance, her tension increasing as he watched her with silent interest.

'I expect the situation in London is very different,' he said after a long pause, his smile implying he knew there was more behind her answer but deciding, much to her relief, to let her off the hook. For now.

'I've seen several malaria cases in practice there, plus a couple of more unusual diseases.'

Leaning against the sofa, Conor regarded her, his green eyes steady. 'I know you talked with Fred yesterday and I believe he explained our routines and back-up staff. Aside from general surgeries and home visits, I'm responsible for the diabetic clinic and the diet and fitness group, while Fred holds the ante—and postnatal clinics. The mother and baby group is covered by us both. We share other things like the stopping-smoking, well-woman, male-health clinics and so on. And minor surgery.' His gaze turned speculative. 'I understand the latter doesn't interest you.'

'No.' Kate fought the sickness in her stomach. The prof

might think she was capable but she had lost her nerve for surgery. What scared her was whether she had lost her nerve to be any kind of doctor. 'I don't do surgery.'

Her response had been stiff and she could feel Conor looking at her, knew he had questions. She held her breath, releasing it when he finally moved on. 'We only handle minor procedures—Fred and I will cover those. Dorothy Scott, our nurse practitioner, deals with any small injuries, so you won't be faced with anything but the odd bit of stitching in an emergency. Would that be all right?'

'Yes, of course.'

'Ease yourself in at your own pace, Kate, and always ask if there is anything you want to know.' That unsettling gaze focused on her again. 'We want your stay to be a happy one.'

All she wanted was to keep her head down but she nodded all the same. 'I understand there won't be out-of-hours work?'

'No.' Conor shifted, folding his arms across his chest, a frown on his face. 'We signed on for cover when the new system came in. Fred was finding the long hours increasingly tiring. I— Well, never mind. We rotate Saturday morning surgery between us, so you'll only do one in three. Saturday is for emergency drop-ins, rather than appointments. You won't be asked to work evenings or Sundays.'

Not that she would mind. She preferred maintaining involvement with patients but the current working arrangements were widely adopted and she could understand an older man like Fred choosing to slow down. What had Conor been going to say about himself before he'd thought better of it? No doubt he valued the extra time to devote to his hectic social life.

'Have you settled in upstairs?'

She swallowed as Conor squeezed his hands into the pockets of his jeans, tightening the fabric across his hips, drawing her attention back to his body. 'The flat is very comfortable, thank you.'

'I hope you won't find Glentown too quiet after the city life you are used to.'

The doubt in his voice made her wonder if Conor had less confidence in her position here than Fred did. 'I'm sure I won't.'

Far from it, if only he knew. The quiet life, rural location and the solitude of walking in the hills were major draws of this job. Peace and space were what she needed to regroup, restore her shattered spirit and think about the rest of her life.

'Let us know if there is anything you need or anything we can do to for you while you are here.'

'I will.' He meant the flat, the job, she reminded herself, trying not to react to the husky suggestiveness of his voice. 'Everything is fine.'

Everything except Conor himself—and the fact that she was scared witless about her adequacy as a doctor. Why had she let her father and the professor talk her into taking this post? It was easy for them to tell her it was time to move on but she felt she had failed, was unsure she had anything left to give.

A fresh wave of panic welled inside her and she curled her hands into fists, battling the overwhelming urge to run—to run from facing a challenge that felt too big, too soon, too scary. Helplessly, she looked at Conor. His clear eyes watched her and she could see curiosity mix with a warm compassion that caused an uncharacteristic threat of tears. Blinking them away, she started as he reached out and took her hand, his fingers giving hers a reassuring squeeze.

'First days are always difficult.'

Kate shrugged, not trusting herself to speak, frightened she would do the unthinkable and blurt everything out, confide in him, explain this wasn't first-day nerves. What was it about this man that got inside her skin? But she couldn't forget his reputation, how very wrong he would be for her, or why she was here and what she had to do to get her life back on track and mend her battered soul.

* * *

Conor wasn't sure what had happened but he was positive Kate had been on the verge of confiding something before there had been an emotional withdrawal and a shoring up of her defences. He sensed that whatever had caused that sudden welling of panic and anxiety was about more than new job unease. Now barriers were being placed between them, Kate's inner disquiet and wariness obvious. Something much deeper was going on here but it would take time and patience to gain her trust and break through her reserve—if he wanted to take things further. Which he did. More than anything. His innate concern for anyone or anything in pain meant he couldn't leave her hurting, but getting past her defences and persuading her there was something special here worth exploring wouldn't be easy.

Aware of her tension, he brushed the pad of his thumb across the back of her hand before he let her go and forced himself to give her space. He missed the contact, missed being close enough that the citrusy fragrance of her toyed with his senses, but he needed to keep things businesslike…for now.

'We have a busy morning and plenty of patients waiting. Do you feel ready to make a start?'

'OK.' Her eyes closed for a moment and when she opened them again he was struck by the thread of fear in the dark brown depths.

Concerned for her, he tried to ease the tension with humour. 'Don't worry, Kate, I don't bite. Not like that, anyway!'

His teasing comment backfired. All he could think about were the many parts of Kate he desperately yearned to taste and to nibble, the fire of desire reigniting inside him. Hell! He saw the flush tinge her cheeks before his gaze captured hers. The disapproval in her eyes amused and troubled him. He had diverted her from her fear but only at the expense of making her think he was some kind of lech, which was not what he had intended at all. Sighing, he led the way back to his consulting room, unable to get the sight, sound and scent of Kate Fisher out of his mind.

Instead of finding answers, meeting this woman had raised more questions. Everything about Kate intrigued him…and made him more certain than ever that she was hiding something, that there were secrets waiting to be unravelled.

CHAPTER TWO

KATE tried to wrench her gaze from the distraction of Conor's sublime rear view as she followed him along the wide, airy corridor. She had been unsettled by his throw-away comment. She was sure he hadn't meant anything sexual by it but all she could think about was what his mouth might taste like, how his lips and teeth would feel caressing her skin. This was appalling. It had to stop. Now. She was here to get her career back on track, to see if she could be a doctor after the traumatic events of the last months. It may have been too long since she had been held and loved, but now was not the time to start yearning for male companionship. And Conor was *not* the right man to turn to, not with his apparent legion of ladies and aversion to commitment. He confused her. She had been forewarned of his heartbreaker reputation, she disapproved of his womanising, the unprofessional, casual way he dressed and approached being a doctor, and yet he had displayed a sensitivity to her feelings she would never have expected. She took a seat in Conor's consulting room and tried to focus on the job ahead, nerves clenching in her stomach and making her feel sick, her doubts returning with a vengeance.

'All right?' Conor asked, taking the first packet of notes from the full tray on his desk.

Taking a deep breath, aware he again seemed attuned to

her mood, Kate nodded. ‘Fine,’ she lied, feeling the intensity of his regard before he reached for the phone.

‘Hi, Jenny,’ he said and Kate visualised the young receptionist with the long blonde hair who had been Conor’s chief fan the previous afternoon. ‘We’re ready for Andrea now. Thanks, sweetie.’

‘Andrea?’ Kate queried as they waited, trying to ignore his throw-away endearments and the intimate familiarity in his voice when he spoke to women.

‘Mmm.’ He took the notes out of their folder. ‘One of my ladies.’

‘I see,’ she murmured stiffly, unable to prevent her feelings showing in her tone.

‘Do you?’

Kate’s expression closed, her mouth tightening in disapproval. She had heard he was unorthodox but surely he wasn’t so unprofessional that he had any kind of relationship with a patient? Glancing up, she saw the knowing expression in his green eyes, her breath catching when he flashed her a naughty grin before he stood up and walked towards the door.

‘The very lady I’ve been longing to see.’ Kate watched him smile at whoever was approaching along the corridor, his tone affectionate. ‘Now I know why I make sure you’re my first appointment in the morning. Gets my day off to a good start to see a beautiful woman. Come on in, Andrea.’

Steeling herself to be polite to some flirty bimbo, Kate struggled to prevent her mouth dropping open as Conor guided an older lady inside. She was clearly in pain, two walking sticks held with difficulty in her weakened hands. There was a quiet dignity in her thin face and pale blue eyes as Conor helped her across the room to a chair.

‘Seems you’ve already found yourself a beautiful woman,’ Andrea commented with a friendly smile, shifting around to find a more comfy position. ‘Trust you, Conor!’

Kate was subjected to the full force of Conor’s sultry green eyes. 'You're both beautiful. I'm a lucky man this morning. Andrea, say hello to our new doctor, Kate Fisher. Kate, Andrea Milne,' he introduced them, rounding his desk to sit down.

'I'm pleased to meet you,' Kate managed, trying to ignore the wild beat of her pulse after Conor's intense look, the exchange with Andrea adding fuel to the rumours about his reputation.

'You, too, dear. Good to see a fresh face…and such a pretty one.'

Kate noticed Conor smile before he glanced at Andrea's notes then returned his full attention to his patient. 'How is my favourite lady today?'

'Better for seeing you.' Andrea chuckled, colour washing her pale cheeks. 'I wish I was thirty again, not sixty!'

Conor winked at her, his smile teasing. 'Me, too.'

Kate waited while Conor chatted about Andrea's symptoms, watching as he knelt on the floor to conduct a gentle examination of the lady's troublesome hands and feet. There were signs of subluxation of the wrist, along with muscle wastage and the beginnings of deformity in the hands. She feared Andrea might go on to develop the classic swan-neck shape to the fingers typical of rheumatoid arthritis.

'Any more trouble with your knee?' Conor's question was casual but Kate could see the care with which he checked the joint and listened to the reply.

'Some twinges, but nothing like before,' Andrea explained.

'And your wrists?'

'The splints you recommended have been a real help.'

Conor sat back on his heels, pushing a wayward fall of hair back from his forehead as he smiled. 'Good. We'll keep a close eye on the knee. If it flares up again we can consider an injection of steroids into the joint to help the problem. How's your other pain, Andrea? Any problems?'

'I'm coping, dear,' she allowed with a brave smile.

'We want to do our best for you.' Kate's breath caught as Conor turned to her. 'We caught Andrea's condition early when she began having problems. The deterioration has been gradual, with a few more acute relapses from time to time. We referred her to the rheumatologist and started disease-modifying drugs,' he explained, and Kate nodded, knowing the DMARDs worked slowly over months to gain their effect, hopefully slowing the progression of the disease and aiding stiffness and inflammation. 'Andrea has been settled on methotrexate for a while now, which was combined with a low-dose steroid. We do regular checks on her blood pressure and symptom progression, plus the usual bloods, biochemistry and so on every three months.' He paused again to smile at Andrea, resting a hand on her forearm. 'You've not had any side-effects or new symptoms?'

'No, dear. Just the usual stiffness and discomfort.'

Conor frowned with concern. 'Andrea's had reduced appetite, tiredness and a loss of grip and mobility, but we try to balance a programme of medication to help manage her pain and use a team approach with the nurses and our visiting physiotherapist involved in keeping her as mobile as possible.'

'And wonderful you all are,' Andrea praised, her gratitude evident, along with her fondness for Conor.

Kate felt chastened at the way she had judged Conor's aptitude as a doctor. She had expected a self-interested romeo, if not playing at being a doctor then certainly not taking the job seriously. She had never imagined he would care this much. True, he dripped sex appeal from every pore, but behind the casual clothes, irreverent humour and wicked smile was a watchful, concerned doctor who worked to put people at their ease, valuing the whole person. And he took his time. If all his consultations were like this, they were in for a long day, but she didn't mind because patient care was her top priority, too. She had been wrong about his professional skills, but although she could learn a lot from this man she knew it was a bad idea to spend more time than necessary in his company.

After Conor has escorted Andrea along to Dorothy, the nurse practitioner, who would take care of the blood tests, he returned to the room and called for their next patient, a middle-aged man with breathing problems. Kate soon discovered Conor was as caring and irreverent with his male patients as his female ones.

'We've had the X-rays back, Jim. I'm glad to say that there are no signs of growths or tumours.'

The man's relief was palpable. 'Thank goodness for that' He tried to laugh but stopped short, wheezing uncomfortably.

'You do have a nasty infection and some fluid on the lungs,' Conor continued, listening to Jim's chest and taking his blood pressure. 'I'm going to prescribe some new medication and I want you to come back and see me next week—call me sooner if you don't notice any improvement or you are worried, OK?'

'Sure, Doc. Thanks.'

Conor tapped some instructions on his keyboard then signed the prescription form that emerged from the printer, handing it over with a rueful smile. 'I suppose you haven't stopped smoking, Jim?'

'Well…' The man looked sheepish. 'I am trying, Doc but it's not easy to give up. I've smoked since I was fourteen. I know it's naughty but I enjoy it.'

'Many naughty activities are pleasurable,' Conor murmured as he rose to his feet, and Kate willed herself not to blush when he glanced at her with a cheeky smile, leaving her in no doubt what he was thinking. 'In your case, though, Jim, smoking is damaging your health. I know it's difficult, but do the best you can. If there's anything I can do, referring you or trying patches, come and talk to me.'

'I will, Doc. Thank you. Good to meet you, lass,' Jim added, as Conor showed him from the room.

Kate kept her eyes averted when Conor returned to his desk. She was struggling with his wicked aside, her mind disobeying her as she imagined in vivid detail far too many sinfully pleasurable and very naughty things she was sure Conor would be all too expert at doing.

Heat flared inside her but she fought to ignore the unwanted desire. No way was she going there. Especially with him. She had too many issues to face while she was here without allowing herself to become one of the bevy of women Conor was rumoured to juggle in his life and adding another notch to his legendary bedpost.

Her head knew all that...she just hoped the rest of her body would behave.

'How about taking the next consultation yourself?' Conor suggested, watching the play of emotions across Kate's face.

She had been annoyed with him earlier and he had known straight away that she had misinterpreted his comments about Andrea. It troubled him that Kate could imagine he behaved improperly with patients. Was it just him or had something happened that made her view male doctors with disdain and distrust? He hadn't been able to resist teasing her. Keeping her off balance, combined with her genuine interest in the consultations, had banished her alarm, but now that he had suggested she take the next patient, the anxiety and flash of fear were back in those far-too-serious brown eyes.

'Sure.'

She wouldn't look at him and he sensed the veneer of outward assurance was wafer-thin. Kate had a crisis of confidence. He had no idea why. Not yet. But he'd find out. 'Our next patient is Julie MacIntyre. She's 23 and a first-time mother. Her son Dominic is three months old.'

'Any idea why she's coming in today?'

'No.' He swallowed as Kate flicked strands of satiny hair behind her shoulder, exposing the curve of her neck. His heart started thudding again and he cursed under his breath. He had to stop looking at her and concentrate on the job. Thankful when Julie arrived, he rose to his feet, sweeping Dominic out of the young woman's arms to hug him, something else that surprised Kate, he noticed. 'Goodness, haven't you grown, young man?'

'He gets heavier by the day.' Julie laughed.

'Julie, meet our new doctor, Kate Fisher,' Conor said, balancing chubby little Dominic against his chest, immediately understanding why Julie had brought her son to see them. 'If it's all right with you, Kate will take your consultation today.'

'That's fine.' The young woman smiled. 'Hello, Dr Fisher.'

'Kate, please.'

Relieved at the friendly opening, Conor realised he had yet to see Kate smile. As he relinquished Dominic back to Julie and returned to his chair, he watched Kate nervously begin the consultation, determined that his goal for the first week was to make her smile. Somehow. Even once.

'What can we do for you today, Julie?' Kate asked.

'I'm really worried about Dominic's eye,' the young woman explained, her anxiety obvious. 'I thought I should bring him right away.'

'You did the best thing. That's what we're here for,' Kate reassured her, as she moved round the desk, asking Julie more questions while she focused on the baby. 'Has Dominic ever had this problem before?'

'No, there's been no trouble with his eyes at all,' Julie confirmed.

'I'll take a swab to be on the safe side,' Kate explained, following Connor's directions to fetch what she needed, 'but I'm pretty sure it's a blocked tear duct. It's what we call sticky eye and it's not uncommon. Usually the passage hollows out around the time the baby is born but sometimes this can be delayed and become blocked. It's a problem that normally rights itself by the time the baby is a year or so old.

Dominic's eye doesn't look infected, so I won't be prescribing antibiotic drops just yet.'

Impressed, Conor sat back and let her get on with the job, enjoying watching the graceful way she moved, her ease with the baby, her gentleness and the thoughtful way she explained things to Julie. Whatever panic Kate had experienced before the consultation had begun had vanished once she had got into her stride, though he was still interested to know its cause.

'What will happen?' Julie asked, jigging the happy baby on her knee once Kate had finished taking the swab with gentle care.

'The best thing is for you to bathe his eye with boiled water to remove any debris. Make sure your hands are clean and keep the water comfortably warm. You can do it several times a day, perhaps when you have Dominic down to change his nappy.'

Julie let out a sigh of relief. 'Is that all?'

'It should clear up on its own,' Kate reassured her, almost managing a smile, Conor noted. 'Come back any time if you are worried. We'll see Dominic again in a few days to check how things are, and I'll let you know when we have the results of the swab—but I'm pretty sure it is a blocked duct.'

'Thank you so much.'

'No problem.'

When Kate moved to see them out, Julie hesitated, grinning as she held Dominic out to Connor for a final cuddle, and Conor smiled, brushing a finger down one warm, pudgy cheek. 'Take care, young man. You, too, Julie.'

'We will. Bye, Conor. Thanks again.'

As Kate returned to the desk, he waited for her to complete the necessary paperwork for the swab and make up the notes. 'Nicely done, Kate.'

She murmured an acknowledgement, appearing embarrassed by his praise, still not meeting his gaze. He was impatient to find out more about her but there was no time to waste as their next patient arrived.

Conor made sure Kate took various cases for the rest of morning surgery, satisfied as time went by that they had an exceptionally good doctor in their midst. Whether she believed in herself was another matter. When their list was over, they snatched a few moments for a hasty drink before house calls and he discovered Kate shared his taste for hot chocolate. Other staff were on a break and he noted Kate's wariness if anyone asked a direct question about her life or her work.

She was tense when they left the surgery but by the time they had completed most of the visits on the list and were in the car heading back towards Glentown-on-Firth for their final call, Conor was even more impressed with her work. She established a rapport with patients, and he was delighted with her kindness, her ability to listen and the way she treated everyone with genuine respect and patience. Although she still hadn't smiled. Nothing more than a tilt of her lips that failed to strip the deep inner sadness from her eyes.

'This is a beautiful area.'

Startled that she had initiated a conversation, he flicked her a glance before returning his attention to the narrow country road.

'It's wonderful. So are the people. I came here nine years ago and can't imagine ever living anywhere else,' he told her, keen to keep her talking, hoping to change the poor opinion she had formed of him. 'It's a diverse region with many varied environments.'

'You don't come from around here?'

His childhood had not been stable or happy but that wasn't something he wanted to talk about. 'No. I trained in Aberdeen—that's where I met Kyle Sinclair, one of the GPs at the practice in Rigtownbrae. We both wanted to work in a rural area and were lucky to settle near each other. I love the hills, the outdoors. I have the best of both worlds in Glentown, the natural environment plus the satisfaction of community medicine, getting to know the patients and their families, being involved in their lives.'

'It must be rewarding,' she allowed, a wistful note in her voice.

'To me it is.' He glanced at her again, wishing he could get inside her head, know what she was thinking and feeling. 'Maybe you'll find it so, too.'

A sigh whispered from her lips. 'Maybe I will.'

'I know from your CV that you trained in London,' he probed, recalling the recent employment gaps that puzzled him. 'Has it always been the City for you?'

'Yes.'

The reply was clipped, her voice stiff, and he knew she was lying. As he slowed the car at a crossroads, he looked at her but she turned her head away. Her hands betrayed her, though. They were clasped in her lap, her knuckles white with tension. Driving on, he was convinced Kate's doubt and anxiety were deep-seated. This woman had secrets. Painful ones. His heart ached in response and he reached out a hand to cover hers, only to have her pull away from the contact, denying the comfort and understanding he yearned to offer.

'Kate, I—'

His was interrupted by the intrusion of his mobile phone and he cursed in frustration. As he searched for somewhere to pull off the narrow lane, Kate unwound her fingers and reached to take the phone from its rest.

'Shall I do it?'

'Thanks.'

'It's Jenny,' she told him after a moment, frowning as she listened. 'Yes, I'll tell him. Just a minute.'

'What is it?'

'Joyce Bingham has phoned to say that Lizzie Dalglish has fallen down the stairs. She's distressed and asking for you.'

New concern tightened in his chest. 'Tell Jenny we'll go

straight there, please, Kate, and ask her to ring Douglas, our next appointment, and tell him we'll be late.'

'OK.'

'And let Joyce know we'll be there soon.'

As Kate relayed the messages, Conor put his foot down, anxious about what they would find when they arrived.

CHAPTER THREE

'IS IT FAR?' Kate tightened her hold as Conor guided the four-wheel-drive with skill along the rural roads.

'About two miles. Joyce Bingham is Lizzie's next-door neighbour.'

The reply had been terse and she dared a glance at his set face. Lizzie was someone he cared about but, then, he had demonstrated time and again his dedication to his patients. The morning had been full of surprises, misjudgements and close shaves, and she felt mentally exhausted from the time spent with Conor, fighting to ignore the sexual tension that crackled between them and desperate to deflect his probing questions and not divulge more about herself.

Within minutes Conor drew up outside three old farm-workers' cottages and Kate followed in his wake as he grabbed his bag and hurried up the path to the middle house, where the front door stood ajar.

'Conor, thank goodness you're here,' an anxious, middle-aged woman greeted them.

Kate saw him smile and give the woman's shoulder a re-assuring squeeze. 'Hello, Joyce. What happened?'

'I heard this fearful crash,' the woman explained. 'I knew Billy was at work and Yvonne had gone shopping, so I rushed round. Poor Lizzie's in a state. I've called the ambulance but she was asking for you. She wanted to move but I told her to stay where she was until you came.'

'You did perfectly,' he praised, introducing Kate as they stepped from the porch into a small sitting room. 'Joyce, could you be an angel and track down Yvonne for me?'

'Yes, of course.'

The woman seemed relieved to have something to do. Kate followed Conor as he made his way to the foot of the stairs, finding the frail figure of an elderly lady lying there, her head propped on a pillow, a blanket covering her. She watched as Conor knelt down and took one thin, papery hand in his.

'Lizzie? Can you hear me?'

'Conor?' The thready voice was a mere whisper as pale blue eyes opened and struggled to focus.

'I'm here,' he soothed. 'What have you been doing to yourself?'

A grimace crossed the pain-ravaged face. 'So silly. Should have waited for Yvonne,' she confided, her voice a little stronger.

'Don't worry now. Did you trip on something? Can you remember? Did you feel dizzy or black out?'

'No, I wasn't dizzy. I caught my foot.'

'All right, Lizzie, we'll get you sorted out as quickly as we can,' Conor promised, reaching for his medical bag and turning back the blanket so he could check the elderly woman's condition and vital signs.

'Sorry to be such a nuisance.'

He tutted in disapproval. 'You're never a nuisance. Can you tell me where it hurts?'

'M-my right leg,' she managed, her face twisting with pain again.

Kate shifted to give Conor more room as he began to examine the woman's injuries. From where she stood, Kate could tell the femur was broken by the hip, the external rotation and shortening evident. Her gaze met Conor's as he glanced up with a grimace, sadness dulling his green eyes.

As he returned his attention to Lizzie, Kate stepped carefully round the other side and knelt down, ready to help if he needed anything, wriggling closer in the tight space between their patient and the wall. 'Hello, Lizzie, I'm Kate, the new locum. I'm helping Conor today.'

'Lucky Conor.'

Kate heard him chuckle at the spirited reply. 'Does anything else hurt, Lizzie? Did you hit your head when you fell?' Connor probed. Kate could see nasty bruises along the frail limbs.

'No. Just my leg.'

After checking Lizzie's eyes and the reaction of her pupils, Conor monitored heart, lungs and blood pressure again, hooking the stethoscope round his neck and recovering Lizzie with the blanket. 'How bad's the pain, Lizzie?'

'Grim,' she confirmed, sounding tired.

'We'll give you something for that now,' he promised, and Kate drew up some analgesia, handing him the syringe so he could check and administer it. For a moment he looked right at her, his expression so warmly intimate that she forgot how to breathe. 'Thanks, Kate.'

'No problem.'

She lowered her lashes and forced herself to focus on writing up notes of what they had done, drugs used and doses given—information that would be required by the paramedics and hospital doctor. Anything but look at or think about Conor.

'It should start to ease now, Lizzie,' he was saying, sitting back on his heels after another check of her vital signs and holding her hand again. 'The ambulance will be here soon.'

The woman shook her head. 'No! Conor, I don't want to go to hospital.'

'I know you don't, sweetie,' he said gently, his voice calm in response to Lizzie's distress. 'But there's nothing else for it, I'm afraid. You've broken your thigh bone right by the hip and it has to be X-rayed and properly seen to.'

Lizzie's eyes closed and she was silent for a few moments. 'I'm not going to be claiming that dance from you any time soon, then, am I?' she rallied with a weak smile.

Moved both by Lizzie's spirit and Conor's compassion, Kate watched as he brushed some thinning strands of white hair back from the pale face, his softly accented voice husky with affection. 'I'll save you one, I promise.'

'Conor?' Joyce called, returning to the room. 'The ambulance is pulling up. I've rung the Glentown post office and Jeanie Harris is searching the village for Yvonne.'

'Thanks, Joyce, you're a star.'

Conor concentrated on keeping Lizzie as calm as possible as the paramedics arrived and prepared to transfer the fragile lady to the ambulance, putting in an IV line to give her fluids and placing her on oxygen. Kate accompanied them outside, noting how Conor held Lizzie's hand until the last moment.

'We'll take good care of her, Conor,' one of the paramedics promised, closing the back doors of the ambulance.

'I know you will.' Conor smiled, handing over his hastily scribbled letter plus the notes Kate had already prepared. 'Thanks, guys.'

They watched as the ambulance left, Joyce coming to stand beside them. 'Poor old Lizzie,' she sighed.

'Thanks for your help, you were great,' Conor said. 'Are you OK? You've had a shock.'

'Nothing a strong cup of tea won't help. Would you both like one?'

Glancing at his watch, he shook his head. 'We'd better not, Joyce, but thank you. I need to tell Yvonne about her mum, then we have a call to make before we get back for afternoon surgery. Ring me if you need anything, all right?'

'I will. Thank you, Conor.'

After packing up the medical bag, they left the house in time to see another car arrive, a woman in her mid-forties scrambling out and hurrying up the path towards them, tears shimmering in her eyes. 'Oh, Conor, I've just heard! Is Ma going to be all right? I never thought she'd do anything like this. I was only going out for some essentials.'

'It's not your fault, Yvonne. Lizzie's in the best possible hands,' he reassured her, giving her a sympathetic hug. 'Are you going to be able to get to the hospital?'

'Yes, thank you, I rang Billy and he's coming home straight away. We'll go together,' she told him with a watery smile.

'Billy is Yvonne's husband, manager of the village bank,' Conor explained, introducing them. 'Call if I can help. I'll ring the hospital later and be in to visit Lizzie when I can.'

'Bless you, Conor. I'm so relieved you were here.'

'Your mum's a special lady, Yvonne.'

A special lady but a frail one, Kate thought, climbing back into the car. 'Do you think Lizzie will be all right?'

'I hope so.' He shrugged, but she could see the concern on his face. She'd only been working with him half a day but her misjudgement of him as a doctor had been glaring. He cared deeply about these people. 'Lizzie's long-term prognosis is worrying. You know as well as I do the high mortality and disability rates after these sorts of fractures in a person of her age. Her bones are fragile and she's become infirm and unsteady recently—that's why she left her own house in the village to move in with Yvonne and Billy. It's not an ideal situation for any of them.'

'The stairs can't help.'

'No, they don't. Lizzie has a bed-sitting room upstairs as the only bathroom facilities are up there. It means she's restricted. And she misses the village activity and her friends.'

He lapsed into silence, a frown on his face, and she suspected he was wondering about a solution…if and when Lizzie was well enough to come home.

The rest of the day was hectic with the completion of the home visits followed by clinics, consultations and a couple of minor emergencies, but Kate welcomed the busy pace because it gave her little time to worry about the job or fret about Conor. It was well after six before she was ready to leave, and when she discovered Conor was giving advice to a patient on the telephone she took the opportunity to escape. She nodded goodbye from the corridor, ignoring his gesture for her to wait, slipping past his consulting-room door before he could detain her and subject her to any more uncomfortable questions. She needed to recharge her mental batteries before facing him again.

After saying goodnight to those members of staff yet to head for home, she declined their offers to join them for a meal or a drink at the village pub, needing to be alone to assess her first day. She walked round the side of the building and down the path, unlocked the door and went up the stairs to the spacious two-bedroom flat that was her home in Glentown-on-Firth.

The village nestled at the foot of a wooded valley, bounded along the southern edge by the coastline of the Solway Firth, while to the north lay farmland, woods and the stunning Galloway hills. Situated in the heart of the village, the Solway Medical Centre was housed in an impressive two-storey granite building under a slate roof. Originally two residential villas, they had been combined and renovated with a modern extension added at the rear during a recent expansion of the practice.

Having telephoned her father in London to reassure him she had survived her first day, the sound of his voice and his concerned support making her homesick, she prepared a light meal and sat at the large bay window in the living room, blind to the magnificent views because her mind was buzzing with thoughts and images—far too many of them featuring Conor Anderson.

She would never forget her first sight of him. Or the instant wave of desire she had experienced, more powerful than anything she had felt before, but she was not ready to think about involvement with a man again. Not yet. And certainly not with a casual romeo like Conor who appeared to have half the women of south-west Scotland at his beck and call, each hoping to be the one to tame him but getting a broken heart for her trouble. No, she had enough problems sorting out her career and deciding what to do with the rest of her life.

Today she had learned that Conor's care for his patients was genuine. If there was anything to be done to make life easier for Lizzie and her family, Kate had no doubt he would do it. She had been concerned about Conor's casualness but the patients loved his easygoing, touchy-feely approach to their care. He was a maverick, not at all what she was used to, but she respected him as a doctor. As a man he scared the hell out of her. She had never responded so intensely to someone. Her stay here was always going to be difficult professionally—the unwanted physical attraction to Conor made the weeks ahead even more alarming.

'How did things go today?'

Conor seated himself in Fred's kitchen and gratefully accepted the drink offered to him. 'Thanks. It went well. We had a busy day, routine for the most part, but I'm afraid that Lizzie Dalglish had a fall down the stairs and has broken her femur.'

'Oh, no.' Fred frowned, stirring a teaspoon of sugar into his steaming drink. 'Have you heard how she is?'

'I rang the hospital before I left the surgery. She's come through the operation which is a good start. We'll have to see how her rehabilitation goes. I'll visit when Lizzie is well enough.'

Fred ran the palm of one hand over his balding pate, a characteristic habit when he was anxious or lost in thought. 'How did Kate get on?'

'I was very impressed; she's an excellent doctor.' He paused, declining to mention his intense and immediate attraction to her. Meeting Fred's blue gaze, he watched the older man's expression. 'I'm not sure Kate knows it, though.'

'Why do you say that?'

'She was tense, nervous about her work—at least until she got started,' he explained, knowing Fred well enough to tell when he was being evasive.

Looking away, Fred shrugged. 'That's not unusual for first days.'

'It was more than that,' Conor persisted, puzzling over his unanswered questions and still miffed at the way Kate had sneaked home, denying him the chance to speak with her again. 'She's more than capable of holding her own consultations, but I'll keep taking her on house calls until she's better acquainted with the area.'

'Good. That's fine. But I don't want to rush her.'

Again Conor sensed that his partner was protecting Kate. But from what? Why? 'Do you know her history?'

'Kate's?' Fred parried, delaying a response when Conor nodded. 'Not much.'

Frustrated, Conor frowned and rested his arms on the table. 'So tell me what you do know.'

'I can't tell you any more than I already have, Conor.'

'Come on, Fred! I'm a partner here, too.'

'Yes, you are. But I can't break a confidence, you know that.' The older man sighed.

'Kate's confidence…or the professor's?'

Fred's blue eyes were troubled. 'Both, I suppose. Kate hasn't spoken to me—and she doesn't know James has told me more than he said he would,' he admitted, clearly uncomfortable with the situation.

'But—'

'All we need to know is that Kate's not incompetent or in any kind of trouble.'

'I never thought she was incompetent.'

Conor's frowned deepened. He could never imagine Kate doing anything wrong, let alone being negligent. After her initial hesitancy he had seen how natural and thorough and caring she was, but she was definitely in trouble, if not professionally then in some other part of her life. He knew it. What he didn't know was the nature of the problem. Yet. With or without Fred's help, though, he intended to find out.

'Has Kate been ill?' he asked, remembering his initial concern about her pallor.

'She's a good doctor, Conor,' Fred insisted. 'Better than good. We are lucky to have her.'

'I know that.'

'She needs some time.'

Which told him precisely nothing. 'But—'

'If Kate wants to talk, she will. Stop pushing, OK?'

Conor wasn't satisfied that it was OK. Kate was hurting. Anyone could see that. And it wasn't in his nature to stand by and do nothing.

'Leave her alone, Conor.' Fred's voice was uncharacteristically stern. 'Kate's not someone for you to play with.'

Irritated, Conor rose to his feet. 'I'm not playing, Fred. Far from it.'

'Then give the woman some space.'

Kate was soon taking her own surgeries and settled into the new routine, grateful for the friendliness of staff and patients. Sometimes she struggled with an accent or unfamiliar phrase but misunderstandings were laughingly overcome. If only the minor incidents with language were her only problem. Even though Fred was back, she still found herself accompanying Conor on home visits and, much to her chagrin, it was becoming harder to maintain her resolve and her resistance. She tried to avoid him but he seemed intent on hanging around, driving her to distraction. She was novelty value, she reassured herself. It would soon wear off. What about his busy social life? How did he fit all the women in when he seemed to work such long hours? It was none of her business. Thankfully he had refrained from asking any more awkward questions, although she sensed that his curiosity simmered under the outward charm.

'If you have any thoughts about Charlie, I'd be pleased to hear them,' Conor said, interrupting her reverie as they headed back to the surgery on a grey, wet Friday afternoon.

Their last visit had been to a man in his early sixties, physically healthy but suffering from depression. Conor had explained how Charlie had spent his life farming, building up a reputation for a prize herd of Ayrshire cattle, only to lose everything when the area had been hit by an outbreak of foot and mouth disease. With his stock culled, his life's work decimated, his farm silent and lifeless, Charlie had given up. Increasingly lethargic, he refused to take an interest in anything, rarely speaking and not eating properly. He had no family but his loyal friends were worried. So, Kate knew, was Conor.

'It's horribly sad.' She imagined how different Charlie must have been when full of vigour and enthusiasm compared with the shell of the man she had just met. 'Losing everything that way, his whole purpose for being.'

'I know. I don't want to impose something drastic on him at this stage and risk alienating him. At the moment he'll let me in, take his medication, but he won't consider seeing our visiting counsellor, Sarah Baxter. The situation has worsened since Christmas.'

'What happened at Christmas?'

'His dog died.' Conor sighed. 'Max had been keeping Charlie going. After losing him, he just sat down and became even more uncommunicative.'

Having come to know more about Conor as a doctor in the last few days, she could tell how frustrated he was, feeling he had been unable to help Charlie through this difficult time. 'I'll give it some thought,' she promised as they arrived back at the surgery, pondering on the problem as she preceded him inside. They heard a fearful screaming echoing down the corridor from the direction of the nurses' treatment room.

'I'm so glad you're back,' a harassed Aileen greeted them. 'Conor, can you do anything?'

'What's the problem?' he asked, handing over the patient notes for filing.

'Little Callie McIntosh.' The practice manager grimaced. 'She's cut her arm and it needs stitching but she won't let anyone near her. Fred has tried, so have Dorothy and the other nurses, Kristen and Sandra.'

Kate went with Conor to the treatment room but hesitated in the doorway, the young girl's distress stirring unwanted memories and making her feel panicky. About three, the child was red-faced from screaming, a mix of fear and fury in her wide blue eyes, a bloodstained dressing roughly wrapped round one arm. Callie's mother was frazzled, while nurse practitioner Dorothy's look of relief when she saw Conor was comical. Feeling more in control as she forced herself to concentrate on the present, thankful Conor had not noticed her momentary lapse, Kate watched as he took charge. Talking to calm Callie, he knelt down beside her, smiled and turned his attention to the child's well-loved teddy bear, which was clutched tightly in the hand of her uninjured arm.

'What's his name?'

'B-Bear,' she whispered.

'It looks like Bear needs a little help.' Conor pointed to a split in the seam of one leg where the filling was poking through. 'Shall I make him better?'

Wide-eyed, Callie nodded. 'Can you?'

'Sure I can. A few quick stitches and he'll be as good as new.'

Amazed, Kate looked on as Conor pretended to give the teddy a local anaesthetic and then swiftly put a few stitches in the furry leg. She knew how pushed he was for time, and yet he gave of himself to this troubled child. It was a side of him she had never anticipated but was now coming to know so well.

'There!' He smiled when he was done. 'That wasn't difficult, was it? And Bear was so brave. Do you think you can be as clever as him and let me make you better, too?'

'S'pose.'

'Good girl.'

There were a few more tears but Conor talked to Callie, working gently but swiftly, and the job was soon finished. The little girl even had a smile on her tear-stained face as Conor proudly stuck a colourful sticker on her T-shirt for being so brave and gave her a sugar-free lollipop.

'What a star,' he praised, ruffling the blonde curls.

Unsettled, Kate left Conor talking over Callie's follow-up care with her mother and Dorothy, slipping away to the staff-room to help herself to a quick mug of hot chocolate before her first afternoon appointment arrived. For once the room was empty and, while the kettle boiled, she browsed the huge pinboard stuffed with photos of the staff from holidays and various activities which she had not had the chance to look at before. Her attention caught, she paused to examine one photo more closely, her eyes widening in surprise. Unless she was mistaken it was of Conor, completely bald, posing with a young girl wearing a headscarf.

'We tease Conor about that,' Aileen informed, startling her. 'But we were very proud of him. He has a special way with people.'

'What happened?' Kate asked, interested despite her determination not to get involved.

'About four years ago Conor was caring for Lucy, a thirteen-year-old with cancer. She was terrified about the treatment, tearful about her looks and losing her hair, so Conor did a deal with her—said he'd shave his head in support to keep her company.'

Unwanted emotion welled inside her at yet more evidence of Conor's caring. She didn't know many doctors who would go to those lengths for someone.

'We always say Conor should be available on the NHS

by prescription!' Aileen joked. 'He's wonderful at making people feel better about themselves. You wouldn't believe the number of patients who have benefited from Conor giving them some time, be it a game of golf, a trip out somewhere or just a chat at home.'

Kate wondered if some of the teasing about 'dates' referred to this and not to romantic entanglements at all. She had discovered firsthand how special time with Conor could make a person feel, having been on the receiving end of some of that one-to-one attention herself that week. She didn't want to admit that the intimate smiles and warm looks made her insides throb with desire and made her wish for things that were out of bounds.

'I'm surprised he doesn't have a family of his own, given how good he is with children,' Kate ventured, annoyed with herself for fishing.

'There'd be many a lady applying for that job!' Aileen laughed. 'Conor's not serious about any of his dates so I can't see that happening.'

After Aileen had gone, Kate made her drink, cradling her mug in her hands, a frown on her face. What had she expected? She had heard enough about Conor to confirm her opinion of him as a womaniser who was shy of commitment. Not that it mattered to her. The way he ran his life was none of her business, but it was warning enough, if any more was needed, to redouble her guard against his easy charm.

Her frown deepening, she returned to the photos, her gaze straying to another one of Conor, this time with two other gorgeous-looking men, walking out on the hills. Her gaze moved on, lingering on a photo of someone in a protective body suit and helmet, holding some kind of tray-like object, taken at a winter sports centre.

'What on earth is that?' she murmured to herself, leaning in for a closer inspection.

'Hi.'

She jumped, nearly dropping her mug as Conor's husky voice sounded in her ear, so close his breath fanned her cheek. She stepped away, horribly aware of him, his earthy fragrance teasing her senses, her pulse racing. 'I didn't hear you come in.'

'Sorry.' His teasing smile belied his apology. 'Fancy having a go with me?'

'I beg your pardon?'

His smile widened at her wary suspicion and he pointed to the photo she had been looking at, then the one next to it of the figure sledging down an ice chute.

'That's you?'

'It is.'

'You flung yourself head first down an ice track on a teatray?' Kate gasped in amazement.

'It's not a teatray!' Laughing, he stepped up close behind her, looking over her shoulder. Her body tingled in response. 'It's an expensive, high-tech piece of equipment called a skeleton bob, and it's fun.'

'It's barking mad crazy is what it is. And "skeleton" is an accurate description of what you'd be if you did it. Why don't you play football or golf like a normal person?'

He laughed again and she could feel the rumble of it against her back. 'I do those, too… I love sport. I go curling, mountain-biking, walking, all sorts.'

No wonder he was so fit, his body so superbly athletic. Anxious at the way she was reacting to the proximity of that body, scared she would weaken and forget the many reasons why she had to resist him, she slid to the side and put more space between them, her heart hammering as she concentrated on washing up her mug, keeping her gaze averted.

'Kate,' he murmured, his voice huskily intimate. 'I wanted to ask you—'

'There you both are!' Jenny announced, appearing in the doorway, and Kate breathed sigh of relief at the reprieve.

Conor sounded anything but relieved, frustration ringing in his tone. 'What's the problem, Jenny?'

'There's no problem.' The young receptionist smiled, oblivious of the charged atmosphere. 'Kate, Fred wants to see you in his room before you begin your consultations.'

'Thanks, Jenny. I'm finished here.'

She dried her hands, refusing to look at Conor, and headed for the door, hearing Jenny's eager invitation behind her.

'Conor, some of us are getting together for a drink after work. Will you come?'

'I'm sorry but I already have plans tonight. Another time, though, I promise.'

'It's OK if you have a date. Which lucky lady has drawn the winning ticket this time?' Jenny teased, although disappointment underlaid the joking.

Conor murmured something Kate couldn't catch then added, 'I can't let her down, Jenny.'

She walked on, thankful to hear no more of the conversation. Professionally he was an incredible doctor but privately he was a player, a natural flirt, and the last thing she needed was another one of those in her life. Squaring her shoulders, determined to push thoughts of Conor from her mind, she knocked on Fred's door and stepped inside.

'Kate's here now, James. Yes, we're delighted,' Fred said enthusiastically over the phone. 'I'll pass you over and give you some time to talk.' Putting his hand over the mouthpiece, he stood up and smiled. 'James would like a word with you, my dear. Take your time. I'll go and get myself a cup of tea before surgery and give you some privacy.'

'Thank you, Fred.'

She waited until the door closed then picked up the phone, moving to stare out of the window at the view down a side road towards the sea.

'Kate?' a familiar voice barked in her ear.

'I'm here, James. How are you?'

'Busy. I phoned to hear how your first week has been,' he said without preamble. 'How have you been coping?'

'Things haven't been as bad as I anticipated…so far.'

'Kate, nothing is going to change what happened but you *can* change how you react to it. You're a wonderful doctor and Glentown-on-Firth is the perfect place for you to ease back into work and find some peace with yourself.'

'I guess time will tell,' she allowed, wishing she could feel as confident about herself and her abilities as the prof and her father did.

'The circumstances were extraordinary, Kate, you can't blame yourself,' the prof chastised for the umpteenth time. 'Anyone would have been traumatised by what happened. Most would never have lasted as long as you did, kept their heads and saved so many lives.'

Kate bit her lip. It was easy for other people to tell her what she should and shouldn't have done, how she should and shouldn't feel, but they hadn't been there. No one else knew what it had been like. She had been back in the UK for two months and she still had nightmares, still doubted her decisions…still grieved. Grieved for Wesley, her brother, for the colleagues and patients she felt she had failed. She may have healed physically but she hadn't come close to dealing with the memories and self-doubt.

'I don't have all day, Kate.' His impatient voice snapped her from her thoughts. 'I'm due in Theatre in an hour. An interesting case, multiple fractures. A shame you aren't here, I could use you.'

A cold shiver ran along her spine. 'You know I can't do that. I'll never do surgery again.'

'I think you're wrong but I accept that's your choice. Now, how are you finding everyone up there?'

'Fred's lovely.' She smiled, already fond of the paternal doctor. 'The other staff have been very welcoming.'

'Including Conor Anderson?' he queried, amusement in his gravelly voice.

'You knew about him, didn't you?' A hint of accusation laced her tone. 'Conor is like Darren all over again.'

'Don't talk such bloody rubbish.' The prof seldom minced his words and Kate couldn't prevent a smile as she imagined his fierce blue eyes, the bushy grey brows knotted together in annoyance. She remembered how terrified she had been when she had first met Professor James Fielding-Smythe during her training, a man whose reputation, not only as a peerless surgeon but as a taskmaster able to reduce the toughest of junior doctors to a trembling wreck with one withering glance or cutting word, was legendary. Since then he had become a trusted adviser. 'Conor Anderson is as far from Darren as it is possible to be. He's a special doctor, Kate. He could be good for you.'

'I gather Conor's a little too good to all the women around here,' she riposted with asperity.

'I doubt the man's a monk but that doesn't make him the kind of unscrupulous, cheating bastard Darren proved to be. Sacking him was the best decision I made—and the most satisfying,' he added with a ruthless chuckle. Kate winced as she recalled the terrible scene. 'My worst decision was letting you leave my team to return to general practice and then back your yen to join the aid agency. I should have fought to keep you. You had the makings of a first-class surgeon.'

Kate swallowed. Sometimes she wished the professor wasn't quite so blunt. 'James—'

'I've known Fred Murdoch nearly forty years, we trained together, fulfilled the best-man role for each other when we married our respective wives,' he informed her, his voice turning reminiscent as he moved the conversation in a fresh direction, giving her little time to adjust her thoughts. 'I may have told you that Cordelia and I visit Glentown-on-Firth every year. Fred and I have a week or two salmon fishing. Our wives enjoyed shopping trips to Edinburgh or Glasgow—until Fred's wife, Annette, died two years ago. Cancer. Very quick. Conor was a tremendous support to Fred when Annette was ill. And afterwards. Give him a chance. More importantly, give yourself a chance.'

'I'm trying to. I'm not sure I still have what it takes to be a doctor.'

'You must find that out for yourself. Being a GP was always your original goal but you were sidetracked by Darren and his ambitions. Make the most of this fresh start, Kate.'

The professor hung up with customary abruptness after instructing her to send regular email reports on her progress. Kate stared at the phone feeling unsettled and confused, James's wise if impatient advice ringing in her ears. A tap on the door announced Fred's return and she looked up as he came back into the room. She had not known about his wife and a wave of compassion washed over her as she studied him, seeing an underlying tiredness, noticing the way his suit hung on him as if he had shrunk from the person he had once been.

'All right, my dear? Jenny told me the call was finished.'

'I'm fine,' she fibbed. 'Thank you.'

Fred moved to his desk and sat down, his expression benevolent but curious. 'Kate, I'm not going to pry but James mentioned that you wanted to come here because you needed to think about some changes in your life and to decide on the direction of your career.'

'Something like that, yes,' she managed, uncomfortable under the gentle regard.

'I hope you will come to think of us as your friends. If there is ever a time you would like to talk, about anything at all, I hope you will feel you can come to me. Or Conor—most of you young women seem to gravitate to him!'

Kate closed her eyes, ignoring his final words. 'Thank you, Fred.'

Emotion threatened to choke her at the feeling she was there under false presences and was taking advantage of this man's kindness.

CHAPTER FOUR

LOCKING up the surgery on Sunday morning, Conor slipped the keys in his pocket and walked round to the flat. Out on calls on Friday and in the staffroom later, he had felt closer to Kate than at any time during the week and he was frustrated that Jenny had interrupted them. He had not seen Kate since but when he had phoned her a while ago to tell her he was downstairs, she had been tense, her voice distant.

He hesitated at the front door, pondering the wisdom of his actions. Kate had not given him the slightest encouragement but he couldn't keep away from her. Before he could change his mind, he rang the bell, his pulse rate increasing when he heard footsteps on the stairs, his breath burning in his lungs when she opened the door looking soft, cuddly and vulnerable. It was the first time he had seen her out of the smart suits she wore to work, and the figure-hugging jeans teamed with a white shirt that offset the olive tones of her skin had the ever-present desire tightening inside him.

'Hi.' He smiled, resisting the urge to touch her. 'May I come in?'

Wary indecision shadowed her dark brown eyes. After several moments she stepped back, turning and heading up the stairs, leaving him to close the door and follow in her wake, puzzled by her renewed defensiveness. He had a great relationship with his colleagues, friends and patients. And he loved women. All women. He enjoyed their company but he was very choosy about who he became involved with. It sounded corny but he was looking for the one woman he could spend the rest of his life with and with whom he could have the family he craved. His social life was active but he rarely took things further than friendship.

The scars of the past had deep roots and after the disaster of his parents' marriage and their subsequent succession of partners and failed relationships he was determined not to settle for second best, not to repeat their mistakes. He'd thought he'd found his ideal woman once, at med school, but fed up with the long hours and his desire to be a rural GP his girlfriend had dumped him for someone richer and more upwardly mobile. He'd learned the lesson. And the padlock round his heart had never been opened again. He had planned it would stay locked until *the one* came along. If she didn't, he would bitterly regret not having children but better that than raise them in the kind of broken and unhappy home he had endured.

It was amazing, inconvenient and unsettling, but he had known from the first second he'd met her that Kate was *the one*. Disapproval and distrust registered in her soulful brown eyes whenever she looked at him—which wasn't often as her gaze was usually fixed on some point behind his shoulder or down at the floor. It would be easy to retreat from that touch-me-not front, but he was intrigued by her and sensed that, like an iceberg, much more of her lay below the surface than she ever allowed the world to see. Concerned for her well-being, he was determined to find the real Kate. He knew she was worth fighting for. Whether he could ever win her round was another matter entirely. Filled with nervous uncertainty, he watched her now, arms folded across her chest, every atom of her being tense, the shadow of pain dulling her lonely brown eyes. Everything about her drew him like a moth to a flame.

'What do you want?'

He swallowed down an inappropriate chuckle. Better not tell her how badly he wanted to take her to bed. 'I'm sorry I disturbed you earlier, but I didn't want you to worry if you heard noises downstairs.'

'That was thoughtful, thank you,' she allowed, unbending a little. 'Was everything all right?'

'Allan Mountford, a farmer from outside the village, cut himself on some machinery and his leg needed stitching. It's such a long drive to A and E so it makes sense to take care of it here. Easier and quicker for everyone.'

'Except for you.' A slight frown creased the smoothness of her brow. 'I thought the service handled out-of-hours work.'

'Officially it does,' he admitted, looking away from her, embarrassed to admit how he couldn't let go. 'Fred needed to cut back his hours so I went along with his choice to sign on with the service, but I like to keep up with my own patients. I tend to take some evening and weekend calls.'

'I see.'

He could tell from her tone that the information didn't square with her image of him. He walked across to the window and admired the view. 'Are you all right here alone?' he murmured, hating to think of her by herself. Lonely.

'Some people like being alone,' she pointed out coolly. 'Not everyone has to have company all the time or needs to be the centre of attention.'

'Ouch!' He turned to face her, his smile rueful. 'You don't approve of me, do you?'

'I don't know you.'

He captured her unwilling gaze. 'So why not reserve judgement until you do?'

'Conor—'

'You're an excellent doctor, Kate. Why do you doubt yourself?'

She looked scared, her eyes widening with alarm. 'I don't know what you mean,' she riposted in that stiff, cool tone he was coming to know so well, the one she used when she wanted to keep people at bay or avoid something…or when she was lying. At the moment she was doing all three.

'I think you do.'

'I— I was thinking about Charlie.' Panic brought an edge to her voice and a desperation to her eyes, her fingers nervously tucking a few silken strands of hair behind her ear as she changed the subject. 'Your farmer.'

Aching for whatever was eating her up inside, he moved closer, taking her trembling hand in his, feeling the rapid and uneven beat of the pulse at her wrist. 'I know who Charlie is, Kate.'

'You mentioned his dog.' Her voice was husky as she slipped her fingers from his and stepped away.

'Yes.' Disappointed, he allowed her retreat. 'Max had been Charlie's constant companion for fourteen years. Losing him at Christmas was the final straw.'

'Perhaps it's time he had a new dog, a new life to worry about. So he feels needed.'

He thrust his hands into his pockets to stop himself reaching for her again. 'It's not something he'll talk about.'

'But if he was faced with it, if someone presented him with a dog that has had a bad start or been rescued from something and needs someone special to give it a home and care and…'

Her words trailed off, her troubled gaze flicking to his then away again, and he had the sudden knowledge there was a resonance here, maybe one she had not intended but which had hit her too—a damaged life that needed healing. Just like Kate. Kate, who so clearly needed some loving care but was unable to reach out and take what he so desperately wanted to give her. Sensing her unease, he forced himself to focus on Charlie, realising that it was not only an excellent plan but was a way he could involve Kate and spend time with her outside work.

'You're brilliant!' He smiled at the surprise on her face. 'It's definitely worth a try. And I know just the person who can help us.'

Aware of her watching him, wary but interested, he took out his mobile phone and brought up a number from the memory, waiting several moments until the call was answered.

'Is that the Lochanrig home for waifs and strays?'

'Conor?' The voice registered a mix of harassment, welcome and laughter.

'Hello, Hannah. I need your help. You know that puppy you were telling me about? Have you found a home for him yet?'

'Nic thought he'd found somewhere a couple of weeks ago but it fell through,' Hannah informed him. 'I wish we could keep him but he's causing havoc with Wallace!'

Knowing what a character their ginger cat was, Conor laughed. 'I think I might have the perfect home for the puppy if you are interested.'

'That would be fantastic. Have you really?'

'It's all thanks to Kate, our new doctor,' he continued, winking at her as he explained Charlie's situation. 'Is the puppy ready to home?'

'The sooner the better!' Hannah laughed, sounding frazzled again.

'Would it be OK if we came over and collected him today?'

'Sure. Come to lunch, Conor. We'd love to see you. And meet your Kate!'

'Unfortunately not. Yet.'

'Oh, dear!' Hannah sounded knowing and amused. 'Like that, is it?'

His looked at Kate and the customary wave of longing swamped him. One week and his entire life had been turned upside down. 'Yeah, it is. See you in a while, Hannah.'

* * *

Kate shifted under the heat of desire in Conor's green eyes as he looked at her before ending his call. It was hard enough coping with her own confused feelings for him, the physical want warring with emotional doubt, knowing he was the last man on earth she should let close to her because she would find herself back in the painful place she had been before. Conor had the power to hurt her. And at the moment she was too vulnerable, her life too shaky, to take the temporary pleasure he would offer.

She was taken by surprise as he hugged her and dropped a brief kiss on her cheek before letting her go, his touch leaving her skin tingling.

'You're a star, Kate. Come on, grab your things, we can go now.'

'What? But—'

'You have to come,' he protested before she could summon an excuse. 'It was your idea and I'll need some help with the puppy on the drive back.'

Bemused, Kate found herself railroaded into accompanying him, with time only to pull on a knee-length cardigan, ankle boots and collect her bag. She had to be mad, spending more time with Conor, she fretted, confused by him, thrown by his insight and probing questions, alarmed by her unwanted physical reaction to him. As they drove east out of Glentown-on-Firth towards the larger town of Rigtownbrae some miles away, she felt tongue-tied, unable to think of any subject outside their work environment that was safe. Impatient and annoyed with herself, she looked out of the window at the impressive landscape.

'I didn't get a chance to catch up with you on Friday.' Conor's voice drew her from her thoughts. 'I was going to ask you to come with me in the evening.'

Shocked, she stared at him. He'd planned on taking her out on his date? She opened her mouth to speak but could think of nothing appropriate and closed it again. The man had some nerve! How could he be so brazen about it?

'What's wrong?'

'Nothing,' she murmured, unable to keep the terseness from her voice. 'Why would I have wanted to go with you?'

A laugh rumbled from inside him. 'You certainly know how to deflate an ego!'

'Conor…' She sucked in a deep breath and closed her eyes. The man was impossible.

'Anyway,' he continued, undaunted by her manner, 'I went over to the county infirmary to visit Lizzie.'

Kate opened her eyes and stared at him in amazement. 'You went to see Lizzie?'

'Of course. That's what I was trying to tell you in the staffroom.'

'On Friday?'

He glanced at her with a puzzled frown. 'That's right. I thought you might be interested.'

'I am.' She struggled to find her voice, confused by the feelings churning inside her: shame that she had misjudged him again; pleasure that he had not only taken time to see the elderly lady but that he had considered taking her with him; stupid relief that he had not been out smooching with one of his women. 'How is she?'

'Holding her own and in good spirits.'

'I'm so pleased. She's a lovely lady,' Kate enthused, not wanting to examine why her own spirits had suddenly lifted.

'She is.' Pulling up to negotiate a road junction, he glanced at her and smiled. 'It's too soon to know what the long-term prognosis will be but I was pleased to find her coping so well. I'll let you know next time I'm going over and if you want to come, you'd be welcome.'

A warm feeling settled inside her. 'Thanks. So what is this place we're going to today?' she ventured after a few moments, trying to steer things on to safer ground.

'Lochanrig is a village about eight miles north-east of Rigtownbrae. Hannah Frost has been GP there for some years—her grandfather founded the practice and her father carried it on. Nic di Angelis is Italian and he arrived about eighteen months ago as a locum and swept reserved, workaholic Hannah off her feet! They've been married about nine months now, although Hannah keeps Frost as her working name to avoid confusion.'

'I see.' Kate tried to absorb all the information. 'So what do they have to do with this puppy?'

Conor chuckled again. 'They are always taking in waifs and strays. Nic rescued the first one not long after he arrived, the only survivor of a litter of kittens he found dumped in a sack by the road.'

'How awful.'

'Wallace is a real character! They've acquired various other animals in the intervening months and they told me about this puppy recently. He'll be about four or five months old now,' he explained, negotiating the main street of Rigtownbrae, nearly deserted on a sleepy Sunday, before taking the rural lanes towards Lochanrig. 'I thought of it when you had your brainwave about Charlie. This may well be just what he needs.'

When they arrived at a large stone-built house set in its own grounds on the edge of Lochanrig village, the front door was open, an adapted child gate covered in wire mesh blocking the gap. Conor rang the bell and a disembodied voice greeted them from inside, vying with the distant barking of a dog.

'Conor, if that's you, I'm in the kitchen. Please, shut the gate after you!'

Stepping back to let her through ahead of him, Conor guided her inside, closing the inner door and the gate behind them. Kate was conscious of his hand at the small of her back, steering her towards a door that led to a large, airy country kitchen where an attractive woman with long chestnut hair, tied back in a loose ponytail, was sitting at a rustic table, a cloth draped over one shoulder, a tiny scrap of tabby fur cradled in her hands.

'Hi. Nearly finished.' She smiled as the kitten took the last of its milk.

Kate watched, fascinated, as the woman gently wiped the kitten's face then rose to her feet and set it back inside a large pen that already contained a bundle of assorted-coloured kittens, and she tried to count how many there were in the tangle of legs. Five. As Hannah moved to wash her hands, Kate edged across to take a closer look at the tiny bodies. They were so gorgeous. She turned round to ask Hannah about them, in time to see the woman laugh as Conor swept her into his arms for a hug. The insidious curl of jealousy that clenched inside her was dismaying. She didn't want to feel anything. It was ridiculous. Conor was of no interest to her beyond work and Hannah was happily married to someone else.

'It's good to see you, Conor,' Hannah said. 'Sorry about the muddle.'

Keeping his arm around the woman's waist and cuddling her close, Conor peered into the pen. 'Are you going to keep any of them?'

'Would you believe me if I said no?'

'Nope!'

Hannah pushed a fall of escaped chestnut waves back from her face. 'I thought not. I get so attached but I know we can't keep them all. It's not possible. It's only been eighteen months and we've already got Wallace, Hoppity, Sparky, the puppy and now these kittens. Someone rescued them from being drowned and brought them to us because we've earned a reputation for not turning anything away. I dread to think what Nic's going to bring home next! Speaking of whom, he had to pop out to see a patient—he'll be back soon.'

'I'm already here,' an accented voice announced from behind them, and Kate looked round to see a stunningly good-looking man approach, recognising him from one of the photos with Conor on the pinboard in the staffroom back at Glentown.

Conor sighed in mock disappointment. 'I suppose you want your wife back?'

'When you can spare her,' the dark-haired man agreed wryly.

As Conor released Hannah, Kate was surprised when the men shared a brief, manly hug before the sexy Italian took Hannah in his arms and kissed her.

'Kate, come and meet Nic and Hannah,' Conor invited, drawing her closer, reigniting her awareness as he rested a hand at her waist. 'This is Kate Fisher, our new doctor.'

'Welcome to the madhouse, Kate.' Hannah laughed.

The couple were friendly and fun, but Kate couldn't halt the lingering envy at how clearly they loved each other, how tactile they were, always touching, sharing private glances.

'How were the Pattersons?' Hannah asked, moving to the oven to check on the delicious-smelling chicken that was roasting.

'Sandy is deteriorating,' Nic admitted sadly. 'Alexandra is coping as only she can.'

Hannah drew her hair back from her face and retied the rough ponytail. 'Alex is amazing. She gave up her job as a district nurse in the south of England to come home and care for her dad and keep their small farm going,' she explained to them as Nic left the room. 'I've no idea how she manages everything. We don't know how long Sandy has, but Alex will be there to the last. I don't suppose you have any nurse vacancies coming up, do you?'

Conor shook his head. 'Not right now. Why?'

'As and when the time comes, Alex is going to need a job. We'd take her ourselves, she's terrific, but we're not likely to have any places either. If it comes to it I'll have a word with Kyle and see if there's anything going in Rigtownbrae. Not that

I'd wish anyone on poison Penny. She's a district nurse there,' Hannah explained at Kate's murmur of curiosity, the accompanying grimace implying that easygoing Hannah had a problem with the nurse. Before she could question her, Hannah turned to Conor and moved on. 'Have you seen Kyle lately?'

'Last Monday,' Conor confirmed, getting his wrist slapped as he tried to help himself to a roast potato. Kate hid a smile as he winked at her. 'We went walking.'

'How is he?'

'Low. The whole marriage and pregnancy thing has hit him hard on top of everything else.' A disapproving frown darkened his face and Kate wondered what the story was with his friend, deflated by further evidence of Conor's antipathy to lasting relationships and families.

Nic returned, having changed into jeans and jumper. 'Is Kyle coming to the charity dinner?'

'I doubt it,' Conor replied. 'I don't think he's ready for anything like that. You're both going, right?'

Hannah nodded and smiled at her. 'Are you coming, Kate?'

'I don't know anything about it,' she admitted, feeling uncomfortable.

'Of course she is,' Conor protested.

Kate glared at him. 'I don't think so.'

'She will.'

'Conor—'

'Why not come and see the rest of the menagerie while we wait for lunch to be ready?' Hannah suggested, and Kate was grateful for the change of subject.

'We've had to separate them. The puppy is in the dining room—he and Wallace don't get on. Sparky, Hoppity and Wally are in the living room.'

Hannah opened the door to be greeted by an enthusiastic Border terrier and Kate looked around the spacious room, seeing an elegant ginger cat curled up on a cushion on the settee enjoying the sunshine that streamed through the window.

'This is Wallace,' Nic said, stroking the ginger cat who began purring like a road drill. Smiling, Nic moved across and picked up a small black and white cat which, to her surprise, was wearing a colourful jumper. Amused at her reaction, Nic cradled the little cat in his arms as he continued. 'Meet Sparky. He was badly burned but is healing well. He is the proud owner of many woolly jumpers knitted for him by the local Women's Rural! He must wear them until his skin settles and his hair begins to grow back.'

As Hannah dropped to the floor to cuddle the energetic little dog, Kate turned to watch, listening as the story of how the sandy-haired terrier had come to them was recounted.

'Hoppity had a horrible time with her injuries,' Hannah began, gently stroking the dog's rough coat as it climbed into her lap. 'Nic found her quite by chance. She'd been caught fast in some fencing wire and several times we were scared she might die. She had to have her leg amputated, but it's never slowed her down or stopped her doing anything.' Hannah smiled but Kate felt familiar panic overwhelming her. 'You'd never know, would you? She's amazing.'

Listening to the story of the brave little dog's struggle for survival, Conor glanced at Kate, frowning as he found her staring into space, her face pale. Exchanging a puzzled glance with Hannah and Nic, he moved across to her.

'You OK?' he murmured, grateful that his friends continued to fuss over the animals and chat as if nothing unusual was happening.

Kate, however, didn't respond. She appeared to be in some kind of trance and he took her hand, finding it shaking and cold. Concerned, he gently squeezed her fingers. 'Kate?'

She blinked, slowly focusing on him, the trauma and hurt

in her eyes making him want to take her in his arms and make everything better.

'What's wrong, sweetheart?'

'Nothing.'

That cool, stiff voice again. 'Kate—'

'I'm fine.' She snatched her hand free and crouched down beside Hannah to make a fuss of Hoppity.

He didn't believe her for a second but under the circumstances, with Nic and Hannah looking on, there was little he could do about it at the moment. What had happened? Worried, he thought back over the conversation but nothing struck him as unusual or likely to have upset Kate to that extent. It was clearly nothing to do with being scared of the dog because she was now taking the wriggling body from Hannah and cuddling it against her. The first genuine smile he had seen from her curved her mouth as Hoppity nuzzled inside the long pale blue cardigan she had pulled on over her shirt and jeans and began licking her face, the stubby tail wagging furiously. He shoved his hands in his pockets, cursing himself as all kinds of fool for being jealous of a dog, for goodness' sake! And the smile did crazy things to his insides. He'd waited all week for it and only wished she would look at him like that.

When Hannah and Kate rose to their feet and moved out of the room to go and inspect the puppy they had come to collect for Charlie, Nic gave Sparky a final cuddle and set him back on the floor to play with a toy.

'What was that about with Kate?' he asked with concern.

'I have no idea.'

'She reminds me a little of Hannah when I first met her.'

Interested, Conor glanced at Nic. 'In what way?'

'She is sad inside.'

'I know.'

Nic moved to the settee and made a fuss of Wallace. 'I do not forget you, little man. Come, Conor, we go and see your puppy, yes?' he suggested, leading the way out of the room and closing the door. 'So what is Kate's story?'

'That I don't know—yet.' They paused in the dining-room doorway and his gaze settled on Kate where she fussed over a young tri-colour Border collie. 'But I intend to find out.'

Nic's smile was amused. 'That is the way of it?'

'It is,' Conor admitted ruefully. 'Not that I'm getting very far. But I knew the second I first saw her. I shook her hand and it was like being plugged into the national grid.'

'For me also.' Nic's dark eyes filled with love as he looked at his wife. 'It just took us a while to get there.'

'Kate's worth waiting for. I'm just not sure what to do, how things will work out.'

'Mmm!'

He glanced at Nic and caught his grin. 'What's funny?'

'The mysterious way these things work. Usually you are fighting women off with a stick.'

'It's not like that,' Conor protested with an embarrassed laugh. 'You make me sound like some kind of gigolo!'

Nic's expression sobered. 'Not at all, my friend. They may chase you but I know you never encourage them and seldom follow up on the attention. But now, how do you say, the boot is on the other foot? For the first time you have to do the chasing, no?' he teased in his lilting, accented voice.

'Nic, could you bear to go and check on the chicken while I tell them about puppy?' Hannah called, turning to smile at them and bringing their quiet talk to an end.

'Of course, *cara*.' Nic turned and rested a hand on Conor's shoulder. 'If it is meant to be, so it will be.'

Nic left on his errand and Conor moved further into the room, eager not to be too far from Kate, doubt and uncertainty remaining despite his friend's advice.

'We'd keep him ourselves,' Hannah was explaining and he tried to set his thoughts aside and concentrate on the puppy. 'But aside from the fact that Wally hates him for some reason, working the hours we do and with the new orphan kittens we just don't have the time needed to devote to another dog. And he'll need much more attention than little Hoppity.'

'What happened to him?' Conor asked, as Kate knelt beside the shy young dog. He noticed how calm and gentle she was, taking care not to touch the healing wounds on the thin, gangly body.

Hannah grimaced and looked up at him. 'Believe me, you really don't want to know.'

'That bad?'

'Worse. I've never seen Nic so angry.' Hannah shook her head. 'The puppy was a horrible mess when we first brought him home, Conor, but he has plenty of spirit and a strong will to live. He's been under the care of Alistair Brown, the vet in Rigtownbrae. Alistair is happy for the puppy to go home now as it's just a matter of healing. And time. And plenty of tender loving care.'

'I think he's going to give Charlie a whole new purpose in life,' Conor commented, wishing his job allowed him to keep the dog himself. 'Is he still on medication?'

'Yes, but he's good to go. I've written everything out. Is Charlie going to be able to take him back to Alistair for a check-up in a couple of weeks before transferring to your local vet?'

'I'll take them both myself if necessary,' Conor promised.

'And if it doesn't work with Charlie?' Hannah worried. 'What will happen to the puppy then?'

'I'll let you know every step of the way what happens. I have a plan B, but if it turns out Charlie doesn't come round then I can always bring the puppy back to you if that's what you choose.'

Hannah nodded, her eyes misting. 'I purposely didn't name him because I knew he couldn't stay, but I'm going to miss the little chap.'

'Come and visit. You and Nic haven't been over in a while. We'd love to see you.'

'That would be good.' Hannah brightened. 'We'll organise something. Are you going to cook?'

Conor smiled. 'If you're nice to me.'

'Your fish pie?'

'If that's what you want!'

'Has Conor cooked for you yet?' Hannah asked Kate, and he watched as Kate shook her head, concentrating on the dog.

'I'm just here to work.'

'You have to eat!' Hannah exclaimed, brushing the protest aside and glancing up at him with a querying frown. 'And you haven't lived if you haven't tasted Conor's food.'

Kate looked up then and he smiled at her surprise. Clearly, being able to cook was something else that didn't fit with the distorted image she had of him, along with cuddling babies and rehoming animals. 'I'll be pleased to display my culinary skills any time, Kate.'

Kate kept her eyes averted, not wanting to think about Conor's skills, culinary or otherwise. It was far too dangerous. She was relieved when Nic called them from the kitchen and Conor sauntered off ahead to join him.

'Conor's great, isn't he?' Hannah smiled, casting her a inquisitive glance.

'I don't really know him.' Flustered, Kate focused on the puppy. 'He's a good doctor.'

'That's for sure. The best.'

Her own curiosity getting the better of her, Kate risked some probing of her own. 'Did the two of you date or something?'

'Goodness, no! Whatever gave you that idea?'

'You just seem…close,' she murmured, embarrassed and wishing she hadn't asked.

Hannah sat back on her heels, her expression sobering. 'I didn't date anyone. I wouldn't even have been able to hug Conor a year or two ago,' she told her, and Kate listened in growing horror as the other woman gave her a brief account of what had happened to her at medical school.

'That's appalling, Hannah.'

'It seems another life away now. Thanks to Nic.' A loving, satisfied smile curved her mouth and her green eyes twinkled. 'I was so scared and I put up a fight but he won me round in the end. Thank goodness!' Hannah paused a moment as she settled the puppy back in his large open pen full of toys then turned to smile at her. 'Conor's very like Nic that way.'

'How do you mean?'

'The need to care for anyone or anything they see hurting.' Hannah's words were direct as they both rose to their feet. 'Take it from one who knows, Kate. Don't run too hard: it is so worth being caught. I never imagined I could be this happy, this whole.'

Kate looked away from the other woman's understanding smile, feeling uncomfortable as they walked back to the kitchen. She couldn't imagine ever feeling whole again. As she took her place next to Conor at the table in the kitchen she sensed him looking at her, nervous when his hand reached for hers, warm and gentle as he gave her fingers a brief squeeze.

'OK?'

'Fine,' she fibbed.

She heard his sigh but was thankful that he released her hand, although she remained tinglingly conscious of his presence close beside her.

Lunch was delicious. She listened more than she talked as the conversation and laughter flowed around her, unable to get Hannah's words and experiences out of her mind. As they lingered over coffee after the meal, she met Nic's kind but knowing gaze, seeing the speculation in his dark eyes, relieved when Conor drew the Italian's attention, chatting to him about motorbikes as he flipped through the latest copy of *Performance Bikes* magazine that sat on top of a pile of medical journals at one end of the table.

'You haven't got the new Ducatti?' Conor exclaimed, awe and envy in his tone.

'I have. You want to come and see it?' Conor was already on his feet and Nic laughed as he turned to Hannah. 'You do not mind, do you, *cara?*'

Hannah rolled her eyes in mock despair. 'Bloody motorbikes. And typical men. Leave us poor women to do the washing-up!'

'My wife jokes with you.' Nic smiled with amused indulgence. 'She has turned into something of a biker chick herself.'

'I have not!' Hannah protested at his teasing.

'No? You do not beg to share a ride with me, *innamorata?*'

Kate saw Hannah's cheeks warm in response to her husband's suggestive murmur, the look passing between them leaving her in little doubt at the hidden meanings and sexy undertones.

'Go and look at the damn bike.' Hannah laughed, pushing him towards the door.

Kate discovered that Hannah wasn't the least bothered about clearing the table, turning her attention instead to the kittens who had woken up from their nap. 'Want to hold them?' she invited, and Kate nodded enthusiastically.

'May I?'

'Of course! Take your pick.'

Unable to resist, she chose two grey kittens that appealed to her, one of which had a tiny white patch on its chest. Cuddling them close, she wished she could take them home. They were so beautiful. She glanced up, embarrassed to find the men had returned and Conor was watching her from the doorway. Her heart skittered as he closed the gap between them, perching on the edge of the table as he helped tease one of the kitten's claws free from her cardigan, cradling the tiny body in the palm of one hand. Kate swallowed and dragged her gaze away.

'Hannah, if you and Nic do decide to rehome some of the

kittens, I'd like to take these two girls when they are old enough to leave,' Conor announced, and Kate's eyes widened in astonishment.

'That's great!' Hannah looked delighted. 'I knew I'd tempt you one day!'

Kate's stomach tightened when Conor looked at her, his smile private and warm. 'I'm tempted. Perhaps you could bring them over in a few weeks.'

'A good idea, my friend,' Nic agreed. 'Then we can see you, Kate and the puppy at the same time, no?'

Conor nodded, moving across the room, and after a final cuddle handed the kitten back to Hannah. 'We'll look forward to it. Now, I'm afraid, we ought to be getting back so we have time to call in to Charlie's and put plan A into action. And if that tin contains some of your coconut and lime cake, please can I take a piece home?' he added with a boyish grin.

As a laughing Nic went off to get the puppy ready for his journey and collect up his toys, food and medication, Hannah shook her head, reaching for a knife and a couple of food bags. 'Conor, you are terrible. Don't you ever think of anything but food?'

'Sometimes.' Kate saw the wicked glint of amusement and hot desire appear in those arresting green eyes. 'Quite often of late.'

She couldn't halt her blush, scared she knew just what he was thinking…because she was thinking it, too. And she shouldn't be. Because it was never going to happen. Not with things the way they were in her life. No matter what Hannah said about him, however seductive his appeal, Conor was not for her.

CHAPTER FIVE

'I CAN'T believe how well that went,' Conor exclaimed with relief. 'For one awful moment I thought it wasn't going to work. Charlie was resistant at first but you were brilliant, Kate, bringing him round,' he praised, glancing at her sitting beside him in the car as they headed back to Glentown-on-Firth at dusk. 'Charlie hasn't been so animated in a long time.'

'The puppy's story affected him,' Kate agreed, and he could hear surprise in her voice, see the appealing glow of pleasure on her face.

It had worked perfectly, the shy little dog and the lonely man who had lost his purpose gravitating towards each other as if each recognised the other's need. As he himself recognised a need in Kate and desperately wanted to take care of her. She hadn't wanted to be drawn into conversation on the journey back from Lochanrig, her attention devoted to the puppy she'd had cradled on the back seat. As much as he longed to talk to her, especially about what had happened during that strange moment in Nic and Hannah's living room, the time wasn't right. Again. It was frustrating but he had to be patient if he wanted to unravel her mysteries and find answers to his ever-growing list of questions about this woman.

'Thank you, Kate.' Parking the car at the surgery, he turned to look at her. 'I've fretted over Charlie for so long.'

'Let's hope it works out. I'm glad he took the puppy or I'd have been horribly tempted myself and it wouldn't be possible for me to have him.'

He heard the wistful note in her voice and smiled. 'Me, too. Have you always loved animals?'

'Yes. There were dogs, cats, guinea pigs and all sorts at home when I was young.'

'You had a good childhood?' he probed gently, welcoming the opportunity to keep her talking about herself.

'Very much so.'

Her reminiscent smile made his stomach turn over. She was so beautiful. And he ached to see her smile more, to hear her laugh, to strip that inner sadness away. He was delighted her home life had been so contented but he couldn't help envying her, too, wishing he had known a settled childhood.

'Where are your family from, Kate?'

'I grew up in Surrey. It's just me and Dad now; he lives in London and is a head teacher. My mum died when I was thirteen.'

'You were an only child?' he chanced, dismayed when he saw her tense, her jaw tightening as she looked away from him.

'No.'

The stiff, cold tone was back and she pushed open the passenger door, sliding out before he had a chance to speak. Hell! OK—so this was another no-go area. He ran the fingers of one hand across his forehead. It was like walking on eggshells around her. If she hadn't been an only child but she described her family as being just her and her father now, what had happened? It was something that upset her, that she was not prepared to talk about and, not wanting to end such a good day on a sour note, he left the car and followed her rigid frame down the path. He could tell she wasn't pleased but she didn't object when he followed her inside and up the stairs to the flat, helping as she silently set about making hot chocolate.

He was no closer to learning what troubled her, which made things very difficult in knowing what to say and how to approach her. She was as skittish as a fawn when things became uncomfortable for her. If she was concerned about being trapped or thrust into some kind of relationship too quickly, he would need to keep things casual, take things slowly, not put any pressure on her. If he told her too soon just how far ahead and how permanently he was thinking, she would run a mile. She would certainly think he was some kind of crazy man if he told her that he had known from the first second that he wanted to spend the rest of his life with her. Hell, he probably was crazy.

Frowning, he ran a hand through his wayward hair. She made him feel things he had never felt before. And everything was so out of his control that it scared him. His whole life had turned inside out the moment he had met her and he wanted more than anything to be with her, to take away her pain, to know her in every way possible.

Patience and care, he told himself, spooning chocolate into the mugs. It went against the grain for him, was contrary to his nature, but if it was what Kate needed, he would keep things light and casual and fun for now. The last thing he wanted was to scare her with serious declarations of undying love, certainly no talk of marriage and a few dozen babies—not yet, anyway.

'It'll be good when Nic and Hannah come over in a few weeks' time,' he commented, cupping his mug in his hands, eager to steer the conversation back to safer ground.

Wary brown eyes looked at him. 'You're serious about having the kittens?'

'Of course I am.' Hoping to engineer another opportunity to spend time with Kate outside work, he voiced a brewing idea. 'Perhaps you'd come to the pet shop with me and help pick out the things I'm going to need.'

'Why did you do that? Offer them a home, I mean,' she asked after a moment and he hoped it was a good sign that she hadn't refused outright.

'I couldn't resist them.' It was pretty impossible to resist her, too, especially when she blew on her drink like that and then licked dusky-rose lips with the tip of her tongue. A groan nearly escaped him. He wanted—needed—to kiss her. His hands tightened round his mug. This was torture. He forced himself to focus, watching her expression as he continued. 'Besides, I could see how much you wanted them.'

The thought that Conor may have decided to rehome the kittens because of her made Kate feel warm inside. 'But I'm not going to be here,' she murmured in confusion, trying to keep up the barriers between them.

'You will be for a while. You can share them.'

She shouldn't even think of agreeing but the lure of the kittens was compelling. 'We'll see.'

'I bet you've thought of names for them, haven't you?' He raised an eyebrow, a twinkle in his eyes. 'I'll tell you mine if you tell me yours.'

She couldn't help but smile. He may confuse her and scare her and challenge her, but he could be irresistible sometimes. 'Willow.'

'Smoky.' He smiled back, his expression so warmly intimate that she couldn't breathe.

It wasn't a good idea to get too involved or close to this man. She had managed to escape from the difficult moment over her family, nearly revealing far too much about herself, terrified Conor was going to pursue the subject and that she would have to talk about Wesley. The aching hole opened up inside her as it always did when she thought about her brother. She missed him so much. Loved him. Was so angry with him. So many emotions jumbled up together. And always the guilt. As ever, the memories threatened to rise up and choke her but she battled against the images, at least while Conor was there. They never left her, invading her sleep every night, affecting every part of her life these last months.

'Are you all right, Kate?'

Conor's husky concern shivered through her. He was too observant, too attuned to her moods. Unable to look at him as she tried to mask her emotions, she nodded. 'I'm fine.' Sensing his hesitation, she held her breath, willing him not to question her further.

'I've really enjoyed today,' Conor commented with obvious sincerity, and she sighed with relief as he turned to wash his mug in the sink before leaving it on the drainer. 'Thank you for the idea and for seeing it through with me.'

'That's OK. It was good meeting Nic and Hannah, I really liked them.' Nervous, she set down her own mug as Conor moved closer and she realised her escape route was blocked.

'They liked you, too. But that's no surprise—you're easy to like.'

Her pulse started racing as her gaze slid inexorably to his and she recognised the burn of desire in his green eyes, fighting against her own response. 'Conor—'

'I know you feel it…' The fingers of one hand tucked some strands of hair behind her ear, lingering to brush against her cheek, making her flesh burn 'This amazing connection between us.'

'Maybe. But I'm adult enough not to act on it.'

'Why?'

She paused, taking a deep breath, desperate not to weaken. 'Look, Conor, I'm only here for a short time.'

'We can take things a day at a time, have some fun,' he suggested, which was exactly what she had expected of him.

The knowledge she had been right and he wanted a temporary diversion enabled her to harden her heart and shore up her fragile resolve. As the pad of his thumb began to trace the swell of her lower lip, she caught his hand and removed it, disconcerted when his fingers closed around hers, preventing her withdrawal, holding her palm against his chest so she could feel the rhythmic beat of his heart. Her body throbbed from his touch, his closeness, the subtle earthy fragrance of him wrapping around her. Part of her wished she was the kind of person to throw caution to the winds and enjoy a few commitment-free nights in his bed. She had no doubt she would enjoy it. But she couldn't do it. Not now. Maybe if Darren had never happened, maybe if the last frightful months had never happened, perhaps then she could have accepted the brief, casual fling Conor was offering, satisfying the yearning ache of want inside her.

But those things *had* happened and for now her life was complicated by so many other issues and problems that this was one step too far, no matter how gorgeous and sexy and tempting Conor was. Meeting his seductive green gaze, she called on all her determination and found the strength to pull her hand free, breaking the electrifying contact.

'I didn't come here for this.'

'What did you come here for, Kate?'

The softly voiced question caught her unawares and she regretted again that Conor saw far more than she wanted him to, understanding and compassion mixing with the desire in his eyes. For a moment she thought of Hannah's story and advice. But her own situation was different and she couldn't take the risk with Conor or open herself up to more hurt.

'I'm just here to work. Adding extra variety to your social life is not part of my job description,' she insisted, wishing she could put more distance between them. Although he wasn't physically touching her, he was far too close, far too tempting.

Amusement sparked in his eyes. 'What do you know about my social life?'

'Nothing.' Cursing the flush that warmed her cheeks at his light-hearted teasing, she looked away from him. 'And that's the way it's going to stay.'

'What about your social life?'

'What about it?' she parried, her discomfort increasing.

'Apart from today, you've done nothing but work this week.'

'I'm here to work, nothing more.'

His head tilted slightly on one side, he looked at her, his expression thoughtful. 'This is a great area, you know. There's lots to see and do. It would be a shame not to enjoy some of it while you're here.'

'Conor—'

'I'd be happy to show you around,' he added with a boyish smile.

She sighed, wondering how long she was going to be able to resist his gentle persistence. 'In the unlikely event I need a tour guide, I'll let you know.' Straightening her shoulders, she forced herself to face him and inject some authority into her voice. 'I don't date colleagues.' Not now, she added silently. A shame she hadn't introduced that rule sooner.

'Will you promise me one thing?'

'What?' Kate asked warily, trembling as his hands skimmed up her arms to her shoulders, moving on to cup her neck and face, his thumbs under her chin forcing her to look at him.

'Don't close your mind to this.'

She tried to ignore the way his touch made her feel all shivery and hot and needy. 'It wouldn't work, Conor.'

'You can't know that.' His voice was husky and persuasive, his eyes sincere. 'Take the time you need, but give us a chance. Please.'

'Conor, I—' She snapped off her words, alarmed how shaky her voice was, fearing he had detected the underlying emotion she had been unable to contain.

Frowning, he tipped up her face, gazing into her eyes. 'Tears, Kate?'

'I don't cry,' she snapped, struggling for control.

'Maybe it's time you did.'

Shocked, she stared at him. 'Why?'

'To get it out.'

'What?'

'Whatever it is that's eating you up inside. Something is haunting you, making you sad,' he clarified, shocking her anew with his frightening perception.

Her hands shook as she caught his wrists, trying unsuccessfully to free herself from his hold. 'I don't know what you mean.'

'Yes, you do.' He stroked her face, his fingers warm, caressing, strong yet exquisitely gentle. 'Let me in, Kate. Tell me what's wrong.'

'Nothing's wrong,' she lied, trying to shore up her battered inner defences, feeling closer to letting go than she had in ages. She had been on the ragged edge for too many weeks but she hadn't cried, terrified that if she ever started she would never stop, that all the pain and grief and horror and guilt suppressed within her would come pouring out and swamp her and she would never be able to cope. She had buried everything inside because that was the only way she could function and go on. She was just a novelty, a diversion, something for Conor to tinker with while she was there, but this was her life and she wasn't strong enough to handle it. Sucking in a ragged breath, she injected some steel into her tone. 'I'm not some project for you to fix, Conor.'

'Is that what you think?' He frowned, hurt and puzzlement in his eyes following her terse comment. 'You're wrong, Kate. I want to help because I care, because I want—' He ceased abruptly, looking uncertain. After a brief hesitation he sighed, closing his eyes for a moment as if struggling for control. When he opened them again they were dark green, warm but troubled. 'I'm not going to hurt you. I'd never do that.'

But he would. Because she knew with utter certainty that she could care for him. Impossibly. Deeply. Irrevocably. That was why he was so dangerous and why she had to stop anything before it started. Physically she wanted him with a desperation that shocked her but emotionally she was too vulnerable. It would hurt too much when the time came for her to walk away. A few nights of pleasure would never be enough with this man. No matter how much he planned not to, he would hurt her—terribly—and she was too fragile to survive any more pain.

Staring into his mesmerising green eyes, dreading to imagine what was showing in her own, she knew she had to send him away. 'Forget about me, Conor.'

'I can't do that.'

'You must,' she whispered, trembling under the touch of his hands on her face, seeing his wry smile.

'It's not humanly possible.'

Scared her heart was going to stop, unable to suck air into her lungs, she stood motionless as he bent his head and pressed a firm but brief kiss to her mouth, releasing her before her body could betray her and respond as every atom of her being craved her to do. He held her gaze for one timeless moment, a welter of emotion and desire churning in the depths of his moss-green eyes, then he turned and walked away, leaving her wanting so much more…and knowing she could never have it.

The days passed quickly and Kate was grateful because being busy gave her little time to brood about her problems…including Conor. Which didn't mean she could put any of them out of her head. Somehow she got through each day and coped with her work, but inside she felt as if she was hanging on by a thread. She was relieved to go out on house visits with the district nurses Jillian, Elaine and Ritchie for a few days, learning more about their regular patients and increasing her knowledge of the area.

By the end of her second week Fred decided she was ready to handle visits on her own and however much she told herself she was thankful, an insidious, traitorous part of her missed Conor's company. When he wasn't flirting with her or trying to get her to go out with him, he was funny and smart and always told her such interesting things about the local history and environment. He also gave her confidence about her work. Shadowing him had been interesting…when she could forget about the man and concentrate on what an amazing doctor he was.

Over two weeks after the visit to Nic and Hannah and seeing the rescued puppy settled with Charlie, Kate had still not been able to put the incident with Conor in her kitchen out of her mind. He remained patiently persistent, somehow managing to give her personal space and yet always be around, lounging in her consulting room at the end of the day, talking about work with his mouth while his eyes said very different things. No matter how hard she tried, how many times she told herself she was doing the right thing, being sensible and thinking of her self-preservation, she couldn't forget that too-short, too-chaste brush of his lips on hers.

Impatient with herself, she parked her car outside the surgery at Thursday lunchtime, using her key to unlock the door as she was running late and the staff had begun their break. She left the tray of patient notes behind Reception to be filed away, then set off along the deserted corridor towards her consulting room. She heard a murmur of voices as she approached Conor's room and she glanced through the open door, pausing in shock as she saw him standing just inside, Jenny in his arms. The young receptionist was clinging to him, her face buried against his chest and one of his hands was stroking her blonde hair. Rooted to the spot, Kate was disturbed by the wave of hurt and disappointment that lanced inside her. He hadn't wasted any time, had he? Only days ago he'd been asking her out, wanting her to give things a chance between them, but it seemed he had moved on. Her heart clenched as she heard some of their conversation.

'I don't know what I'll do,' Jenny murmured in distress.

'Let's wait until the result is back and take it from there,' Conor soothed. 'Whatever happens, I'll be here for you.'

The exchange brought back painful memories. Was something going on between Conor and Jenny? Might Jenny be pregnant? Kate's thoughts turned to Darren and what a fool he had made of her, working his way through a string of junior nurses and doctors behind her back, getting at least one of them pregnant, before she had found him in bed with his latest conquest…a former friend and colleague.

When Conor turned his head and saw her, Kate felt embarrassed at being caught, her heart thudding under her ribs as she met his disapproving green gaze. Looking grim, he moved slightly, reaching out to push his door closed with one foot, shutting her out. She felt rejected and hurt. It wasn't her business what he did. She had wanted him to leave her alone, to turn his attention to someone else, so it was crazy to feel like this because he had.

Once in the sanctuary of her own room, she drew in a steadying breath, unable to concentrate on her paperwork or banish her unease at what she had seen. She wrestled with her thoughts, wondering if she should mention the incident to Fred. But what if she was making too much of it? If she was going to do anything, she needed to know the truth—which meant confronting Conor, asking him to explain what had been going on. Nerves made her tense and uncertain. She would think about it some more. See what happened. Her spirits low, she sighed when her mobile phone rang but brightened when a glance at the display told her the call was from her father in London, who was home from school as the Easter holidays had begun.

'Kate, darling! Is this a bad time?' her father greeted her, his familiar voice tightening her chest with emotion.

'No, it's fine. I've just arrived back from home visits.'

'Are you all right?' She heard his deep-seated concern. 'You sound a bit down.'

'Just a difficult day,' she excused herself.

'How are things going? Are you coping?'

She closed her mind to thoughts of Conor. 'I'm doing all right,' she reassured him, with more conviction than she felt.

They talked for a while and Kate found that hearing his news and talking with him had a calming influence on her inner turmoil.

'I rang because I've planned a little surprise, Kate,' her father announced. 'I thought I'd come up tomorrow and stay for the weekend. Would you like that? Would it be convenient?'

'That would be fantastic! Could you really? I miss you so much!' She laughed, relief and happiness welling inside her. She desperately needed to see him, talk with him. 'Tell me what time your plane arrives and I'll arrange to be there to meet you.'

Chuckling at her enthusiasm, her father gave her the details. 'See you soon, Kate. I love you.'

'I love you, too.'

'I presume there's some reason other than for the pleasure of my company that you've come over here, face like thunder, to raid my fridge and wear a groove in my flooring?' Kyle Sinclair drawled, lounging back in an armchair and taking a pull of his drink.

Scowling, Conor paced up and down Kyle's small living room, tense and moody. It was Friday night and all he had done since the previous afternoon had been to pace and fret and torment himself with dark thoughts.

'For goodness' sake, Conor,' Kyle complained. 'Sit down and talk to me.'

'You don't want to hear about it.'

His friend gave a rough laugh. 'I sure as hell don't want to sit here and watch you walking up and down all evening. You've listened to me moan on about the mess I made of my marriage and the dismal state of my love life for heaven knows how many months. It'll make a change to talk about yours. I assume this is about a woman?' he added with a knowing smile.

Conor paused in his pacing to frown at Kyle. 'What makes you assume a thing like that?'

'Because you're not usually so grumpy and I've never seen you like this before.'

'Bloody women.' Sighing, Conor dropped on to the sofa and picked up his own drink.

'Amen to that,' Kyle agreed with feeling, leaning forward to chink bottles. 'So, what's her name?'

'Kate.'

'Your new locum?'

'Yeah.'

Conor's frown deepened as he thought about the previous afternoon. He had been consoling Jenny when he had seen Kate in the corridor. He'd seen right away she had got the wrong idea about what had been going on and it had ticked him off no end, but he had also been concerned by the paleness of Kate's face and the pain in her huge brown eyes. Unable to leave Jenny, who had needed privacy and time, he had gone along to Kate's consulting room afterwards to find out what was wrong and challenge her about her misjudgement of him, but she had been on the phone, making arrangements for a visit from her father. With a busy afternoon of consultations and clinics, plus a minor emergency coming in, he had been unable to talk with her and things had been strained between them since.

'I just don't understand why she thinks the worst of me and has some warped view of me as some kind of rampant womaniser,' he complained to Kyle, recounting the sorry tale, scared all his hopes and dreams were going to come to nothing and he might never win Kate round. If he didn't, he was going to be the one who ended up with his heart broken.

'You know that's not me. I'm not going to tell her one

moment that I want to spend time with her and then be messing with someone else.' He let out a disgruntled huff of breath. 'The signals Kate's been giving are far from clear but she admitted she felt the connection between us, even if she's wary of acting on it. Whether that's because she's here for a short time or because she's been hurt before I don't know.' He slumped back against the cushions, feeling deflated. 'Anyway, that's why I'm here, as nervous and uncertain as a pathetic adolescent.'

Kyle smiled, his dark blue gaze amused but sympathetic. 'Why don't you do something about it if you care for her so much?'

'Like what?' Conor growled.

'Throw her over your shoulder and whisk her off until she surrenders,' his friend teased, earning himself another scowl.

'I'm not the caveman type. And I don't want to upset her.' He dragged his fingers through his hair in agitation. 'I know something's wrong, Kyle, something bad that's making her hurt inside. She needs gentle handling, not have me charging in like some unfeeling macho idiot. Especially if she already has the wrong impression of me.'

'Talk to her, then.'

Conor sighed, setting down his drink. 'Believe me, I've tried, but I don't get anywhere. There are so many mysteries about Kate and it's so difficult to get close to her. It's like peeling back layers of tissue paper but the image underneath never clears because there are always more and more layers.'

'I hope you're not setting yourself up for trouble, Conor. You said before there were unanswered questions about her CV and why she was working with you. Are you really sure about her?' Kyle fretted, leaning forward and resting his elbows on his knees.

'I've never felt like this before, Kyle, but I just know Kate's the one for me. Whether I can ever convince her of that is another matter,' he admitted, voicing his inner fears.

'I'm hardly qualified to give advice when it comes to relationships after the way I've screwed up mine.' Kyle took another drink, a frown on his face. 'But if you feel this strongly, follow your heart. Just be careful. Please. I don't want to see you get hurt, Conor.'

'Kate's an excellent doctor—although she doesn't believe in herself right now—and the patients love her.' Hell, he loved her, but he wasn't confessing that aloud, not while he was so wary of his ground and of ever winning Kate's trust. 'She's smart and kind and she has a true natural beauty. But something is hurting inside her. I can't find out what it is but I can see the building tension and panic in her eyes. She's trying hard to fight it but it's as if she's hanging onto her control like a climber without a safety rope who's gripping the only available hand hold with her fingertips and is starting to slip. I'm scared for her, Kyle. What's going to happen to her when that inevitable fall comes?'

'You be there to catch her, buddy, and you hang on tight.'

'I plan to—' he looked up, meeting his friend's understanding dark blue gaze '—if she'll let me.'

CHAPTER SIX

KATE looked at the surly teenager slumped on the chair by her desk and smothered a sigh. Fred had offered to switch Saturday surgery with her, knowing of her weekend visitor, but she had declined, anxious to pull her weight and having taken the previous afternoon off to collect her father from Prestwick airport. It had been wonderful to see him. This morning he was content to wander along the seafront and explore the village while she worked, but faced with Lindsay Graham and her mother she was beginning to wish she had accepted Fred's offer after all.

Her list had included two patients with gastroenteritis, one with angina, one with allergic rhinitis, one sent to hospital with suspected appendicitis, a baby with earache and a young man suffering the after-effects of a binge-drinking night out, which had resulted in him falling off the sea wall, grazing his face, spraining his wrist and bruising his ego. She had been unable to cure the latter symptom but had recommended a more modest consumption rate and some self-control in future. Self-control made her think of Conor, which was not a good idea, given how close her own was to slipping where he was concerned, even though she had yet to solve the Jenny issue, which had given her two sleepless nights so far. She pushed the thoughts aside and concentrated on the glowering teenager and her over-anxious mother.

'Mrs Graham,' she began again, summoning her patience and resisting the temptation to call for reinforcements. 'I think it would be better if you waited outside while I see Lindsay.'

'But she's my daughter, she's only fourteen! She doesn't have secrets from me,' the woman wailed, and Kate glanced at Lindsay who rolled her eyes as only a teenager could, willing to bet there were all manner of secrets between mother and daughter. 'It's my right to be here.'

'It's my right to some privacy and I don't want you here,' Lindsay riposted rudely.

Rising to her feet, Kate rounded the desk, her tone placating. 'This isn't getting us anywhere, is it? Mrs Graham, please, will you sit in the waiting room for a short while? I'll call you back in when we're ready.'

Kate accompanied the reluctant Sara Graham to Reception where Aileen took charge, assessing the situation at once and organising a cup of coffee for the nervy mother, sitting her down with some magazines so Kate could escape back to her consulting room to face the difficult teenager.

'OK, Lindsay,' she began. 'Let's start again. Can you tell me how you are feeling?'

The girl gave a nonchalant shrug. 'I just feel off-colour. Achy and low. And I've had a sore throat for a while.'

'Is it all right if I check you over?'

'S'pose,' she agreed uncooperatively.

Kate carried out her examination, finding that the glands in Lindsay's neck were a little enlarged and tender. Her throat was inflamed but not infected, and there were characteristic petechiae or small reddish-purple spots in the mouth, which helped confirm her suspicions on the cause of the teenager's problems.

'Has swallowing been painful, Lindsay?'

Again the disinterested shrug. 'It's sore but it hasn't stopped me eating or talking.'

'And you've had some pain? Does that include headaches?'

'Yes,' the girl agreed.

Kate nodded. 'Have you felt feverish at all?'

'A bit. Yes. I'm so tired and haven't any energy to do anything. What do you think it is?'

'I suspect you have glandular fever, Lindsay. I'm sure you feel quite weak and achy but that will pass,' Kate reassured her. The girl's symptoms were fairly moderate and she had detected no enlargement or tenderness of the spleen. 'I need to take some blood to be tested to ensure nothing else is going on.'

Lindsay remained quiet as Kate did a few more routine checks, taking the blood sample before drawing off her gloves and returning to her desk. She was about to explain what Lindsay needed to do when the phone rang.

'Excuse me a moment, Lindsay,' she apologised.

'Kate, I'm sorry,' Aileen said when she answered the phone. 'Conor's here and has calmed Sara Graham down, but she's anxious to return to her daughter.'

'Just a moment.' Kate put her hand over the mouthpiece and looked at Lindsay. 'Do you mind if your mother comes back now we've finished the examination?' She took the half-hearted nod as agreement. 'All right, Aileen. Thank you.'

Sara Graham arrived, with Conor following. Wondering why he was there on his Saturday off, Kate met his gaze, seeing his sympathetic smile, knowing he understood and was waiting to see if there was anything he could do. Rather than seeing it as interference, Kate welcomed the back-up, even if she was very aware of him.

'Sit down, please, Mrs Graham,' Kate said.

'What's the matter with Lindsay?'

'It's nothing very serious,' she said soothingly. 'Lindsay has glandular fever and—'

'But that's the kissing disease, isn't it?' The woman's eyes widened and she swung round to engage her daughter. 'What have you been doing, Lindsay? Have you been seeing a boy?'

Lindsay slouched on the chair. 'Mother, you are so ridiculous.'

'That's only one of the ways of catching it,' Kate intervened, keen to prevent another family dispute.

'See.' Lindsay smirked at her mother. 'Don't you know anything?'

'But, Lindsay!' Mrs Graham fretted.

Conor stepped forward and Kate nodded as he raised a querying eyebrow, welcoming his help. 'Sara, this isn't relevant. Why not let Kate explain what help Lindsay needs now?'

'All right.' The woman glanced up at Conor with a tremulous smile. 'If you think so.'

'Daddy said she only insisted on bringing me so she could flutter her eyelashes at you, Dr Anderson.'

Mrs Graham flushed and turned to remonstrate with her daughter. Kate tried not to look at Conor but couldn't help it, seeing him make a face behind Mrs Graham's back, doing an impossibly good impression of Lindsay rolling her eyes. She looked away, managing to turn her burst of laughter into a smothered cough. The man was outrageous. Clearing her throat, she focused on the notes, composing herself before returning her attention to her patient, trying to ignore Conor's distracting presence.

'Mrs Graham, we'll test the blood sample to ensure there is nothing else. For now Lindsay needs lots of rest and plenty of fluids. I'll prescribe paracetamol for the aches and temperature.'

'What about antibiotics?' the woman fussed.

'Glandular fever is caused by a virus, Mrs Graham. Antibiotics don't kill viruses, they help treat bacterial infections.'

Mrs Graham turned to look at Conor. 'Is that right?'

'Exactly as Kate told you,' he replied, and Kate appreciated the way he insisted the woman take note of her own opinion and not keep questioning him.

'But Lindsay could be ill for months with glandular fever, couldn't she?' Sara fretted. 'What will we do?'

Unable to prevent a glance towards Conor, she warmed at the encouragement in his eyes. 'Most people recover in a few weeks and do not go on to have complications. Lindsay will feel tired during that time, and maybe for a short while afterwards, but she should soon show signs of improvement.' Kate turned to the sulky teenager. 'Lindsay, you must drink plenty of fluids and rest. No rough or contact sports for at least a couple of months. You should both know that it is advisable not to share towels, cups and so on and…' She paused, daring another look at Conor for support, anxious not to spark off another mother/daughter row. 'Avoid close contact and kissing.'

'We need to discuss that,' Mrs Graham stated.

Lindsay rolled her eyes again. 'Mother.'

'Close contact and kissing also means with family and friends,' Conor clarified, hopefully excavating them from another difficult moment.

Kate smiled and rose to her feet, eager to end the torturous consultation. 'Come back and see me in ten days, Lindsay. We'll assess how you feel then, and we'll have the result of your blood test. If you feel worse in the meantime or want anything explained, phone me or come to the surgery,' she added, handing over the paracetamol prescription.

Thankful that Conor followed the Grahams down the corridor to Reception to see them out, Kate sat down and phoned through to Aileen. 'Is that it or do I have anyone else to see?'

'No, pet,' the practice manager reassured her. 'You get yourself home and enjoy your weekend. Tom is here, waiting to take you to lunch.'

'Thanks, Aileen.'

Eager to see her father, she wrote up her notes, logged off her computer and left the room.

* * *

Conor held the door open for Sara and Lindsay Graham, thankful when they took their leave. Poor Kate! Things might be tense between them but at least he'd made her laugh. Smiling, he turned towards the reception desk and saw that Aileen was talking with a distinguished-looking man he didn't recognise. Dark-haired and dressed in casual but smart clothes, the man was tall and trim.

Aileen smiled and beckoned him over. 'Have you met Kate's father?'

Interested, Conor walked across to join them just as Kate came along the corridor. Her smile faltered as she saw them together and Conor's curiosity increased. He waited in silence as Tom enveloped her in a hug, admitting to himself that he had popped in to return some notes, after being called out in the early hours, on the off chance there might be an opportunity to meet Tom Fisher.

'Hello, darling. I gather you've had a busy morning.'

'It's been quite eventful.' Kate drew back and Conor noted her wary expression as she glanced at him. 'Thanks for your help with the Grahams.'

'No problem.'

She looked uncomfortable, stepping closer to her father as if for comfort or protection. Either way, Conor didn't like it. 'Have you been introduced, Dad?'

'Not yet.' Her father smiled, the expression in his brown eyes, so like Kate's, curious and open. 'We were just about to take care of that when you joined us.'

'This is Dr Conor Anderson. He's one of the partners here at the Solway.'

'Delighted to meet you.' Tom smiled, holding out his hand.

Conor shook it, aware of Kate's nervousness. 'Hello, Mr Fisher. It's good you could visit. I hope you enjoy your stay in Glentown.'

'Tom, please. And, thank you, I'm sure I shall have a

lovely time.' Tom turned to Kate and rested an arm around her shoulders. 'My daughter settling in all right?'

'Kate's doing very well. We're lucky to have her with us,' Conor replied, meeting her anxious gaze with a smile.

'Good, good. It's a relief to know she's making friends.' The accompanying smile included Aileen. 'Perhaps you'd care to join us for lunch? We're having a snack at the local pub before going to explore St Ninian's Cave while the weather holds.'

'Dad, I'm sure Conor has other plans.'

Kate's rush to dismiss him brought out his stubborn streak. 'Not at all. I'd be delighted to accept,' he agreed, seeing Kate's expression close.

'Splendid!' The older man turned to Aileen. 'Would you be free to come, too, my dear?'

'Well, I— That's very kind of you,' Aileen murmured, clearly flustered, her freckled cheeks pinkening.

Conor glanced at Kate, pleased that she was more amused than upset by her father's interest in Aileen. He wished he could invite them all to his house for a meal, not having had the chance to take Kate there yet, but he held back, knowing Kate would want to spend time alone with her father that weekend. As they waited for Aileen to collect her things, Conor saw Kate murmuring to her father. He met Tom's gaze and saw the older man's puzzled expression. What had she said?

If he hoped to learn more about Kate's mysterious past over lunch, he was disappointed. They had an enjoyable time but there was no opportunity to steer the conversation towards more personal topics. Tom was warm and funny—it was easy to see where Kate had acquired her intelligence and kindness of spirit—and Conor took to the man straight away, finding someone who shared his interest in the environment and who was keen to learn about local history. Kate seemed on edge throughout their meal and he wondered if she was scared her father would let something slip. Frustration gnawed at him. He still didn't know what the problems were and what Kate was hiding.

When they'd finished their lunch and left the pub, Tom took his arm, allowing the two women to walk on ahead. 'A quiet word?'

'Of course. Is something wrong?' Conor asked, seeing worry cloud the older man's eyes.

'I can see you care about my daughter,' Tom murmured, his gaze following Kate as she talked with Aileen. 'Conor, look after Kate for me.'

'I plan to,' he said, his own concern for her increasing with her father's obvious anxiety.

The man nodded, understanding in his eyes. Conor wanted to ask more about what was going on and why Tom was worried but Kate turned at that moment, looking nervous when she saw them talking together. Saying no more, Tom moved across to join her and, as the pair set off to the Isle of Whithorn to explore the historic site of St Ninian's Cave, Conor walked Aileen home.

'You really care about Kate, don't you?'

Surprised and alarmed at Aileen's perception, Conor glanced at her, about to deny it, then changed his mind. 'Yes, I do.'

'There'll be mourning across the county when you settle down,' Aileen predicted with an affectionate smile, slipping her arm through his. 'I think Kate needs you, Conor. You'd be good together. I hope it works out.'

'Thanks, Aileen. So do I. You seem taken with Tom, if I may say so,' he teased, laughing as Aileen's cheeks flushed with warmth again.

'Isn't it foolish, at my age?'

'Age has nothing to do with it and you have a lot of living ahead of you. You deserve to be happy—Craig would have wanted that.' He had spent many hours helping Aileen through her grief after her husband had been lost at sea while out on a hazardous RNLI rescue five years previously. 'It's time you had someone new in your life. And Tom's a really nice man.'

Aileen looked up at him with a watery smile. 'He is, isn't he? Like father, like daughter, it seems. I'll have to get my matchmaking hat on and give you and Kate a helping hand!'

'You don't think I'm capable of winning her round?' The joking tone hid his inner concern that Kate would never return his feelings.

'If anyone can, it's you.' Aileen's smile was rueful. 'I was thinking that if Kate stayed on here, there would be more chance of Tom visiting.'

'An ulterior motive if ever I heard one!' He waited while she found her front door key and unlocked the door, bending to drop a kiss on her cheek. 'I'd be delighted if things developed for you and Tom, Aileen, but I'll do my own wooing, thanks.'

As Conor headed home, he reflected on the impact the Fisher family had made on the inhabitants of Glentown-on-Firth. He only hoped, despite his nervousness and misgivings, that the outcome for them all would be a happy one.

Monday morning arrived too soon. Kate felt bereft with her father gone, although their final talk before his flight had left her unsettled. The conversation replayed itself in her head as she prepared for work.

'It's been wonderful spending this time with you, Kate.'

'Come up whenever you can,' she said with a smile, hoping to see him often.

Uncertainty shadowed his eyes. 'Would you mind if I kept in touch with Aileen?'

'Of course not.' Her smile widened to a grin. 'I thought you were getting on well!'

'She's a delightful lady. I've left a little something, if you wouldn't mind delivering it.'

'No problem!'

'Your Conor seems a lovely young man,' her father teased.

Kate tensed, her smile fading. 'He's not "my" Conor.'

'I'm sure he'd like to be! He's very smitten with you.'

'I don't think so, Dad.' She cursed the warmth that flushed her cheeks. 'We work together. That's all. He's a good doctor but he's just like Darren, stringing along half the women in the district.'

Her father frowned, the look in his eyes speculative as he watched her. 'Conor didn't strike me as being remotely like Darren. Far from it. I found Conor sincere and caring. Are you not using that as an excuse to prevent him getting close to you?'

Her blush deepened. 'I'm only here for a short time. It wouldn't work.'

'Nonsense. The change in you this last month has been remarkable. You've lost that pallor and you've put some weight back on. What we need now is something to put a sparkle back in your eyes.'

'I'm fine.'

His smile was sad but resigned. 'We both know that isn't true, darling. You've never talked about what happened—and you told me on Saturday not to mention it, that no one here knows anything, not even about Wesley. Do you think that's healthy?'

'There's no need for them to know anything.' She sucked in a deep breath. 'I'm here because I need to know if I can still be a doctor.'

'You're an excellent doctor. Remember the lives you saved, Kate.'

For a moment she closed her eyes, but the mental images of those lives she had not saved were too vivid and she opened them again. 'But it wasn't enough. And now I'm running away.'

'You're not running,' her father scolded, his frown deepening.

She shook her head, denying the comfort. 'What would you call it?'

'Recovering. Moving on. Being human.' His hand cupped her cheek, lingering sadness in his eyes and pain in his voice. 'Don't let this rule the rest of your life, Kate. I don't want to lose you, too.'

'I'm sorry, Dad.'

'It's not your fault, darling. None of it is. Please, believe that.' He drew her into his arms, hugging her tight. 'I love you.'

She hugged him back. 'I love you, too.'

All her life he had been there for her, picking her up when she had fallen or when she had broken up with a boyfriend. But a sticking plaster and some soothing words wouldn't help fix this.

'James was right—this place is good for you. Open yourself up, Kate, let people get close to you. There's nothing to say you couldn't stay here if you wanted to.' Hugging her one last time, he stepped back. 'Whatever you choose, I'll always be here for you.'

By 'people' her father had meant Conor, she knew, and his parting advice nagged at her. Was he right? Was she making excuses to keep Conor at bay? She was uncertain of him and his motives, and she was too fragile for a temporary fling, unable to handle the inevitable pain that would follow. She had enough worries, getting her career back on track and facing all the demons she held so tightly inside. Frowning, she left the flat and walked round to the surgery, finding Aileen at Reception.

'Oh, my goodness!' The older woman flushed as Kate handed her the plant and card from her father. 'How sweet of him.'

'Dad was very taken with you.' She smiled, wondering if anything would come of the friendship.

'Would it be all right…? I mean, would you mind if I sent a note to thank him?'

Amused that the efficient practice manager looked as flustered as a teenager, Kate shook her head. 'Of course not. Dad devoted himself to family and work after my mother died. He has many hobbies and friends, but he's never been interested in another woman before. I'd be delighted for him if he found happiness—and for you.'

'Thank you. You're a lovely lassie.' Aileen's eyes glittered. 'I'll put the plant in the staffroom before the rush starts.'

Left alone, Kate was checking some mail when Jenny took her place at Reception, her face pale, her eyes red-rimmed. Concerned, Kate was wondering whether to intervene when Conor arrived, his green gaze meeting hers.

'Hi.'

'Morning,' she managed, wondering how one word delivered in that husky tone and soft accent could make her shiver with awareness.

'Good weekend?'

'Lovely.'

He nodded, his attention switching to Jenny. 'All right, sweetie?'

'I'm OK.' Jenny found a semblance of a smile for him.

Leaning over the desk, he stroked her cheek with his fingers. 'Good girl. I'll see you later.'

'Eleven-thirty?'

'No problem.'

Picking up his note tray, he headed to his room. Disturbed, Kate collected her own notes and as patients began arriving she followed down the corridor, pausing at Conor's open door.

'Everything all right?'

He glanced up, his green eyes cool. 'Fine, thanks. You?'

'I suppose. I…'

'What?'

She sucked in a breath, nervous about confronting him. 'About Jenny.'

'What about her?' He leaned back in his chair and linked his hands behind his head, the action tightening his T-shirt across the muscled contours of his chest.

'I just wondered if it was…appropriate,' she murmured, feeling foolish.

'Appropriate?'

He sounded more amused than annoyed. 'Do you always—?' She broke off. 'Manhandle' was a bit too strong a word and she searched in vain for something else to say.

'Do I always what, Kate?' he challenged, the amusement fading. 'Jenny is a valued member of staff and a friend.'

'And that's how you behave with your staff?'

'If they are upset and in need of a cuddle, yes.' He leaned forward and rested his forearms on his desk. 'You have some problem with that?'

Kate bit her lip, wishing she had never started this appalling conversation. Why should she care a jot what the wretched man did and with whom he did it? 'No, no problem,' she lied.

'Good.' He paused, enigmatic green eyes darkening, holding her captive. 'Perhaps you'd like to try it some time.'

It was clear what he meant and the suggestiveness in his voice made a knot of longing tighten in her stomach. 'No, thanks.'

Her hackles rose as she heard him chuckle and she continued down the corridor, slamming her bag and notes on her desk. Damn the man. He thought far too much of himself. And she was still unsettled about the Jenny thing. Was it perfectly innocent? Was she just over-sensitive about anything that smacked of impropriety because of Darren?

Throughout a long and varied morning surgery, Conor refused to let his preoccupation detract from his care of his patients, but he was concerned and puzzled about Kate, as well as anxious about his eleven-thirty appointment. He hadn't received the phone call he had been expecting when, his consultations having overrun by thirty minutes, his final patient arrived.

'I've decided to come in on my own if that's all right,' the blond-haired young man commented, closing the door behind him.

'Of course, Mark.' Conor smiled, gesturing towards a chair. 'I've not heard from the hospital yet but I'll ring now you are here. They promised your results would be ready this morning. How have things been this last week?'

'A bit gruesome, to be honest,' he admitted with a grimace, his hands clenched.

Conor nodded sympathetically. 'It must be difficult. Let's hope we can put your worries to rest now.'

Waiting to be connected to the right department at the hospital, he tried to imagine how he would have felt at twenty-four, his whole life ahead of him, moving in with his childhood sweetheart and suddenly finding a testicular lump, immediately thinking the worst. He hadn't wanted to give Mark false hope but, having examined him before fasttracking him to the hospital, he was as confident as he could be that it was not cancer. The ultrasound could confirm his hunch that Mark had either an inguinoscrotal hernia or an epididymal cyst. Smiling his encouragement as the call was answered, he prayed his instinct was right.

'I don't believe it,' Mark murmured for the hundredth time, and Conor smiled as he walked him to the door.

'I'm going to the staffroom to have a drink before my house calls. Come and get me if you want me to explain anything again.'

Looking bemused, Mark nodded. 'Thanks, Conor.'

Relieved the confirmation had come through and Mark's diagnosis was an inguinal hernia in the scrotum, Conor headed for the staffroom, finding Kate and a couple of the nurses there.

'Hi.' He noted how Kate's wary brown gaze skittered away from him. 'Busy morning?'

'The usual. You?' she asked after a pause, looking even more restless as Kristen and Sandra pulled on their coats and headed out for lunch, leaving them alone.

'Busy but good.' He prepared his hot chocolate and turned to watch her. 'Kate, I want to—'

'Conor?'

He saw Kate tense as Jenny's voice reached them. 'In here,' he answered, setting his mug aside just in time as the young receptionist rushed into the room and flung herself into his arms. Delighted for Jenny but frustrated at yet another interruption when he had hoped to talk with Kate, he smiled as Mark appeared in the staffroom doorway.

'We can't thank you enough, Conor.' Jenny smiled through her tears as she hugged him.

'I told you it would be all right.' He let her go and glanced at Kate, who was watching in confusion as Jenny moved back to Mark and wrapped her arms around him. 'I'm delighted for you both.'

'It's definitely not a tumour?' Jenny said, her anxious gaze flicking between them.

Conor was swift to reassure her. 'Definitely not. Mark will need an operation to surgically repair the hernia but that's all.'

'You've been brilliant,' Mark said as Jenny sagged against him. 'It's been a hellish week. Jenny's told me what a support you have been to her.'

Conor risked another glance at Kate who had risen to her feet and was quietly slipping on her coat. 'That's what friends are for.'

'Finding the lump gave us such a scare and I don't know what we would have done if you hadn't helped. It's made us realise how short time could be and what is important.' Blushing, Jenny smiled up at him. 'Mark and I have decided to get married in the summer and start a family as soon as possible.'

'Just be happy—you both deserve it.'

His enjoyment in his friends' news was dampened when Kate slipped out of the room. He wanted to follow her, talk to her, discover what was hurting her, ask why she'd misjudged him, but rudeness prevented him deserting Jenny and Mark, who still had questions for him. But some time soon he was determined to engineer time alone with Kate to try and get closer to her. Her father's words came back to him, the request he take care of Kate. He planned to, but he wished he knew what it was that she needed protecting from, what had happened to cause her such inner hurt and turmoil.

CHAPTER SEVEN

WITH Fred taking a few days off, the rest of the week was frantic. Kate was relieved as it helped her avoid Conor and allowed little time for him to continue his habit of lounging in her consulting room at the end of the day for a chat. She felt guilty about the Jenny situation, having allowed her own past experience and the rumours she had heard about Conor to mistrust him and wrongly judge him. She had been touched by the scene she had witnessed in the staffroom. There were many more depths to Conor than she would have expected. His care of his patients, staff and friends was beyond compare and he gave selflessly of himself. The more she came to know him the less like Darren he seemed, both as a doctor and a person, but that only made her more edgy because it was becoming harder to keep up her barriers and hold Conor at a distance.

As her final patient of Friday morning arrived, Kate noticed that the large young woman who entered the room and closed the door appeared exceptionally nervous and was shaking with fright. Short platinum curls framed a round, attractive face but her skin was very pale and her dove-grey eyes were wide with anxiety. She sat down with obvious reluctance and Kate glanced at the notes. Louise Kerr was twenty-two and rarely visited the surgery. The last notation was from two years ago, written by a Dr Myers, and Kate felt anger burning inside her at the comment written in a tight, neat hand. 'Told patient she was disgustingly obese and not to come back until she lost weight.' Smothering a curse, she pushed aside her fury and disbelief, focusing on the trembling young woman.

'Hi,' she said with a smile, keeping things friendly. 'May I call you Louise?'

'F-fine.'

'Good to see you, Louise. I'm Kate. How can I help you today?'

The young woman shredded a paper tissue in her fingers. 'I didn't want to come, only my friend Julie MacIntyre—you saw her little boy Dominic recently—said how nice you were. I'm sorry to bother you but the pain is getting worse,' she confided after a long pause, the whispered words so soft Kate had to strain to hear her.

'You are not being a bother, Louise,' she said reassuringly, although if the single line in the notes from her previous visit was any indication of the reception the poor girl had received last time she had sought help, it was not surprising she was so scared. 'You are as valuable and deserving as any other patient and I'm here to do all I can to help.'

Fearful grey eyes widened in surprise. 'I— The last doctor I saw here…' Her fingers resumed the shredding as her words trailed off.

'Go on,' Kate encouraged.

'Dr Myers. She said all that was the matter with me was that I was so fat and I was just wasting her time.'

Kate wanted to hit something. Preferably Dr Myers. She sucked in a breath and tried to cool her temper. 'I'm very sorry that Dr Myers failed you, Louise, it must have been a horrible experience being treated so badly and not taken seriously. Did you not feel able to talk to Dr Murdoch or Dr Anderson?'

'Oh, no! Dr Murdoch is a friend of my parents, I've

known him all my life, and I couldn't possibly see Conor—Dr Anderson.'

A flush stained Louise's cheeks and Kate frowned again. From all she had discovered of his skills as a doctor she couldn't believe Conor had been lacking in tact and understanding, too. Before she could voice her concern, Louise continued.

'I mean, Conor's always so wonderfully kind but I'd be far too embarrassed to let him see me. He's so gorgeous,' she confided, displaying all the signs of a smitten female. 'I couldn't talk to him about that sort of thing and definitely never take my clothes off and let him see how revolting I am.'

'Louise, you are a human being, a lovely young lady, and we are here to help you.'

Tears shimmered in her eyes. 'I don't like to waste your time.'

'You are not wasting my time. I can see from your notes that you aren't someone who makes a fuss and you don't seek the help you are entitled to. But you're back today. That's good. It must have been hard for you to come,' she said, working to set the anxious girl at her ease and gain some trust. 'Let's try and make a new start. Begin at the beginning. All right?'

Louise nodded and bit her lip, tears spiking her lashes. As Kate encouraged her to talk, years of bullying, shame and fear poured out along with the health problems, and Kate struggled to keep an upwelling of emotion in check.

'I've tried every diet imaginable, tried exercising, but I'm laughed at if I go to the gym and nothing works long term, more just goes back on again if I lose any weight. It's like a vicious circle. And the more problems I have with my health, the more people taunt me, the less motivation there is.'

'OK.' Kate blew out a breath, her mind sorting out all the issues here. 'Let's deal with one thing at a time. You have problems with your periods?'

Blushing, Louise lowered her gaze and nodded. 'They are

irregular but when I do have one it's very heavy and lasts ages. And the breaks between are getting shorter and shorter. I never know what is going to happen or when, but when it starts, it's just awful. It's got so bad I can't hold down a job and I can't leave the house for days sometimes.'

'Do you have any pain with them?'

'I have pelvic pain most of the time,' Louise admitted, her voice a little stronger as she talked. 'It's hard to describe but I feel it deep inside, all around the pelvis and through my lower back.'

Kate nodded, making notes. 'And is that the pain you mentioned earlier, the pain that has become so bad you were brave enough to come here today?'

'No,' Louise admitted, lowering her gaze.

'Tell me about this other pain, Louise.'

As she ran through the symptoms, her eating patterns and the times of pain, the more Kate suspected gallstones. Louise was very young but all the signs were there. There was so much going on she wasn't sure where to begin.

'Is it all right if I do a few checks, Louise? I'd like to test your blood pressure,' she explained, taking things one step at a time so as not to alarm her, careful not to cause embarrassment as she substituted a larger cuff to fit Louise's arm. There were no previous readings to compare with but Kate was concerned that the level was on the high side and made a note to keep a regular watch on Louise's BP over the coming months. She checked the girl's eyes, unsurprised to find the conjunctivae pale. 'Is it all right if I take a blood sample?'

'Why do you need to do that?'

'Losing so much blood could make you anaemic and that would make you feel low and tired. A simple test will confirm it and a course of iron tablets will help. I want to check your hormone levels, see if something there is adding to the problems with your periods,' she explained, preparing what she needed, making a mental note to check thyroid function, too.

'All right,' Louise agreed.

'Thank you.' She set about taking the blood sample and smiled as she finished up. 'All done. You are doing really well, Louise. I'd also like you to provide a urine sample for me. No hurry right now, but I'll give you a sample bottle and you can drop it in when you can. I need that because I want to ensure there is nothing there that we don't know about,' she explained, thinking about any signs of diabetes.

'OK.'

Knowing this was going to be difficult, she tackled the next problem. 'I don't want to rush you, but I would like to examine you, Louise, so I can help find out what's making you so uncomfortable. Will you let me do that?'

'I don't know if I can.' The words were whispered, the grey eyes filling with tears once more. 'Do I h-have to?'

'I would never make you do anything against your will, Louise, but we need to sort out this pain. I'm not going to think anything and I'm definitely not judging you. I just want to help. Please?'

When Louise finally agreed, Kate kept things as business-like and dignified as she could so as not to cause more stress than necessary, leaving any question of an internal exam for when Louise was more trusting and relaxed. Keeping a blanket drawn up to Louise's waist, Kate felt her abdomen, finding tenderness in the upper-right quadrant. It was true that Louise's shape made it hard to feel but, combined with the other reported symptoms, she was pretty certain of her diagnosis.

'OK, Louise, you've been great. You can straighten your clothes now and sit down when you are ready.' Kate gave her some space and returned to her desk, jotting notes as she waited for Louise to rejoin her. 'Now, then, one thing at a time. We'll test for the anaemia and hormone levels, plus monitor your thyroid activity, and I'll check the urine sample as soon as you provide it,' she said, handing over the sample pack which the young woman slipped into her bag. 'While we wait for the test results I'm going to start you on a course of iron tablets and I'll write you a prescription for a low-dose contraceptive pill and we'll use it temporarily to begin to get your periods under control.'

'What could be making them bad?'

'I'm not sure yet.' Kate smiled in reassurance, anxious not to worry Louise until they knew more but considering the possibility of endometriosis or fibroids. 'When we have a clearer idea what's going on, we'll probably change you to a different medication but we'll wait for the results and see how the Pill helps you in the short term.'

'Gosh,' Louise murmured, tucking the prescription into her bag to join the sample pack.

'I know, it's a lot to take in.' Kate gave her a moment to absorb what she had heard. 'Now, about your upper abdominal pain, nausea and so on. I think you might have gallstones, Louise. It's a horrible pain, but we can do something about it. I do need to refer you to the hospital, though, to have a scan.'

Grey eyes widened in alarm. 'Oh, I can't do that!'

'It's painless, Louise. They just put some gel on your skin and the ultrasound can look inside and see if you have the stones or not.'

'It's not that. I—'

As the young woman broke off, Kate nodded, understanding her fear of being examined. 'I'll contact them myself and explain the situation, I promise.'

'And if I do have these stones?' she said after several moments.

'We'll cross that bridge if and when we come to it. The important thing now is to know what we are dealing with.'

Louise nodded, her fingers twisting together in agitation. 'I'll try.'

'Good girl. In the meantime, there are things you can do about the attacks of pain. With gallstones, it helps if you cut out fatty foods because they aggravates the condition. I'll give you a leaflet about it. Anything you can do to remove trigger foods will make a difference to the pain.'

'Really?'

Kate smiled at Louise's surprise. 'Really. I want you to take one iron tablet three times a day—they might make you a bit constipated so make sure you eat plenty of fibre while you are taking them and lots of vitamin C, which helps your body absorb the iron. Eat plenty of fruit and vegetables, whole grains, white meat, fish, and cut back all you can on dairy products and fatty foods,' she advised, handing over the leaflet.

'I'll do that.'

'Is there anything you want to ask me, Louise?'

Frowning in consideration, she shook her head. 'No. I don't think so.'

'OK, we'll leave it there today. You've done really well, Louise, I'm so glad you came to see me. Things will get better, I promise.'

'I don't know what to say,' the young woman whispered. 'You've been so kind, I never expected…'

'You have every right to expect. I want you to come and see me again in a week, but if you have any concerns in the meantime or any pain that worries you, just call me. And you'll drop that sample in for me?' Kate stressed, walking with Louise to the deserted reception area.

'I will. Thank you so much.'

Kate gave her shoulder a gentle squeeze. 'It's no problem, honestly.'

Surprised how late it was and discovering everyone had gone to lunch, Kate unlocked the front door, seeing Conor approaching from the car park.

'Hi, Louise,' he said. 'We haven't seen you for a while. Everything all right?'

Kate noticed Louise blush scarlet at Conor's attention and warm smile.

'Yes, thank you. Kate's been lovely.'

'That's good.'

She almost flushed herself at the approval and slow burn of heat in Conor's green eyes as his gaze met hers before he walked on into the building. Pulling herself together, she held the door open for Louise. 'I'll see you soon.'

She watched the young woman walk away, head down, shoulders hunched. There would be a lot of work ahead on all kinds of issues and she wanted to ensure that Louise would be able to seek help from one of the other doctors when she herself was no longer there. Frowning at the welter of emotions churning inside her at the thought of leaving Glentown-on-Firth, she locked the door and returned to her consulting room, staring down at her notes, her chin resting in her hands. She was seething with fury at the treatment Louise had experienced in the past, shocked at the lack of care and understanding demonstrated by Dr Myers.

A brief tap on the door was the only warning she received before Conor came in. She was amazed when he handed her a pack of sandwiches and a fresh fruit smoothie.

Disconcerted, she met his gaze. 'What's this for?'

'You missed lunch.'

'I can't stop now,' she said, unsettled by his thoughtfulness. 'I have a couple of house calls to catch up on before afternoon surgery.'

'I've done them.'

To her chagrin, he sat himself on her desk, far too close, far too familiar. 'You have?'

'Mmm.' Feeling him assessing her, she concentrated on the refreshing tangy drink. 'It was clear you needed time—Louise was here over an hour—so I did the calls.'

'I'm sorry,' she responded, unable to keep the stiffness from her voice.

'There's nothing to apologise for, it wasn't a criticism,' he said, his voice warm and concerned. 'You gave Louise what she needed.' He paused and she couldn't stop herself looking up at him, his nearness making her pulse race. 'So, what's the story? Everything all right with Louise?'

'Yes,' she lied. Green eyes studied her as he waited and she sighed. 'Sort of. Why?'

'What's wrong?'

Did the wretched man always have to read her so easily, know what she was thinking? She shook her head in denial but he wasn't buying it.

'Kate, talk to me.'

'What was Dr Myers like?'

Conor let out an exclamation of surprise. 'I've not heard her name mentioned in a while.'

'And?'

'She was hopeless,' he admitted, frustration evident in his tone as he folded his arms across his chest. 'Well qualified on paper but she hadn't a clue about community medicine or interacting with people. She didn't last more than a couple of weeks.'

'Well, she left her mark,' Kate informed him, thinking of the time it had taken poor Louise to find the courage to come back for help.

'What do you mean?'

Kate told him the bare bones of what had happened, seeing the thunderous look on his face, listening to the angry tirade against Dr Myers as he slid off the desk and paced her room. 'I had no idea.'

'It's not your fault, Conor. How could you have known?'

'Poor Louise.' Swearing under his breath, he dragged the fingers of one hand through his wayward hair and she looked away, dismayed how much her own fingers itched to follow the path of his. 'Why didn't she come to me or Fred?'

Reining in her inappropriate thoughts, Kate frowned, unsure how much to tell him because she guessed Louise wouldn't want Conor to know about her crush on him. 'It's been hard for her, Conor. I think she finds it easier talking to a woman.'

'I'm glad you were here for her.' His voice husky, he closed the gap between them again. 'Thank you.'

Staring into mesmerising green eyes, she feared she was in danger of losing something of herself. 'Just doing my job,' she replied, unable to look away.

'No. It's more than that. And I appreciate it. Louise and your other patients are very lucky.'

She felt herself flushing at his compliment. 'Thank you. Um, do you know who would be likely to do the ultrasound when I refer Louise?' she asked, trying to restore order to her thoughts and banish the unwanted awareness of Conor as a man.

'Dee Miller would be your best bet,' he advised, making her nervous as he perched himself back on her desk, far too close for comfort.

'When we have an appointment confirmed I thought I would ring and have a chat to explain Louise's genuine anxiety. I hope they'll be a bit gentle with her.'

'Good idea.' His approval and understanding warmed some of the chill spots deep inside her, places she'd never expected to feel anything again. 'I'm sure they'll do all they can to put her at ease. Maybe you could persuade Louise to have an ultrasound to check for fibroids at the same time and save her the anxiety of two visits.'

Kate wasn't sure if Louise could handle more than one thing at a time. 'I'll think about it.'

'There's an excellent female gynae consultant at the county hospital. Let me know if you want me to introduce you.'

'I'll remember that, thanks.'

Kate was amazing. Conor couldn't stop looking at her, wishing he could linger there all day, talking with her. It was true he'd had reservations about her appointment—was still concerned on a personal level about her secrets and inner pain—but she was an incredible doctor, the best locum they had ever had. He was livid about Dr Myers, concerned what else the woman had done in the short time she had been with them, and he planned to review as many of the cases she had handled as possible to ensure no one else had been suffering in silence, as Louise Kerr had done. Kate was the complete opposite of Dr Myers—caring, thoughtful, dedicated. What she had done for Louise today had been important, special. He planned to do everything he could to make Kate a permanent fixture, not just at the practice but in his life…his perfect partner.

'May I cook you dinner tonight?' he asked, watching as she picked at her sandwich.

'I don't think so.'

A pout of dissatisfaction shaped his mouth. 'Why not?'

'I have things to do.'

'What things?' he pressed, unwilling to be fobbed off.

Her nervous glance flicked over him and away again. 'Private things.'

'Right.' He folded his arms, amused at her feeble excuse, noting the tinge of colour wash her cheeks. 'I'd really like to cook for you.'

'It wouldn't be a good idea, Conor,' she insisted, her voice flat and guarded.

He raised an eyebrow, teasing her. 'I'm not going to poison you.'

'I didn't mean that.'

'Kate, am I paying for someone else's sins?'

She looked shocked and wary as she glanced up in response to his softly voiced question. 'What you mean?'

'You labelled me from day one. I don't know why. But the image you have of me is wrong.' Shifting, he slid his hands under his legs, heat flooding his veins as he caught the way her gaze lingered on his thigh before she swallowed and closed her eyes. He might be as frustrated as hell but it gave him a measure of satisfaction to know Kate was not as unaffected as she pretended to be. 'You thought something was going on between me and Jenny, didn't you?' he continued, seeing her flush. 'And that wasn't the first time. So why do you always think the worst of me?'

He thought she wasn't going to answer, she was silent for so long, then she sighed and pushed the remains of her sandwich aside. 'Let's just say I knew someone who cut a swathe through the medical and clerical staff.'

'He hurt you.'

'At the time. I learned the lesson, though.'

'What lesson?' He wished she would look at him so he could gauge her expression. 'That all men are the same?'

She shook her head, one hand moving to flick a fall of hair back behind her shoulder. 'Not to get involved with colleagues.'

'Doesn't that rather depend on the circumstances and the person?' he challenged softly.

'Conor…'

As her voice trailed off, he reached out and caught her chin, tipping her face up so he could look into her eyes. Clearly her past experience was making her wary about trusting him now but he could see that this issue was not the main cause of her inner pain and the loss of professional confidence. Unfortunately they were pressed for time now and, hearing staff moving along the corridor, he reluctantly released his hold on Kate's silky-smooth skin and slid off her desk. He'd made some headway today—at least he knew why she was wary of embarking on a relationship—but there was still a long way to go if he was ever going to get beneath the surface and discover the secrets Kate kept hidden.

CHAPTER EIGHT

BEFORE dusk fell on the Saturday after Easter, Kate strolled along the sandy beach that edged the curve of the bay to where the ground rose up to a craggy headland. After a wet, grey week today had been sunny, but the April air was chilly and she drew her coat around her, sinking her hands deep into her pockets. Apart from the couple of days her father had been there, she had not yet explored this beautiful and varied landscape. Her gaze strayed out over the Solway Firth. On a clear day, she could see the Cambrian mountains on the English side to the south. Aside from a couple of people walking their dogs, the beach was deserted. She welcomed the solitude after the hectic week, although time alone with her troubled thoughts was not always a good thing. What had possessed her to reveal anything to Conor? Far from putting him off, her explanation had intrigued him further. Stopping for a moment, she breathed in the clear fresh air.

The sudden arrival of an enthusiastic and very wet dog startled her. The black-and-white cocker spaniel dropped a disreputable-looking tennis ball at her feet and grinned up at her, tongue lolling as it panted happily, stubby tail wagging twenty to the dozen.

'Hello there.' She smiled, bending to stroke the dog. 'Where did you come from?'

She glanced around to see if the owner was in sight, alarmed when she recognised Conor approaching. Oh, help. Her insides tightened at the sight of him dressed in a pair of faded jeans that lovingly hugged his legs like a second skin and a well-worn waxed jacket pulled over a fleecy jumper. He was impossibly good-looking. As he neared her, she noticed the frayed rip in one leg of his jeans, which afforded a tantalising glimpse of his thigh. Her traitorous fingers itched to touch, to explore. She turned to avoid his gaze and continued walking, unsurprised when he fell into step beside her, and she watched out of the corner of her eye as he threw the ball, the dog bounding away to retrieve it.

'Hi, Kate.'

The warm huskiness of his accented voice raised prickles on her skin. 'Hi. Have you suddenly acquired a dog?' she said, cursing her inane words.

'Sadly not. This is Toby,' he said as the dog raced back to them. Conor threw the ball once more. 'He belongs to old Dave Mackay in the village. Dave can't get out much now so he lets me borrow Toby for a walk.'

Making out that Dave was doing him the favour and not the other way round, which was typical of the Conor she was coming to know and which made him all the more dangerous to her resolve to stay away from him. They walked on for a while in silence, enjoying the tranquillity, and she indulged herself, watching Conor play with Toby. Concerned things were becoming too companionable, she decided to leave Conor to his walk with the dog and turn back before she reached the rugged headland where the rocky cliff sloped down to meet the sea.

'I'm going to head home now.' She halted, raising a hand to push her windblown hair out of her eyes.

'I'll walk back with you.'

Her heart thudded. 'You don't have to do that.'

'I know.' Conor faced her, the expression in those incredible green eyes far too intimate. She held her breath as he reached out to catch a wayward strand of hair, his fingers brushing her skin as he tucked it behind her ear. 'I want to. Besides,' he added, fingers lingering before he turned and whistled for the dog, 'I don't keep Toby out too long. He's Dave's only company.'

She bit her lip to silence further protests as they retraced their path back along the shore towards the village, which nestled in the wooded glen at the foot of the hills.

'What are you doing tomorrow?' Conor asked, throwing the tennis ball for Toby again.

Kate glanced at him warily. Did he never give up? 'Just some things at home.'

'It's supposed to be a beautiful day, according to the weather forecast. A shame to spend it all indoors.' He slipped Toby's lead back on as they moved up off the beach. 'If you like walking, you ought to see Glen Trool while you're here and get up in the hills.'

'It sounds interesting. I'll do that some time,' she agreed, keen to put distance between them.

'I'll pick you up at nine tomorrow. Dress warm and wear walking boots if you have them.'

Shocked, she stared at him, disconcerted by the teasing smile and the knowing look in his green eyes. 'But I—'

'See you in the morning.'

Without giving her a chance to respond, he dropped a brief kiss on her startled lips and then strode off up a side road, Toby trotting beside him. Bewildered, she watched his retreating figure, the fingers of one hand pressing to her mouth where the feel of his gentle kiss lingered. Pulling herself together, she walked the short distance to the surgery, anxious for the sanctuary of her flat above. Conor made her feel out of control and she didn't like it. Why was he so determined to spend time with her? She wouldn't go tomorrow. Of course she wouldn't. She'd make up an excuse and put him off.

Avoiding him would be much better for both of them. Feeling better about things, she made herself some hot chocolate and settled down to catch up on her medical journals. Everything would be fine. She would tell Conor she had changed her mind.

So why did she find herself sitting beside him on Sunday morning as he drove through the forest to a car park by Loch Trool? When Conor had arrived she had opened her mouth to tell him she wasn't going but her protests had been silenced by his boyish enthusiasm and her common sense had vanished—again. There had been a difficult moment when she had put on her walking boots, her gaze drawn to the dust of Africa that still lingered in the grooves and crevices from the last time she had worn them.

'What's wrong?'

'N-nothing.' Fingers shaking, she had tied the laces, pushing the memories aside, her throat tightening when she had straightened and her gaze had clashed with his, the green eyes reflecting a disturbing mix of concern, puzzlement and interest.

Conor eased her nerves by keeping off personal topics on the drive, telling her about the area they were visiting, the history of the Galloway hills, the Covenanters and Robert the Bruce, the bloodshed of centuries past hard to imagine with the tranquil beauty around them.

'What on earth have you got in here?' she complained as she helped heave his rucksack out of the boot of the car.

Green eyes shone with amusement. 'A few essentials. And a picnic lunch.'

'You said a walk, not a day trip!'

'You'll love it,' he promised. 'Everything we'll need is in there and I've left note of our route and expected return time.'

Even the weather had obeyed him. It was a warm spring day, the sky was clear and the sun shone over some of the most glorious scenery she had ever seen. Conor shouldered his pack as if it weighed nothing and gestured across the car park.

'Before we head up in the hills, come and see Bruce's Stone,' he suggested, leading the way a few hundred metres down the path and out to a small promontory where the stone stood.

'Wow,' she breathed, taking in the view across the loch.

'Lovely, isn't it?' Conor smiled and she was far too aware of his presence beside her. 'Wait until we get higher up.'

Conor breathed in the freshness of the air and tried to remember when he had last felt so contented. He didn't push the pace, aware Kate wasn't used to this, delighted to spend time with her, especially being able to share one of his favourite places. It was clear she had been going to back out that morning but he'd managed to breeze it out. There had been a peculiar moment when she had put on her boots. She had gone into a trance, just like that day at Nic and Hannah's, but the dark inner pain in her eyes when she had looked up had torn at his gut. Now she seemed to be enjoying her surroundings. After her initial fears that first day she had settled beautifully into her doctor role and everyone loved her, patients and staff alike. Outside work she held something of herself back and he knew she refused offers of social company, not just his own. She wasn't unfriendly, just private and guarded, protecting herself. Kate intrigued him more with every passing day.

'The Merrick is the highest mountain in south-west Scotland,' he told her when they stopped for a break. 'In fact, the Galloway hills are known as "The Highlands of the South".'

They walked on, pausing often to admire the views, and he pointed out things of note, finding Kate an avid listener. She showed a keen interest in everything, asking questions as they passed from the glen to the uplands, the glacial landscape becoming more remote, changing to moorland and mountains. He was surprised to discover that Kate wasn't as physically fit as he'd anticipated, so he kept things gentle and watched her closely to ensure she was comfortable. Again he remembered how pale and stressed she had been when she had first arrived in Glentown. She had more colour now and she had put on some weight, which certainly suited her, he decided, casting an appreciative glance over her delicious curves. He wondered again if she had been unwell. More than once he noticed her left hand stray to her side and he paused as they passed Loch Neldricken to give her another chance to rest before they headed on along the slope of Ewe Rig, enjoying the solitude, and then began the harder climb towards Redstone Rig.

Finding it hard to catch her breath on the steepest parts, Kate was grateful that Conor kept the pace gentle, although she envied the effortless way he moved up the trail ahead of her. She hadn't realised how much the events of recent months had taken out of her but now she felt her legs would seize any moment. She had healed physically but had not done much exercise in the last weeks and now she was feeling it. Maybe this had been a touch ambitious. But saying so would require an explanation and that she couldn't give, so she kept going. Unconsciously her hand clasped her left side below her ribs where an ache twinged.

'Something wrong, Kate?'

Alarmed that Conor had seen her action, she removed her hand. 'Nothing,' she lied, but she could tell he didn't believe her and was both curious and concerned. 'Just a stitch,' she fabricated, hoping to divert his attention and head off any further questions.

'A bit out of practice?' he teased, going along with her subterfuge as he shrugged off his rucksack and waited for her to join him. 'We'll have to make sure you get more physical activity while you're here.'

She could feel a flush colour her already heated cheeks at

the wicked glint in his eyes. She could just imagine the kind of physical activity he had in mind and no way was that going to happen! 'I'm fine.' At least she had diverted him from anything else that might be wrong.

'Well, what do you think?'

'About what?' She propped herself against the nearest available outcrop for support.

'Him,' Conor elaborated, pointing towards a rock formation which, in profile, created the perfect likeness of a wizened, aged face. 'The Grey Man.'

Momentarily blind to the breathtaking scenery all around her, Kate stared. 'You brought me all the way up here to see a rock?'

'It's not just a rock.' He laughed, disgustingly unflustered. 'Isn't it fabulous?'

It was impressive, she had to concede, her equilibrium returning after a short rest. Her father would love it, too. Conor was in his element here. He not only knew so much about the landscape and history but she realised how much of his rare free time he spent walking in the hills and forests or along the coastal paths, either alone or with his friends and fellow GPs Kyle and Nic. Did that mean his other ladies came here, too? Not that she was one of them, she added with a frown. But if he worked so hard, walked so much and played other sports, how did he have time for all his liaisons? He'd been to visit Lizzie in hospital, done other favours for people, but she couldn't remember hearing of Conor actually dating anyone in the whole time she had been there. So was she wrong about him? If she was, it made him more dangerous and her more vulnerable.

Conor found a sheltered spot and they settled down to their picnic lunch, enjoying the sunshine and the incredible views. Ribbons of gossamer cloud streamed around the highest peaks, some of which still had a coating of snow, looking as if some giant celestial hand had dusted them with icing sugar. They chatted about the scenery, the remote tranquillity inspiring awe and reverence, and then talk turned to work and Conor mentioned Fred.

'He's been fabulous to work with.' Conor leaned back, resting on his elbows. 'But he has been slowing down these last months and I worry about him. I know the day will come, probably quite soon, when he'll decide to go part time or give up completely. Not that I begrudge him his retirement but I'll miss him.'

'I was very sorry to hear about his wife.'

'Yeah. He's never picked up from losing Annette,' Conor confided, his voice wistful and sad. 'It was a bad time.'

'What will you do when Fred retires? Practice-wise, I mean.'

He glanced at her, his eyes hooded. 'I'm hoping my perfect partner will never want to leave.'

Kate looked away, unnerved by the edge to his voice, unwilling to acknowledge how much this place and these people had come to mean to her in just six weeks, how hard it was going to be for her to walk away when her contract ended. Her father had hinted she could stay on if she wanted to. Maybe she could have, if things had been different… But they weren't, so there was no point dwelling in fantasy land.

'I'm sure you'll find someone suitable when the time comes.'

She drew her knees up and wrapped her arms around them, gazing unseeing at the hills, not wanting to think about who would come after her to fill her shoes on a permanent basis and find their niche in this wonderful community…and be Conor's partner. Unsettled by her thoughts, far too conscious of him close beside her, she began packing away the things then scrabbled to her feet.

Taking a different route, they began the walk back down in silence, a growing tension fizzing between them. When she skidded on some loose shale, Conor was there to catch her, his arm strong and secure around her waist as he held her far too close for several breath-sapping moments before she managed to extract herself and put some distance between them.

'Thanks,' she mumbled, unable to look at him.

'No problem.'

His own voice was rough, letting her know he was affected and aware. This was ridiculous. She swallowed, sucking in a few deep breaths, trying to regain some control as they continued the descent, surprised when Conor took her hand to help her over the rocky path down the Buchan Burn. He failed to release her, his fingers linking with hers as they paused to look at the waterfall. Her traitorous body reacted to his touch, her pulse racing, her flesh tingling, her hormones rampaging out of control.

She was relieved when they reached the car park. The walk had been wonderful, the views amazing, and she wouldn't have missed seeing any of this for the world. The problem was her awareness of Conor, her dwindling willpower to keep him at bay. Thankful for some respite, she leaned against the car and waited while he stowed his pack in the boot, expecting him to continue round to the driver's side to unlock the doors. So when he walked towards her, moving in close, her heart began beating a wild tattoo in her chest.

He was way too close. Kate swallowed, nerves jangling inside her. He put his hands on the car roof either side of her head, holding her captive. She couldn't breathe. Mesmerising green eyes were dark and intent. Whatever fragments of self-control she had left were shot to pieces. If he touched her now she was going to explode. Scared how vulnerable she was to him, her hands rose to his chest in a futile effort to maintain some distance between them.

'Conor—'

'I enjoyed myself today.'

'Um, yes, it was good. Walking,' she managed, her voice far too husky and unsteady.

His sultry gaze dropped to her mouth as she moistened dry lips. 'I meant being with you.'

'I don't think—'

'Good,' he interrupted, brushing the pad of his thumb across her mouth to silence her. 'Don't think, Kate. Just feel.'

The first touch of his mouth on hers threatened to make her breathless all over again. His initial kiss was hesitant, as if assessing her reaction, his lips warm and coaxing as he encouraged a response. Not that he needed to. Much to her despair, her body was betraying her brain. No matter how much she denied this, her mouth was taking on a will of its own as her lips parted in shameless invitation, seeking more, demanding more.

She heard Conor's soft moan as he gave her what she craved. One arm slid round her waist and drew her closer against him, while his other hand sank into her hair, cupping the back of her neck as he changed the angle, deepening the kiss, moving from teasing gentleness to heated demand. It wasn't fair. He was far, far too good at this.

She whimpered, her whole body on fire as Conor sucked erotically on her lower lip before his tongue slid into her mouth, placing teasing strokes on hers, encouraging it to join in a sensual dance. The passion erupted between them, flaring out of control. It wasn't enough. She wanted more, wanted everything, needed to climb right inside his skin.

Forgetting where they were, her hands burrowed under his jacket, her fingers pulling restlessly at the hem of his jumper and the shirt beneath, impatient to feel the touch of his skin, finding his back warm and supple, the muscles flexing. His earthy scent made her light-headed, his taste made her feel drunk. It had been a while since she had been with a man, been held and kissed. Not that she'd ever been kissed like *this* before. It was all heat and fire and sensual seduction. Slow, deep, thorough, unbelievably sexual as he made love to her with his mouth. And she wanted more. Much more.

Conor shifted even closer, the length of his athletic body pressing along hers, leaving her in no doubt about the extent of his arousal. But he still wasn't close enough. She moved more firmly against him, desperate to ease the terrible burning ache that raged inside her, moaning in relief as he slid one leg between hers. Too needy to care what she was doing, she wantonly rubbed herself on his thigh, matching the suggestive rhythm of his movements. The hand at her waist slid down to cup her rear, pulling her tighter. He tilted his chest to one side and she gasped into his mouth as his other hand burrowed under her jacket to shape the fullness of her breast, her hardened nipple urgently seeking his palm, a fiery ache of sensation short-circuiting to her womb.

She wanted to tell him there were too many clothes between them but no way on earth could she break this earth-shatteringly sensual kiss. Their mouths fitted like two halves of a whole, lips clinging, caressing, taking and giving everything, tongues tasting, teasing, joining in an impassioned exploration. But the urge to satisfy the burning need was becoming too much to bear. Her fingers moved more insistently on his back as she lost herself in the magic of getting physical with Conor Anderson, sharing what was the most intensely erotic and arousing experience of her life. Just when she was unable to help herself squirming more blatantly against him, her hands working round to the fastening of his jeans, Conor was pulling away.

'No!' Unaware of what she was doing, she protested, trying to hold onto him. 'Please.'

His hands cupped her face and she struggled to open her eyes, staring dazedly into the heated green depths of his, her heart racing, each ragged breath searing her lungs. He held her away from him, fighting for control. Part of her wanted to weep because he had stopped and she needed him so badly, while another part of her was ashamed that she had so lost control that she would have let him—made him—take her here in a public car park, and damn the consequences.

* * *

Conor wanted to cry with frustration. Dazed, disbelieving, he held onto Kate and fought to regain his senses, cursing fate for doing this to them.

'I'm sorry, we have to stop.'

'Conor?'

'We're needed. Listen.'

His shaky, breathless words seemed to permeate Kate's confusion as she turned her head towards the source of the insistent background noise before glazed brown eyes struggled to focus on his face. 'What?'

'Someone's in trouble.'

The last thing in the world he wanted was to let her go. He wasn't even sure he could move because his knees were so shaky and he was so painfully aroused, all his senses in a spin after what had to be the most mind-numbing kiss he'd ever shared in his life.

What the hell had happened to them? It was crazy. One moment he'd brushed her lips with his, the next it had been as if the whole universe had imploded, spinning him away in a vortex of heat and pleasure, and he'd been lost in her sweetness, the clamouring rush of sexual demand. Dear heaven.

He looked down at her flushed face and the dusky-rose lips still trembling and swollen, groaning aloud as he forced himself to move, to set her away from him before he lost it again, still shocked that he'd been so carried away that he'd forgotten where they were. As much as he needed her, he certainly didn't want their first time together to be some rushed and thoughtless moment against his car in a public place. No way. He wanted to take his time and savour every inch of her body, every second of loving her.

Dragging a shaky hand through his tousled hair, he stumbled away from her, every atom of him screaming to finish what they had started, but he could see the woman who had been calling for help as she emerged from the path into the car park. In her sixties, dishevelled, tears streaming down her face, she hurried towards them.

'Please, someone, help!'

'What's happened?' Conor called.

'My husband, Angus,' the woman sobbed. 'It's his heart.'

Taking the woman by the arm, he steered her to the car, somehow managing to organise his thoughts as he used his mobile to call for emergency assistance, asking for the local park ranger as well as the nearest paramedics or the air ambulance, whichever would be quicker to reach this remote spot. He was thankful to note that Kate had similarly snapped into professional mode, at least on the outside. Inside he imagined she was as wired as he was. His whole body throbbed with unfulfilled want, her fragrance and her taste filling his senses. As Kate took his keys and went to the boot of the car, he pushed his own needs aside and focused on the distressed woman, trying to extract a medical history.

'What's your name?'

'R-Rose,' the woman cried.

'OK, Rose. We're both doctors. We'll do all we can to help him. Does Angus have a history of heart trouble?'

The woman nodded, her whole body trembling as she leaned against the car. 'Yes. For years. He's already had one triple bypass,' she explained, giving details of his medications.

'Does he have a pacemaker fitted?' The woman shook her head and he was sympathetic to her distress while cursing the wasted time. 'Whereabouts is Angus, Rose?'

'Down the path by Bruce's Stone.'

He nodded as Kate took the emergency bag and automated external defibrillator from the secure compartment in the boot of his car before running on ahead. 'I'll bring the oxygen and be right behind you,' he told her, turning back to Rose. 'I know this is hard but I need you to keep calm. Please, wait here and direct the park ranger or paramedics to us. Can you do that?'

'Yes. B-but—'

'Rose, we've no time to waste if we're to help Angus.'

Leaving the poor woman at the car, he grabbed the oxygen from the boot and took off after Kate. When he caught up with her, she was kneeling by the man who was lying on the path. She already had his shirt open and the adhesive electrode pads that recorded ECG and delivered the shock attached to the chest.

'How is he?'

'Unresponsive. No pulse and he's not breathing.' She checked the trace on the machine while administering chest compressions. 'Conor, he's in VF.'

While the machine charged, ready to deliver a shock, Conor tilted the man's head back and raised his chin, working swiftly to clear the airway and insert an endotracheal tube. 'Bilateral breath sounds,' he confirmed once the oxygen was attached and he monitored the adequate chest rises.

'I'll get a line in if you can take over here.'

He prepared to continue uninterrupted chest compressions, calling 'Clear' as the machine readied for the first shock and he watched Kate attend to the oxygen before pressing the button. The machine recharged and a series of three shocks was delivered without altering the VF rhythm. Resuming the oxygen supply, he returned to chest compressions as Kate struggled to find a vein, muttering darkly as her first two attempts failed. 'Cannula in. 1milligram of adrenalin?'

'Yes. Flush with 20 to 30 mils of saline.'

'OK.'

There were no anti-arrythmic drugs in the bag so they continued with the cycle of shocks, compressions and flush of adrenalin, the trace on the machine showing the irregular wave form of VF. Once they appeared to have Angus back, the AED trace confirming a change in rhythm, a carotid pulse vaguely discernible, but within minutes the machine alerted them to a return of VF and they renewed the sequence of adrenalin, shock and compressions.

'Hello?' a voice called, and Conor glanced up, seeing one of the park rangers he knew running down the path.

'Here, Gavin.'

'I didn't know it was you, Conor. That's a blessing. Air ambulance ETA is five minutes. They were nearby after a patient transfer. The closest landing site with road access is three miles away,' the ranger explained with a grimace. 'We've arranged to drive them up straight away and will transport your patient down when you're set to go.'

Conor nodded. 'Thanks, Gavin. Is someone taking care of the wife, Rose?'

'It's being done.'

Gavin went to organise things but it seemed for ever before two paramedics arrived, a couple of volunteers waiting nearby to help with the stretcher. 'What have we got, Doc?'

Conor filled them in on Angus's known history, what they had done, the drugs administered and the time they had been attempting resuscitation. 'Do you have amiodarone?'

'I do. Standard 300 milligrams IV bolus diluted in 20 mils of 5 per cent dextrose?'

'Thanks.'

'Lucky you happened to be here,' the first paramedic commented, and Conor glanced at Kate, seeing her flush, remembering all too clearly what they had been doing before they had been interrupted by the emergency.

They worked as a team to do all they could for Angus, but Conor feared the outcome was not hopeful, despite all their efforts. When the AED trace confirmed Angus had the return of an output, Conor began clearing his things. 'Let's get going before we lose him again.'

As post-resuscitation care continued, willing hands helped carry the stretcher to the car park and slid it into a park vehicle for the journey to the air ambulance.

'We have room if one of you wants to come with us,' a paramedic suggested.

'I'll go,' Kate offered. 'Then you can bring Rose in the car.'

Not wanting to waste time, Conor nodded, following the convoy of park vehicles to the site where the yellow helicopter awaited them. Asking a distressed Rose to wait for him, Conor ran to help the others load Angus on board, checking his precarious condition and ensuring Kate was OK.

'You sure you're all right to do this?' he said.

'I'll be fine.'

'I'll drive his wife down and meet you there.'

He hated sending Kate off without him but in the circumstances there was no time to waste. Every second counted for Angus. Conor squeezed Kate's hand for a second before he was forced to stand back as she climbed inside. All he could see was Kate's face at the window as, moments later, the aircraft lifted into the sky and headed south-east. Filled with an urgency to go to her, he hurried back to the car, doing his best to comfort Rose as they started the longer road journey to town.

CHAPTER NINE

ANOTHER day was over but even with Fred back full time, work was still hectic. Louise Kerr had been for another follow-up consultation, still nervous but happy to report some improvement in her various symptoms. The urine sample had shown no signs of diabetes and Kate hoped she could persuade the young woman to go for the ultrasound when the appointment came through from the hospital. It was going to be a long haul but it was rewarding being able to help someone in need. She was sad she wouldn't be there long term to see Louise through her whole journey.

Frowning, she raised her arms above her head, closing her eyes as she stretched her body, trying to tease out some of the knots that tightened her muscles—muscles that hadn't fully recovered from the hours hiking in the hills with Conor three days ago. No. She didn't want to remember Sunday for all sorts of reasons.

'Would you like me to give you a massage?'

The teasing suggestion had her eyes snapping open, warmth heating her cheeks as Conor appeared at her consulting-room doorway, two steaming mugs held in his hands.

'No, thanks,' she declined, suppressing a shiver at the thought of feeling Conor's touch on her body again.

'You only have to ask if you change your mind.'

Kate knew he was talking about much more than the massage and her stomach tightened, warmth prickling through her. Wary, she watched as he crossed the room, the scent of hot chocolate teasing her and making her mouth water almost as much as the memory of their erotic kiss.

'Thanks,' she murmured as he set a mug down for her, perturbed at their shared passion for hot chocolate.

Shared passions with Conor was a taboo subject. Especially after Sunday's lapse in self-control. She could feel his gaze on her as he sat down, cupping his own mug in his hands, and she prayed he wasn't going to raise the thorny subject of the kiss again. He was frustrated with her because she had panicked at what could have happened, at her brazen behaviour, and she had insisted she didn't want to talk about it—or repeat it. Which was a lie, because her body wanted to, whatever her head tried to tell it. Everything was so complicated in her life and she felt so edgy, but she was grateful that, although Conor didn't understand, he'd respected her wishes. So far. How long either of them could keep up the pretence she was too nervous to consider.

'I had a chat with Rose today,' he said after a few tense moments of silence, and a wave of sadness hit her, her own concerns set aside as she glanced up and saw the understanding in Conor's green eyes.

'How is she coping?'

'As well as can be expected. She's going home to Manchester tomorrow. Her son has flown home from his business trip to Germany and is coming up to fetch her.' He paused a moment, sipping his drink. 'You were out on house calls when she rang but she asked me to thank you for all you did.'

Kate frowned. 'Whatever that was.'

Angus had never regained consciousness. His condition had remained unstable on the short helicopter journey and he had crashed again at the hospital, the efforts of the emergency team failing to resuscitate him. The latest massive event had been too much for Angus's heart to bear and by the time Conor had arrived at A and E with Rose, Angus had died.

'We did all we could, Kate,' Conor reassured her, the warm huskiness of his voice sending a customary tingle down her spine. 'With his past medical history and the state in which we found him, Angus's chances of survival were poor from the outset.'

'I know.'

The incident with Angus had made her think of other lives she might have saved had her skills and her nerve been adequate, but she couldn't explain that to Conor, had never talked about it, not even with her father or the professor. She couldn't talk about it. Couldn't face it herself. Closing her eyes to evade Conor's observation, she leaned back and tasted her drink, her thoughts returning to Sunday. It had been late by the time they'd arrived back in Glentown and she had insisted Conor drop her at the flat, knowing he had been confused and concerned by the distance she had placed between them. But she hadn't been able to face him, too vulnerable to put herself in the danger zone again and be tempted to forget everything in his arms. It would be good but reality would return afterwards. Somehow, if she wanted to regain her career and her life, she had to face all the issues that Conor had so scarily and correctly identified were eating her up inside.

Her eyes opened, finding him watching her, and a ripple of unease went through her. She wasn't sure she had the courage to confront those demons, scared that if she let go she would never put the pieces back together again.

Conor watched the play of emotions cross Kate's face, having a good idea where her thoughts were travelling. She had panicked after Sunday's explosive kiss, refusing to talk about it, her assertion that it was unimportant, a momentary lapse, making him annoyed and frustrated. He had reluctantly backed off, concerned he would push her further away if he pressured her because instinct told him there were other issues complicating things. But now Sunday had become yet another no-go area. If Kate thought she could lie to herself that the kiss hadn't meant anything, so be it, but no way was he going to accept that. What they shared was special and now he'd had a taste of paradise, he was going to fight to keep it. If that meant changing tactics in an attempt to draw her out of her comfort zone until she faced up to whatever she was burying, then he would do it. And to hell with playing fair. This was too important…for both of them.

Sensing her unease, Conor sipped his chocolate, his gaze watchful as he planned the next stage of his campaign. 'I also heard from Nic and Hannah today,' he told her, seeing interest vie with the wariness in her soulful brown eyes.

'Are they OK?'

'Fine. They're coming over at the weekend with the kittens.' He smiled at the flash of excitement she couldn't hide and leaned forward to set his empty mug on the desk. 'They said to say hello and that they are looking forward to seeing you.'

Wariness came to the fore again. 'Oh, but—'

'I was hoping you'd visit the pet shop with me. I'd be grateful for your help deciding what the kittens will need,' he interrupted, tempting her before she could formulate an excuse.

'Well…' She trailed off, even white teeth nibbling her lower lip and making his gut—and other parts of him—tighten with desire. 'When did you have in mind?'

Keeping things light and trying not to show his elation that she hadn't flat out refused, he gave a casual shrug. 'I thought we could go to Rigtownbrae on Saturday after surgery finishes at lunchtime.'

'I guess that would be OK.'

'Great. Thanks, Kate.' Hiding his relief at her agreement, he rose to his feet, forcing himself to leave it there and not push yet about joining Nic and Hannah at his house for a meal. He had to take a step at a time if he hoped to regain lost ground and reach a point where she trusted him enough to let go and confide in him.

Noting the surprise and confusion on her face as he made to leave, he gave her a friendly smile and headed for the door. 'I'll look forward to Saturday.'

'We've bought an awful lot,' Kate said as she helped Conor unload their purchases of food, bowls, litter trays, beds, toys and other accessories when they returned to Glentown-on-Firth late on Saturday afternoon.

'I'm glad you were there to help me. Thank you.'

She frowned as he smiled and continued to take things out of the car. His behaviour over the last few days had confused her. She had expected him to pressure her but he'd been friendly and warm without overstepping her boundaries. It should have pleased her but she felt even more unsettled and fidgety. Did it mean he'd lost interest? If so, that was a good thing. Wasn't it? Her frown deepened. If only she could get the feel of him, the taste of him, the memory of that sexy kiss out of her mind. But she couldn't. And she was even more confused. She wasn't sure it was a good idea to spend time with him but the thought of the kittens was irresistible.

They had been late leaving as Sheena McIntosh had brought little Callie to the surgery, the child who had made a fuss having her arm stitched. With her teddy bear, still sporting Conor's stitches, clutched in one hand, she had handed over a sheet of paper covered in abstract blotches of bright colours.

'I drawed this for you,' she announced proudly.

Smiling, Conor dropped to his knees in front of her. 'Thank you, sweetie. I'll put it in my kitchen.'

Kate's heart had turned, watching him with Callie, devoting his attention and sweeping her into his arms for a cuddle. He'd make such a wonderful father—if only he wasn't so against commitment. She looked at him now, adding Callie's messy picture to the pile of things to be taken inside, knowing many other people would have thrown it away when the child had gone. Turning away in confusion, she concentrated instead on her first sight of his house.

Situated on rising ground at the edge of the village and reached by a short, secluded drive, the house was set back from the road and out of sight of its neighbours. Built of granite, partly painted white, it was long and low, one half single-storey with a flat roof and the other half double-storey under a pitched slate roof with two squat chimneys. From the sweep of the gravel drive she could see part of the huge garden, which was sheltered by trees and shrubs and afforded views over the Firth to the south and to the woods and hills to the north. It was stunning and she loved it the moment she set eyes on it.

'Come along in,' Conor invited her, hoisting several bags into his arms and leading the way.

Picking up a few packages, she followed him and found herself in a big, homely kitchen with a slate floor, rustic table and filled with welcoming warmth from a Rayburn. The room had pale wood units, slate worktops and was decorated in creams, pastel yellows and pastel blues. Sunshine flooded in through a large window and a pair of glass doors at one end that looked out towards the coast. Kate had no idea what she had expected of the place Conor lived, but it wasn't this. She felt at home, at peace. Which was scary. Sensing him watching her, she turned away and set down the bags, nervous now she was alone with him on his own territory. He collected the last of the things, returning to the kitchen to unpack everything, glancing at her with a sheepish smile.

'It does look rather a lot, doesn't it?'

'They're going to be two very spoiled kittens.'

Warm green eyes looked at her. 'I like spoiling those special to me.'

Her pulse rate rose and a tingle of awareness shivered through her. For a moment she didn't think she could breathe, then Conor moved away, releasing her from his spell, and she sucked air into her parched lungs. Feeling shaky, she watched as he fixed Callie's artwork to the big fridge with a couple of magnets, the painting joining an assorted collection of photos, cards and funny quotations. Next he took out a couple of glasses and then opened a bottle of red wine, letting it stand for a few moments while he returned to the fridge, taking out an enormous dish topped with mashed potatoes which he put into one of the Rayburn's ovens.

'Hannah will skin me alive if her fish pie isn't ready!' He smiled, returning to pour the wine. 'She and Nic will be here soon.'

'I was going to go home. I thought—' Her words snapped off and she wondered how she was to extract herself from this situation.

'That would be a shame—they'd be upset not to see you.'

She bit her lip, suspicious that Conor had tricked her into this. 'I didn't realise they were bringing the kittens today.'

'That's why I was in a rush to get the things.' His expression looked innocent as he handed her a glass. 'Here you go. Try this.'

'Thanks.'

Conor turned away, moving back to the fridge and taking out salad ingredients. 'I arranged for them to go and see Charlie—he's called the puppy Ben, by the way. Nic and Hannah are coming here afterwards. Feel free to wander around and make yourself at home.'

Kate hovered for a moment, torn between wanting to escape and genuine pleasure at the thought of seeing Hannah and Nic again. Not to mention the kittens. She took a fortifying sip of wine, watching from beneath her lashes as Conor prepared the food, impressed with his easy dexterity. Curious to see more of the house and needing space from the intensity of being close to him, she wandered out of the kitchen that was at the single-storey end of the house. A light passageway led to a small formal dining room and a flight of stairs led up from the hall to the upper storey. She bypassed the stairs, finding a small cloakroom and then a study, where Conor clearly spent a fair amount of time. A similar-sized room came next and was packed with shelves of books. She browsed a while, finding a mix of local history, environment, biographies, sport and some novels. Moving on, the last remaining room was the living room. It was beautiful. In the old part of the house, the beamed ceilings were lower but the room was light, large windows and French doors looking out over the wonderful garden and the views to the south and south-west. The plain walls, painted a pale terracotta, made the atmosphere even more cosy and warm. At the other end was an inviting inglenook fireplace and she could imagine curling up on one of the sofas and snuggling up in front of that fire on a freezing winter night. Alarmed at the direction of her thoughts, she spun away and crossed to gaze out at the garden.

She sensed rather than heard Conor's approach, glancing over her shoulder as he came into the room with an armful of logs.

'OK, sweetheart?'

'Fine,' she murmured, watching as he knelt down by the fire and swiftly coaxed it to life. 'Your house is lovely.'

'Thank you. I fell in love with it as soon as I saw it and I'm really happy here. Did you see upstairs?'

'No.' Upstairs meant bedrooms and that was far too dangerous and tempting.

'The views from the terrace are wonderful.'

It wasn't the views she was worried about! She was saved from further difficulties by the sound of a car arriving outside, and Conor rose to his feet, setting a guard in front of the fire.

'Let's go and see our kittens!'

Kate wanted to point out that they were nothing to do with

her, but he had already set off along the passageway. She followed more slowly, feeling out of place, but Hannah and Nic greeted her with enthusiasm and she was soon drawn into their circle, her nerves dissipating.

'I can't believe how much they've grown in such a short time!' she exclaimed as Nic set down the travel basket and Hannah handed one frisky grey kitten to Conor and one to her.

She cradled it in her arms, realising it was the one with the little white mark on its front. They seemed not to have been bothered by their journey, settling down for a cuddle, trying to outdo each other with the loudness of their purring.

'You're certainly well prepared! You have a whole pet shop in here.' Hannah laughed, looking around the kitchen. 'What are you going to call them, Conor?'

'I've chosen Smoky for this little girl,' he answered with a smile, looking like a proud father as he sat at the rustic table, the kitten cuddled against his chest, and Kate felt her heart clench as his green gaze met hers. 'Kate picked the other name.'

She flushed as Nic and Hannah looked at her with interested speculation, concerned they may get the wrong idea about her and Conor. 'I suggested Willow,' she replied, looking down at the contented kitten.

'Willow is a lovely name,' Nic said, his Italian accent warm and attractive.

'It suits her,' Hannah agreed with a smile. 'And Ben suits our little dog. He's looking amazing, Conor. It was so lovely to see him again, happy and settled in his new home. Charlie was full of Ben's progress and antics!'

'The change in Charlie is amazing. Thanks to Kate. The idea was inspired,' Conor added, his approval making Kate's cheeks warm and setting her pulse skittering again.

They chatted about Ben and the animals until it was time to eat. With the kittens settled in their new beds and curled up asleep after their adventurous day, Conor served up the salad and some fresh granary bread, then took the steaming, mouth-watering pie from the oven. The aroma was enough to set Kate's taste buds zinging and she wasn't the only one as Hannah took her place at the table with enthusiasm.

'Ooh, you don't know how I've been looking forward to this!' she sighed, as Conor set the dish on the table.

Laughing, Nic poured the wine before taking a seat beside his wife. 'The way she raves about your food, my friend, makes me feel inadequate,' he teased, his brown eyes full of mischief.

'If I wasn't already stuck with you, I'd marry Conor just for his cooking!' Hannah giggled at the possessive look on her husband's face. 'Don't be silly, Nic, I'm only teasing. Conor wouldn't have me anyway!'

Kate was disconcerted when Hannah smiled at her, a knowing look in her eyes. Was the other woman alluding to the fact that Conor was shy of marriage and families? She felt his gaze on her but didn't look up, concentrating on her meal as Hannah tucked into the food with appreciative sighs of enjoyment. Kate took her first mouthful of Conor's fish pie and thought she had gone to heaven. Oh, my! She closed her eyes, savouring the subtle but delectable flavours that melted on her tongue. Realising the room had gone quiet, she opened her eyes, flushing as she discovered the others watching her with amusement.

'Well?' Hannah demanded with a grin.

Kate flicked a brief glance towards Conor. 'It's lovely.'

Thankful when the conversation moved on and she was no longer the centre of attention, Kate concentrated on enjoying her food, lingering over every forkful. She didn't remember ever having tasted anything so delicious. Except for Conor himself. Heat flooded through her and she couldn't stop herself looking at him, seeing desire flare in the depths of his green eyes as his gaze met hers. She feared he knew just what she was thinking about.

Feeling edgy, Kate was glad when the evening came to an

end, fretting about whether Conor would try to delay her, surprised when he suggested Nic and Hannah drop her at the surgery on their way through the village. As the others lingered in the living room, Kate went to the kitchen to collect her things and say goodbye to the kittens. It was a wrench, leaving them, and she wished she could take them home, envying Conor their company. As she was about to leave the kitchen to rejoin the others, she heard their voices approaching.

'Kate?'

She straightened at Conor's call, casting a final glance at the sleeping kittens. 'I'm coming.'

Rejoining them in the hallway, she was grateful that Hannah and Nic bustled her out to the car without further delay, although Conor's apparent disinterest contrarily played on her mind.

Hannah turned to smile at her as Nic drove down the drive to the lane. 'Tell me you are going to come to the fundraising dinner and keep me company.'

'I don't think so.'

'Please. It wouldn't be the same without you, would it, Nic?' Hannah demanded.

She saw Nic shake his head in the dimness of the car. 'It would make us very happy to have you join us, Kate.'

'What exactly is this dinner?' she queried, not wanting to commit herself.

'Hasn't Conor told you?' Hannah protested, tutting in frustration. 'It's a charity event we have twice a year for all the local services: health professionals from hospitals and general practices; the fire service; mountain rescue; RNLI; police. Members of the public can buy tickets, too, and we raise money for necessary equipment for the hospital or the air ambulance, that kind of thing.'

'I didn't bring anything to wear to something like that,' Kate prevaricated, hoping that would be an end to it, but she had counted without Hannah's determination.

'That's no problem,' the other woman said dismissively. 'It's not formal ballgowns or anything. I know the perfect place—I'll email you the details. Aileen will tell you more about it.'

Kate was thankful when the car drew up at the surgery. 'I'll see. Thanks for the lift. It was good seeing you both again.'

'You too, Kate,' Hannah replied, warmth in her voice.

Kate opened the door, surprised when Nic climbed out as well. 'I'll walk you down, *cara.*'

'Thanks.'

At her door she searched her bag for her key before smiling at him. 'Goodnight.'

In the security light, Nic's dark eyes were kind and understanding. 'Take care, Kate. We'll hope to see you soon. Don't forget you have friends here.'

She watched him walk into the darkness, his parting words ringing in her ears. Her mind buzzing with myriad thoughts, she went inside, locked up and prepared for bed.

True to her promise, Kate found an email from Hannah in her inbox on Monday morning, giving the details of somewhere she could get a suitable outfit. Kate still wasn't sure whether to go. There were also emails from James and a couple of friends, but with a busy surgery ahead she left those for that evening when she would have more time. The final email was from Conor. She felt nervous when she opened it, wondering why he was contacting her that way, but a smile curved her mouth when she discovered he had taken digital photos of the kittens and had sent her some. After emailing a brief note of thanks, she changed her desktop screensaver to an image of Smoky and Willow then buzzed her first patient through.

As she had predicted, her morning was hectic. After her consultations she went out on home visits and it was lunchtime when she arrived back at the surgery. It was quiet when she walked in so she left her tray of notes for Jenny or Aileen to file and some correspondence she needed Barbara Allcott, their medical secretary, to prepare, then walked down the corridor towards her room. As she passed Conor's door, he glanced up and beckoned her in.

'Hi,' he greeted. 'Do you have a minute?'

'Sure,' she agreed, feeling wary as she sat down.

'I gather you've been out to see feisty Mrs Lucas at the residential home this morning?'

Kate nodded, frowning. 'Is there a problem?'

'No, of course not!' Conor looked at her in surprise. 'I wanted your impressions of the place. It's not been open long.'

'I've been there a couple of times now and I've found it excellent.'

His eyes crinkled at the corners as he smiled, leaning back in his chair and linking his hands behind his head. 'Don't look so worried. I've had an idea.'

'What about?' she queried, trying to relax and not notice the way the fabric of his T-shirt pulled across the muscles of his chest.

'Lizzie Dalglish.' Conor sat forward, taking out a set of notes. 'You know we were talking about the problems of her living with Yvonne and Billy, plus the issue of the stairs?'

'I remember. How is she coping since leaving hospital?'

'That's just it. She's been staying at the residential place to convalesce. I saw her yesterday afternoon and she was in better spirits, being back in the village with her friends able to visit her and update her on the local gossip!'

Smiling, Kate nodded. 'I can imagine. I wish I'd known she was there, I'd have stopped by. What's the problem?'

'Yvonne is talking about taking her home and either making alterations to the house or moving to a bungalow.'

'And Lizzie doesn't want to go,' Kate supplied.

Conor's smile was appreciative. 'We're clearly on the same wavelength. Lizzie is enjoying being in the hub of things—she has a unit of her own on the ground floor and is able to have some independence but with help on hand twenty-four hours a day. It's an ideal solution for her—but she's worried how Yvonne will react.' A pout of consideration shaped his mouth and drew her attention to his lips, bringing the memory of their feel and taste.

'Um, well…' She cleared her throat, forcing herself to look away. 'Have you spoken to Yvonne?'

'She and Billy have felt the burden of Lizzie's care this past year but she's adamant Lizzie should be with them,' he explained.

'Probably neither party wants to hurt the other's feelings,' Kate mused. 'Would they be all right financially if Lizzie stayed on permanently at the home? It's an impressive place.'

Conor nodded, twisting a pen through his fingers. 'I gather Lizzie has the money from the sale of her home. I'll have another chat with Yvonne this week and try to get her and Lizzie talking honestly to each other about their real feelings. Sometimes you can get so close to things you can't see the solution.'

'Right.' She rose to her feet, unsettled by the underlying edge in his voice, scared he might be alluding to her own unwillingness to confide in him. Despite being eager to escape, she lingered a moment, unable to help herself. 'Thanks for the photos. How are the kittens?'

'It's been an exhausting round of playing, eating and sleeping so far!'

'They must be a handful,' she agreed, hearing her own wistfulness.

Green eyes turned warm. 'Any time you want to come and play with them you're more than welcome.'

'Thanks.' It was tempting. But so was Conor and being at his house wasn't sensible. 'I'd best get on.'

'Hannah emailed this morning. She says you're coming to the dinner.'

His words stopped her before she reached the door. 'She asked me, but I haven't decided.'

'I hope you'll say yes, Kate.'

The sultry green gaze and husky voice made her hot right through. Temptation was becoming harder and harder to resist.

CHAPTER TEN

DEAR God!

Conor felt his whole body going into meltdown as he looked at Kate. Having managed, with Hannah's help, to cajole her into attending the fundraising dinner, he'd forced himself into a dreaded suit for the occasion, anticipation bringing him to the flat several minutes early.

'I won't be long, I'm not quite ready,' she said, and he was thankful she was unaware of his predicament, his raging desire mixed with stunned shock.

He tried to draw air into starved lungs, his gaze following her, devouring her. From the first day he had admired her natural beauty but never more so than now, the bare minimum of make-up needed to enhance brown eyes he wanted to drown in and dusky-rose lips he couldn't wait to taste again. Her dark brown hair was loose, just the way he loved it, falling in a glossy curtain to frame her face and brush her bare shoulders, a wispy fringe feathering her brow. His fingers itched to bury themselves in the silken thickness. As for her outfit… Conor swallowed the restriction in his throat. How those two minute little straps secured the low-cut bodice in place he had no idea, but it clung to accentuate the generous swell of her breasts and brought him out in a sweat. His mouth went dry. Heart pounding, his pulse raced as his gaze continued down, seeing how the fabric skimmed the gentle flare of her hips and the trousers shaped the lush curve of her rear before moulding the length of her long legs. The creamy colour of the one-piece suit brought out the olive tones of her skin, the fabric covered in silver-grey threads that shimmered as she moved. Conor stared, overcome with heat and arousal. The temptation to touch was unbearable. No way was he going to get through this evening. Smothering a groan, he thrust his hands into his pockets in an attempt to stop himself giving in to his baser instincts. All he wanted was to lock the door, strip off her clothes and spend the whole night lovingly and thoroughly exploring every inch of her.

'Are the kittens all right?'

'The kittens?' He struggled to find his voice and force his mind to focus on something other than anticipating the pleasure of making love with Kate. 'Um, yes, they're fine. They've had a mad run around and a good supper and were asleep when I left.'

His gaze followed as she moved around the room, collecting her things. He couldn't forget how she had felt in his arms, how she had tasted that day in the car park when passion had raged between them. How could she deny what they had? She had been as aroused as him, urgently pulling at his clothes, rubbing herself on him as her body had sought the fulfilment they had both craved. He wanted her so badly it was a physical ache. And now he had to spend the evening with her dressed like that and not touch her? No way was he going to survive this. And no way was any other man laying hands on her. Nic could be trusted for a couple of dances but that was it. Whether she liked it or not, he was staking his claim on Kate and woe betide anyone who tried to move in on his territory tonight.

Kate collected her jacket and bag, checking she had her mobile in case of emergencies, and turned to face Conor, halting at the raw expression in his sultry green eyes. It was hot and sexy and scarily intent. Hell, she had known this outfit was a mistake. Having braved the subject with Aileen and been told several members of the surgery staff would be attending the dinner with their partners, Kate had found herself at the address Hannah had given her and been taken under the wing of Moira Montgomery, the elegant, middle-aged woman who owned the select clothes shop. She had fallen for the shimmery trouser suit the second she had seen it. On the rail it had looked classy but once on her eyes had widened in alarm when she had looked at herself in the mirror.

'I don't think I should wear this,' she had breathed, concerned it was too revealing.

'Nonsense, lovey,' Moira had insisted, fussing around her. 'You look magnificent. It could have been made for you.'

Now every millimetre of her flesh tingled under Conor's inspection. His obvious hunger was exciting yet scary, but she was even more frightened by her own response, the rush of desire she was unable to control. Burning with arousal, she could imagine the whisper of his touch on her skin, the caress of his hands, the taste of his mouth, and her pulse rocketed, her breath lodging in her throat. He looked impressive but unfamiliar in his dark grey suit, white shirt and grey tie. Having disapproved of his style of dress when she had first met him, she now couldn't adjust to him wearing anything else, acknowledging how the casual clothes suited his personality. His hair was semi-tamed but still flopped across his forehead. Her fingers itched to brush it back. What she really wanted to do was rip his clothes off and never leave there tonight at all.

Alarmed at the dangerous electricity sizzling between them, she turned away and fussed with her jacket, thankful when she was covered up.

'Shall we go?' she suggested, her voice crisper than she'd intended as she struggled to hide her reaction and fragile self control.

* * *

Conor found his protective and proprietorial instincts were well to the fore when he escorted Kate out of the flat into the dark evening to the car. He feared the journey would seem a long one and not just because of the wet and windy weather. Initial attempts at conversation, even with safe topics like Lizzie or the kittens, soon fizzled out, which was unsurprising given that the atmosphere between them was charged with tension and desire. Glancing across at her, he noted that her hands were clenched in her lap and, along with his physical hunger, he experienced a deepening need to watch over her. Suddenly troubled, he remembered his conversation with Kyle, his instinct that if and when Kate let go of the pain inside her the fall was going to be a big one. A shiver rippled down his spine and he was alarmed by the inexplicable feeling that something important and life-changing was about to happen. Affected by the charged atmosphere, he flicked on the CD player, hoping the background music would help fill the deafening silence and help them relax. Hands tightening on the wheel, he focused on negotiating the narrow lanes in the difficult conditions, trying to shrug off his unease and push his jumbled thoughts to the back of his mind.

'Hell!' he exclaimed, bringing the car safely to a halt as they rounded a bend to find the road blocked by a serious accident. He turned to Kate, his hand resting on her arm. 'You OK?'

'Fine.'

Her gaze was fixed on the scene and Conor's attention shifted, too, as blue lights from an attending fire engine, ambulance and police car reflected off the wet road in the darkness of the evening.

'I'll see what's going on,' he said, aware Kate was following as he left the car.

It took a moment to make sense of the tangled mess but it appeared a tractor pulling a trailer had crossed the road. A car coming round the bend had seen it too late and the collision had impacted the vehicle under the trailer. Firefighters worked with obvious urgency on the wreckage and Conor could see one paramedic inside the remains of the car. His colleague was running from the ambulance towards the crash site, carrying some equipment.

Recognising the paramedic, Conor joined him. 'What's happening, Ally?'

'Conor. Thank God.' Ally looked stressed and anxious. 'We're in a hell of a mess here, Doc. Ten-year-old boy trapped by his leg in the car. We have fluids up. Airway clear, no head injury. But he's deteriorating fast and he's in shock; his BP is dropping, he's pale and cold. The trapped leg looks non-viable, but we can't access it or the other leg. We fear massive internal bleeding following blunt trauma to his abdomen after the rapid deceleration—could be spleen, liver, bowel, anything. The fire service are working as fast as they can but they can't get him out for some time. And there's a major incident elsewhere taking up much-needed personnel. We have no road assistance or air ambulance coming here sooner than twenty minutes. That's far too long. We need him out. Now. Leg or no leg. But none of us have surgical skills.' Worried hazel eyes stared at him. 'He's going to die if we don't do something in a hurry.'

Before Conor could reply, he heard a moan of distress and turned to see that Kate was just behind him. Her face was deathly pale and, as she swayed, he wrapped an arm around her waist, holding her close, feeling her trembling.

'Kate? What's wrong?'

She didn't appear to hear him. He looked into her eyes, alarmed at the look of stark anguish in them. Ignoring him, she turned to Ally, licking her lips and sucking in a deep breath before could speak, her voice rough and shaky.

'Capillary refill?' she demanded.

Ally shot him a querying glance and Conor nodded, not understanding but going along with any idea she might have to help. 'This is Dr Kate Fisher—she's working with us at Glentown.'

'Very prolonged,' Ally informed her, answering her rapid questions, and Conor listened to the brisk conversation, knowing that if it took six seconds or longer for the skin to turn pink after being pressed, as the blood refilled the capillaries, it was a dangerous sign. As Ally had indicated. 'He's top priority, immediate extraction.'

Which meant they had to get him out and off to hospital without any more delay. Another glance at Kate's face and Conor noticed her unnatural pallor, her lips bloodless. But her eyes had changed, now totally blank of emotion and expression, as if she was shutting everything down inside her. It scared him. He remembered the times she had blanked out before but this was different. Worse.

'I need gloves,' she said as Ally's succinct briefing came to an end, and continued to list things she wanted.

'Kate, I don't think—' Conor began, but she was shrugging away from him, moving to the car as Ally rushed off to get what she had asked for. Anxious, Conor turned to her. 'Kate!'

Before he could stop her she was throwing off her jacket and wriggling inside the car to examine the boy and talk to Dave, the other paramedic. Feeling helpless, Conor stood by the wreckage unable to hear what Kate was saying as the firefighters worked on, trying to cut the tangled metal free and gain access to the trapped boy's legs. Remembering where they were meant to be, he took out his mobile and sent a text to Nic to let him know they were helping at an accident scene and might not make it to the dinner. At least their friends and colleagues wouldn't worry if they didn't show. All the worry was his at the moment. For Kate.

Ally returned, handing the gloves and other things inside to Kate and Dave. 'Any other casualties?' Conor asked as they waited for Kate's next move.

'Tractor driver is in shock—one of the policemen has taken him home,' Ally explained, pointing towards the nearby farmhouse. 'The boy's name is Russ. His father, Bryan, is in the back of the ambulance—shock and minor cuts and bruises.'

Kate's starkly white face appeared at the gap where the twisted car door had been removed, that frighteningly blank look still in her eyes as she asked for ketamine, saline and other items. 'And I need more light in here,' she instructed, unrecognisable as the woman he knew.

When Ally had delivered the things Kate had requested, the fire crew stopped work. Kate calculated dosages and administered the ketamine through the IV to anaesthetise Russ, with Dave responsible for monitoring the oxygen and breathing. Once Russ was under, Conor held the light steady and observed as Kate used a tourniquet above the knee, then flushed the open, traumatic wound site with saline before she set to work.

'Air ambulance less than fifteen minutes,' Ally whispered to Conor.

He nodded, all his attention focused on what was happening in the car. 'Right.'

'Is Kate a surgeon?'

He opened his mouth to say no but closed it again, frowning. Did this explain the gaps in her CV? Maybe this was why she knew Professor Fielding-Smythe so well. Struck dumb, he watched as Kate carried out the impossible procedure with a speed and skill he could only marvel at. She didn't even have the right equipment but she never hesitated, Dave and Ally doing exactly what she told them while he directed the light and watched in awe and confusion. If Kate had the training to attempt what she was doing now, why on earth was she working as a GP locum in their rural Scottish practice?

Fighting down the fear and the nausea, Kate tried to blank everything out and do what needed to be done. She had heard the words 'He'll die if we don't do something in a hurry' and she had known she had to act. No one else here could do it. She could. *If* she could find the courage. Too many people had died already. She couldn't stand by and do nothing, knowing that if she had acted the boy might have had a chance. But she didn't know how to make herself face it either.

Her first sight of Russ's injuries had convinced her that the leg was not viable and, with his internal injuries and deteriorating condition, the seriousness of the situation was indisputable. Russ came out now or he died. He might still die, but this way he had a chance—if she could do it and if the air ambulance arrived on time.

Paralysing fear threatened to overwhelm her and she wanted to leave the car. To run. Again. She closed her eyes. The only way she could do this was to blank everything from her mind, operate, literally, on autopilot, forgetting the past, forgetting Conor.

Lying at an uncomfortable angle inside the wreck, her fingers feeling numb and lifeless, she worked on bones shattered beyond repair, tying off blood vessels, saving nerves and tendons, doing the best she could to preserve muscle and take enough viable skin for the surgeons at the hospital to work with.

When Russ was finally able to be removed from the car with the utmost care, they found his other leg had suffered a more minor open fracture and she welcomed help from Conor, Dave and Ally to treat the leg and maintain the boy's fragile clinical condition.

By the time the air ambulance arrived, complete with an experienced trauma doctor on the crew, Russ was ready to go, critically ill but with a chance of survival he would not have had were he still trapped in the car with time running out. She gave her report to the attending doctor in a monotone, never more relieved to abdicate her care of a patient. While Conor and the others were occupied with the transfer, she slipped away, making it nearly as far as the car before reaction set in. Slumping to her knees on the ground, she was violently ill. Then the shaking started. Images and memories flooded her brain. It was too much. Self-preservation kicked in, something inside her switching off, closing her down.

'Where's Kate?' Conor demanded.

'Don't know, Doc.' Ally frowned. 'I haven't seen her since we began the transfer. She was awesome in there.'

Conor glanced round, unable to find her. Russ was safely installed in the air ambulance *en route* to the specialist help he needed—only alive thanks to Kate's skill and quick thinking. Dave and Ally were clearing up and taking Russ's father, Bryan, to hospital by road, while the firefighters and police were making the scene safe. Taking his leave, he picked up their discarded jackets and went in search of Kate, his heart pounding as his worry increased, his mind buzzing with questions. As he neared the car, he saw her slumped at the side of the road and he ran forward.

'Kate!'

She didn't answer. Kneeling down in front of her on the wet grass, he saw she hadn't even taken her gloves off. She looked bedraggled, streaked with blood, and although her eyes were open, she wasn't seeing or hearing anything. She was horribly pale, her body shaking, and she had a haunted look that scared him. Hating to leave her even for a moment, he eased off her gloves then opened the car, put their things inside and returned with a dry blanket. Wrapping it around her, he drew her into his arms and held her close, rocking her, feeling inadequate because he had no idea what was going on and how to help her.

'Katy?' he whispered, voice choked with emotion. She shivered but didn't respond. He stroked the damp strands of hair back from her face and brushed his lips over her cold, pale cheek. 'I'll take care of you. Everything's going to be OK.'

He hoped to God that was true. Rising to his feet, he lifted her into his arms and carried her to the car, gently setting her on the passenger seat and wrapping the blanket around her before securing the seat belt. The drive to his house seemed to take for ever. Kate never stirred, just sat staring into the darkness, deep in one of her trance-like states. When they pulled up at the house, he left her in the car while he opened the front door and turned on the lights, then he went back for her, carrying her inside and up to his bedroom.

'Can you stand for me?' he asked, setting her on her feet in the *en suite* bathroom, holding onto her as she swayed. 'We need to get you cleaned up and warm.'

Her beautiful trouser suit was ruined—wet, dirty, torn and covered in blood. Concerned for her physical well-being and emotional state, knowing she wasn't fit to do anything for herself, he hid his own emotions and began gently stripping off her ruined clothes. She stood like a child while he helped her, his fingers unsteady as he slipped off her shoes and then moved to find and struggle with the side fastening of her one-piece outfit. He soon discovered why the fabric clung to her like a sheer glove—she was wearing virtually nothing underneath it.

This was going to kill him. No matter how much he told himself he was a doctor, that he had to do this for Kate's sake, that it wasn't personal, it was impossible to ignore his feelings. She was so incredibly beautiful.

Don't look! He repeated the words over and over like a mantra in his head. Close your eyes, he told himself. It didn't help. Not one bit. He tossed the garments aside and quickly followed them with his own, keeping his boxers on to maintain some propriety—not that Kate was in a fit state to care.

The most important thing was to get her warmed up and as it didn't seem likely that she could stand safely on her own in the shower, much less wash herself, he needed to get in there with her. Maintaining as safe a distance between their bodies as he could, he drew her under the water, keeping his touch as impersonal as possible as he cleaned her, avoiding the most dangerous no-go areas. A frown creased his brow as he noticed a scar on her left side halfway between her hip and her lower rib, wondering what had caused it, remembering how she had held herself there, passing it off as a stitch, the day they had walked up to the Grey Man. In the circumstances he couldn't look closely but from what he could see the wound wasn't very old and hadn't been professionally tended to when fresh. More unanswered questions jostled in his head. Frowning, he rinsed her hair with care then snapped off the shower. He wrapped a towel around her head then reached for another large fluffy one to encase her body before stripping off his wet boxers and knotting a towel around himself.

As she seemed more steady on her feet, he slowly walked her to the bedroom and sat her on the bed, drying her and swapping the towel for a large T-shirt before turning his attention to her hair, combing it through and drying it. When he finally tucked her into his bed, she lay on her back, staring up at the ceiling, her hands shaking as they clutched the duvet. He was loath to give her any medication until he had a better idea what was wrong. Her pulse and her breathing were normal. This was something deeply emotional, part of the cracking process he so feared might happen if she didn't release whatever inner pressure she was carrying. And she still hadn't cried, was keeping everything buried inside her. He knew a little more now, at least in terms of the professional skills she had hidden, but not enough for any of the jigsaw pieces to fit and the picture to make sense. For a while he sat in silence, stroking her hair until she seemed to settle, some of the tension leaving her body, her hands relaxing their death-like grip on the duvet.

'Kate, can you hear me?' An imperceptible nod was his only answer, but at least a response was there, a sign she was emerging from the dark, lonely place in which she had shut herself. 'Would you like a drink?' Again the tiny nod. But his suggestion of water brought a negative shake. 'Hot chocolate?' This time the nod was firmer. 'Just rest. I'll be back in a couple of minutes, I promise.'

Conor hated leaving her. Covered only with the towel around his waist, he hurried downstairs, locking up his car and the house before going to the kitchen. The kittens were fine, stirring while he made the hot chocolate then settling back in their beds. He laced her drink with a splash of brandy before carrying the mug upstairs and setting it on the side cabinet. Kate hadn't moved but she seemed less rigid and unfocused. Taking a chance, he slid into bed beside her, helping her sit up before handing her the mug. As she cradled it in trembling hands, he drew her into his arms, holding her as she slowly sipped her drink, the aroma of the chocolate mingling with the citrusy fragrance of her hair and skin.

When she had finished, he took the empty mug from her and set it aside, surprised but delighted when she snuggled closer rather than pulling away, as he had feared she would. There were so many things he needed to know but he held his tongue, rocking her gently, one hand stroking her hair as she relaxed more against him. He closed his eyes, only to open them again as all he could see in his mind was Kate—not just her beauty and how she had looked and felt, but he would never forget the terrible pain and stark trauma in her eyes back at the accident site.

Kate allowed herself to rest in the comforting circle of Conor's arms, reality and memory returning, having shut down after the horror had become too much to bear. She had done what had needed to be done but it had taken everything out of her, brought back all her nightmares, and she could never have moved, never have functioned if Conor hadn't taken over.

Embarrassment churned inside her at how helpless she had been, how many liberties she had granted him. And now she was in his bed, wearing nothing but a T-shirt that carried the lingering earthy scent of him. She couldn't believe she had allowed him to undress her, wash her, care for her. He'd been amazing, though, not pressing her for answers to the questions he must have, caring for her with a gentle kindness and compassion that made her want to weep. But she couldn't cry. Even now. If she did, she would never stop.

As her senses reawakened, she became more aware of Conor's presence, the safety she felt in his arms, the warmth and scent of his body, the feel of his bare chest beneath her cheek—warm skin, rippling muscle, the dusting of hair. The temptation to turn her head and press her mouth to his flesh was overpowering. Despite her efforts to keep him at a distance, her body gravitated to his and she curled into him, seeking comfort, lulled and aroused at the same time. As she fought to keep the memories at bay, she knew she would have to leave Glentown, that her haven of calm was over. There would be questions, interest, intrusions she couldn't cope with. The thought of leaving this place and these people, especially Conor, was painful, but her nightmares were worse, driving her on, keeping her moving because she wasn't strong enough to confront them.

She snuggled closer. For tonight she could banish everything from her mind. It was wrong but for these few hours she could take what Conor offered, what she needed so badly. Just one night. Then she would have to go—to find somewhere else where she could start over, make fresh decisions about what she was going to do with her life, whether she could even carry on being a doctor if she was going to go to pieces every time something like this happened.

'Do you want to talk?'

Conor's words, husky and soft, drew her from her thoughts and she shook her head. 'No,' she murmured, feeling the thud of his heart, knowing her own pulse was speeding up at what she was thinking and doing, her breath catching in her chest.

'Maybe you should sleep now,' he suggested, his voice unsteady.

'No.' She turned into him, looking into his darkening green eyes. 'Stay with me.'

She felt him tense, heard the longing underlying his words. 'You don't know what you're asking.'

'I do.' Her hand moved, her fingertips exploring his chest.

'Not now,' he said, catching her hand in his. 'I don't want to take advantage of this.'

Ignoring his protest, she wriggled closer, pressing her mouth to the strong column of his throat, loving his taste. 'Please, Conor, make me forget.'

'Tonight?'

'Everything.' She leaned in, nibbling along his bottom lip, hearing his breath catch. 'Just for a while, make it all go away.'

'Kate, don't,' he groaned.

'I need this…need you.'

'Kate…'

Conor struggled to maintain his willpower. It was torture to hold back but he didn't want to abuse her trust. She'd been distressed, she was… Dear heaven! Kate's tongue teased the outline of his mouth. His hands moved to her sides to keep some distance between them but they tightened as her fingers returned to their exploration of his chest, his heart pounding as they brushed around and across a sensitive nipple. She smiled against his mouth at his involuntary response.

'Please, Conor.'

As if he could deny her anything. As if he didn't want her like a crazy person. Any chance he had of being honourable evaporated as she kissed him, teasing forgotten, and his mouth opened hotly under hers, swallowing her whimpers of encouragement. She wriggled on top of him, pressing her body against his, setting him on fire. Her T-shirt rode up so he felt peachy-soft skin under his hands. He was a flesh-and-blood man, not a bloody saint. A man pushed beyond the limit of his endurance. Wresting control from her, he rolled them over until she was beneath him, welcoming the feel of her hands on his skin. Passion flared in an instant. The kiss deepened, hot and demanding, her tongue twining with his, her fingers urgent as they roamed his body. He shuddered as she dragged her nails down his spine. Her touch, her taste, her fragrance drove him insane but he wanted more. Much more. Wrenching his mouth free, he looked into sensual brown eyes, hands unsteady as he drew off the T-shirt, tossing it aside.

'Katy,' he whispered. 'You're so beautiful.'

She gasped, her body arching to him as his fingers traced the outline of her breasts, seeing the flush of arousal on her skin, dusky-rose nipples peaking in anticipation of his touch. Her hands pulled at him but he took his time, savouring her as he had longed to do, smiling at her impatience as his fingertips spiralled slowly inwards to where she most craved them. She cried out when he reached his goal, so responsive to him. One hand sank into his hair, urging his mouth down, and he gave her what she needed, what they both needed, circling her areola with his tongue tip before opening his mouth on her flesh and hungrily drawing the swollen nipple deep inside, drunk on the taste of her, the feel of her.

'Conor!'

'Is that good?' he mouthed against her skin.

She writhed beneath him, struggling to get closer. 'Yes! More…please,' she whimpered.

He could do this for hours; would never get enough of her. He turned his attention to her other breast as her hands grazed urgently down his back and struggled to free the towel. Moving to help her, he groaned as she pulled it free and there was nothing more between them, feeling her heat as she shifted to bring them intimately into contact. If he wasn't careful this was going to be over in five minutes and he didn't want that. He slid lower, taking his time kissing and caressing his way down to her navel, finding her just as sensitive and responsive there, her body squirming to his as he licked, nibbled and sucked on her skin.

Kate whimpered as his fingers found the scar on her side, her body tensing as his lips whispered across the wound. Her hands fisted in his hair and he looked up, seeing the denial in her eyes.

'Don't.'

'What happened?'

She shook her head and he allowed her to distract him. Deliciously. 'No more waiting,' she urged, her hands gliding down, driving him to the edge of reason.

Aroused beyond bearing, he gave in. Later, he promised himself. Later there would be time to love her for hours as he yearned to, to ask all his questions. Reaching out, he dragged open the bedside drawer, scrabbling inside.

'Pray there are some condoms in here,' he told her hoarsely, unable to remember how long ago it had been since he'd needed them. 'And that they're not past their use-by date.'

Impatient, wanting Conor with a desperation she had never experienced before, Kate moaned with frustration. 'Hurry,' she begged, unable to hold on much longer.

Relieved when he found what he was looking for, she took it from him, looking into his eyes as she rolled it on, fingers lingering, feeling his response, welcoming his weight as she drew him down, mouths meeting hotly. She wanted this, needed it. Her body had known from the first; for tonight her head ceased arguing and putting obstacles in the way.

'You're sure?' Conor's voice was rough with tension, green eyes dark with passion.

'Yes.' Her hands moved down to encourage him, gasping as he moved into her and smoothly united them. 'Yes!'

'Katy,' he groaned, one arm sliding under her hips, his free hand sinking in her hair.

She wrapped her legs around him, demanding everything, giving everything. Nothing had ever been like this. The terrible burning inside her threatened to consume her and only Conor could ease the ache, extinguish the fire. She couldn't stand it. Moving with him, desperate for release, she clung on to him, burying her face in his shoulder, sobbing as he took her higher and higher. For what felt like an eternity she teetered on the precipice, balancing on the edge of an unimaginable abyss, until Conor, at last, allowed her to plummet over the edge, his hold tightening, keeping her safe, as they fell together into the most intense, impossible explosion of pleasure, beyond anything she had ever imagined. Incredible. Frightening. Wonderful. They collapsed together, hearts pounding, breathing laboured, bodies entwined. Kate closed her eyes, surrendering to the magic of this night with Conor, knowing she could never repeat it.

CHAPTER ELEVEN

CONOR struggled awake, bitter disappointment surging through him when he discovered he was alone. Frowning, concerned for Kate and worried about the future, he hugged her pillow, drawing in her lingering scent, an ache of longing leaving a hollow loss inside him. Closing his eyes, he relived the most amazing night of his life. Kate was incredible; uninhibited, intensely sensual. Their passion had been hot and insatiable. After the first urgent coming together, they had spent hours learning each other; he had loved every inch of her, while her hands and her mouth had brought him to the edge time and again. Rather than feeling sated, he yearned for more. More of Kate. For ever wouldn't be long enough. But she had gone.

His mobile phone beeped with an incoming text and he was both relieved and annoyed to discover it was from Kate.

I'm at the flat. I'm fine. I need time alone. Please. K.

Shit!

Conor didn't believe for one second she was fine. Cursing, he slid from the bed, anxious about her emotional and physical state. Scared that she was backing off again, he went to shower, his heart clenching as he found her ruined outfit on the floor. The last thing Kate needed to be was on her own. He tipped his face to the water, angry with himself for giving in to temptation last night. Yes, he'd wanted her, but he had known there were unresolved issues and he had been frightened she had been reacting to circumstances and would regret it. Too late he knew he had been right. He had to be with her, knew his own feelings, but Kate kept pushing him away and he was scared he was being a fool, that he was opening himself up to heartbreak.

Back in the bedroom he sat on the bed, frowning over what to do. He wanted to go round there straight away but was worried he would make things worse if he pushed her. Whatever had affected her so deeply at the accident site—and the times she had blanked out before—was important and bad and buried inside her. Hiding her surgical skills lay at the root of her inner torment. Had some procedure gone wrong? Did she blame herself? There was so much he needed to know, but reacting the wrong way now could ruin everything. But he couldn't do nothing. Full of uncertainty, he reached for his mobile and composed a text of his own.

Kate, I'm worried about you. I'll give you space today if that's what you want but I'm always here for you if you need anything at all. Please call me. Any time. Love, Cx.

They needed to talk. Most of all Kate needed to release whatever was causing her so much pain. How much did Fred know? Anxious not to leave the house in case Kate returned or called him, he paced away the day, worrying and thinking, even the antics and company of Smoky and Willow failing to cheer him. He spoke briefly to Kyle and to Nic about what had happened, his anxieties over Kate and his feelings, then phoned Fred to give him basic details of the accident the previous evening, hearing his partner's genuine distress.

'Did you know Kate has surgical skills?' he asked, trying to keep any accusation and resentment from his tone.

'I knew she had done some training on James's team; he said she could have been a good surgeon but her heart was in general practice. She had some crisis of confidence, through no fault of her own, but I don't know more than that, Conor. Truly. How is she?' the older man added after a short pause, concern in his voice.

'Not good.'

'You've fallen for her, haven't you?'

Conor closed his eyes, feeling as if his heart was cracking. 'Yes, Fred, I have. And I'm going to do everything I can to help her. Can we shelter her from this at the surgery?'

'Of course. There's bound to be interest—what Kate did was amazing, especially as everyone believes she is just a normal GP—but I'll speak to all the staff today and make sure no one questions her,' he promised.

'Thanks.'

'What are you going to do?'

He ran a hand through his hair, an idea forming in his mind. 'I'll see how Kate is tomorrow, but I might need a day or two off.'

'No problem, Conor. Whatever you have to do for Kate. Any news of the boy?'

'I rang the hospital. He's come through the operation and is stable but critical in Intensive Care,' Conor replied, knowing Russ only had this chance thanks to Kate's actions.

After a sleepless night Conor arrived at the surgery on Monday morning to find a worried Aileen waiting for him.

'Fred told me yesterday. You look terrible,' she fretted, her grey eyes anxious.

Conor manufactured a wry smile. 'Thanks.'

'We'll look after Kate, pet, don't worry,' Aileen reassured him. 'I'm fielding all calls. We've had a couple of press queries.'

'I was afraid of that. Let's keep Kate out of it if we can. Put anything through to me…or Fred if I'm not here.' His gaze strayed down the corridor. 'Is Kate in yet?'

'She is.'

Nervous tension made him feel sick. 'I need a few minutes to talk to her.'

'Let me know if there's anything I can do to help,' the perceptive woman offered, her smile understanding.

'There is one thing…'

After outlining his plan and gaining Aileen's enthusiastic support, Conor went to Kate's consulting room, taking a deep breath before knocking on the door. He stepped inside, his throat closing as he saw her pallor, the dark circles under her eyes. Her gaze slid from his as she clasped tremulous hands together on her desk. Uncertain, he sat down, wondering how to get through to her.

'No one is going to be bothering you about Saturday,' he began, wishing she would look at him. 'Aileen is monitoring the calls and if there are any questions, Fred or I will deal with them.'

'Thanks.' The word whispered out, husky and raw.

'There are bound to be questions, but we'll do all we can to field them…if that's what you want.'

'Yes.'

'Kate, we need to talk.'

She shook her head, her hair falling to shield her face. 'There's nothing to say.'

'Please, don't do this,' he begged, fear making him edgy.

'It was just a night, Conor,' she insisted, voice shaky. 'I'm sorry. It shouldn't have happened. It didn't mean anything.'

Conor stared in disbelief. This was worse than he'd expected. 'I don't believe that and I don't think you do either. What we have is special, Kate.'

'It can't be.'

The panic in her voice tore at his heart and he rose to his feet, rounding the desk to crouch beside her, taking one cool, trembling hand in his. 'I know you're scared about something. Hurting. Let me help you. Please.'

'You can't,' she insisted, withdrawing her hand from his.

Frustrated, concerned, confused, he wanted to pull her into his arms, hold her, shake her, demand answers, anything to break through her emotional barriers, but he returned to his chair to stop himself doing something dumb. It was time to change tactics and put his plan into action. No matter how Kate tried to deny it, he knew what they had was amazing and he wasn't going to give up until she faced whatever inner torment was keeping them apart. It hurt that she couldn't trust him and he was scared she was going to run, so he had to act now if he hoped to help her and give them any chance for a future together.

'I know this isn't the best time, Kate, but would you do me a favour?'

She glanced at him for the first time, wariness in her eyes. 'What kind of favour?'

'I have to go away for a few days and—'

'You're going away?' she interrupted, with a mix of shock, relief and alarm.

'Not for long.' He couldn't bear the thought of leaving her, even for a short time, but it was essential. 'Would you look after Willow and Smoky for me?'

'Of course.' She frowned, wrong-footed by his request. 'When?'

Conor hid his relief, hoping the kittens would be his insurance policy and that she cared too much to abandon them and run while he was gone. 'I'll bring them and their things over at lunchtime.'

'Right.'

'I'll leave you to get on, then.'

With a supreme effort of will he rose to his feet. Aware she was puzzled and unsettled, he left the room and went in search of Aileen, getting the information he needed before making arrangements with Fred. He was going to fight for Kate Fisher.

Unable to sleep, Kate sat in the dark living room, two sleepy kittens cuddled in her lap. She welcomed their warmth and company. Not for the first time she felt horribly alone but this time it was more cutting, more raw. Conor had gone away. One moment he claimed he cared, the next that he was going on holiday. She cursed her contrariness. She had told him to leave her alone, had said she didn't want him, and that was the best thing for both of them. But she had never expected to feel so bereft. To need him so much. She was so confused. And scared. Making love with Conor had been a stupid mistake. How had she ever thought she could take one night and it wouldn't matter? Making love with Conor had been the most stupendous thing that had ever happened to her, the explosion of hot passion indescribable. Her own behaviour had been out of character: she had responded to him with wild abandon and a complete lack of inhibition. Thinking about the things they had done brought a flush to her face and she pressed cool palms to her cheeks, trying to block out the memory of the unimaginable pleasure she had experienced with him.

Had circumstances been different, she could have settled in her rural Scottish haven, but Saturday night had far-reaching consequences. There would be repercussions, no matter how Conor and her colleagues tried to shelter her. They couldn't protect her from her own nightmares. People would start asking questions, wondering about her, wanting to know how a supposedly ordinary GP had carried out such a surgical procedure. There would be questions about her past. And Conor would have all manner of questions of his own that she couldn't face answering. However painful, she had to leave before the past caught up with her. If only she had never succumbed to temptation in Conor's bed. She had known one night wouldn't be enough but in her weakest moment she had grasped what he had offered, needing to forget everything else. In the process she had opened herself up to more hurt because she had done the most unforgivable thing of all. She had fallen in love with Conor Anderson.

* * *

Unable to book the flights he wanted, Conor opted for the freedom to move where and when he needed and drove. By the time he reached London on Monday night he was physically tired and mentally exhausted. He parked outside the address he had been given and, taking his overnight bag, he walked up the path and rang the front doorbell.

'Welcome, Conor,' his host greeted him, stepping back to let him in. 'I've been expecting you.'

'Thank you.' After shaking hands, Conor followed Kate's father to a cosy sitting room.

'You must be tired and hungry. What can I get you?' Tom offered.

Worried about leaving Kate, Conor ran a hand through his wayward hair. 'I'm sorry it's so late. I don't want to put you out.'

'You're not, believe me. How about a sandwich and a coffee?'

'That sounds great,' he admitted with a weary smile.

'Make yourself at home—there's a cloakroom across the hall,' the older man said. 'I'll be back in a few moments.'

Left alone, he thought of Kate, wondering how she was coping. He scanned the bookshelves along one wall of Tom's sitting room before surveying the rest of the room, noticing the photo frames on the piano. He walked across, his heart lurching as his gaze zeroed in on one of Kate. She looked happy, her eyes bright, revealing none of their current soulful pain, as she snuggled up with an attractive young man. A mix of emotions chased through him: gut-wrenching jealousy; aching hurt for whatever had happened to turn this carefree woman into the one who had arrived in Glentown-on-Firth; a determination that Kate would look like this again, would laugh with him and be free.

'Conor?'

He jumped at the sound of Tom's voice, guiltily setting the photo back on the piano. 'Sorry.'

'Not at all.' Tom's gaze flicked to the photograph then back to him, a knowing smile curving his mouth. 'You're in love with my daughter.'

Conor swallowed. 'I am,' he agreed, relieved when Tom nodded in apparent approval and set down a tray containing a plate of sandwiches and a pot of coffee.

'So,' Tom commented once they were settled, 'I assume something has happened to bring you here in a hurry?'

'Yes. We had an…incident. On Saturday night,' Conor continued, filling Kate's father in on the details of the accident—but not what had happened afterwards between Kate and himself.

Tom's brown eyes, so like Kate's, clouded with concern. 'That will really have spooked her, Conor, and brought back a lot of hurt. She might run.'

'That's my fear.' He paused, trying to collate his thoughts. 'I've known from the first that something was wrong. Aside from the gaps in her CV, one look at her eyes told me she was hurting. I've tried to encourage her to talk but she won't. I want to help her but I don't know her history, what it is that went wrong.'

'I can tell you some of it. The rest I don't know myself because she's refused to talk since she came home,' Tom admitted.

Conor frowned. 'Home from where?'

'With Kate it was always going to be medicine,' Tom explained after a pause. 'Her goal was always general practice but she met Darren and was swayed by his ambition for a while.'

'Darren?' He forced the question, glancing back at the photo on the piano, wondering if he had a name for the face.

'I never liked him. Darren was not right man for Kate. He was on the professor's team, on his way to being a surgeon. James had been impressed with Kate during her initial training and Darren persuaded her to change her career path. At the end of her GP training, she joined the surgery rotation instead of going straight to a GP job as she'd planned. Darren was charming and knew how to get what he wanted. He had grand schemes for a fancy private clinic, was very self-centred and materialistic, but Kate wised up and ended her relationship with Darren.'

'What happened?'

'My daughter has always been traditional at heart; she's focused on her career but she's always wanted a family of her own. She found out Darren had been playing the field around the hospital behind her back, then she discovered him in compromising circumstances with one of her colleagues. That was two years ago.'

So Darren was the doctor Kate had mentioned. 'Kate thinks I'm like him,' he murmured, remembering her distrust and disapproval, her reaction seeing him with Jenny, jumping to the wrong conclusions.

'You're nothing like him, Conor. I'm sure she knows that deep down but is using it as an excuse to maintain some distance.'

'Maybe.' He frowned, unconvinced, groaning inwardly when he recalled how he'd been so worried about putting pressure on her by getting too serious too soon that he'd suggested they have some fun, keep it casual—the very thing bound to put her off. Cursing himself for getting things so wrong, he broke off his troubled thoughts as Tom continued with the story.

'The professor has been a mentor to Kate but he was disappointed when she left his team. She returned to general practice but didn't settle. I wasn't surprised when she decided to join an international aid agency—she always had strong views about injustice. Her first trip to Africa was hard but rewarding—the second was much worse. Wes, always the adventurous one, the risk-taker, was already there. Photojournalism gave him the buzz in the field he sought.'

Puzzled by the turn of the conversation, Conor frowned. 'Wes?'

'Wesley. My son,' Tom informed, gesturing to the photo.

So the guy cuddling Kate was her brother? A surge of relief washed through him.

'Wes often spoke of the terrible need and lack of health care in parts of Africa, and Kate had done her elective there during training, so when this posting came up she took it. She was part of a very small team in a remote area and they had been there for some weeks when there was an uprising. The fighting was terrible. Wes was there, covering it for his newspaper. As next of kin, the aid agency told me Kate's group were stranded, under attack, coping with unimaginable casualties, amputations, all sorts. She has never spoken of it.'

Conor felt sick as he listened, sure it was much worse than Tom knew. Kate had kept the real horror inside her. Saturday's accident had made her face it again. No wonder it had tipped her over the edge. He wished he was there with her now, keeping her safe.

'Wes was killed. So was Kate's fellow doctor and untold numbers of civilians and rebels. Kate was injured but she carried on alone, unable to get out. I know from speaking with the agency director that she had to do surgery way beyond her training, that there was no one else to help all those people.' Tom paused, emotion raw in his voice. 'When they finally got to her, she was in bad shape, traumatized, when they evacuated her home nearly four months ago. For a while she said she couldn't be a doctor any more, would never do surgery again. As she healed physically, the prof persuaded her to have a complete change of scene.'

'So she came to us,' Connor filled in, choked up as he struggled to absorb the enormity of all Kate had been through.

'Yes.' Tom smiled, his expression clearing. 'It's been good for her, Conor. I couldn't believe the change in her when I came up—it was like beginning to have my daughter back again. She's bottled everything up inside, about Wes and Africa. It's not healthy.'

As he lay in bed later, trying to get some sleep before the long drive back to Scotland, Conor's mind refused to shut down. He understood the omissions from her CV, the professor's concern to get her the job, why Kate had been terrified that first day with all the doubts inside her about being a doctor. And losing her brother on top of the other horrors, shutting that grief and trauma inside. He physically hurt at the knowledge of what Kate had endured, her amazing strength and courage. And her pain. So much pain and loss. He couldn't begin to imagine what she had seen and done and lost. He couldn't bear to think of her so alone, so scared. She wouldn't be any more—not if he had his way.

'You have my blessing, Conor, and my gratitude,' Tom said as they parted company on Tuesday morning, shaking hands. 'You're just what Kate needs.'

'I hope so, Tom.'

Setting off later than he had intended, Conor prayed that he could help Kate before it was too late.

'Fred, could I have a moment?' Kate asked after final surgery had finished on Tuesday, nerves tightening inside her as he glanced up from his paperwork and smiled, waving her to a chair.

'Of course, my dear. How are you?'

She lowered her gaze, hating lying to him. 'I'm fine.' Taking a deep breath, she steeled herself to get things over with. 'I'm really sorry to cause any difficulties, but I'm going to have to leave,' she told him, cursing the unsteadiness of her voice.

'Oh, Kate.' The heartfelt compassion in his words was nearly her undoing. 'If this is about Saturday, aren't you being too hasty?'

'No.'

'Have you spoken to James about this?' Fred asked after several moments of uncomfortable silence.

'No,' she repeated, suppressing a shiver when she imagined the professor's reaction. 'Not yet.'

Sighing, Fred ran a hand over his bald pate. 'Why not take a few days off when Conor comes back and think this over more carefully?'

'That wouldn't help.' Not with Conor being part of the problem, even the mention of his name spearing her insides with pain.

'Kate?' Reluctantly, her gaze met his, seeing the kindness and understanding in his blue eyes. 'Aside from the fact that we don't want to lose you, do you really feel things are going to be better anywhere else? We all care about you here—why not stay and let us help you?'

Fearing Fred knew rather more than she had thought, she shook her head. 'I can't. You can't.'

'I'm truly sorry you feel that way.' He shook his head, his eyes sad, and she felt a fresh wave of guilt. Fred, Aileen, everyone had been so kind to her. 'If you change your mind, you only have to say. Otherwise, if you're still sure it's what you want, we'll talk again when Conor comes back.'

'Do you know when that will be? Or where he's gone?'

She bit her lip, cursing herself for asking, her chest tightening when Fred's gaze slid from hers. 'Um, no. No, I don't, not exactly,' he murmured, looking evasive, and Kate suspected he did know but for some reason she didn't understand he had chosen not to tell her.

Leaving the surgery and returning to the flat, seeking solace in the kittens' antics, she wondered how she could have made such a mess of everything. She had come there to get her life back on track but had succeeded in making everything a hundred times worse, not only failing to deal with the issues in her professional life but by falling for the one man she felt she couldn't have.

* * *

Maybe things had worked out for the best time wise, Conor decided as he parked outside the surgery after what had felt an interminable journey. He checked his watch. After nine o'clock. A good thing to catch Kate by surprise and off guard. There was a light on in the bedroom of the flat upstairs and he walked round the side of the old granite building to the door of her flat. He rang the bell, waiting a tense few moments before he heard her light footsteps on the stairs and his pulse rate kicked up.

'Who is it?' she asked, sounding husky.

'Conor.'

'Oh!'

Her surprise and dismay were evident and when he didn't hear the bolt being drawn, he stepped closer. 'Open the door, Kate.'

He didn't actually hear her sigh but he could imagine it. Her reluctance was palpable as the door finally opened. Despite the dark circles under her eyes and her paleness, she looked beautiful, her hair mussed, a sleepy bloom on her face. His gaze skimmed down over the baggy T-shirt that fell halfway down her thighs, then lifted to her face, seeing nervousness, confusion and anxiety in her wary brown eyes.

'Is something wrong?' she asked, one hand settling at her throat as if shielding herself.

'Can I come in?'

'I—'

'Please, Kate.' He remembered the kittens and realised they were a way in. 'How are Smoky and Willow?'

Something shuttered in her eyes. 'Fine. You want to see them now?'

'Please. I've missed my girls,' he told her, holding her gaze, her being the most important of them.

'Of course.'

As she stepped back he moved inside, locking the door

behind him before he followed her up the stairs, looking at her shapely calves and the soft curves of her bare thighs. Upstairs she turned and faced him, crossing her arms defensively across her chest.

'Couldn't this have waited until tomorrow morning?'

'Sorry, no.' He managed a passable attempt at an apologetic smile, deliberately misleading her. 'You go back to bed. I'll see to things.'

'What?'

'I said—'

'I heard what you said,' she riposted with a frown. 'I meant, why?'

'Because you're sleepy and I didn't mean to disturb you. Off you go and get comfy. I won't be long with the kittens.'

She looked grumpy as she stared at him. 'Lock the door behind you when you go.'

Kate stomped back to the bedroom. So much for her early night and the hope she might get some much-needed sleep after the turmoil of the last few days. Stupid of her to think Conor was here to see her. She was so contrary. She'd told the man she wasn't interested in him—what did she expect if she didn't even know her own mind? Bemused and not a little anxious, she wriggled back into bed and drew the duvet up to her chin. Why was Conor there? Was it for Smoky and Willow? And where had he been? Thirty-six hours wasn't much of a holiday. She frowned again, hearing him moving about in the kitchen. What was he doing in there? It shouldn't take that long to pack up the kittens' things and go.

Kate tensed in surprise when Conor appeared in her bedroom, carrying two mugs of hot chocolate, and tried to close her mind to how much she still wanted him. It was impossible. Confused, she watched him, wary and uncertain, wondering what he was going to do next. When he handed her both mugs and then sat down on her bed with his back to her and began to take off his clothes, her eyes widened in shock.

CHAPTER TWELVE

'CONOR!' Kate protested, struggling to avoid spilling the drinks in her agitation.

'Mmm?'

Shoes hit the floor before his jumper was pulled over his head and tossed aside. Her gaze strayed inexorably to his broad back, the warm, smooth flesh and play of muscle whose feel she remembered too well, her traitorous fingers itching to touch, hot colour staining her cheeks as she saw the faint marks her nails had left on his skin. When his hands moved to the waistband of his jeans, panic surged through her and she found her voice.

'What the hell are you doing?'

'What does it look like?' he responded with maddening unconcern, as he shrugged out of his jeans and boxers then drew back the duvet so he could slide in beside her. 'Shift over.'

'Conor, we are *not* doing this.'

They weren't, she promised herself, fighting the shameful weakness of temptation, scared that he only had to touch her and her resolve would crumble to dust. Ignoring her anxiety, he adjusted his pillow, took one of the mugs out of her hands and leaned back to sip his drink. The nerve of the man left her speechless. Bewildered, she concentrated on her own drink as the silence stretched between them, but she was painfully aware of his nearness, of that ever-present shimmer of desire that crackled between them like an electric current. She could almost hear the thunder of her heartbeat in the silence of the room. Why the hell was she sitting there? She should leap out of this bed right now and demand he leave. So why couldn't she move? The seconds ticked by until, drinks finished, Conor set their mugs aside. Her pulse skittered as he slid an arm around her, shifting them until her head was resting against him and his fingers were stroking her hair.

'I've resigned,' she murmured, trying to put some distance between them, even if it wasn't physical.

'Have you?' He sounded insultingly unconcerned at the news. 'Don't worry. We can unresign you tomorrow.'

'Sorry?'

'When you change your mind,' he elaborated.

'Why would I want to change my mind?'

'Because you're happy here.' Pausing a moment, the fingers at her hair moved to caress her neck, making her flesh prickle. His voice dropped, soft yet husky. 'Because it's time to stop running.'

Kate stiffened in his hold. 'I don't know what you mean.'

'Yes, you do.' His fingers maintained their soothing caress, lulling her into a false sense of security. 'Do you want to know where I've been?'

'Not particularly,' she lied, feeling the chuckle rumble inside him, her fingers defying her, unable to resist their own explorations over the warm, supple, hair-brushed skin of his chest.

'I went to London.'

Kate tensed, her fingers stilling. 'Really?' Anxiety curled inside her.

'Mmm.'

'W-why?' Her eyes closed as she tried to shut out what she feared was to come.

'I had a very interesting talk with your father.'

Every particle of her being went rigid with shock and dismay. 'Conor—'

'Shh.' He stilled her protests, his hold tightening as she struggled to draw away from him.

'Why?' she whispered again, a shiver of foreboding rippling through her.

'I needed to understand,' he explained, his fingers resuming their rhythmic caress. 'And you need to talk.'

She shook her head, denying him, denying the emotions that threatened to overwhelm her. 'I can't.'

'Yes, you can. You are the bravest, most courageous person I've ever met, Kate.' His voice rang with sincerity and she was frightened at the sting of tears pricking her eyes, scared she couldn't hold on. 'I can't imagine what it must have been like for you out there but I could never have coped as you did.'

'But I didn't cope,' she interjected, emotion threatening to overwhelm her.

'From what I heard, you held everything together in terrible circumstances until help came.'

The guilt and the helplessness and the fear threatened to well up all over again, her voice rising with self-recrimination. 'There was so much death, so much killing. Such senseless waste. I should have helped more but I hadn't a clue what I was doing. I panicked, Conor. Cool Kate, always so calm in a crisis, wanted to abandon ship, hide, *die*—anything to get out of there. Then I came home and I lost it, running away from everything like a coward because I can't hack it any more.'

'Oh, Katy, that's not true,' he murmured roughly, his arms tightening, his hands comforting. 'Listen to me. You were alone in a terrifying and dangerous situation, trying to do things beyond your training level. You were physically exhausted, wounded, had little help and you were grieving for your brother and your colleagues. You were understandably scared and tired and ill. Yet you still carried on, saving as many lives as you could until help arrived. You did more—unspeakably more—than any one person could ever be expected to do. You are remarkable, Kate, and I'm so proud of you. Anyone would have been overtaken by the enormity of even a fraction of what you went through. It's hardly surprising that reaction set in once it was over and your body just shut down. It was too much. And you still haven't cried, you're still holding it all inside. You have nothing to feel guilty for, you are not to blame. It's time to let go. Time to acknowledge that you did what you could—and that that was truly amazing.'

'No!'

'Yes,' he pressed, refusing her any respite. 'You have to release this burden.'

She shook her head, trying to fight the emotion, to block out his rawly determined words. 'I can't,' she cried, angry at him for pressuring her, panic clawing ever closer.

'Why not?'

'Because I'm scared it won't stop, that I'll never pick myself up again,' she argued, her words catching, her body shaking with the effort of keeping herself together.

Gentle fingers stroked her face as he held her close, his voice husky in her ear. 'I'll always pick you up, Katy.'

'Conor—'

'Let it go. Trust me.'

She felt as if her last handhold had been ripped from her. The ground slipped away beneath her and she was in free fall. Tears started to flow, huge, hot tears coursing down her cheeks. It was like a dam had been breached, all her defences crumbling under the weight of the torrent, and everything came gushing out, all the pent-up pain, guilt, fear and grief. She turned in Conor's arms, burrowing into him as she sobbed out the hurt.

'It's OK,' he soothed, sounding as if he himself was on the point of cracking. 'I'm here. I've got you. I'm not going to let anything happen to you.'

She had no idea how long the storm lasted but Conor held her, keeping her safe, his warmth and strength seeping into her. Almost without conscious thought or free will, she found herself telling him everything, all the things she had never been able to tell anyone else, that she had never come to terms with: the terror of the gunfire and shelling; the noise; the smells; the blood; the suffering; people dying all around her; the mindless cruelty; the loneliness; anger; fear; and always the guilt that she hadn't been good enough.

'I was so scared, so useless,' she sobbed. 'There was so much I couldn't do.'

'But so much you *did* do to help many, many people who would have had nothing had you not been there,' he insisted quietly.

'But what good did I do them, Conor? What kind of life did I give them?' she demanded, wiping furiously at her tears. 'I didn't become a doctor to cut shattered limbs off innocent children.'

'Oh, Kate.' His voice was thick with answering emotion and he wrapped his arms more securely around her, as if trying to absorb her pain.

'Wesley, he—' She snapped off the words, unable to say it.

'He what?'

She shook her head, ashamed of her feelings. 'Nothing.'

'You're angry with him.'

'Sometimes,' she admitted, surprised anew at his perception. 'I miss him so much. He was brave, foolishly so sometimes. I told him not to go after that final story but he wouldn't listen. Everything was an adventure to him.' Fresh emotion welled inside her. 'I'm mad at him for leaving me there, for abandoning me, for not coming back. What does that make me?'

'Human, Kate, like the rest of us.'

She sniffed, taking the umpteenth tissue he had offered her. 'When I got home London seemed too oppressive and mad. Everything that had once been familiar and comfortable was suddenly alien and distressing. I'd lost a bit of weight, felt run down and stressed out.'

'And you had your injury.'

'Yes.' A flush tinged her tear-stained cheeks, a very different kind of shiver rippling through her as his fingers slid under her T-shirt and caressed the scar on her side.

'You didn't take care of yourself,' he chided.

'There was only me, Conor, and medications were so short. Others had far more need of them than I did. It was a flesh wound—the bullet missed anything vital.'

She felt a tremor run through him as she talked about her injury. 'It became infected?' he asked with obvious concern.

'Yes. But I'm fine now,' she murmured, distracted by the feel of his touch on her skin.

'I can understand why you wanted to shield your dad from all this, especially as he was grieving for Wesley, too, but wasn't there a friend, anyone, you could talk to?'

'Most people can't understand or don't want to. They prefer not to acknowledge how bad things are in other parts of the world, they don't want it to upset their cosy lives. Either they see what aid workers do as crazy or they think we are some kind of heroes, and neither is true. People volunteer for many different reasons.' She frowned, feeling exhausted as she rested against him. 'There just seemed a distance between me and the people I'd known before. I'd been away nearly a year by then, our lives were so different, we didn't connect any more.'

Held safe in his arms in the darkness of the night, she expunged the pain, exorcised the ghosts. And something she had never expected began to happen. A new calmness and sense of peace slowly began to ease the maelstrom of torment inside her, as if everything that had been eating away at her had been washed away. She felt almost ill from the crying that had ravaged her but there was a sense of release, of things shifting back into balance.

'Do you want to go back?' Conor asked after a while.

'Not to aid work.' She welcomed the way he linked the fingers of one hand with hers, giving her strength. 'I've done my bit. I couldn't live that life any more. But I think I'd like to go back to Africa one day. Make some new memories. Some better ones.'

His free hand returned to stroke her hair, his fingertips caressing her neck. 'What about your career?'

'I wondered for a time if I could still be a doctor.'

'And now?'

She sighed, trying to organise her jumbled thoughts—not easy the way her body responded to his touch. 'I can't face surgery any more but being a GP…I've enjoyed it.'

'You're an amazing doctor, Kate.' A warm glow burned inside her at his words. 'Russ is holding his own. He's going to have a long recovery, but he's alive thanks to you. His parents want to meet you and thank you. And all your patients love you—you've given the people here so much.'

'They're easy to care about.'

'So why don't you stay?'

It was tempting but she couldn't see him every day and not be more to him than a practice partner. Neither could she watch him with other women. 'I don't think so.'

'I want you here, Kate.' He sounded so serious, so sincere that she lifted her head from his chest, her teary gaze drawn to his. The emotion in the green depths amazed her. 'With me. Please.'

'W-with you?' she said in a shocked whisper.

A wry smile curved his mouth. 'Is the idea so terrible?' he teased, failing to mask the edge of anxiety.

'It's not that, but…' Her words trailed off as she struggled to voice her concerns. 'You want a quick fling—'

'Do I?'

'Don't you?'

'No.' He released her hand, his fingers lifting to brush the lingering wetness from her cheeks. 'What do you want?'

Everything, the whole happy ending, but it wasn't going to happen. She tried to move away because being so close to him made it impossible to think straight, but his hold tightened, keeping her close. 'It doesn't matter.'

'It does to me.'

'It wouldn't work, Conor, we're too different. You flit from woman to woman. You're phobic about commitment and—'

'You think I don't want commitment?' he interrupted.

Kate frowned in confusion at the surprise and challenge in his voice. 'Do you?'

'I want you to be a partner in the practice, if that's what you'd like, but most of all I need you in my life,' he insisted, his lips whispering against her skin. 'I love you, Kate. More than anything I want to settle down with you and have a family.'

Tears stung her eyes and she shook her head, trying to take it in. This wasn't what she'd expected, but he sounded genuine. 'Why haven't you, then? Settled down, I mean.'

'All I remember from my childhood is my parents' terrible marriage, the vindictive divorce and the stream of failed relationships and marriages that followed for both of them. I've lost count of the number of times my mother has married, the trail of devastation left in her wake.' His thumb brushed her cheek as he continued. 'I vowed that would never happen to me, that I wouldn't make those mistakes. I want it to be right, Kate. I don't want to put any child through the kind of thing I faced.'

Kate struggled to concentrate. 'But I thought—'

'You thought I was another Darren,' he chided.

'But all the women.'

'Just because I went on dates and have women friends doesn't mean I sleep with them, or even kiss them, for that matter. I've been much more choosy than you give me credit for. Why do you think I was in such a panic on Saturday night that the condoms might have been past their use-by date?'

The very thought of that night made her blush. She

frowned, thinking back, realising she had been so desperate for him that his scramble for the box in the drawer hadn't really registered. Could it really be true that he loved her? She hardly dared to believe it.

'But you said you just wanted some fun while I was here,' she reminded him, seeing him wince.

'A stupid misjudgement on my part.' He smiled, brushing some wayward strands of hair back from her face. 'You were so wary, so skittish, I thought you'd freak if I told you how serious I was and I'd frighten you away, so I planned to take it slowly, keep it casual. I didn't know that was exactly the wrong thing to do after what you had been through.'

'I don't understand.'

He smiled patiently at her frown. 'I knew from the first second I saw you that I was going to marry you.'

'W-what?' She stared at him, open-mouthed in shock, her heart thudding uncontrollably. 'But you don't even know me.'

'Don't be silly, Kate,' he chastised with a gentle smile. 'You're the other part of me that makes me feel whole and complete for the first time in my life.'

Kate swallowed, sure she was going to cry again. 'I am?'

'Convincing you has been another matter entirely.' The fingers of one hand slid back under her T-shirt, tracing distracting circles on her skin. 'I thought you'd say I was crazy if I dropped to my knees that first morning and begged you to marry me. You were so beautiful, so sad, so scared. I love you, Kate. All of you. Everything about you. Your compassion and ability as a doctor, your goodness as a person, your courage, your humour, your intelligence. As for what you do to me…' He drew her hand to his chest and she felt the rapid thud of his heart under her palm. 'I've never felt anything like this before. You turn my insides to mush. Kissing you, touching you, making love with you—nothing has ever been like this, Kate. I want to spend the rest of my life with you, loving you.'

'Oh, Conor.' The words escaped as a half laugh, half sob, her mind clearing, her fears fading. She couldn't doubt Conor's sincerity, could no longer deny her feelings for him, the amazing chemistry and bond between them. 'I love you, too.'

Overwhelmed with relief and happiness, Conor sank a hand into Kate's silken hair and drew her head down for a kiss, sighing with contentment as her mouth opened on his, hot and demanding, and the hungry desire flared out of control in an instant, just as it always did. She whimpered, pressing her body against his, her fingers gliding over his skin. There was only one place this was going but while he had a fragment of sense left he needed to know something. Rolling them over, he pinned her under him, catching her hands and linking his fingers with hers, smiling as she looked up at him through sultry brown eyes.

'What?' she demanded impatiently, wriggling under him, arousing him beyond bearing.

'Wait a minute.' He gave her more of his weight, keeping her still. 'Will you marry me?'

Disbelief vied with happiness as she looked up at him. 'Yes!'

'And we'll have dozens of babies?'

'I don't know about dozens.' She laughed through her tears. 'But definitely some.'

He had been scared about what would happen when Kate's fall hit her, had never imagined the secrets and the pain she had held inside her had been so traumatic. His heart had nearly broken at her anguish but they were through the worst now. It would take time but they would face it together and could look towards a brighter future. Peeling off her T-shirt, he lost himself in the magic of making love with Kate and, when they were finally joined together as one again, Kate wrapping around him, he gave thanks to whatever fates had brought this special woman into his life.

EPILOGUE

ONE late summer evening Kate stood on the roof terrace outside the bedroom, looking at the view.

Their wedding a few weeks ago had been the most special day of her life, her new community and all the practice staff having turned out in force to celebrate the marriage of two of their doctors. Her father had enjoyed every moment, his friendship with Aileen flourishing, and he was visiting often, talking about retiring to the village in the near future. Fred was ecstatic, taking more time to relax and cut back his hours, content that the Solway Medical Centre was in good hands. James, who had flown up with his wife for the weekend, had told everyone who would listen that he was responsible for bringing the happy couple together. Charlie had waited outside the church, Ben devotedly at his heels, while Lizzie Dalglish had been pushed up from the residential home in her wheelchair, grinning her delight as she sat beside Andrea Milne in pride of place. Louise Kerr, gaining in self-esteem as her health improved, had joined them, while Jenny and Mark had rushed back from their own honeymoon to celebrate. Nic and Hannah had been there and Kyle, still recovering from his own problems, had stood up as Conor's best man. There hadn't been a dry eye in Glentown.

Kate smiled, leaning on the railing as her thoughts turned

to their honeymoon. They had gone to Africa, visiting the country she had worked in on her last aid agency assignment, meeting former local colleagues and some of the people she had treated, including children she had felt so guilty about but who were facing their futures with amazing fortitude and thankfulness. There had been moments of sadness for Wesley and colleagues lost, but the trip had allowed her to put things in perspective, to balance bad memories with good ones. After that first week spent facing her past, Conor had surprised her with a special three-night visit to the incredible Ngorongoro Crater in Tanzania, which had been an unforgettable experience. Then they had spent four days in Kenya, where they had visited the Sheldrick elephant nursery in Nairobi. Kate laughed. Only Hannah and Nic would give someone a orphaned elephant as a wedding present! They had some wonderful photographs to show their friends that evening of their fostered baby elephant enjoying her daily mudbath.

Kate felt a deep peace and happiness she had never imagined she could know. She loved her work, her home, her community. She loved Smoky and Willow, who caused havoc wherever they went. Most of all she loved Conor. With every fibre of her being. Sensing his approach behind her, she leaned back against him as his arms enclosed her.

His lips nuzzled the sensitive spot behind her ear. 'Kate, are you all right?'

'I'm fine.' She smiled to herself, relieved now she knew just how fine.

'You've been distracted since we came home,' he said. 'What's wrong?'

'Nothing. Honestly. Not now.'

'Not now?' She heard the concern in his voice, his arms tightening. 'So there was something?'

'I was worried about my anti-malaria medication.'

'You're not feeling well? Why didn't you tell me?'

A smile curved her mouth as she turned to face him. 'I wanted to be sure. Now I am.'

'Sure of what?' he questioned with a frown.

'That everything was all right with the timing being so dodgy.'

Conor's frown deepened, his hands cupping her rear and pulling her closer. 'You're talking in riddles. What timing?'

'You know the dangers of the prophylactic drugs for some people.' She couldn't help teasing him a moment longer, hot desire flaring inside her at his touch. 'Pregnant people.'

Conor stilled, one hand moving round to curve protectively over her belly, a suspicion of moisture filming his green eyes as he stared at her in joyful anticipation. 'You're serious?'

'I am.'

'We're going to have a baby?'

'We are!' His urgent, excited kiss took her breath away.

'Hannah and Nic are coming to dinner!' Kate protested, laughing when he whisked her inside and began stripping off her clothes, her fingers sinking into the thickness of his dark blond hair as he dropped to his knees and pressed his mouth to her navel.

'They'll understand. I intend to celebrate baby number one first,' he murmured, his breath warm against her skin. 'I wonder how it happened.'

'You need me to explain the facts of life, Dr Anderson?' She laughed at his expression.

'It must have been that day you got so wild and the condom broke!' he teased, and a tide of colour warmed her face. 'I can't believe you can still blush! Not after the sinful, shameless things you do to me!'

'Conor!'

Laughing, he tipped her onto the bed, shed his own clothes and followed her down. 'You've made my life so special and happy.'

'I aim to please.'

'Oh, you more than please, sweetheart!'

His suggestive chuckle set her pulse racing, her fingers tightening on his shoulders as he set his mouth to the hollow of her throat. 'You're not too bad yourself.'

'Yeah?'

'Yeah.' She slid her hands down his back and wriggled provocatively under him, smiling at the evidence of his arousal.

'Now you've done it,' he groaned.

'I do hope so!'

For a moment he paused and raised his head, the look in his sexy green eyes warming her from the inside out. 'I love you, Katy. My perfect partner in every way.'

'I love you, too.'

And then they no longer needed words, their bodies taking over and demonstrating the intensity of their feelings and the loving bond between them that grew more special with every passing day. The events of the past had led her to Conor, who had helped her to heal. The past would always be with her, she would never forget, but thanks to Conor she had faced her demons… He had taken all the broken pieces of her life, her very self, and had put her back together, making her whole again. Out of pain and loss had come hope and love…a love now growing new life inside her and cementing the promise of a long and happy future together.

DR CAMPBELL'S SECRET SON

BY
ANNE FRASER

Anne Fraser was born in Scotland, but brought up in South Africa. After she left school she returned to the birthplace of her parents, the remote Western Islands of Scotland. She left there to train as a nurse before going on to university to study English Literature. After the birth of her first child, she and her doctor husband travelled the world, working in rural Africa, Australia and Northern Canada. *Dr Campbell's Secret Son* is her first novel, and the hospital which has such a strong hold on Jamie's loyalty is based on the place Anne and her husband lived and worked for a year and a half. It is also the setting for her next book. Anne still works in the health sector. To relax, she enjoys spending time with her family, reading, walking and travelling.

To my sisters—
without whom this book
may never have been written!

CHAPTER ONE

SARAH JANE CARRUTHERS took a deep breath before pushing open the double doors and entering the accident and emergency department.

'You'll be OK, girl,' she told herself. After all, it was what she had been working for as long as she could remember. It was the culmination of years of hard work and personal sacrifice. And nobody, except perhaps her mother, knew just how much it had cost her to be here today. One of the youngest and most highly regarded accident and emergency consultants in the country.

Her mind flew back to her mother and baby. It was the first time she had left Calum for a whole day since he had been born six months ago. Although she had tried to prepare them both for this day, she had been surprised at how emotional she had felt leaving her baby. She had been close to tears as she'd handed the small bundle over to her mother.

'We'll be fine, Sarah Jane,' her mother had attempted to comfort her. 'I've got the milk in the fridge and, remember, I have done this once or twice before!' She was the only person who ever called her by her full given name. Sarah preferred to leave out the 'Jane', especially professionally. It made her sound too young.

'I know Mum. It's just that he's so small still. He needs me so much. Maybe I should have stayed off another couple of months. Just until he was a little bigger.'

'It's never going to get any easier, darling. Your work needs you, too. Oh, by the way, did I tell you? You look fantastic.'

Having spent the last few months in jeans and T-shirts, Sarah had taken a great deal of time over her appearance that morning, dressing carefully in a smartly tailored black suit that emphasised her slim figure. She had added a blouse of emerald green which perfectly matched her eyes and tied her thick blonde hair into a neat chignon at the nape of her neck.

Although she had the utmost confidence in her medical ability, this was the first time, as a new consultant, that the buck would stop with her. Her team would be looking to her to take the lead and to inspire confidence. At the very least, she thought with some satisfaction when she had checked her appearance in the mirror, she would look the part, even if she didn't feel it.

However, the moment she stepped into the department it was as if she had never been away. The rush of adrenaline she had always felt coursed through her body, reminding her that despite her love for Calum she also loved being a doctor. And she knew she was a damn good one.

A red-haired nurse, who she recognised from her previous visit to the department, came rushing up to her.

'Dr Carruthers. Welcome to the department. It's good to have you on board. I'm not sure you remember from your visit, but I'm Sister Elizabeth York. My friends call me Lizzie.'

Lizzie's bright smile was infectious and as Sarah smiled back she felt herself relax. 'It's good to be here,' she replied, surprised to find herself really meaning it.

'Dr MacDonald will be so sorry he can't be here to help you settle in, but the locum who is covering for him is excellent.'

Sarah felt a small flicker of anxiety. Dr MacDonald was the senior consultant and Sarah had relied on him being there. Unfortunately he'd had a small stroke a couple of weeks before and was unlikely to be returning to work. There was nothing for it—she would just have to cope.

'No problem. I'm sure we'll manage. Perhaps you could show me around and introduce me to everyone?'

'Of course, I'd love to. Er, just one thing before we get started,' Lizzie said with a broad grin. 'You have something suspect on the shoulder of your jacket.'

Sarah glanced down. She was aghast to find that Calum had left a little of his breakfast on her shoulder. So far her day wasn't starting exactly as planned! 'Oops. Must have happened when I gave my son a last cuddle on the way out.'

'It's a relief to know you're not perfect after all. We've heard so much about the wonderful Dr Carruthers I was beginning to believe you couldn't be human. One of those wonderwomen, juggling a high-flying career and family while managing to look completely gorgeous and immaculate at the same time!'

Sarah laughed. She suspected that she had found a friend and ally in Lizzie. 'Oh, I'm human all right—as you're sure to find out. Give me a few minutes to clean up and then perhaps you can introduce me to the rest of the staff. And thanks. Wasn't exactly the first impression I was hoping to create. I was going with the high-flying immaculate career-woman.'

By the time Sarah returned, Lizzie had assembled the rest of the staff. 'Everyone's here, with the exception of the locum consultant. I'm a bit surprised—he's usually the first to arrive. Perhaps he's been delayed in the traffic. Mind you, it's not quite nine o'clock yet.'

'Well, first of all I'd like to say how pleased I am to be here and to meet you all. However, I do run a tight ship. I expect excellence from myself and all my staff. Professional conduct at all times.'

Looking around the serious faces, Sarah noted a mixed reaction. Some looked pleased at her words, but there were one or two who shuffled their feet uncomfortably—an older female nurse and one of the plaster-room technicians. She made a mental note to keep an eye on them.

She smiled to soften the impact of her words. 'On the other hand, if anyone has any problems, personal or professional, please, let me know. There's bound to be times when we all need a bit of support.' She saw a couple of staff nodding their heads in agreement.

'I think you'll find me very hands on,' she went on. 'I know some consultants leave a lot to their junior staff, but I like to keep up my clinical skills, so if you have any problems, let me know. Oh, and by the way, I take my coffee black.' Her last comment, spoken lightly, elicited a smile from her colleagues.

As the staff went about their business, Sarah unclenched her fists, which she had hidden behind her back. She shrugged the tension out of her shoulders. It was important to get off to the right start and it would take time for the team to get to know and trust her. She knew that Dr MacDonald had been in the department for years and was well loved by staff and patients alike. She had been told, however, by the senior managers who had formed part of her interview committee that some of his practices were considered outmoded. She, together with the locum consultant, would be expected to bring the department up to date.

'I'm getting a little long in the tooth for all this,' Dr MacDonald had confided in her when she had gone to see him about the job. 'I find it hard to keep up with the new technology that's sweeping into emergency medicine. I worry sometimes that we depend on it too much. Forget the basic principles of medical practice and lose sight of the patient at the end of all these machines and monitors. Always remember, Dr Carruthers, there is nothing better than your intuition. You strike me as a sensible girl despite your impressive credentials. I'm due to retire about a month after you take up your post, so I'll be there to help in the beginning. After that it will be up to you and whoever replaces me to make the department your own.'

Sarah had been grateful when she'd thought that Dr MacDonald would be around for a while. Regardless of what senior management thought, she knew him to be an excellent consultant with a national reputation. If only she could run the department half as well as he had, she would be happy.

'Come on, then, Dr Carruthers.' Lizzie interrupted her thoughts. 'I'll show you Resus first.'

'Please, Lizzie, except when we're in front of patients, call me Sarah.'

Lizzie showed Sarah around the department. She was pleased to see that everything was immaculate. All the equipment and drugs were stored neatly in the right places and the department was obviously kept well stocked. Lizzie was clearly a woman after her own heart.

'It's quiet so why don't we grab a cup of coffee while we can? I can fill you in on the rest of the information,' Lizzie suggested 'We're lucky enough to have a small staffroom right next to the duty room.'

Lizzie ushered Sarah into the staffroom. Painted in the ubiquitous hospital green, it was simply furnished with a couple of worn armchairs and a small coffee-table. A kettle and some mugs rested on top of a small fridge.

But it wasn't the room that caught Sarah's attention. Sitting in one of the armchairs, long legs stretched in front of him, was a figure that made Sarah's heart bang painfully in her chest. Jamie! What on earth was he doing here? The last time Sarah had heard, he had still been in Africa.

Jamie stood up, uncoiling his lean frame. He seemed unsurprised to see her. She caught a flicker of wry amusement in his deep brown eyes.

'Ah, our new consultant,' he drawled in his deep gravelly voice that, to her dismay, still had the power to send shivers up her spine.

'Sarah, may I introduce Dr Jamie Campbell, our locum consultant. He's only been here a couple of weeks, but we're all hoping he'll take Dr MacDonald's job when he officially retires. Jamie, this is Dr Sarah Carruthers—our new head of department.'

Sarah was speechless. He was the last person she had expected to meet. As Jamie engulfed her hand in his, feelings that she had thought she had managed to suppress came flooding back. He couldn't be here. She wasn't ready.

'Jamie. What brings you to the Royal?' she said, striving to keep her voice even.

'Work.' he said dryly. 'I need to keep my skills up to date, so I agreed to fill in here for a few weeks. But I'm going back to Africa as soon as I can. So, don't worry, whoever gets Dr MacDonald's job, it won't be me.'

Lizzie looked at Sarah, puzzlement furrowing her brow. 'You two know each other?'

'We've worked together before.' Jamie answered before Sarah could respond. 'I guess you could say we know each other pretty well.' He smiled politely, but his eyes were hooded.

'By the way, what happened to you this morning? We missed you at rounds.' Lizzie rushed on, seemingly unaware of the tension between her two colleagues.

Jamie looked a little sheepish. 'I was in early, so I took the opportunity to pop in to see Mrs MacLeod across the road. You remember, the old lady who broke her leg last week? I knew she had been discharged home yesterday and I just wanted to check up on her. She lives alone. And she's a stubborn one. The nurses told me she'd refused home help. I think I've managed to talk her around.'

It was unusual—if not unheard of—for A and E doctors to make house calls. But as Sarah well knew, Jamie had never gone by the book. It was one of the things she loved—*had loved*, she corrected herself—about him. She had known that she would have to see him again, but she'd always imagined that it would be at a time of her choosing. A time when she was prepared, when she could face him cool, calm and collected. Not like this, when he still had the power to set her pulse racing, make her go weak at the knees and, worst of all, send her thoughts spinning in every direction, except the sane, sensible path that she needed to keep him at a distance.

His skin, tanned by the African sun, added to his rugged good looks, making him drop-dead gorgeous. He had changed into theatre greens in preparation for the day ahead and the V of the tunic top revealed the dark crisp hairs on his chest. The trousers were too short for his tall frame, stopping just above his ankles, the thin fabric clinging to the muscles of his legs and hugging his hips. Images of being held in his strong arms, her head against his muscular chest, came rushing back. He was still the most disgustingly attractive man Sarah had ever met.

Before Sarah could think of anything to say, a nurse rushed in. 'Ambulance Control has just phoned. Multiple RTA—ETA five minutes.'

Sarah felt a jolt of adrenaline at the familiar words. Ambulances would be bringing in the casualties from a multiple traffic accident to the department within five minutes. Thinking about Jamie would have to wait.

'How many casualties are we expecting?'

'Three, the two drivers and one of the passengers—a child of about five.'

'OK everyone, let's get ready. Lizzie, could you let theatre know that we might need an emergency theatre? After you've done that, meet me at the entrance.' Jamie was already moving. His laconic manner had disappeared, replaced with an intensity that Sarah knew well. Despite the turmoil he had raised within her, she was glad that he would be working beside her for her first real challenge as a consultant. Whatever else she might feel about him—*And what would that be?* a small voice whispered—Sarah knew that Jamie was one of the best A and E doctors around.

As Sarah and Jamie stood waiting for the casualties to arrive, Sarah turned to Jamie. 'I had no idea you were back in the country.'

'And I had no idea until a few days ago that you had been appointed as the new consultant here. If I'd known, I wouldn't have taken the post. Well done, by the way. I know it's what you always wanted.'

I wanted you, she thought bitterly. She was dismayed to find how much his words hurt. 'I'm sure we can both manage to put the past behind us,' she said briskly. And then she thought of Calum. God—Calum. Jamie had no idea. How could they possibly put the past behind them?

'We need to talk.'

Jamie narrowed his eyes. 'I thought we had said everything that had to be said. But, sure. Name your time and place.'

The loud wail of sirens signalled the arrival of the road traffic victims, cutting off any further opportunity for discussion.

As the paramedics opened the doors of the ambulances, Jamie and Sarah swung into action. Sarah took the first ambulance, leaving Jamie and Lizzie the remaining two. Lying on a stretcher was a pale woman in her early thirties. She was unconscious. She had a large wound in her forehead which had bled copiously.

While Sarah bent to examine the patient, the paramedic rattled off all the information he had. 'This is the driver of one of the cars. Her son was with her. He's in one of the other ambulances. She's been unconscious but breathing on her own, Glasgow coma scale of 7. Head wound looks superficial but she obviously hit her head quite hard—it was an older car so no airbag. She also has a broken leg. Not sure of other injuries. Pulse is 110 and blood pressure 110 over 50. Oh, and as you can see, she's pregnant. Pretty far on, by the look of things.'

'OK let's get her into Resus.' Sarah turned to one of the junior doctors she had been introduced to earlier. 'Dr Thompson, could you take her in? I'll be with you in just a tick, once I've assessed the other casualties.'

Sarah moved over to the other ambulances. The other driver, an elderly man in his seventies, was sitting up on his trolley, his face covered with an oxygen mask. Lizzie was talking to him reassuringly. She looked up as Sarah approached.

'Mr James here is complaining of chest pain, but he doesn't seem to have any injuries. I'm just taking him into Resus as a precaution. Jamie has already taken the child through.'

Sarah bent over Mr James and listened to his chest. 'Thanks, Lizzie. Could you organise an ECG? I'll be along in a minute.'

Sarah hurried inside to join her patient. She passed Jamie examining a small child in one of the cubicles. The child was distressed but conscious. Jamie looked up. 'Neil here is fine. A bit shaken, but no damage done. His car seat kept him well protected. We'll just keep him under observation for an hour or two. He said his mummy fell asleep, but that's all I can get out of him so far. Except for a name—Lucy Croy. Do you need any help?'

'Yes, please. If you feel Neil will be OK for the time being with the nursing staff? I could use you in Resus.'

'I'll be back just as soon as I can, Neil.' Jamie said soothingly. 'I'm just going to check up on your mum. Nurse Winter here will look after you. She's got a little boy of just your age.'

As Jamie walked with Sarah she filled him in on the condition of the two other accident victims.

The resus room was a hive of activity when they entered. Doctors and nurses surrounded the two patients, taking blood and setting up drips. Although the air of tension in the room was palpable, everyone was working calmly and efficiently. Mr James had been connected to an ECG machine, which was checking his heart rhythm. One of the junior doctors, a cheerful-looking woman in her mid-twenties who had been introduced to Sarah as Dr Karen Davidson, looked up.

'I'll have the results of his ECG in a few moments and have also taken blood to check his troponin level.'

As one, Jamie and Sarah decided to concentrate on Lucy, who appeared to have regained consciousness but was thrashing around confused.

'We've started a drip on this lady. We've taken blood and urine samples. I've rung Obstetrics and they're sending someone down. Any clue as to what happened?' Dr Thompson asked.

'All we know so far is what the son has told us. He said she fell asleep, but whether he means before the accident or after is unclear. He said her name is Lucy, Lucy Croy,' Jamie replied.

'My son, is he OK? Please, I need to see him.' Lucy's eyes darted around the room, searching for her little boy. She tried to sit up. Gently Sarah pressed her back onto the trolley.

'Just relax. Neil is absolutely fine. You can see him shortly. But first we need to check you over. Can you remember what happened?'

'Not really. No. Nothing until I woke up here. My baby—is my baby OK?' Lucy clutched her abdomen.

Lizzie bent over Lucy, using the Doptone to search for the baby's heartbeat. She glanced up at Sarah. 'Baby's heartbeat seems fine. But I think we should get Lucy attached to a foetal monitor to be on the safe side.'

'Good idea.' She looked enquiringly at Jamie, who had been examining Lucy's head wound.

'Seems superficial, although it's bled quite a lot. I'd be surprised if it's serious enough to have caused the loss of consciousness, though. We'll get a head CT just to be sure.'

'Dr Carruthers, I have the results of Mr James's tests, if you have a moment,' Dr Davidson called over.

'You go on. We're fine here.' Jamie said. 'We'll know more once we get the blood and urine results.'

Sarah introduced herself to the elderly man lying on the trolley.

'I'm just going to examine you, Mr James. Can you tell me how you're feeling?'

'It's Bill,' he gasped, clearly in some pain. 'I'm all right—a little groggy perhaps. But my chest. It's awfully sore.'

He didn't appear to have any chest injury—she'd checked for bruising or chest tenderness automatically in her rapid but thorough initial assessment.

'Please—could somebody phone my wife? She'll be worried sick. I was only going to the garage to get some petrol. She'd have expected me to be back a long time ago.' Bill was clearly getting increasingly anxious. He struggled to get off the trolley. 'I need to be getting back...'

'Please, Mr James—Bill—try and relax. We'll let your wife know where you are,' Sarah said reassuringly.

She nodded to Dr Davidson. 'Could you ask one of the

nursing staff to try and reach Mrs James? I'd just like to re-examine Bill.'

Sarah's brow furrowed as she reviewed Mr James's ECG. She was at a loss to explain his chest pain. He was a little muddled and was unable to give a clear account of the accident. She fully expected the ECG to show ischaemic changes and was baffled when it appeared normal. But the old man continued to complain of severe chest pain. His blood pressure was low, where she would have expected it to be higher. Karen was looking to her to explain the symptoms, but she couldn't. It was her first real test as a consultant and she was scared she was going to fail it. If only Dr MacDonald were here! She looked up from studying Mr James's X-ray to find Jamie at her elbow.

'Problems?' he asked quietly. Jamie had always been protective of her, right through medical school and beyond. It was on the tip of her tongue to retort that she was managing just fine. It was *she* who was the senior doctor after all! But she knew her reaction was more likely a response to his proximity. Although she wanted nothing more than to put a million miles between them again, Sarah was too much of a professional to ever let personal feelings get in the way of patient care. And, she admitted to herself, there was no one whose medical opinion she trusted more than Jamie's.

'His symptoms don't quite fit. I've looked at his ECG and there isn't anything I wouldn't expect in someone of his age.'

'OK if I examine him?'

'Please. I need all the help I can get.'

Jamie returned a few minutes later, looking worried. 'You're right, it is puzzling, but I have come across something like it once before. I can't be sure, though, until I see his chest X-ray.'

'I've got it up here.'

As Jamie moved closer to scrutinise the X-ray, he brushed against her. Sarah felt an electric shock go through her body that made her toes curl.

'Tell me what you see,' Jamie prompted.

Sarah studied the X-ray for a few moments. 'His aorta seems a little wider than I would have expected—but I can't be sure.'

'That's what I thought,' agreed Jamie. 'But it would be helpful to know if it's always been like that or whether this is something new.'

'Hey, doesn't the department have a computer link with Radiology?' Sarah said.

'Good thinking. We should be able to compare this with any previous X-ray films.' Jamie and Sarah grinned at each other and she felt the past drift away. God, it felt good to be working with Jamie again. *Just that?* The treacherous inner voice was back.

Sarah called Lizzie over, who confirmed that they were able to do what she had asked. Minutes later Mr James's previous X-rays were displayed on the computer screen.

'Bingo!' Sarah exclaimed. 'There, you can see that his aorta is definitely wider than before. Looks like it's ruptured. That would explain his symptoms. We'd better get someone from Cardio. The sooner he's taken to Theatre the better. Could you page for someone, Lizzie? And let Theatre know?' She turned to Jamie and saw her delight mirrored in his eyes.

'Well spotted,' he said warmly.

'Team effort.' she replied sincerely

'We always did make a good team, didn't we?'

Jamie's words hung in the air. Although she knew that

he could be referring to when they had been trainees together, the look in his eyes told her that he meant something quite different.

'Jamie, I…' she started to say just as the cardiothoracic consultant, with an entourage of students, rushed in.

'I believe you've got a damaged aorta for me?'

'I'll leave you to it while I check up on Mrs. Croy, shall I?' Jamie dropped one eye in a slow wink before walking away.

'We're pretty certain.' Quickly and concisely Sarah explained Mr James's history.

'You're absolutely right,' the surgeon congratulated her. 'Well picked up. It's a pretty subtle sign on the X-ray and quite often gets missed until the patient's collapsed.'

'I wouldn't have picked it up without Dr Campbell suggesting it might be a possibility. It's not something I've ever come across. Luckily he had once before.'

Once Bill had been taken up to Theatre, Sarah returned to Lucy's bedside.

'She'll be going up to X-Ray soon,' Jamie informed Sarah. 'In the meantime, we'll keep her under close observation.' One of the nursing staff had brought Neil in to see her and he was sitting quietly, holding his mother's hand and watching the activity in the room with wide-eyed interest. Lucy seemed a lot calmer now that she had her son by her side. Sarah stretched to ease the kinks in her back.

'Well done, everyone. Great work.' Sarah glanced at her watch. 'Good grief, is that the time?' Hours had passed since the ambulances had arrived and Sarah was suddenly conscious of feeling ravenous. Besides, she wanted to check on Calum. 'If you guys want to go for lunch, I'll man the fort until you come back.'

Jamie eyed Sarah. She was still as beautiful as he remembered in a delicate way that belied the iron resolve he knew underpinned everything she did. She looked tired, dark circles bruised the delicate skin under her eyes. But despite the tiredness there was a new fullness to her breasts and roundness to her cheeks that hadn't been there before. At one time he had known every inch of her body and these curves were most definitely new. Nice, but new. He longed to run his hands over her body to refamiliarise himself with her contours. Damn it! He wanted to do more than that, he admitted to himself.

'I had a huge breakfast,' he said, patting his lean abdomen. 'I'm quite happy to wait an hour or so. Why don't you go with Lizzie? She can continue filling you in about the department while I check at Reception and deal with any waiting patients.'

'No, you and Sarah go, Jamie.' Lizzie suggested. 'I've checked and there's nobody waiting to see a doctor just now. I'll stay with Lucy. Besides, I'm on a diet,' she said, indicating her curves. 'Need to get into my dress for the wedding so I brought a salad. I can always page you if I need you. Go on the pair of you—shoo.'

Sarah didn't feel ready to be alone with Jamie. There were things she needed to tell him, but she wanted to be away from the distractions of the hospital so they could talk without interruption. Furthermore, she couldn't think clearly in his presence. She desperately wanted time alone to gather her thoughts.

And her feet were killing her. The new shoes she hadn't been able to resist to go with her new suit were rubbing painfully. She'd forgotten what it was like to be constantly on your feet. It would be comfortable if unfashionable shoes from now on, she promised herself. She flicked off one high-heeled shoe and rubbed her sore toes on the back of a trousered leg.

'I'm quite happy to put my feet up for a few moments in the staffroom with a cup of coffee.'

But Jamie clearly had other ideas. 'You need to eat.' he said firmly. 'I'll go to the canteen and get some sandwiches—you put the kettle on. Then you can put your feet up while you're eating. There's a spare pair of theatre sandals in the cupboard if you like.'

Good grief, did nothing escape the man? Sore feet or not, nothing would persuade her to clump around in theatre sandals. She glared at Jamie, making it clear that she found his suggestion preposterous. Noting the twinkle in Jamie's eyes, she smiled ruefully. He obviously remembered the fetish she had always had for shoes.

'You win. Five minutes in the staffroom?'

Sarah filled the kettle and set out the mugs for coffee before reaching for the phone. Although she had promised not to call, she couldn't help herself. She just had to check that Calum wasn't upset and crying for her.

As she waited for the call to be answered, Jamie arrived back with a pile of sandwiches and some fruit, which he dumped on the coffee-table.

'There, that should see us through the next few hours,' he said. 'Sorry, I didn't notice you were on the phone.'

'There's no answer,' Sarah replied, replacing the receiver, small lines of anxiety creasing her brow. Could Calum be sick? Had her mother taken him to the doctor? Don't be silly, she admonished herself. Perhaps they'd gone for a walk or her mother was changing Calum and couldn't come to the phone.

There could be a hundred reasons. That didn't stop her from worrying, however.

'Is anything wrong?' Jamie asked, as ever tuned into her moods.

'My mother isn't answering the phone.'

'Is that a problem? Is she ill?' Jamie had met Sarah's mother often and the last he'd known she had been in the best of health. Still, she was getting older and it had been a long time since he had last seen her.

'No it's not that. It's…' Sarah tailed off.

Jamie looked at her quizzically, cocking an eyebrow.

Just as Sarah was formulating the words to tell Jamie about Calum, there was a soft tap on the door and one of the male nurses popped his head into the room.

'Visitor, or should I say visitors, for you, Dr Carruthers. And can I just say he's absolutely gorgeous.' He stepped back, allowing Sarah's mother, with Calum in her arms, to enter.

'Mum! What is it? Is Calum all right?' Sarah said anxiously, reaching for her son. But it was immediately apparent from the smiles and gurgles as big brown eyes gazed into hers adoringly that her child was in perfect health.

'We were out for a walk, so I thought we'd just step in for a moment and say hello. We'd have crept away without disturbing you if you'd been busy. But I thought it would put your mind at rest if you could see for yourself how perfectly content Calum is.'

Catching sight of Jamie, Sarah's mother's lips formed a large O. 'Well, I never! Jamie. I must say I didn't expect to find you here.' She looked from Sarah to Jamie, perplexed.

For a moment Sarah froze. In her anxiety for her son, she had completely forgotten about Jamie's presence. She resisted the desire to grab her son and bolt from the room. Anything to put off the moment when she'd have to tell him. She sneaked a look at Jamie, who was looking confused. 'Jamie is the locum consultant here, Mum. He started a few weeks ago. Jamie, this is Calum, my son.'

'Your son!' Jamie said disbelievingly. Well, why not? He hadn't expected her to live the life of a nun. Heaven knew, *he* hadn't. But he hadn't expected her to find someone else so soon. Had she been that desperate to have children? How old was the child? Around six months, he guessed, although he was no expert. He started doing some mental arithmetic in his head. That meant she must have fallen pregnant soon after he'd left. That *was* quick.

Sarah busied herself pouring coffee. She turned her back on Jamie, taking a few deep breaths to steady her nerves. The teacup rattled in the saucer.

'Mama.' Calum gave a plaintive cry, reaching once more for his mother.

'You take your child. I'll get the coffee,' Jamie offered. Sarah scooped Calum into her arms. She covered his face with kisses, murmuring soothing endearments until he stopped fretting. Calum turned his wide brown eyes on Jamie. He had seen those eyes before. Then suddenly it hit him. Those were the same eyes he saw in the mirror every morning when he shaved.

Sarah stole a glance at Jamie. The colour had drained from his face as he looked from her to Calum. His lips tightened and his eyes were as grim as she had ever seen them. She felt the blood run cold in her veins. Not just angry she thought—furious.

'Mrs Carruthers, could you excuse us, please?' Jamie said, a river of steel running through his voice. 'I think Sarah and I have to talk.'

CHAPTER TWO

'WE DO have to talk, Jamie, but this is not the time or the place.' Sarah said, unwrapping the small arms from around her neck. 'Mum, could you take Calum home now, please?'

Mrs Carruthers moved to take Calum from his mother's arms but the baby, sensing the tension in the room, clung tighter to his mother.

'I'll just step out for a minute, shall I?' Calum's grandmother said, beating a hasty retreat and closing the door behind her.

'You had no right.' Jamie's eyes were almost black with fury—and something else. Could it be fear? wondered Sarah. Was he *that* terrified of becoming a father? Well, he needn't worry. She and Calum had managed just fine without him and would continue to manage without him. Or so she tried to convince herself, deliberately forcing back the memories of the lonely nights when she had longed for his strong body next to hers, his comforting arms around her, sharing the joys and anxieties of parenthood as well as her bed.

'It is nothing to do with you, Jamie. You made it perfectly clear that you didn't want children—or me, for that matter.'

Sarah fought hard to keep her voice steady. She had no intention of letting him know how much he had hurt her when he had left.

'Were you ever going to let me know?'

'Let you know what exactly?'

'That I had fathered a child.'

'Are you so sure that it's yours?' Sarah bit back, and then immediately regretted the words. Of course he had to know Calum was his. Despite the fact he had made it clear that he never wanted children, he did have the right to know. Even if he wanted nothing to do with either of them.

'Not mine?' For a moment hope flared in his deep brown eyes. Sarah felt as if her heart had been squeezed.

Jamie strode towards her, his mouth set in a grim line. Involuntarily, Sarah stepped back, hugging Calum protectively. Jamie shot her a look of questioning anguish before gently moving aside the blanket covering the small body. The baby gazed up at him with solemn brown eyes. A tiny hand reached out and wrapped itself around one of Jamie's fingers. The child pulled the finger into his mouth and gnawed with the nub of a tooth. Jamie's heart lurched. He felt ill.

'Oh, Sarah, what *have* you done?' he said, his voice edged with despair.

Sarah had imagined this moment for months. But never quite like this. In the small hours of the night, when she had lain in her big empty bed almost overwhelmed with the responsibility for the small life that depended so utterly on her, she'd imagined Jamie coming back into her life and, if not loving her, at least loving his child. She had never expected, or wanted, his financial help—she earned enough to provide quite comfortably for her and her child—but Calum needed a father figure. Someone who would play football with him, take him fishing, all the things that she imagined other fathers did.

'It's not just what *I* did, Jamie. You of all people should know that it takes two to make a baby,' she said, a small smile twisting her mouth.

Jamie had removed himself to the other side of the room, putting as much physical distance as possible between him and Sarah and the baby. He looked at her coldly. 'You told me you were on the Pill,' Jamie said flatly. 'I would never…'

'Never what, Jamie? Made love to me? If I remember correctly, that last night when you came round, you couldn't wait to get me back in your bed.'

Sarah's cheeks burned at the memory of their last night together. Of him standing in her small sitting room, looking as beautiful and dangerously enticing as Lucifer. Of her capitulation and their frenzied love-making before he had left her in the early hours of the morning. She had woken to find him staring down at her. Had it been a trick of the moonlight that had made her imagine the tenderness in his eyes as he'd gazed down at her? She had reached up and pulled him towards her. 'I could come with you,' she had whispered, not caring that she was laying her heart at his feet. He had gently detached her hands from around his neck.

'You are about to achieve everything you ever dreamed of in your career, Sarah. I can't give you what you want from me. Not when I'm…' He had hesitated. 'Not the committing kind.' And so he had left with one last lingering kiss.

Sarah forced her thoughts back to the present.

'And I *was* on the Pill,' she stressed 'until you told me it was over between us. And I thought it really was. That last evening was, well, unexpected.' Once more her cheeks flared as she stumbled over her words. Calum was getting restless in his mother's arms, beginning to squirm.

'Why didn't you tell me when you found out you were pregnant?' Sarah winced as Jamie ground out the words. 'Didn't you think I had the right to know?' He stood, arms crossed, looking at Sarah. She had seen that look before, usually when he had been justifiably ticking off some junior doctor for failing in some way. It was the first time she had ever had his disapproval directed at her. She lifted her chin.

'And what would you have done?' she asked scathingly 'Come rushing back? Offered to make an honest woman of me? No, Jamie. You made it crystal clear that marriage and children weren't part of your plans.'

'You could have had a termination.' Jamie's voice was emotionless. Sarah felt as if she had been kicked in the stomach.

'A termination? Oh, believe me, I thought about it. I wasn't ready to be a mum. And certainly not a single mother. But when it came down to it I just couldn't do it. She clutched Calum closer, unable to imagine a life without him. 'Is that what you would have wanted me to do? How can you bear to think that? Especially now that you've seen him? No, Jamie, having Calum was the best decision I ever made in my life. If you feel differently, I was right not to tell you.'

Jamie rubbed his face tiredly. Suddenly all the anger seemed to drain out of him.

'You don't understand…' he began, but before he could finish there was an urgent rap at the door and Lizzie pushed the door open.

'Jamie, Sarah, sorry to interrupt,' she said, taking in the atmosphere in the room with a quizzical eye, 'but I'm a bit worried about Mrs Croy—the pregnant lady.'

Jamie and Sarah immediately focused their attention on the young nurse, following her out of the room towards Resus.

'Could you take Calum home, Mum?' Sarah said as she passed her mother in the corridor. Calum immediately let out a loud wail at being removed from his mother's arms and Sarah couldn't suppress the pang she felt as she passed him over.

'I can handle this,' Jamie said tightly.

'I know you can, but it's my job, too. Calum will be fine in a moment.'

'Are you sure?' Jamie asked, his voice softening. But Sarah was already striding off in front of him without a backward glance at her snuffling baby. Surreptitiously she blinked back the tears that threatened to fall. She was determined not to let anyone see, least of all Jamie, how much Calum's cries tore at her heart. Millions of women had to leave their babies to work. As she had told Jamie, she had a job to do.

Her baby's plaintive cries still ringing in her ears, she bent over the frightened woman lying on the gurney in front of her.

Lucy looked from Sarah to Jamie, her eyes full of terror.

'I haven't felt my baby move since I came in. That's not normal, is it?' She reached over and clutched Jamie's arm with a strength that her small frame belied. 'Please, Doctor, don't let anything happen to my baby.'

'Try not to worry,' Jamie said softly. 'We're going to do everything in our power to make sure your baby stays healthy.'

'The obstetrician was down earlier, but thought everything

was fine. He was happy for Mrs Croy to stay in the department while she had all her tests. We kept the monitor on, though, as he suggested,' Lizzie told the doctors. Sarah could read the anxiety in her eyes. Clearly she felt something was wrong, too.

'Could I see the tracing?' Sarah asked. It had been a long time since she had done obstetrics and she prayed she remembered enough.

Lizzie handed Sarah the tracing of the baby's heartbeat. The lines looked ominously flat, suggesting the baby was in some distress. Wordlessly she passed it to Jamie. 'Get the obstetrican back down here stat, please, Lizzie. As well as a paediatrician and anaesthetist,' she added quietly, not wishing to further alarm the already terrified mother.

Jamie looked at the tracing and nodded at Sarah.

'I'd just like to have another look at your tummy if I may, Lucy.'

Jamie lifted Lucy's gown and felt her abdomen. 'Her abdomen feels soft and normal but…' He stepped back, looking puzzled for a moment. 'Sarah, what do you make of this?' Sarah bent over the woman. She could just make out a line of discolouration underneath Lucy's swollen abdomen.

'It looks like bruising from the seat belt.'

Jamie nodded grimly.

'It wasn't here when I first examined her. But bruising can take an hour or two to develop.' Sarah knew immediately what was causing his frown of concern.

'Lucy, I just want to examine you down below.'

Lucy's frantic eyes darted from Jamie to Sarah. It was clear she could sense their concern.

'She has some bleeding.' Sarah finished examining Lucy and looked at Jamie. She read the confirmation in his eyes.

'Lucy,' Jamie said gently, 'we think you might have had an abruption. It's where the placenta—the bit that nourishes the baby—breaks away from the wall of the uterus. It means we are going to have to get your baby delivered straight away.'

'Is my baby going to die?' Lucy whispered.

'Not if we've got anything to do with it. We're going to have to perform a Caesarean section and get the baby out. Lizzie, could you set up Resus for the op?'

Damn, where was the obstetrician? Sarah thought. It had been a few years since she had done a section. As an accident and emergency trainee she had been taught how to do it for emergencies such as this. But it had always been under the supervision of a consultant obstetrician.

Jamie caught her look and smiled reassuringly as he started scrubbing up. He seemed to read her mind. 'We don't have time to wait. Hopefully Donald will be here shortly, but I've done dozens of C-sections in Africa. We didn't have the luxury of obstetricians in the hospital I worked in, so we all had plenty of practice. How do you feel about assisting?'

'Like a hole in the head,' Sarah muttered under her breath. Some first day! Could it possibly get any worse? But she couldn't let her anxiety show. Not when everyone was watching her closely. 'Of course I'm happy to assist.'

'Better still, why don't you do it and I'll talk you through it?' Jamie suggested.

He was right, of course. It would be a good way for her to brush up on her technique while having someone experienced standing by. She had always loved the surgical part of her training, taking pride in her neat needlework.

His confidence in her helped her make up her mind. 'OK. Lizzie, could you call in the medical staff who are free to observe?' It would be good experience for them. They were part of a teaching hospital after all. Part of the consultants' responsibilities was to ensure that junior medical staff got thorough training in all aspects of emergency medicine. She looked at Lucy, who had been listening in, clearly terrified.

'Do we have your permission, Lucy?' she asked gently. 'It really is necessary to get baby out as soon as possible.'

Lucy looked from Sarah to Jamie for a moment before making up her mind. Mutely, she nodded her agreement. 'Just save my baby,' she pleaded.

Within minutes the young mother was draped and the staff gowned up. The anaesthetist arrived and gave her a spinal anaesthetic to deaden the feeling below her waist. The medical and nursing staff stood around to observe. Sarah knew they'd be interested to see how their new boss coped with the emergency.

Sarah took the scalpel Jamie held out for her and made a neat incision across Lucy's abdomen roughly where the seat belt had caused the bruising. Jamie used his hands to hold the layers of muscle and fat so that Sarah could see more easily what she was doing. Just as she made the final incision into the uterus, the obstetrician, Donald, appeared gowned and gloved.

'Sorry, folks. It's bedlam upstairs. Everything was perfectly quiet until an hour ago then all hell broke loose…' He watched Sarah for a few moments. 'Looks like you've got everything under control here. Are you OK to close up or would you like me to hang around? It's just that they could do with my help upstairs and you guys seem to be handling everything here.'

Almost before he had finished speaking, Sarah removed the baby, nodding her agreement to the harassed obstetrician while smiling her pleasure at the new arrival. Jamie checked the baby was starting to breathe as he prepared to cut the cord. 'You have a beautiful, healthy baby girl Lucy. You have a quick hold of her and then we'll let the paediatrician give her a quick once-over while Dr Carruthers stitches you up.'

He turned to Donald. 'It's all right. You can go. We'll finish up here then get Mrs Croy and baby up to the postnatal ward.'

Jamie watched as Sarah stitched Mrs Croy's abdomen together, her small hands working quickly. Unbidden, the image of those same hands fluttering across his chest and moving downwards rushed back. She had always had the power to surprise him. Underneath that cool professional exterior was a woman of hidden passion and innovation. At the memory he almost groaned aloud. Ye gods, he thought to himself, he had to concentrate on work. Seeing he was no longer required, he quietly left the room.

Later, Jamie went in search of the solitude of the staffroom. He needed time to think. He had managed to avoid being alone with Sarah for the rest of the shift. It hadn't been difficult. By the time Mrs Croy had been taken up to the postnatal ward, a queue of non-urgent patients had formed and he and all the other doctors had had to work flat out to ensure that they were all seen and treated.

But by six in the evening all the patients requiring the consultants' expertise had either been sent home or dispatched to the wards for follow-up care. Most of the junior day medical staff had gone, replaced by the night shift.

He was pretty certain that Sarah had left for the day. The full implications of seeing her again and finding out that she had a son—*they* had a son—had hit him hard. But now wasn't the time for rational discussion. Not before he knew exactly what he was going to do.

To his dismay, when he opened the door to the staffroom, he found Sarah sitting in one of the armchairs, holding a cup of coffee loosely in her hands. Her head was leaning back, exposing her long, delicate neck, and her eyes were closed, her breathing steady. Her thick blonde hair had come loose from the rather severe chignon she'd had when she'd arrived that morning and fell in wisps about her face. It made her look younger than her twenty-nine years and very vulnerable. As he watched her sleeping form he realised that despite the fifteen months and the continents that had he had put between them, he still cared for her. His heart twisted. How would she feel when she knew the truth? And one way or another, eventually she would have to know

'SJ?' he said quietly as he reached forward and gently removed the mug from her fingers, unsure if she was asleep. Her eyes fluttered open and for a long moment her green eyes, heavily fringed with dark lashes, gazed into his.

'Jamie,' she murmured dreamily.

Then suddenly she sprang to her feet.

'How long have you been watching me?'

'I've just come in. I thought you'd be long gone by now. Don't you have someone you need to get home to?' he said gently.

'Calum! He'll be waiting for me.' She looked at her watch. 'Is that the time already? It'll be his bedtime soon,' she said wistfully.

'Off you go. I'll finish up here,' Jamie offered

'I won't be treated any differently. I am fully prepared to take my share of the workload. I'll go home when I'm good and ready,' she told him, eyes flashing. But Jamie could see the fatigue in the deepening circles around her eyes and the way she moved to try and ease her aching back. Before he could stop himself he came up behind her and started massaging her shoulders with strong fingers.

He felt a shudder go through her slight frame and for a moment she leaned against him. He breathed in the heady scent of her perfume and the fragrance of her shampoo. He felt himself grow hard at the memories the feel of her body evoked. Aghast, he pushed her away from him.

She looked at him, confusion in her emerald green eyes.

'Go home, Sarah,' he said huskily.

'I need to write up some notes before I can leave,' she responded tiredly.

'Leave them. I'll do them. Now, go home, woman, before I lift you bodily out of this department.' It wasn't the right thing to say. For a moment he detected a glint of rebellion in her eyes before the shutters came down.

She held her hands up. 'OK. OK, I'm going!' she said, slipping a note in his hand before she left. 'My new address and telephone number. We will have to talk some time, but preferably not in the hospital.'

After Sarah left, Jamie sank back into the chair, still warm from Sarah's body, his head in his hands. Why couldn't he have stayed away from her that last night?

He had been a fool. A selfish fool. Now everything had changed. With a sigh he picked up the phone.

'Robert? Jamie,' he said when the phone was answered. 'Look, I need a favour from you. Never mind what it is right now, but could you come around to my flat, say, about eight this evening? Great I'll fill you in then.' He replaced the receiver. There was one thing he still had to do before he left for the night. He left the staffroom and made his way to the nurses' station. Checking to make sure that there was no one around, he selected a couple of needles, syringes and vials for collecting blood, and slipped them into his pocket.

Sarah moved around the kitchen, putting laundry away and making up the next day's bottles. It had taken longer than usual to settle Calum, who had been fractious and unsettled after a day without his mother. She was exhausted. It had not been a good first day, she thought. Oh, the work had been demanding, but she had loved every minute of it. She supposed practising medicine was like riding a bike—you never really forgot what to do. And as long as you kept up with the latest medical journals… She cast a guilty eye at the unread pile sitting on her coffee-table.

No, it wasn't work that had left her feeling as if she had done a few rounds with a heavy weight boxer, it had been meeting Jamie again on top of the emotional upheaval of leaving Calum. Her son and her job was as much as she could cope with right now. The last thing she needed, in her already over-complicated life, was Jamie Campbell stirring up old emotions.

'You should go to bed, darling,' her mother said, entering the kitchen. She, too, looked tired. Something else to feel guilty about. Her mother wasn't getting any younger and, God knew, looking after a six-month-old baby for hours at a time clearly took its toll.

'No, you get yourself home, Mum. I'm fine. Besides…'

'You're hoping he'll phone or call round, aren't you?' her mother said softly. 'But it's almost ten, so it's a little unlikely, don't you think?'

'Why didn't he let me know he was back? I could have broken the news better.'

'I thought you decided you weren't going to tell him?'

'I wasn't. There didn't seem to be a need. I thought if he knew, guilt—or a sense of duty—would make him try to pick up where we left off—he's that kind of man. But it wouldn't be because of me. It would be because of Calum. And I don't want him unless…' Calum stirred in his sleep. Mrs Carruthers followed Sarah into the nursery. They both held their breath as Calum sighed and his breathing grew deep and regular once more. The two women stood over the sleeping form and smiled at each other.

'Unless he can love you, too. Not just because you are the mother of his child,' her mother finished for her.

'Something like that, I guess.' Sarah grinned wryly. 'But we can manage, can't we? I have Calum, you and my career. It's enough. There's no room in my life for a love affair. When would I have the time?' She laughed but there was a break in her voice. 'Anyway,' Sarah went on, 'he clearly wasn't lying when he told me he didn't want children. Did you see his reaction when he realised Calum was his? I know he said he didn't want children, but surely after seeing Calum he must feel something? Oh, Mum, how can he not care? What will I tell Calum when he's older? How can I tell him his father didn't want him—even when he knew about him? Why did he have to come back? We were fine as we were.'

'It'll have been a shock for Jamie,' her mother said placatingly. 'After all, you had almost nine months to get used to the fact you were going to be a mother.'

'You always did defend him,' Sarah replied, hurt.

'I'm not defending him. How could I defend any man who hurt my only daughter as badly as he hurt you? You're better off without him, Sarah. One day you'll find someone to love you who is worthy of you. Someone who'll love Calum as if he were his own.'

'I don't want anyone else. I mean…I don't want anyone. I'm never going to let a man get under my skin again. Least of all Jamie Campbell. And I certainly don't want Calum to have a father who flits in and out of his life, like mine did. Never knowing if or when he'd turn up…'

And usually he hadn't. Sarah winced at the memories of her childhood self, sitting waiting eagerly for her father to take her out for the day. She would have been up for hours, getting dressed in her best dress, hair neatly brushed, almost giddy with excitement. And then, as the hours had passed, she had gradually given up hope until at last she had gone to bed to sob her eight-year-old heart out.

Jean Carruthers looked at her daughter sadly. 'I'm so sorry, Sarah. Your father was a weak man. But…' she shook her head in puzzlement '…Jamie Campbell never struck me as being weak.' She pulled on her coat ready to leave.

'Weak—no. Selfish? Perhaps. Whatever. He has no place in our lives.' Sarah wondered just who she was trying so hard to convince. She kissed her mother goodbye. 'Unfortunately we have to work together until he returns to Africa. I have to be professional about this, but the sooner he goes back, the happier I'll be.'

Jamie placed the tourniquet just above his elbow. Using his teeth, he pulled on one end to make it tight. He tapped at a swollen vein with a finger before inserting the needle. Blood rushed into the tube. As he released the tourniquet there was knock on the door. Jamie carefully placed the vial to one side before answering it. Robert stood there, right on time.

The two men exchanged small talk while Jamie poured them two large measures of malt whiskey.

'You didn't ask me over here to talk pleasantries,' Robert said astutely.

'No.' Jamie admitted. Then he quickly explained what he wanted Robert to do and why.

When he had finished, Robert looked thoughtful.

'I had no idea. You never told anyone, did you?'

'There was no reason to. It was nobody's business except mine.'

'Until now.'

'Until now.' Jamie agreed flatly

'I always did wonder why you let her go. We all thought you'd found your match in Sarah Carruthers.'

'I had. That's why I had to let her go. The other women

didn't matter. They knew that I wasn't in it for the long term. But Sarah—Sarah was different.'

'Why didn't you tell her? She's a doctor. She would've understood—if she truly loved you.'

'How could I tell her? I'm not the kind of man that would prevent a woman from having the children she wanted. The type of man who would tie a woman to him, to have her look after me. Give up her career, her future. No, I could never ask that of any woman. Least of all Sarah.'

'But you could have had the test before now!' Robert continued to insist.

'No,' Jamie said quietly. 'I decided a long time ago that if I had inherited the disease, I'd rather not know. I'd rather live in the here and now. Live every day as if it might be my last. It's the way I am, Robert, for better or worse.'

'Surely you have to tell Sarah now? She has a right to know.'

'What's the point in telling her now? It's too late. If the test is negative then she'll have spent the time worrying unnecessarily. If it's positive…' Jamie shook his head despairingly. 'Well, of course she'll have to know then.' He stood up, indicating the conversation was at an end. 'But this is getting us nowhere. I appreciate your concern but what I need you to do is to take the blood specimens and expedite them through the system as fast as possible.'

'They normally like you to have counselling in advance of the results,' Robert reminded Jamie as he pocketed the specimens and made for the door.

'It's not counselling I need, Robert. It's answers. Just do your best.'

CHAPTER THREE

SARAH was feeding Calum his breakfast next morning when her mother arrived. They'd had a tug of wills over the teaspoon Sarah was using to feed him. Calum had made several attempts to pull it from Sarah's hand and most of his breakfast had landed in his hair. He was delighted with this new game, smiling up at his mother to reveal a single tooth.

'What am I to do with you? Just as well I haven't had my shower yet.'

Calum responded by kicking his legs out in front of him in delight.

'You'd better jump in the shower, Sarah Jane,' her mother advised, eyeing the gloop that clung to one of Sarah's eyebrows. 'I'll finish feeding this young man if you like. I'll give him a bath after you leave.'

After months of searching, Sarah had managed to find a small house for the three of them near the hospital. It was small, but it had a garden and a small granny flat with a separate entrance for her mother. It meant that her mother could always be close at hand to help, but Sarah was also aware that her mother was getting older and if there came a time when she might need Sarah to help her, she would be able to return the favour.

When Sarah arrived at the hospital, the department was already mobbed with patients, although it wasn't quite eight.

She hadn't slept well. Despite her exhaustion it had taken her a long time to fall asleep. Unsettling thoughts of Jamie had tumbled around her head. She still couldn't quite believe that she'd be working with him, seeing him every day. How would she cope, knowing now that the time apart had done little to diminish the feelings she had for him? She had believed that she had got over him, although the daily sight of her child had been a constant reminder of his father. And if she hadn't been ready to see Jamie, she had been less prepared for him to find out about Calum. It had all happened too quickly. Could she really blame Jamie for being shocked and dismayed? When she had at last fallen into a restless sleep, it had only been to dream of him. A Jamie who looked at her with angry, disappointed eyes.

She wanted to find out what was happening before the junior doctors arrived for rounds at eight-thirty so she went in search of the night shift. She was unsurprised to find a dark head bent over case notes.

'Oh, hello, so we didn't scare you off?' Jamie said, looking up.

'Of course not. Yesterday was a fairly typical day, wouldn't you say?'

'Not in every aspect, no.' Jamie returned.

'No, er, well, perhaps not,' Sarah had to agree. She supposed, certainly hoped, it wasn't every day that Jamie found out he was the father of a child. 'Anyway, let's get started, shall we?'

'I've already been around. There's nothing that the juniors

can't handle. I was about to go up to the wards to see our two from yesterday. I've already spoken to the medical staff on Postnatal and Cardiology and apparently all three are doing fine.'

'It would have broken Lucy's heart if she'd lost the baby. Do you mind if I come up with you? I'd love to check up on them for myself, as well as see more of the hospital. We don't get to see the positive results of our work, do we? Patch them up and send them home usually.'

Sarah followed Jamie up to four flights of stairs to the labour ward.

'You wait for the lift if you like,' he offered. But Sarah didn't want to appear a wimp. Besides, she thought, thinking of the couple of extra pounds she wanted to lose after giving birth, she could do with the exercise. Exercise was something else she had to add to her to do list!

Jamie waited at the top of the stairs for her to arrive. He looked amused as she tried to disguise her laboured breath. 'Do you still climb?' Climbing and hill walking had been a shared passion. But Sarah had never taken the risks he had. He had seemed to always push himself. It had been as if he'd been driven. He had always looked for more difficult climbs, higher mountains. He had refused point blank to take her along on his more dangerous expeditions. She had argued with him that his attitude was patronising and sexist. But he had refused to be swayed. Sarah knew him to be a stubborn man once he had made up his mind. Just as he had made up his mind that he didn't want her, she thought bitterly.

'I don't exactly have the time!' she retorted. 'What, between a young baby and a full-time job.'

'Of course you don't. Sorry, that was stupid of me.' He flashed her one of his heart-stoppingly gorgeous broad grins and her heart lurched. She felt a surge of desire that warmed her body to the tips of her toes. Damn the man that he could still make her feel like that.

'We really don't know that much about each other, do we?' she replied coolly. 'Do you know which room Mrs Croy is in?' Sarah peeked into the room opposite the nurses' station where the patients recovering from surgery were always put and, sure enough, she could see Lucy sitting up in bed, holding her tiny baby. What she didn't expect to see were the tears that rolled down the young mother's cheeks.

'Perhaps you could let the staff know we're here?' she suggested to Jamie, nodding her head in the direction of the weeping woman. She wanted a few moments alone with Lucy and, besides, it was hospital etiquette to inform staff that visiting medics were present.

She tapped gently on the door. 'Can I come in, Lucy?'

Lucy sniffed away the tears. 'Dr Carruthers. It's good of you to come and see us.' Sarah slipped over to the side of the bed.

'May I?' she said, holding out her arms for the baby.

Wordlessly Lucy passed her daughter to Sarah. Sarah pushed back the blanket wrapping the baby to reveal a tiny face with rosebud lips. Blue eyes fixed on her face for a few seconds before scrunching up as the infant started to wail.

'Oh, dear,' said Sarah, 'I think I've unsettled her.'

'It's not you,' Lucy replied, joining her baby in loud sobs, 'it's me. She's hungry and I can't get her to feed. I didn't manage to breastfeed Neil,' she hiccuped, 'and I really wanted to feed this baby myself. But I can't.'

'It's not easy these first few days. It took me quite a few goes before I could get the hang of things,' Sarah confided softly.

'You?' Lucy said disbelievingly. 'You look like someone who manages to do everything perfectly first time.' But she looked interested and her tears were beginning to dry up.

Sarah laughed. 'That's just because people think doctors know everything but we don't. We're just the same as everyone else underneath. I promise you, I shed a good few tears when I first tried to feed my baby. But you know what? I had someone who spent quite a bit of time showing me how it was done and sat with me until I felt confident. Would you like me to help you?'

'Could you? I mean, are you sure you're not too busy?'

'Too busy to help a fellow mum? Never. Here, let me help you fix baby on.' Sarah perched on the bed beside Lucy and her infant.

Within a few moments and after only one or two false starts the baby was sucking contentedly at her mother's breast.

Lucy and Sarah smiled at each other. 'There you go! I'll come up later and see how you're getting on.' Sarah noticed Lucy's eyes drift towards the door. She turned around to find Jamie standing there, his expression inscrutable. She had no idea how long he'd been watching them.

'I can see you have your hands full, Mrs Croy,' he said. 'I'll come up and see you another time.' He nodded to Sarah. 'Ready?'

As Sarah and Jamie were about to leave, one of the nursing staff came bustling over. She was small and curvaceous with dark hair tied in a thick plait that fell down her back.

'Jamie, are we still on for tonight?' She touched him on the shoulder with a familiarity that set Sarah's teeth on edge. Was this woman the reason he hadn't called last night? Not that his love life was anything to do with her, she reminded herself.

'Sure. I'm on call, so we can't eat anywhere too far from the hospital.' Jamie slid a look in Sarah's direction. 'By the way, this is my colleague and the accident and emergency's new head of department, Dr Sarah Carruthers. Sarah, this is Annie Walker, midwife in charge of the postnatal ward.'

Annie looked at Sarah appraisingly. 'Pleased to meet you. Nice work yesterday, by the way. I've never seen such beautiful stitching,' she said warmly. 'Lucy has a lot to thank you and Jamie for.' Annie looked at Jamie with blatant admiration. 'Let's not go out. Why don't I cook and we can have a lazy night in?' Her eyes twinkled, leaving Sarah in no doubt as to the kind of lazy night she had in mind.

'Nice to meet you, but if you'll both excuse me, I have work to do.' If Jamie thought she had nothing better to do than be a witness to his love life then he was much mistaken. 'I'll see you back in the department once I've been to see Mr James.' She was aware she sounded a little frosty, but couldn't help herself.

Jamie glanced at her, amusement warming his eyes. A half-smile played on his lips. 'I'll be along in a minute.'

Grief, he couldn't possibly think she was jealous. Sarah glared at him before turning on her heel.

Mr James was still in Intensive Care, but the nursing staff expected him to be moved out to the cardiology ward in a day or two. His wife, an elderly lady with bright eyes and a shock of white hair, was by his bedside.

'This is Dr Carruthers, Mary.' Mr James's voice was raspy from the tube that he'd had in earlier to help him breathe, and

Sarah knew it would take a couple of days for any residual swelling to dissipate. 'She saved my life.'

Mary wrapped Sarah's hands in hers.

'Thank you so much, Doctor. He's a grumpy old so and so, but he's very precious to me.'

'We were only doing our job. But although he seems to be doing well, he's not out of the woods quite yet.' She didn't want to frighten the elderly couple, but a ruptured aorta, serious enough in a younger man, could be devastating in a man of Bill's years. She turned to the old man. 'You had us a little baffled for a while. Luckily for us, Dr Campbell picked up on your husband's condition in time.'

'Where is that young man of yours? I want to thank him, too.'

'Young man of mine?' Sarah said, puzzled. Just what was he talking about?

'Your young man—the other doctor. We'd like to thank him, too.'

'You mean Dr Campbell?' Sarah laughed nervously. 'He's not my young man. Whatever gave you that idea?'

'I wasn't so out of it that I didn't notice the way he was looking at you,' Bill insisted. Sarah felt her cheeks redden.

'Shush Bill,' his wife cautioned. 'You're embarrassing the young doctor. I'm sure she doesn't want to discuss her personal life with an old fool like you.' Despite the words, Sarah could see the very real love that existed between the couple. She sighed. Some people were so lucky. To find love and be able to hang onto it.

'How long have you two been married?'

'Fifty years.' Mary smiled at her husband 'And it seems like yesterday. When you meet the right one, dear, you hang on to him for all you're worth. Real love doesn't come along more than once. I almost lost my Bill during the war. If he hadn't come back to me, that would have been it. I would never have married anyone else.'

Bill looked over Sarah's shoulder. 'Oh, here he is. Your young man.'

Jamie raised a quizzical eyebrow as he entered the room. 'Whose young man?'

Really, the man had the most annoying habit of arriving at the most inopportune moments! Sarah thought irritably.

'I can assure you both that while Dr Campbell has plenty of lady friends, I am not among them.' Now what was she doing? She sounded like something out of a nineteenth-century novel. She could see by the glint in Jamie's eyes that he was enjoying her discomfort.

'And what makes you so sure I have plenty of lady friends? One at a time has always been enough for me,' he replied

'Too much in some cases,' Sarah muttered under her breath to him. 'Anyway,' she said, moving towards the door, 'I really must go and see the patients in the department. You both take care of yourselves. Let me know if you need anything.'

Leaving Jamie chatting with the elderly couple, Sarah found her way back to the emergency department. Lizzie greeted her with a smile.

'How did you find Mr James? And Lucy? I heard that you and Jamie had gone up to see them.'

Sarah brought Lizzie up to date. 'I'm still a little concerned about Bill. He and his wife seem to think that everything's absolutely fine and that he'll be gone home in a few days. I just hope they're right.'

'It's up to the cardiology staff now. We've done our bit. Oh, by the way, Housekeeping brought up some theatre greens for you. It'll save your clothes from getting stained. You know where the changing rooms are.'

'Thanks, Lizzie. Is there anyone I need to see first?'

'Just the usual run-of-the-mill twisted ankles and sore throats. Dr Thompson, Keith, is stitching up a young man who had an accident with a tiling cutter and Karen is supervising the medical students at the moment. We have a couple of patients waiting for X-rays and one in the plaster room,' Lizzie said as she checked the board on which all the patients being seen were logged. 'That's it. Between us we have everything under control. The juniors know to call you or Dr Campbell if they have any concerns and before they discharge anyone home.' She looked at Sarah speculatively. 'By the way, how do you and Jamie know each other?'

It was a question Sarah had been dreading. 'We trained together,' she said evasively. Although she liked and trusted the young nurse in front of her, she wasn't ready to divulge too much of her private life. Hospitals had always been hotbeds of gossip and the last thing she wanted was for her and Jamie to become the main topic.

'He's rather gorgeous, don't you think? Half the female staff are smitten with him. I could fancy him myself if I wasn't already in love.'

Good grief, Sarah thought, exasperated, was everyone determined to discuss Jamie with her? It was bad enough that she had to work with him without having him the subject of every conversation.

'I hadn't noticed,' Sarah lied. 'I'm not interested in men at the moment. Besides, he's not really my type. Too good-looking and impossibly conceited.'

'Conceited?' Lizzie repeated, 'I don't think I'd call him conceited. In fact, I'd say he's got very little idea of the effect he has on women.'

'I think Jamie Campbell has a very good idea of the effect he has on women,' Sarah said, a little more sharply than she'd intended. 'Now, if you'll excuse me, I'll just go and slip these on.' Leaving a bemused Lizzie in her wake, Sarah sought the relative sanctuary of the changing room.

The rest of the day was busy with a constant stream of patients requiring second opinions. She and Jamie fell into an easy working rhythm, dividing patients and the supervision of medical staff between them. When they spoke it was to discuss patients and treatment plans. It was late afternoon before Sarah managed to find time to stop for a sandwich. At least she'd have no problem losing a couple of pounds at this rate, she thought ruefully. She found a convenient vending machine and chose the least uninspiring sandwich she could find—chicken salad.

By the time she made her way back to the staffroom most of the other members of her team, including Jamie, had also taken advantage of the lull to grab a bite or a cup of coffee. Lizzie was happily filling everyone in on the details of her wedding, oblivious to the polite, resigned look on the faces around her. Clearly most, if not all, of the staff had heard it all before. She turned to Sarah, pleased to find a fresh pair of ears to regale.

'The wedding itself is going to be held in the small church in the village I grew up in a few miles out of Glasgow. I'm sorry I can't have you all there, but the church only holds around forty.' Jamie shot Sarah an amused look. She caught herself smiling back. 'The reception will be at a swish hotel on the banks of Loch Lomond.' She named a place that Sarah knew well. It was a five-star establishment which was a favourite venue for wedding receptions amongst the well to do of the city.

'I know somebody who had their wedding there. Cost an arm and a leg,' Karen volunteered. 'I plan on settling for the registry office for mine. Whenever that might be—seeing as I haven't even met him yet!' she added with a self-deprecating chuckle.

'Well, you only get married once, and…' Lizzie looked slightly sheepish, 'I'm an only child and my father is determined to give me a wedding no one will ever forget.'

At the mention of fathers, Sarah felt a pang. She was an only child, too, but it was unlikely that her father would even be at her wedding. Not that she was ever going to get married, she reminded herself. She sneaked a look at Jamie. He was frowning, though whether at the turn the conversation was taking or at some news article in the paper he was reading that annoyed him Sarah couldn't tell.

Lizzie turned to Sarah. 'You will come to the reception, Sarah? Everyone else is. It's on Saturday.'

'I'd love to come, Lizzie. But I'm not sure. There's Calum to think about. He'll have done without me all week. And I need to give my mum a break!'

'Can't you get a babysitter? Oh, please, come even if it's only for an hour or two,' Lizzie cajoled, determined that no one was to miss out on her big day.

'I don't know, Lizzie. I see too little of Calum as it is. I really don't like being away from him when I'm not working.'

Something in the set of Jamie's posture told Sarah he was listening in to the conversation.

'Then bring him,' Lizzie said as irrepressible as ever. 'I'm sure there will be plenty of volunteers to look after him. He's such a beautiful baby.'

Jamie stood, irritably tossing the paper to one side. 'I don't think being dragged along to a wedding is the best place for a baby.'

Sarah stared at him, dumbfounded. The rest of the staff looked uncomfortable as if this was a side to their boss they had rarely seen. 'I think it's time we all went back to work and let Dr Carruthers have her break,' Jamie continued, before leaving the room. The others, apart from Lizzie and Sarah, followed him out.

Sarah was furious. He had no right to tell her how to bring up her child. He may be the genetic father, but that didn't earn him the right to have a say in how Jamie was raised. Lizzie looked a little stricken.

'I'll see what I can do, Lizzie,' she said, 'but I can't promise anything.'

'Look, I'd love to have you there, but if it's no go then too bad.'

Sarah finished rinsing her cup before smiling at Lizzie. 'Come on, let's get back to the fray. Hopefully the patient with the suspected wrist fracture will be back from X-Ray by now.'

Sarah decided to head off at five-thirty. The department was quiet and if she left now she'd have a couple of hours to spend with Calum before bedtime. If she hurried, she just had time to pop in and see Bill on her way out. She changed out of her theatre greens and was calling out goodbye to the nursing staff when Jamie, his face sombre, called her into the duty room.

'Can't it wait, Jamie? I was just about to leave.'

Jamie looked at her, his eyes warm with sympathy.

'What is it, Jamie? What's happened?' she felt her heart begin to thud in her chest.

'I'm afraid I've got some bad news, SJ,' he said quietly.

CHAPTER FOUR

'WHAT is it? What's happened?' Sarah asked.

'I'm afraid Mr James—Bill—has taken a turn for the worse. The staff had thought he was doing well enough to have transferred him out of Intensive Care and into the cardiology ward, but he arrested shortly afterwards. They managed to resuscitate him, but I'm afraid it's only a matter of time. They have decided, with the agreement of Mary, that there is no point in taking him back to Intensive Care, and are going to make him comfortable on the ward.'

'Poor Bill—but I half expected this from the start. His age and the fact that his condition had obviously gone untreated for some time really counted against him. And poor Mary!' Sarah continued, picking up her coat. 'I was planning to go up and see them both before I went home. I'll go up now.'

'Do you have time? Aren't you in a rush to get back to Calum? I'm on call tonight. Why don't you go on home and I'll phone you if there is any change?'

Sarah felt torn. She wanted to go home. She missed her son, and missed spending time with him, even though she had only been back at work a couple of days.

'We both know that being a doctor isn't a nine-to-five job.' Sarah smiled tiredly. 'But neither is being a mother,' she continued with a rueful shake of her head. 'Now I know what these working mothers mean when they wish for a thirty-hour day.' She had always known that it would be difficult, balancing her career with being a single parent, but until today she hadn't realised just how hard it was going to be. Was she always going to feel like this? Torn between her child and her patients, even though Calum would always be her priority. Wearily she got to her feet.

'I'm going to pop up and see Mary for a few minutes at least. Maybe by the time I head off the rush-hour traffic will have eased and I'll get home at the same time anyway. And, yes, if you could ring me if there is any change—it doesn't matter what time—I'd be grateful.'

Jamie looked at her searchingly before replying. 'Of course. Would you like me to come up with you?'

'Thank you but no,' she said formally. 'I know you've got work to finish here. And anyway,' she added dryly, 'don't you have to get ready for your date?'

'Hell, I'd forgotten.' Jamie said. Sarah couldn't help a small pang of pleasure that the voluptuous Nurse Walker could be so easily dismissed from his mind. Serve the vamp right, she thought waspishly.

With a final reminder to Jamie to call her, she made her way to Cardiology where she found Mary sitting in the dim glow of the nightlight, holding her husband's hand. She was talking to him in a soft voice.

'Hold on a little longer, Bill,' she was whispering. 'Jack's on his way. He won't be long. Hold on just a little while longer.'

She looked up as Sarah entered the room and managed a wan smile. 'I was just telling him to wait for Jack,' she said simply.

Sarah pulled up a chair and sat down next to the old lady. She took her free hand in hers feeling the delicate, almost papery skin under her fingers.

'Who's Jack?' she asked softly.

'Our son.' She went on in response to Sarah's look of surprise. 'Oh, yes, we have a son. He lives in the Lake District. Sadly he and his father have never hit it off. Bill was in the army and we always had to move around from place to place. We left Jack in boarding school, we thought it was for the best, but he was really unhappy and always blamed his father. It wasn't fair or right even, but I have two stubborn men. They fell out badly a couple of years ago and neither of them has been prepared to make peace. Each felt it was up to the other. Thankfully, Jack and I have always kept in touch. Occasionally I go and stay with him and his family for a few days. Bill knows and although he has always feigned disinterest, I know he likes to hear about his son and the grandchildren. I keep in touch for both of us. I phoned Jack to let him know about his dad. He's on his way. He just wants a chance to say sorry and to tell his dad that he loves him.' Mary turned back to her sick husband. 'But you know that already, don't you, Bill?' Apart from the flutter of eyelids, there was no response from the sick man.

'I am so sorry.' Sarah said. 'I thought we had managed to save him.'

'Och, don't you worry, dear—I know it's not your fault. We both know that. It's just that Bill's time has come. If you've managed to give him a little longer—just enough to see his son and for Jack to see him one last time—we'll be forever grateful.'

Sarah swallowed the lump in her throat, at a loss for words. The two women sat in silence for a few moments.

'Do you have anyone special in your life?' Mary asked.

'A son. Just over six months old,' Sarah replied.

'And the father?' Mary prompted gently.

'He doesn't live with us.' The dark room and the soft light made Sarah feel that she could confide in the woman looking at her with keen interest. 'He didn't—doesn't—want children,' she said, a slight break in her voice.

'Fathers are important no matter what anyone says. Every child needs a father in their life, and every father…' She hesitated, glancing at her husband's sleeping form. 'Needs his child.'

Sarah's lips twisted. Fathers needing their children? Not in her experience.

Before Sarah could formulate a suitable response, Mary looked past her to the doorway. Her faded blue eyes lit up as she saw who was standing there.

'Jack. My dearest boy, you made it!'

Jack, a man in his early forties, cast an anguished look towards the still form lying in the bed. 'Is he…?' He broke off, clearly unable to formulate the words.

'He's still alive, Jack. But he hasn't got long.'

As Jack enfolded his mother in his arms, Sarah slipped away with a few whispered words to Bill. There was no longer any reason for her to stay. The family needed their privacy now more than anything else.

As she tiptoed away pictures of her father tossing her into the air and her subsequent shrieks of laughter came trickling back. Seeing Bill and his son together after hearing about their long estrangement brought memories to the surface she had kept hidden for a long time. The hurt of his abandonment had been so profound that she had been unable to think of him in anything but the most painful way. But, she realised, it hadn't always been like that. It hadn't always been disappointment and sadness. Her father had been a charismatic man and, she was forced to admit, at least some of her memories involved laughter and fun. Perhaps if he'd been a cruel man she could have borne it better, but he hadn't been cruel, just careless of her and her feelings. Like Jamie.

Before Jamie went to check on Bill and Mary, he called into the postnatal ward to see Annie. They had agreed that she would go over to Jamie's flat after she finished her shift at eight. That way if Jamie was called out he'd be able to go back to work at a moment's notice. But he knew it wasn't fair on Annie to let her continue to believe that there was anything more than friendship on his side. Although at the beginning the attractive midwife had said that she was only interested in a casual relationship, Jamie wondered if her feelings had changed. She had flirted outrageously with him yesterday in front of Sarah and he had to admit he had been slightly disconcerted. Annie had confided in him early on in their friendship that she had recently broken off her relationship with her boyfriend of four years.

'I just got fed up with the amount of time he was playing rugby. Every night and then at weekends. I hardly ever saw him. So I told him it was either rugby or me. And—' he could hear the hurt and indignation under the outrage '—he chose rugby.'

Jamie found Annie in the staffroom, catching up on her notes before going off duty. Not expecting to see him till their date later that evening, Annie grinned wickedly.

'Couldn't wait to see me, Dr Campbell?' she asked teasingly.

'I'm sorry to do this at the last minute, Annie, but something's come up and I can't make it tonight.'

Annie was philosophical about their broken date. 'Only one thing worse than going out with an addicted rugby player—and that's going out with a doctor.'

Jamie was taken aback. Although they had dated once or twice, he had been upfront with Annie right from the start. She knew he would be going back to Africa and wasn't up for a long-term relationship.

'I'm sorry, Annie, I think it's best that we don't see each other again, at least not romantically. I've enjoyed the time we've spent together, you're great company, but you know I'm going back to Africa soon and, besides, my life is just too complicated at the moment. Anyway I suspect, however much you try to pretend otherwise, that your heart lies elsewhere.'

Instead of appearing hurt by his words, Annie shook her head.

'Don't worry, I always knew that our relationship was never going anywhere. It's not as if you were anything less than honest about that.' She looked at him ruefully 'And you're right, if I'm honest with myself, I guess I'm still in love with Mark.' She smiled to show him there were no hard feelings. 'Actually, Mark has been on the phone several times over the last few days—I guess he heard on the hospital grapevine that I've being seeing the gorgeous Dr Campbell, and it seems that rugby doesn't have the same allure as it once had!'

Jamie looked at her suspiciously. 'Correct me if I'm wrong, but is that what yesterday's performance was about?'

Annie dropped her eyes, looking shamefaced, before her face creased into a broad smile. 'Well, it seems to have worked. You don't mind, do you?'

'Of course not. Not if it helped get you and Mark back together. But don't you think those kinds of games can be dangerous?'

'All's fair in love and war. Or so they tell me. You know if ever you need me to do the same for you, I'd be happy to oblige.'

Jamie looked into Annie's twinkling eyes. 'As I said, my life is complicated enough. I only wish *I* could be honest…' He left the sentence unfinished.

Annie looked at him searchingly. She sensed that there was a great deal that Jamie wasn't telling her, but the look in his eyes stopped her from asking. 'If ever you need a friendly ear, Jamie, you know where to find me.'

On impulse Jamie put his arm around her and squeezed her shoulders. 'Thanks, but at the moment there is nothing anyone can do to help.'

Sarah gazed lovingly at her son as he lay in his cot, his long eyelashes casting shadows on his fat pink cheeks as he drifted off to sleep for the night. Her heart felt as if it would burst with love and pride for Calum, and for the thousandth time since his birth she was glad she had made the right decision in having him. If only Jamie would allow himself to love Calum, she thought, he too could experience the wonder of their child.

Leaving the door of the bathroom open in case Calum

woke up, Sarah had a quick shower. As she pulled on pyjama shorts and a camisole top, the doorbell rang. Belting up her short cotton dressing-gown, Sarah frowned as she tiptoed barefoot to the front door. Who on earth could be calling at this time of night? Keeping the chain on, she opened the door just enough to see who was standing there.

'Jamie! What are you doing here?' she asked, although from the sympathetic expression in his deep brown eyes she thought she knew.

'Can I come in for a minute? I know you said to phone, but some news is better delivered in person,' he said quietly.

Sarah unhooked the security chain and opened the door.

'It's Bill isn't it?' she stated. 'He's worse?' She felt her heart begin to thud in her chest.

'I'm so sorry, SJ, but he arrested just before ten. The ward phoned me. They did everything they could but they were unable to bring him around. He died a short while ago.'

Although Sarah had expected the news, it was still a shock. 'Oh, no!' she whispered. She was used to patients dying. She had to be, working as an A and E doctor. But Bill and his wife, and their bittersweet reunion with their estranged son, had crept under her skin. She had hoped against all odds that this was one story with a happy ending. She tried to blink away the tears blurring her vision.

Jamie stepped closer. 'Everybody did everything they could. You did everything you could, and gave him precious extra time to spend with his family.' Without knowing how it happened, Sarah found herself in Jamie's arms. She smelled the leather of his jacket as she rested her head against his chest.

'His poor wife, how will she cope?' she mumbled into his

chest. 'They'd been married for fifty years. They were everything to each other. How does someone go on after their partner of so long leaves them?'

Jamie was a little taken aback by her reaction. He had always known that Sarah let herself become attached to patients. But she usually hid it well, only ever showing a professional, cool exterior. Perhaps motherhood had changed her, softened her? Jamie was unprepared for the surge of protectiveness he felt as he stroked her hair tenderly. As she started to pull away, he cupped her face, gently wiping away her spilt tears with his thumbs. 'At least Mary still has her son and he'll be of some comfort and support to her.' Jamie soothed softly. 'And Bill was able to make his peace before he died.'

Remembering what Mary had said about fathers and sons, Sarah longed to blurt out the words that raged in her heart as she searched Jamie's eyes for some clue as to how he felt about her and Calum. Why couldn't he love her? And their son? Exhaustion and emotion brought fresh tears welling up in her eyes once more. 'Shh, it's OK, SJ,' Jamie said huskily, and before she knew it, he was kissing her salty, wet cheeks, tracing the tears tracks down her face and then finding her lips and tenderly covering her mouth with his own.

Sarah clung to him, breathing in his intoxicating male scent. The smell of him and the taste of his lips sent her dormant hormones into overdrive. All she could think of as Jamie's kisses became deeper, more demanding was how much she wanted him inside her. Maybe it was a reaction to Bill's death, but for the moment neither the past nor the future mattered more than her imperative need.

She slipped her hands under the front of his T-shirt, feeling the muscles of his chest bunch and tense at her touch. She let her hands travel across his skin, first finding the indent of muscle at his lower back and then, as he groaned, pulling her hips towards him, she moved her hands, as light as butterflies, to just above his jeans button to the crisp hair on his abdomen.

Jamie removed his jacket, tossing it onto the floor. In the same swift movement he removed her dressing-gown and pulled her camisole top off over her head. Her nipples tightened with desire as he cupped them gently in hands still rough from years of climbing.

Jamie could not believe he had her in his arms again. And she had come so easily, as if they had never been apart, as if the feelings between them had not lessened with time. How soft and pliant she was, how inviting… The cold intrusive voice of reason made him falter. But was this fair to her? To revive a love affair that should stay ended? What the hell was he doing? He grabbed hold of her hips again but this time it was to peel her away from him.

'I'm sorry, SJ,' he groaned, 'I can't.'

Sarah stepped away from him as if she had been slapped. *He was rejecting her? Again? Did he think she was some sex-starved floozy who had been waiting for him to return so she could grapple him back into bed?*

Before Sarah could think of the words to persuade him that her reaction meant nothing, a loud wail tore through the air.

'What on earth is that?' Jamie asked.

'Calum,' Sarah said quietly. 'He must be looking for his next feed.'

For a moment Sarah and Jamie looked at one another. She felt slightly dazed. With trembling fingers she scooped up her camisole top and hurriedly pulled it on. Her cheeks flushed with embarrassment, Sarah tiptoed silently into the nursery, leaving the door slightly ajar so that she could attend to Calum without switching on the bedside light. As soon as she picked him up, his loud cries changed to whimpers.

Jamie appeared behind her. 'I'd better go,' he said softly.

'Yes, perhaps you should,' Sarah whispered, not trusting herself to look at him. Suddenly she remembered his date with Annie Walker. Unbidden, an image of the gorgeous midwife warming his bed sprang to her mind. Was that why he had pulled back? 'Ah, your prior arrangement with Nurse Walker—she'll be wondering where you are,' she stated flatly, anger rising, overcoming her embarrassment. What a stupid, lust-ridden, idiot he must think her.

Narrowing his eyes, Jamie said tightly, 'Actually, Sarah, I cancelled my date with Annie tonight.'

'Why?' Sarah said, turning away from him so he couldn't read the spurt of happiness she felt in her eyes. His voice was terse. 'Because, like you, I have more than enough to deal with right now without—' Before he could complete the sentence Calum began to cry in earnest.

'Here,' she said, handing him to Jamie 'You hold him while I go heat up a bottle. I don't suppose you can change a nappy?'

Jamie looked at Sarah in dismay. He was holding Calum at arm's length, as if he were some kind of foreign object. 'Change a nappy?' he echoed. 'You're not serious?'

'Why not? You'll have to learn some time. Whatever else you are, Jamie, you are this child's father, whether you like it or not.' Sarah said, and turned on her heel, leaving her son and his father alone together.

Jamie looked at the small bundle he was holding. Calum's cries had stopped and he was looking at Jamie with interest.

'Hello, there,' Jamie said.

Calum kicked his legs vigorously in response. For one horrifying moment Jamie thought he would drop the baby and changed his grip, holding him in his arms the way he had held hundreds of small children in his career. But this wasn't any child. This was *his* child. A surge of love and tenderness for his son caught Jamie unawares. Oh, God, he groaned inwardly. What sort of future had he inflicted on this innocent baby? He *had* to find out the blood results before he became any more involved with either of them. He closed his eyes against the image of life without Sarah or Calum.

'Ubh,' he said as tiny, strong fingers reached forward and gripped his lower lip, yanking it forward. His eyes shot open, to meet those of his son regarding him intently. Strong hands. Jamie thought past the pain. He'll make a good rock climber with a grip like that. And as an image of himself and his son several years older, climbing together, passed through his mind, Jamie realised that for the second time in his life he had fallen hopelessly and irrevocably in love.

Heated bottle in hand, Sarah stood watching Jamie and her son. *Their* son. He seemed so relaxed with his child and Calum in his turn seemed happy and contented with his father. She felt confused. What did it all mean? Jamie taking her in his arms, playing with his child. And how did she feel about it? She needed to know what was going on inside Jamie's head.

'Let me change Calum's nappy and give him his feed. Then perhaps we can talk once he's asleep,' she suggested.

Jamie stood up, handing the baby over.

'Talk about what, Sarah?' he asked softly

'Us. You and me. Well, maybe not us.' She stumbled over the words. That wasn't what she'd intended to say. He obviously had no intention of there being an 'us'. 'You and Calum.'

'Of course I'll make sure you are both well provided for financially.'

'Financially?' Sarah echoed, feeling the blood in her veins turn to ice. 'Is that what you think I want? Financial help with a bit of sex on the side?'

'I'm sorry if I gave you the wrong impression, but I don't think I can give you an answer to what you're asking—not yet.'

Sarah felt her cheeks burn with embarrassment. She had got it wrong—again! For a blind moment she had allowed herself to believe that Jamie wanted her as much as she wanted him. But what was even worse, he didn't seem to want Calum either!

'You can't keep popping in and out of our lives, Jamie. Calum, at least, has a right to either have you in his life with all the commitment that entails or you have to stay out of our lives. For his sake—and mine.' She lifted her chin, determined not to let him know how much her words were costing her. She couldn't—wouldn't—let him see how much she was hurting.

'I need some time SJ. That's all I'm asking. At the moment I can't give either of you what you are looking for.'

'Then I think you'd better leave, don't you?'

Jamie went over to the sofa and retrieved his jacket. 'Of course. I shouldn't have come.' He looked at Sarah and then at his son. Sarah could see something close to anguish reflected in his eyes. 'Goodbye, SJ,' he said softly as he gently closed the door behind him.

CHAPTER FIVE

SARAH crept into the department, praying that she'd be able to avoid Jamie until she had some strong coffee under her belt. What had she been thinking? Falling into his arms like some overwrought child? But she knew her response to Jamie had been anything but that of a child. She almost groaned aloud as she remembered how his body had felt, hard and muscular against hers. She felt her cheeks go pink as she thought of his lips trailing across her shoulders, finding the secret spot at the base of her throat that he knew from past experience drove her wild. Stupid, stupid, stupid, she berated herself. How could she have succumbed so quickly to his touch, thought for one moment that his feelings had changed? That he was ready to make a commitment, if not to her, at least to their son. Nothing more. She felt her blush deepen as she remembered the scene, how easily she had gone into his arms. He wasn't even interested in sex. He had rejected her. She would have gone to bed with him and he knew it. Was the thought of being with her so repulsive to him? Did he think that once they had slept together she would make demands on him? Demands that he clearly didn't want. He had made that perfectly clear.

With a sinking heart she realised she was going to have to find a way to keep him at arm's length. Clearly she couldn't trust the responses of her own traitorous body. Could she persuade him to go back to Africa early? If financial support was all he was prepared to offer, she and Calum would be better off without him. Surely the department could find someone else, even at short notice? But the mere thought of Jamie being thousands of miles away sent her spirits plummeting. She didn't know which would be worse—seeing him every day, yet not being able to have him in the only sense she truly wanted him, completely and wholly hers, or never seeing him at all. Damn him. Why did he have to come back and upset her neatly ordered life? Just when she'd thought she'd got over him.

As she stepped into the department, Lizzie thrust a cup of hot black coffee into her hand.

'Thank you. You must be psychic,' said Sarah. 'How did you know it was the one thing I truly needed right at this moment?'

'I'm getting to know you. You run better when you're kept well fuelled. Besides, we have a young man with multiple injuries coming in in a few minutes. He was found at the bottom of the Clyde Bridge. No one knows what happened. Whether he fell, jumped or was pushed. Looks like we're going to need all hands on deck. So drink up. It might be your last chance for a while.'

Sarah took a couple of sips of her coffee before setting it down and going to change into her theatre greens. Mentally she ran through the possible injuries that she might be faced with in the next few minutes. As she emerged from the changing room, she noticed that Karen was in some sort of heated discussion with a patient. Judging by the expression on her face, Karen's usual good humour seemed to have deserted her, and Sarah thought she knew why.

'Just give me a prescription for the pain, and I'll be on my way,' the patient shouted at Karen.

Sarah went over to them, noticing that the man was scruffily dressed and wore a woollen hat pulled low over his brow.

'Can I help?' she asked politely.

'The doctor here won't give me a prescription for my pain!' the man said angrily

'I'm sure if Dr Davidson here doesn't feel you need a prescription then she is absolutely right, Mr…?'

'Wilson. Kenny Wilson,' The man replied truculently.

'This is the second time Mr Wilson has been here in as many weeks.' Karen said, unmistakably exasperated. 'I've explained that we don't give out strong painkillers for headaches, but he's not happy with my decision.'

'I assume he's been thoroughly examined?'

'Of course. There is absolutely nothing to be found. I've checked with one or two of the other A and E departments and he's a regular attender there, too.' She shot Sarah a significant look. Sarah knew what it meant. Every department had their share of drug-addicted patients. While Sarah sympathised with anyone whose life had hit rock bottom, an A and E department was not the place to get the help they needed.

Kenny took a step towards Sarah, so close she could smell the alcohol on his breath. It took all her nerve not to step back. 'You doctors are all the same,' he hissed.

'I think it's time you left,' a low voice said from behind Sarah. 'Now, are you going to leave quietly or shall I get Security to escort you off the premises?'

Kenny took one look at Jamie's muscular frame and uncompromising expression before deciding that discretion was the better part of valour. He sidled towards the exit, grumbling volubly.

'Thanks, Sarah, Jamie,' said Karen. 'I must admit I was relieved you came along when you did. But now, if you'll excuse me, I have a couple of patients waiting to see me.' As she left them, Jamie looked at Sarah. 'Are you all right?'

'I'm perfectly fine,' she said. It was her turn to be annoyed. 'I know you meant well, Jamie, but when are you going to realise I'm a big girl now and perfectly able to take care of myself and my staff?'

'I've never been in any doubt that you can. You made that crystal clear again last night.'

'Please, forget about last night, Jamie. I should never have…' She searched for the right words. 'Kissed you,' she managed at last, although they both knew it had been much more than that. She would have gone to bed with him, if Jamie hadn't pulled away. She suspected he knew that and cringed inwardly. 'It's just that you caught me at a vulnerable moment.' Sarah said stiffly, her cheeks flushing at the memory.

'It was my fault,' Jamie answered. 'But I'm not sure I want to forget about it entirely.' He smiled lazily.

'Well, it's not going to happen again!' Sarah retorted. 'So can we, please, just stick to talking about work?'

'Sarah I…' Jamie started. 'No, you're right. It's best if we stick to clinical subjects for the time being.' Before Sarah could think about his words he went on, 'You've heard we're expecting a young man with multiple trauma?' He paused as the wail of an ambulance got louder and then shut off abruptly. 'Sounds like he's just arrived. Come on. Let's go.'

While the patient was being wheeled into Resus, the paramedics reeled off information on his status.

'Twenty-four-year-old, name's Tom Kennedy, according to his driving licence. Discovered unconscious at the foot of the Clyde Bridge half an hour ago by a member of the public. Has a GCS of 6, BP 90 over 45, pulse 125 and respirations 18 per minute. Bleeding extensively from a head wound, fractured right tibia and fibula, which have been stabilised. Bruising to abdomen.' The room filled up with medical and nursing staff as they all gathered around the gurney where the patient lay.

'OK,' Sarah said, snapping on gloves. 'Is someone stabilising his head and neck? Good. On my count of three remove the stretcher underneath him.' Once the manoeuvre was completed with practised timing, Lizzie gently and expertly cut away the bloodied clothes from Tom.

The paramedic continued, 'No morphine given due to his poor level of consciousness and respiratory distress. IV fluids given stat and second litre of saline almost through. Twenty-eight per cent Oxygen running at 6 litres via a trauma mask.'

Before Jamie put on the gown and gloves that one of the nursing staff held out for him he passed Sarah a pair of protective goggles. Sarah glanced around the room to ensure that all the staff were wearing theirs.

'I'll take care of his airway and head injury if that's OK with you, Sarah?' Jamie suggested, already preparing to insert an endotracheal tube into the man's airway.

'Fine. Keith and I will check out the rest of his injuries.' Looking up briefly, Sarah turned to Elspeth, one of the older nurses who had worked in the department for years. 'Call Theatre and let them know we might need them. Lizzie, can you—?'

But Lizzie had already anticipated her request and was moving towards the telephone. 'Call X-Ray and arrange a head CT scan, chest and abdo x-rays, and page Orthopaedics—already on it!'

Dr Thompson placed the leads from the cardiac monitor onto Tom's chest. As the Dinamap—the machine that measured blood pressure, oxygen saturation and pulse rate—alarmed, he called out, 'BP dropping—80 over 40, pulse 130.'

'OK.' Sarah remained calm, her fingers deftly examining the abdomen and chest of the patient lying motionless in front of her. 'Let's get some more fluids into him while we're waiting for blood to be cross-matched. A bag of Hartmann's stat, please, Lizzie.' Frowning slightly, Sarah placed her stethoscope on the left side of Tom's chest.

'Need a hand?' Jamie asked, his eyes intent through his protective visor. 'He's intubated, airway patent and clear. His pupils are responding to light but nothing further to be done regarding his head injury until we get that scan.'

Sarah nodded at Jamie. 'He's got a left-sided tension pneumothorax—he needs a chest drain now! Elspeth, can you pass me a kit, please?' Lizzie and Elspeth exchanged worried looks. They knew how serious this condition could be, and there could be other hidden injuries, too.

Swabbing the area over his left side with antiseptic to sterilise the skin, Sarah took the scalpel from Jamie with steady hands. Before she could make contact with the skin, however, the heart monitor emitted a warning bell.

'He's in AF!' Keith called out urgently.

'Carry on, Sarah, we'll keep ventilating him,' Jamie calmly responded, attaching an ambu-bag to the tube he had inserted earlier.

Too focused on her patient to be aware of the mounting tension in the room, she made the small incision into the intercostal space without hesitation. Glancing up she caught Jamie's almost imperceptible nod of encouragement, both knowing how one wrong slip could be catastrophic. But there was no time to waste. They had to get the young man's circulation going again and the insertion of the drain was crucial. Taking a long, thin plastic tube, she pushed it with an equal amount of strength and gentleness between Tom's ribs and into his chest. Suddenly the tube filled with frothy red blood, pouring into the container that it was securely attached to on the floor. Immediately the heart monitor stopped its shrill warning and was replaced by the reassuring beeps that indicate a steady heart rhythm.

'Right, folks, he's stable. Let's get him to Radiology for a CT scan to determine the extent of his head injury.' As Sarah and Jamie rushed the gurney through the bay, Lizzie cleared their path, pushing the resus equipment trolley to one side and sweeping away the discarded debris of dressing packs and empty syringes scattered on the floor with her foot. They were just outside the swing doors of the X-ray department when they were intercepted by one of the triage staff nurses. 'Mrs Kennedy, the patient's mother, has arrived. Can one of you speak to her?' she asked.

'Off you go, Sarah. Keith and I will stay with Tom,' Jamie offered.

'Thanks. Staff Nurse, I'll be along in a minute. In the meantime, can you put Mrs Kennedy in the relatives' room, please?'

Sarah peeled off her gloves and removed her blood-splattered theatre gown, using the brief respite to compose herself. Breaking bad news to relatives was one aspect of her job she found extremely difficult, but at least this time she was confident Tom would survive his injuries. There was every chance he would make a full recovery, although there would be an anxious few hours ahead for all of them. Once Tom had recovered sufficiently, the police would wish to interview him. She wondered what tragic set of circumstances had led to Tom's broken body being found at the foot of the bridge.

After leaving a tearful but grateful Mrs Kennedy a short time later, Sarah went to join Jamie in X-Ray. She found him in discussion with the radiologist, both studying the images displayed on the computer screen.

'What's the verdict?' she asked, peering over Jamie's shoulder.

He glanced back at her, a smile dimpling his cheek. 'Good news—no fracture or evidence of brain swelling. In fact, he's just beginning to regain consciousness. This is one lucky young man, wouldn't you say, SJ?'

'Thank goodness for that,' she said. 'He'll be going to Theatre for the orthopods to set his leg, then hopefully High Dependency will have a bed for him.' Suddenly the adrenaline of the past hour drained away and Sarah felt exhausted, and guessed that Jamie would be feeling the same way. Whatever her personal feelings, they were still professional colleagues who depended on one another. 'Fancy a coffee?' she offered. 'I'll make it this time, after I update his mother.'

'Great. Give me ten while I brief the surgeons on Tom, and I'll meet you in the staffroom.'

Sarah slumped in the saggy chair in the staffroom. She yawned. What she wouldn't do for one completely uninterrupted night's sleep. Lizzie came in and plonked herself down in the chair next to Sarah's with a heavy sigh. Her normally cheerful face was drawn and a frown puckered her brow.

'What it is Lizzie?' Sarah asked, concerned. 'Everything going all right for the wedding? With you and Stewart?'

'Oh, the wedding!' She shook her head dismissively. 'No, the arrangements are going fine. Can't wait for the honeymoon. Chance to put my feet up and get a long rest.' Sarah shot her a mischievous look that brought spots of colour to Lizzie's pale cheeks. 'OK I'm looking forward to the honeymoon for other reasons, too. Stewart and I have hardly spent any time alone in the last month. There always seems to be somebody there, talking about arrangements. I'm beginning to wonder if there is life outside work and the wedding. And I thought I'd never get tired of planning my big day!' She laughed, but then looked serious again. 'No there's something else. A work-related matter I need to discuss with you. And I'm afraid you're not going to be happy when you hear what I have to say.'

'OK. But let me get you a coffee first.' Once the two women had got settled, Lizzie started in a hesitant voice.

'Morphine has gone missing from the resus trolley.'

'Are you sure?' Sarah asked. 'When so many doctors and

nurses are dipping into the trolley during an emergency, isn't it hard to keep track of what's been used?'

'That's just it,' Lizzie continued unhappily. 'It's part of my job to ensure that everything is accounted for and written up correctly. After an emergency, I immediately recheck the trolley and reorder everything that has been removed. But today there was an ampoule of morphine missing—and Tom wasn't given any morphine. I checked first with all the medical staff as perhaps in the commotion it was taken for another patient by one of them, but so far no one is admitting to it. Anyway, at the very least there should be an empty ampoule. I looked everywhere for it—I even tried to empty the sharps bin.'

'That's a bit risky surely? You could get a needle-stick injury.'

Lizzie dismissed Sarah's reproachful tone with a wave of her fingers.

'I took the appropriate precautions. And what's more, this is the second time in two weeks that it's happened. I didn't mention the first incident to anyone but my nurse manager, as I was sure that it was a one-off incident. That someone had simply forgotten to write it up.'

'But now you think differently?' Sarah prompted

'For sure. Once is unlikely, but possible. Twice…' She shook her head. 'And it gets worse.'

Sarah waited for Lizzie to continue. She was obviously choosing her words with care.

'Someone saw Jamie, Dr Campbell, slip a couple of syringes and needles into his pocket the other evening.'

Sarah almost laughed aloud. Surely Lizzie couldn't be suggesting that Jamie had anything to do with the missing drugs?

Lizzie caught Sarah's expression. 'Of course it's ludicrous thinking that Jamie would take the morphine, but if we knew why he took the other stuff, at least we could rule him out.' Lizzie looked at Sarah imploringly. 'I should really go straight to my boss about this, but if there is any chance that you and I could get to the bottom of it first, I'll wait until tomorrow.' She stood up.

'However, if we still don't have an answer as to what happened to the drugs, I'll have no choice but to formally report it.'

'I'm sure that there is a perfectly innocent reason for Jamie's action and I'm confident the mystery of the syringes will be easily cleared up. Perhaps he was going up to one of the wards to take blood from a patient there?'

'Possible, but unlikely. He was off duty, Sarah. On his way home,' Lizzie said miserably. 'And you and I both know that consultants rarely take blood. That's usually left to the junior doctors. Besides, the wards have their own supplies of needles and syringes.'

'There still could be a hundred different innocent reasons why Jamie took the syringes as I'm sure we'll find out when I ask him. In the meantime, do you have any idea who else might be desperate enough to risk their career by stealing controlled drugs?'

'I know my nurses pretty well. Most of them have worked here for years. I just can't believe that any of them would do anything so stupid. One or two of them do have personal problems—as you'd expect to find in any large department. Elspeth, for example has a mother with chronic arthritis who suffers with severe pain. But as I said, she's worked with me for years and I can't see her doing anything so dim-witted, not to mention illegal!'

'What about other staff—porters, clerical staff, plaster-room technicians?'

'I suppose it's always possible. But they aren't usually in Resus. In fact, apart from the odd radiologist, there really is only us doctors and nurses.'

'But there *could* be others. Look, Jamie will be along in a minute and I'll talk to him about it. Ask if he has any ideas.' Sarah reflected for a moment. She hated the thought that any of her staff could be under suspicion—even for a moment.

'Actually, Lizzie, there was a patient in here this morning. Karen saw him. Apparently he had been trying to get her to prescribe him some strong painkillers and she refused. Why don't you track her down and find out when he came in and when he was last here? If she doesn't know, the triage nurses would have made a note of dates and times on his attendance card.'

'I don't see how that will help us *prove* anything,' Lizzie said a little doubtfully.

'At least it will show that someone else apart from staff could be involved. Don't worry, Lizzie,' Sarah said softly, 'one way or another we'll get to the bottom of this.'

'I hope we do,' replied an unconvinced Lizzie, 'I couldn't bear to have this hanging over us all at the wedding.'

Once the nurse had left the room, Sarah sat deep in thought. This was one side of her new role that she would never like. Acting as a policeman, looking at her colleagues, her hard-working and dedicated colleagues, with suspicion was anathema to her. The sooner they got this cleared up the better for the whole department. She jumped when the duty-room door flew open.

'Where's that coffee, then?' Jamie teased, striding into the room.

As Sarah handed him a cup, she paused awkwardly. 'There's something I need to discuss with you.'

Jamie made himself comfortable, stretching his long legs in front of him and putting his arms behind his head before narrowing his eyes at her.

'It's not anything to do with Calum—or last night. I told you I want us to stick to talking about work—and I meant it.' she said through gritted teeth, noting his wary look. 'No, this is something else entirely.'

Jamie visibly relaxed and leaned back in the chair. The movement caused the top of his hospital greens to ride up. Catching a glimpse of tanned muscle, Sarah's couldn't stop her thoughts flying back to the night before. With an effort she forced herself to concentrate on the issue at hand.

'Apparently someone has removed controlled drugs from the resus trolley on two occasions. Two weeks ago and today. And,' she went on baldly 'you were seen slipping some syringes and needles into your pocket the other evening.'

Jamie stared at Sarah, at first with disbelief and then, when he realised she was serious, with deepening anger.

'And you have linked the two events. I was seen taking syringes, *ergo* I must also be a drug addict—or, worse, a drug dealer who has so little regard for his patients or his career that he plunders drugs from the hospital he's working in.'

'Of course I don't suspect you. I can't imagine anyone less likely to be stealing drugs. And once you tell me why you took the syringes, you can help me find out who did really take the drugs.' She looked at Jamie expectantly.

Jamie shook his head. 'I'm afraid I can't tell you why I took the syringes. You are just going to have to trust me that it was not for the purpose of administering drugs, either to myself or anyone else.'

'I'm afraid that's not good enough, Jamie.' Sarah stiffened her resolve in the face of Jamie's anger. Of course she had the right to question him. And he knew it. 'I need to know for sure that you had nothing to do with the missing drugs.'

Jamie glared at her, incredulity written all over his face.

'I can't believe you are even asking the question. Good God, woman, don't you know me better than that?'

'But I don't really know you at all, do I? I thought I did, once. But now I realise I don't know you at all.'

Jamie frowned. 'I didn't take those drugs, Sarah.' He stood up. 'And as far as I'm concerned, that is all you need to know. But may I suggest if you really want to find your thief, you take a look at the CCTV footage from the last couple of days. If you still have no joy, then I suggest you call in the police.' And with one final glare, he turned on his heel and stalked out of the room.

Well! thought Sarah furiously. *Just who did he think he was?* Of course she didn't really believe, not for one moment, that he had taken the drugs, but on the other hand his refusal to tell her why he had taken the needles and syringes, his behaviour over the last few days—there was *something* he wasn't telling her.

Nevertheless, she would do as he'd suggested. Look at what the CCTV cameras had recorded over the last few days. In fact, the more she thought about it, the more she was certain that the only time the trolley had been unlocked had been earlier that day, when the man with the terrible injuries had been treated. It was possible that Kenny had slipped back when their attention had been on Tom. With a bit of luck, something would show up on the security camera.

On her way to see the head of security, Sarah bumped into a harassed-looking Lizzie.

'I've managed to pull Kenny Wilson's records up on the computer. He was in the department on both dates. However, he was signed out of the department shortly after Tom was admitted.'

'I think it's possible that he might have sneaked back in while we were all occupied with Tom. Jamie suggested looking at CCTV footage to see whether there is anything on camera that will help, so I'm just heading off to find the security manager now.'

'Did you ask Jamie about the syringes?'

'Yes, I did, and I have to say I didn't handle it very well.'

'What did he say?'

'Only that he didn't take the drugs, which I knew, and that I should check with Security. Honestly, Lizzie, I do love my job, the medical side at least, but I don't think I realised exactly what I was getting in for when I took the head of department role.'

Lizzie smiled in sympathy. 'Hey, you're doing a great job. Staff morale has never been higher. We all know how hard you work. Jamie, too. I just worry sometimes you try to do too much.'

'It comes with the territory, but thanks for the vote of confidence. On days like today I can do with all the encouragement I can get.'

Soon Sarah was sitting down with the head of hospital

security, a middle-aged man called George, reviewing the tapes. She had had to tell him why she needed to see the footage. It had taken all Sarah's powers of persuasion, but eventually George had reluctantly agreed to spend a few minutes going over the tapes before they involved management and the police.

'You should have come straight to me. Sister York should have come to me after the first incidence. That's what we are here for,' he had grumbled.

'I know, but I'm here now. And if we can get this sorted out without any of the staff feeling that they are under suspicion, then that can only be a good thing, surely?' Sarah had said placatingly.

'You could have trusted me to handle the matter discreetly. I agree with you, though. There's no point in getting staff all hot and bothered before we have to.'

'I'm sorry, George. Next time—God forbid there is a next time—I'll come to you immediately. I promise.'

While they had been talking, George had found and loaded the tapes from the period when Kenny had been in the department up to and including the time when Tom had been in Resus.

She could see blurred images of herself, Jamie and the other medical and nursing staff moving in and out of the picture.

George stopped the tape.

'There. Do you see?'

At first all Sarah could see was the figures of the five or six staff who were working over the trolley on which Tom lay. The security officer pressed a button and the picture panned out, revealing more of the resus room. The emergency trolley had been pushed out of everyone's way and rested near the open door of the room. As the officer showed Sarah the pictures frame by frame, a figure appeared from the door and a hand casually dipped into the trolley and removed a vial. The picture was too grainy for her to make out the contents, but she had a pretty good idea what it was. George manipulated the computer and the face of the figure came into view. Sarah recognised him at once. It was Kenny Wilson. Just as she'd suspected. Then George ran the tapes from the date Lizzie had given her when Kenny had attended previously. It took twenty minutes but eventually they found what they'd been looking for. It was a similar scenario to the one that day. This time two patients with severe injuries had been treated simultaneously and most of the department's medical and nursing staff had been occupied in trying to save their lives. From the footage Sarah could see that Kenny had hung around the department for a considerable time before choosing his moment to remove something from the trolley. He had taken a terrible risk, but had almost got away with it. Sarah felt enormous relief. At least it wasn't a member of staff. But clearly they would have to do something about security. Warn other hospitals in the city. She made a mental note to add it to her management agenda.

As if reading her thoughts, George said, 'Your security isn't up to much, is it? I think I should come around tomorrow and spend the day in the department, reviewing your procedures.'

Sarah sighed. Just one more task to get in the way of her seeing patients. Still, it was a small price to pay for peace of mind. She stood up, thanking George warmly for his help. She needed to find Lizzie and Jamie as soon as she could. At least she knew for certain that Jamie hadn't taken the missing drugs. But why had he taken the syringes? Why didn't he trust her? *And didn't she trust him?* The small niggling voice was back. *With her life, yes. But not her heart, not ever again*

Sarah found Lizzie suturing a patient who had sliced open a finger with a kitchen knife. She waited until the nurse had finished and had sent the patient on her way with instructions to see her GP in seven days to have the stitches removed. Once the treatment room was empty of patients, Sarah filled Lizzie in on what she had found out.

Lizzie gave a sigh of relief, the worry clearing from her eyes. 'Thank goodness. I was going mad, thinking that it might be a colleague stealing drugs.' She frowned again as she remembered her concerns about Jamie. 'Have you told Jamie?'

'Not yet. I will as soon as I catch him on his own. I'm sure he'll be pleased we've found the real culprit. He was furious when he thought I was suspecting him of taking the drugs.'

'To be fair, it wasn't an altogether unreasonable assumption. After all, how well do any of us know him? He's only been here a couple of weeks and although I have nothing but admiration for his clinical skills, we know very little about his personal life. He never talks about himself. But, still, I should have known that he is too fine a doctor to even have been a possibility. It would never have crossed my mind if it hadn't been for the syringes.'

She looked at Sarah who had suddenly busied herself putting away swabs. 'Oh, I'd forgotten. You knew him before, didn't you?'

Sarah thought rapidly. How much should she reveal about her true relationship with Jamie? It was likely that she and Lizzie would be working closely for years to come. But, on the other hand, if she told her, could Lizzie resist telling the others? It wasn't as if Jamie was going to be around for very much longer. She looked at the nurse and met her frank gaze. Somehow she knew instinctively that she could trust Lizzie with her secret.

'Can I trust you to keep something to yourself? I need to know that what I'm about to tell you will go no further.'

'You have my word.' Lizzie grinned. 'Cross my heart and hope to die.' She made the gesture with her fingers. Then the smile left her face. 'You know, Sarah, working in emergency medicine, you get used to hearing and keeping secrets. I promise anything you tell me will go with me to the grave.'

Sarah returned Lizzie's candid look for a few moments before continuing.

'Jamie and I first met while we were both at medical school. We didn't hang out with the same crowd. He and his pals were considered the wild ones. Partying every night and climbing every weekend. My friends were the more studious, quieter set. But somehow,' Sarah recalled smiling, 'he still managed to get the best marks. He did ask me out once, but he had a reputation for being a bit of a womaniser so I said no. Then we met again as registrars. He still seemed a little wild, but instead of directing his energy into parties and womanising, he was putting it into extreme sports when he wasn't working every hour he could. The consultants and the patients loved him. He asked me out again and although I turned him down several times, he persisted until finally I gave in and agreed to go out with him.' Sarah paused.

'We discovered a shared passion for hill walking and he introduced me to climbing. We were inseparable until…'

'Go on.' Lizzie encouraged.

'Until we had finished our training and were eligible for consultant jobs. One day, almost out of the blue, he told me that he was going to Africa to work for a couple of years.'

'Didn't he ask you to go, too?'

'No. From the beginning he made it clear that he wasn't prepared to commit himself to anyone. Would never get married. In fact, I think it was when I raised the possibility of a future and children that he made his decision to go.' She couldn't stop the bitterness seeping into her voice.

'And you thought that you could change him. That you'd be the one that would make him want to commit?'

Sarah smiled wryly. 'I suppose so. It makes me sound a little naïve. He never gave me a reason to think he had changed his mind except…' Sarah's voice cracked a little. 'Except I really thought he loved me. In fact, until he told me he was leaving, I never doubted it for a moment.'

'Sounds like he really hurt you. That he was a bit of a lad on the women front,' Lizzie said sympathetically. 'To be honest, the gossip around here is that he has someone back in Africa. Elspeth overheard him talking on the phone the other day, he seemed to be promising someone that he'd be back soon. And then there's Annie Walker from upstairs.'

Sarah smiled bitterly. 'He does seem to have his hands full and I guess with hindsight it's obvious the suggestion of commitment was enough to make him run a mile. All I know is that I was desperately in love with him. I believed I had found the person I was going to spend the rest of my life with. And I was so sure he felt the same way. How wrong I was.'

'And you never heard from him after he left?'

'Not a word.' It was all Sarah could do to disguise the pain she still felt at his sudden abandonment of her.

'He must have been surprised to find out you had a son.' Lizzie caught the expression on Sarah's face and Sarah could see from her widened eyes that the whole truth was beginning to dawn.

'How long is it since you last saw him?'

'Fifteen months ago,' Sarah admitted reluctantly.

'Calum's his son, isn't he? I thought there was something familiar about your son. But I never guessed.' Lizzie looked dumbfounded. 'Does Jamie know? About Calum? Of course he must know. You'll have told him when you found out you were pregnant.'

Sarah hesitated, thinking back to the day she had taken the pregnancy test. 'I didn't tell him. I decided there was no point. He only found out the day I started work here. He had no idea I had had his child and I had no idea he worked here. So it was a bit of a shock for both of us.'

'And now? Surely, now he knows about Calum, he wants to be part of your lives?'

'Not noticeably. He came around to my flat last night and met Calum properly for the first time. Although he seemed taken with him, he told me he's not ready to make anything but a financial commitment to Calum. As if I need or want his money! Neither do I want someone in Calum's life who is only there when it suits him. Heaven knows, I had enough of that sort of father to realize it's not what I want for my child. Calum deserves a father who is going to be around. Someone who will always be there for him. Not someone who lives halfway across the world and who puts his own needs first.'

'Funny, I would never have thought of him as a man who would abandon his child. But, then, as I said, I don't really know him.'

'I was convinced I knew him. But obviously I don't at all. I suppose there are plenty of men just like him, who run a mile from responsibility. But I'm sorry, I shouldn't have told you so much.' Sarah leaned over and placed a hand on Lizzie's arm. 'Please, don't share this information with anyone else, Lizzie. I couldn't bear it if my personal life became common knowledge. What's more, whatever one can say about Jamie Campbell as a man, he really is one hell of a doctor. And as far as this department is concerned, that's all that matters.'

CHAPTER SIX

KEITH THOMPSON waylaid Sarah as she left Lizzie in the treatment room.

'Do you have a moment, Dr Carruthers?' No matter how often Sarah had tried to tell him to call her by her first name, he insisted on using her full title. It amused her to think that Keith held her in the same awe that she had held her consultants as a junior. She didn't feel that old—or that wise.

'Sure. Is there a problem?'

'I have an elderly lady with cardiac pain who needs to be admitted. The trouble is she's refusing. She's the sole carer of her forty-year-old son who has Down's syndrome. Says he can't be left on his own. He came in the ambulance with her. She won't let me call Social Services either. When I suggested it she became quite agitated. In fact, she's getting dressed to leave and I don't know how to stop her.'

'Would you like me to have a word with her?' Sarah asked.

'Could you?' Keith sighed his relief. 'It's just if she goes home tonight without further tests and treatment, there's no telling what could happen. And it's not as if we could rely on the son to call us if there's a problem. It simply wouldn't be fair on either of them.'

'Which cubicle is she in?'

When Keith introduced her to the patient, a bright-eyed woman in her late seventies, Sarah knew she had a fight on her hands. Mrs Loveday was clearly frightened and upset, but more than that she had the air of a woman who was used to doing battle and getting her own way. Her son sat by her bedside, holding her hand. He had the distinctive features of someone with Down's. He smiled engagingly at Sarah.

'You really need to stay in overnight, Mrs Loveday,' Sarah said gently.

'Can't I come back tomorrow during the day and have the tests then? I really don't see why an overnight stay is necessary. I'd only be using up a bed. There's bound to be people who need it more than I do.'

Sarah hid a smile. Mrs Loveday reminded her of her grandmother. Another feisty soul.

'You need to stay in so we can keep you under observation overnight,' Sarah said carefully. She needed to impress the seriousness of her condition without alarming her even more. 'I know you're worried about your son—David, isn't it? But Social Services will find someone who can stay with him in your home. It will just be for a night or two.'

'If I let Social Services get their hooks into us, they'll never leave us in peace. It'll be meals on wheels, day-care centres and goodness knows what else before we know it. They'll say I'm not fit to look after David and try and take him away from me. The same as they did when he was born. Said he'd never amount to anything—that he was unlikely to talk or dress himself or go to the toilet even. Told me I should put him into care and forget about him. You see…' she grabbed Sarah's hand in a surprisingly strong grip '…I was a single mother, and in those days it was still frowned on. They said being a single mother was hard enough, without trying to bring up a handicapped child on my own.'

Her words brought memories of her own pregnancy flooding back to Sarah.

'Is that what's worrying you? You think they might take David from you permanently? I can see why you're worried, but times have changed a lot in recent years. Social Services are there to help you and David to stay together in your own home. They know that's where he belongs—with his mother.'

Mrs Loveday still didn't look convinced.

'They thought they knew better when he was born, but they were wrong. David manages to do everything by himself. Can't you, sweetheart? He can even drive a car. And he has a job.' David grinned his pleasure at his mother's praise. Then she turned to Sarah again. 'You medical people were wrong before so why should I trust you now?'

Sarah sat down on the bed next to the elderly woman. 'You're absolutely right. We doctors have, and still can, make mistakes. We try our best not to, but at the end of the day we are only human. And when we're wrong and things turn out better for the patient than we'd predicted, we are delighted. The doctors were wrong about David. You were right to fight to keep him. All we could do then was give you an opinion based on the knowledge available at the time, but nowadays we're more clued up and are more conscientious about giving patients as much information as possible so they can make their own decisions.' Sarah thought for a moment. She could see that Mrs Loveday was beginning to waver, but she needed her to be absolutely convinced that she could trust Sarah.

'I have a little boy. He's coming up for seven months now and is a lively wee thing. But there was a time when I was pregnant that I thought he might have Down's syndrome.' Sarah noticed that she had Mrs Loveday's full attention. She stopped pulling on her clothes and sat back down, looking at Sarah with interest.

'They didn't have the tests when you were pregnant but now they do a blood test on all pregnant women that can show them if they are at increased risk of having a child with Down's. Well, my test came back indicating that there was an increased risk. I had to make a decision. I could do two things. Do nothing and wait and see. Have an amniocentesis test, which carried a small risk of miscarriage, and, following that result, decide whether or not to continue the pregnancy. After a lot of thought and after speaking to women like yourself who have Down's syndrome children, I realised what a great deal of pleasure they got from their children, and how most of them grow up, like David, into loving, reasonably independent adults. I decided to take the chance. I had almost decided once before to end the pregnancy because, like you, I was a single mother, but once I decided to go through with the pregnancy, it was as if—I don't know—I had made a commitment to my unborn baby that I would love and cherish it regardless. As they say in the marriage vows. In sickness and in health.'

Sarah paused for a moment and Mrs Loveday patted her hand in sympathy.

'So I know how scared you are. I know that you want to

protect your son, but isn't it better that he gets to know and love and trust other people and places for that time, hopefully a long time from now, when you won't be around?'

'I know you're right, dear. It's just difficult to let them have their independence. You won't know about that now, but just you wait until your son grows up!'

'That time will come for me, too. As it must for all parents eventually. Take a leap of faith and accept the help Social Services can give you now. After all, if you don't look after your health, you might not be around as long as you could be. Let us look after you now and hopefully you will be there for David for many more years.'

'Very well, dear. I guess I don't really have a choice. But only if they'll send someone over to stay in the house. I don't want him upset more than he has to be.'

'I'll make sure of it,' Sarah promised. 'In the meantime, let's get you back into your gown.'

Jamie moved away from the curtain of the cubicle. He had stopped to listen when he'd caught Sarah's words about her pregnancy. He was dismayed. He had no idea that Sarah had had to face so many fears during her pregnancy on her own. He should have been there for her. And now there was a good chance he was about to inflict further months, if not years, of worry and anxiety. He had to find out if he carried the gene, and soon. He would call Robert and let him know that he had to have the result. Stat.

Jamie put the phone down with a frown. He checked in with the hospital back in Africa whenever he could and was usually reassured that they seemed to be coping without him. However, today the conversation he'd had with his colleague had worried him. Greg's usual ebullience seemed to have deserted him and his normally upbeat manner had been subdued. At first he had denied there was anything worrying him until, at Jamie's insistence, he had admitted his concerns.

'One of the more experienced doctors has had to return to Europe unexpectedly—a family emergency,' Greg had told Jamie. 'We were coping, just about, without you, but now being two doctors down is putting a strain on our already over-stretched resources. I simply can't expect anyone to do more. We're all working twelve-hour shifts as it is.'

'Do you need me to come back?' Jamie had asked. 'I still have a couple of weeks left to do here, but perhaps if I explain, they'll let me go earlier.' Even as Jamie had asked the question he had known it wasn't that simple. If it hadn't been for Sarah and Calum he would have already booked the first plane back. He would have hated to let the Glasgow hospital down, but it was far easier for them to find a replacement than the small, poorly funded hospital in Africa.

'No, we can manage for another couple of weeks. Just. As long as we know you'll be coming, we can soldier on.'

'If you're sure?' Jamie said, not really convinced. 'You will let me know if it all becomes too much?'

'Straight away, I promise,' was the reply.

'How's Sibongele?' Jamie asked. 'Is he behaving himself?'

Again there was a slight hesitation. 'He's OK, I guess. He misses you. He asks every day when you're coming back.'

'Any news of family yet?'

'We're still trying to track down his mother's sister. One

of the nurses thinks she knows which village she lives in and we have sent word to her that Sibongele is well enough to leave the hospital and go home. But so far we haven't heard anything. We don't even know if she got the message.'

'If we haven't heard by the time I get back, I'll go to the village myself and try and find her. The boy needs to be with his family.'

'The trouble is, Jamie, I don't think he wants to go. You know he thinks of you as his family since his mother died. He's been at the hospital for so long now, he doesn't remember anything else. He loves helping in the wards. He's bright and recites everything he's learnt from you at the drop of the hat.' Greg laughed. 'I swear some of the patients trust his opinion more than they do ours.'

Jamie smiled, too. He could easily picture fourteen-year-old Sibongele working on the wards with his ready smile and keenness to help. But he was a little concerned at how attached the boy had become to him. Heaven knew why the boy thought he could be a father to him—he couldn't even be sure he could be a father to his own child. But since the child had lost his mother to the TB that had kept Sibongele in the hospital for the past six months, he had developed an attachment to Jamie. And, Jamie had to admit, he was fond of the boy. In fact, although he was keen to see the boy reunited with his aunt, he knew he would miss him when he left.

After he replaced the receiver, Jamie prowled around his small flat. He felt restless and ill at ease. Once or twice he reached for the phone to call Sarah, but pulled back at the last minute. What, after all, could he say to her?

Jamie had always paid little heed to his surroundings, but

today the one bed-roomed apartment seemed to closing in on him. As hospital accommodation went, it was clean and modern with an open-plan sitting room divided by a breakfast bar and a functional kitchenette. The rest of the flat comprised a boxy bedroom and a tiny bathroom with overhead shower.

A steady downpour of rain rattled the window-panes, dampening his spirits even further, and he experienced a sudden yearning for Africa.

As he thought of the country he had spent the last year and a half in, he realised how much he was missing the wide open spaces, and the mission hospital with the staff and patients. They would be struggling to cope without him. There were already too few doctors for too many patients. For a moment he let himself imagine what it would be like to return there with Sarah at his side. She would love the country, he was certain, and as for Calum, he would love it, too. There was an old reservoir that the staff used for dips. He could teach his son to swim. He pushed the thoughts away. It was unlikely to happen. Perhaps he should return sooner than he had planned? Hand in his notice and leave as soon as the hospital managed to find another locum to replace him? There was probably little requirement to further brush up his skills. Even the short time he had spent at the Royal was sufficient for him to be re-assured that his clinical skills were fully up to date.

Why not, then? Why not just go? Remove himself from Sarah and Calum's lives? Let them get on with their lives.

The ringing of the phone rang dragged him away from his brooding thoughts.

'Hi. It's Robert. Can you meet me in the pub across the road in ten minutes?'

'Have you got the results?' Jamie felt his heart begin to beat faster. 'If you have, tell me now, over the phone.'

'Yes, I have the results. But I want to tell you face to face. Can you meet me or not?'

'Do I have an option?'

'Not really. See you in ten.' Jamie heard the click as Robert terminated the call.

As Jamie made the short walk to the pub, his mind was in turmoil. What if the results were positive? How would that affect Calum? He couldn't bear the distress it would cause Sarah when she learned that her child might have a disease that would severely limit her child's future. Would she agree to have him tested? What if she chose to wait until he was old enough to make his own decision? Perhaps his son would choose not to know. Follow in his father's footsteps? Well, he could hardly blame him. If the results were positive, Jamie knew that it was likely he could develop the illness at any time. How could he continue to be part of Calum's life knowing that one day he might become dependent on his child? He shuddered. Anything but that. He would have no option but to remove himself as quickly as possible from their lives. They would forget about him. Make their own future. In time Sarah would find someone else, someone who would be a good father to Calum and a support to her. Despite himself he felt his mind reel away from the image of Sarah in someone else's arms, in someone else's bed. Still, there was no point in torturing himself. In a few minutes he would know his fate.

He swung the pub door open, bringing a blast of cold air into the heavy atmosphere of the bar. It was almost empty apart from one or two couples enjoying their drinks at the small tables set out near the fire. Robert, a solitary figure at the bar, was already in the process of ordering drinks.

'That was quick. What can I get you?' he asked as Jamie approached.

'I could do with a large malt, but as I'm on call, a Coke will have to do.' Jamie waited impatiently. It seemed to take an interminable time for the barman to pour their drinks. He had to stop himself from hauling Robert off the barstool and demanding a response. Eventually they were both seated far away from listening ears in a secluded corner.

'Come on man. Spit it out,' Jamie ground out between clenched teeth.

Ignoring his tone, Robert raised his glass and grinned. 'Cheers.' he said. 'You can relax. The results were negative. You don't carry the gene.'

Jamie felt as if all the breath had been knocked out of his body. He had hardly dared to hope.

'You're sure?' he queried. 'I have to be a hundred per cent certain.'

'I knew you would feel like that, so I used my influence and got them to run the test twice. There's no doubt, you definitely do not have the gene.'

'Thank God for that.' He leant back in the chair. The relief was overwhelming. Now he knew, he could hardly take it all in.

'Hey, you owe me one,' Robert said with a smile of pleasure. 'I can't tell you how many favours I had to call in to get this done. And so quickly.'

'Anything you want. You just name it and it's yours,' Jamie responded fervently. 'Thank you. You have no idea what this means.' As the two men sat in silence Jamie's first thought was for his child. If he didn't have the gene, there was no chance that his son would have it either. Calum was never going to develop Huntington's chorea. He would never know the agony of having his muscles gradually lose control, with the subsequent loss of independence. He would never—as Jamie's father had done in the latter stages of the disease—struggle with the simplest tasks of eating and breathing. There was nothing stopping Calum from having the brightest future.

His thoughts turned to himself. Neither would he know or have to suffer the effects of the devastating illness. He, too, was free to live his life like any other man. Free to love, have children. For the first time since he had learned of his father's illness as a third-year medical student, Jamie knew he had a future. And what would that future hold? Calum certainly. But could that future also include Sarah? Could she learn to trust him again? Fall in love with him once more? Or was it too late? Jamie knew that he had to find out. He needed to see her. Tell her everything. Make her understand why he had acted as he had.

Although he was desperate to talk to Sarah, good manners prevented him from jumping to his feet and leaving his friend to finish his drink alone.

'Can I get you another one?' he offered.

'No, thanks. I can tell you are straining at the bit to get away. Now you know, what are you going to do? Are you going to tell Sarah?'

'At least now I can explain why I behaved as I did. Hell, what must she think of me? First of all I rush away to Africa without a reasonable explanation and then when I return and find out I have a son, I appear to reject him, too. She must think I'm a real bastard.'

'Mmm, I see what you mean. But Sarah is a reasonable woman. Hopefully she'll understand. I suspect, though, that you're going to have to do a fair bit of grovelling first. Anyway, let's finish our drinks and get out of here. It's about time you got on with the rest of your life.'

Jamie felt too restless to go back to the residence. He needed to see Calum and Sarah and he needed to see them straight away. But first he'd pop into the department and make sure there were no patients requiring his expertise. It would mean he was less likely to be interrupted when he saw Sarah.

Jamie used the back entrance of the A and E department, walking past a thankfully empty resus suite. Glancing into the waiting room, he noted a scattering of people sitting patiently while they waited to be seen. Deciding to check the triage area before he left, he noted with surprise a familiar figure sitting at the nurses' station, chatting with Elspeth.

'Dr Campbell, hi—thought you were at home. I was just about to phone you. You have a visitor,' Elspeth explained, tilting her head in the direction of Mrs MacLeod.

'Mrs MacLeod! Is everything all right?' Jamie asked, frowning, wondering if her broken leg was causing her problems.

The elderly lady beamed up at him. 'Och, I'm just grand! Here, this is for you—baked it myself,' she added, holding out a biscuit tin which held a fresh-baked sponge cake. 'I wanted to show you how well I'm doing—and to thank you for everything you did.'

Aware that they were gathering an audience of nursing and medical staff, Jamie shifted uneasily. 'That was really kind of you, Mrs MacLeod. Thank you. But I was just doing my job, you know.'

'Rubbish, young man. What you did for me was way and beyond the call of duty and everyone knows it!' Getting stiffly to her feet, she leaned on her walking stick. 'Well, don't want to take up any more of your valuable time, Doctor. I need to be getting back to let in the home help, although to be honest she's a bit hopeless. It should be me taking care of her!'

Jamie smiled and shook his head in amazement at the spirit and courage of the elderly lady as she walked straight backed down the corridor. Noting the amused expressions of his colleagues gathered round the desk, he turned to Elspeth.

'As you all have nothing better to do than hover about here, I'm off. If you need me you can either page me or call my mobile.'

'Aren't you going to share your cake with us, Doctor?' Elspeth called after his departing back.

Jamie decided to walk the couple of miles to see Sarah. The fresh air and exercise would help clear his head. If the hospital called and he was needed urgently, he would flag a taxi and would be back at the hospital in no time.

Sarah was just finishing giving Calum his bath before getting him ready for bed when the doorbell rang. She wrapped the baby up in a soft white towel and carried him to the door. She expected to see either her mother or one of her friends. What she hadn't expected was Jamie, grinning broadly, holding what seemed to be a cake tin in his hand.

'Hello, you,' he said softly. 'Can I come in?'

He took in the sight of Sarah with their son in her arms. She was barefoot and wearing a pair of faded jeans with a broad leather belt low on her hips. Her white T-shirt rode up slightly, revealing her toned, lightly tanned abdomen. She had her hair tied up in a high ponytail and a blob of foam clung to her fringe. Jamie had never seen her look so desirable. He resisted the urge to pull her into his arms and cover her with kisses.

'As you can see, we are a little tied up at the moment. It's not really a convenient time,' she responded.

Jamie paid no attention to her frosty tone, instead stepping into the flat and taking Calum from her.

'I'll help you put him to bed, if you like.'

Sarah resisted the temptation to pluck Calum back. She refused to treat her child like a ping-pong ball. But who exactly did Jamie think he was? One minute he wanted nothing to do with her or her child, except perhaps a quick romp in the sack with her, and the next minute he was turning up at her door as if he lived there. The man had a nerve.

'What are you doing here, Jamie? If it's Calum you've come to see, we really need to discuss access.'

'You and I need to talk,' Jamie said firmly. 'But let's get this little one off to bed and then we can talk undisturbed. Just tell me what to do.' He had the grace to look a little self-conscious as he said that. Clearly Jamie had no idea what putting a baby to bed actually entailed.

Sarah suppressed a smile. It was an unusual situation, seeing Jamie in a position where he obviously felt clueless. This was completely different to how he normally appeared. Whether at work or in the mountains, Jamie always looked like a man who knew exactly what he was doing.

'OK, you can stay for a while—just this once. We do need to talk about Calum so I suppose tonight is as good a time as any. First I need to finish drying him properly.'

Sarah had lit a fire against the cooling autumnal nights and she reclaimed her son before setting him down on the changing mat she had placed at a safe distance from the hearth. Using the towel, she carefully dried between the baby's toes and folds. Calum squealed with pleasure, kicking with delight in his naked freedom.

Jamie looked at the two figures he was already beginning to think of as his family. The soft light of the flames and the standard lamp cast a glow around the room, chasing the last of the shadows that had hung over him before. Now everything was as it should be, or it would be once he had explained everything. Already he regretted the months of Calum's life that he had missed. Why had he been such a fool? Why hadn't he had the guts to take the test earlier? He would have known that he was free to pursue Sarah and he would have been there for her throughout the pregnancy and birth. He could only begin to imagine how hurt she must've been to not have told him that she was pregnant. And if she had? What then? He would have told her the truth and probably tried to convince her to have a termination. He felt his blood run cold at the mere possibility that his child might never have been.

'Could you watch him? I'm just going to fetch his pyjamas and bottle.' Sarah asked.

She left Jamie crouched over Calum making faces that had her son—their son—smiling. She didn't quite know how she felt about Jamie being there. Had he decided that he wanted to be involved in his child's life after all? And if so, how did she feel about that? She rummaged in a drawer for Calum's pyjamas, pulling out her favourite pair. Tiny blue rabbits frolicked on a white background. She walked back to the sitting room. Jamie had lifted Calum onto his lap. The child fixed his large brown eyes on Jamie's. They seemed in a world of their own. Sarah felt her throat tighten as she took in the scene. She could no longer doubt the affection Jamie had for his child.

She went to the kitchen and tested the temperature of the bottle she had left warming. She had stopped breastfeeding when she had returned to work, but missed the closeness of having the skin-to-skin contact that breastfeeding had involved. Yet another sacrifice she had made in order to return to work. Had it been worth it? If she hadn't gone back to work when she had, would she have missed Jamie's return to the UK? Believing him still in Africa, would she ever have told him about his son? Even now she didn't know what she was going to do about Jamie. She could tell from the way that he looked at Calum that he was smitten. But as far as she knew, he was still planning to go back to Africa. It wouldn't be fair on her son to have a father who dipped in and out of his life. No, Jamie had some tough choices to make. She had to make him see that.

Calum was looking calm and settled when she retrieved him from Jamie and slipped his pyjamas on. His little body was warm from his bath and the fire. He sucked drowsily at the bottle, his eyes beginning to close in sleep. Jamie and Sarah sat quietly as Calum finished his drink and surrendered himself to sleep. Sarah popped him in his cot, turning on the nightlight and leaving the door slightly ajar in case he woke up. By the time she returned to the sitting room Jamie had stoked the fire, which blazed cheerfully. Her thoughts flew back to that last night before Jamie had left for Africa—the night their son had been conceived.

'OK, you can start. I assume you're here to talk about Calum?'

She could see that Jamie was struggling to find words. Perhaps he had come to tell her he was returning to Africa sooner than planned? Once more she felt her heart sink at the prospect. Could she really bear to lose him again?

'There is something I have to tell you,' Jamie began. 'If you can, please, hear me out before saying anything.'

Mutely Sarah nodded her head. Here it was. The goodbye scene all over again.

'My father died three years ago. You know that. But what you didn't know was that he died from Huntington's chorea.'

Sarah couldn't help a gasp of surprise. Why hadn't he told her? Her heart began to race as she realised the full implications of Jamie's words.

'It's OK.' He rushed on, seeing Sarah's expression. 'I have just found out that I don't carry the gene. That's what I was doing when I took syringes and needles from the department.'

'Why on earth didn't you tell me before?'

'I couldn't, Sarah. I'm sorry. I decided a long time ago that I didn't want to know whether I carried the gene. I didn't want to lead my life knowing what could be in store for me. And I couldn't ask you to be with me for the same reason. What if I had it? I would never have allowed you to sacrifice your life to look after me. I would never have stopped you from having the children you so clearly wanted. And children weren't an option for me as long as I thought there was any chance I carried the gene and could pass it on.'

Sarah's mind reeled from what Jamie was telling her. Why couldn't he have told her? Had he that little faith in her? Of course he had always been protective of her, but this was too much. He should have trusted her. Her thoughts veered away from the thought of her son having a terminal illness. If she had known when she'd been pregnant, would she have gone through with the pregnancy? It would have been another thing to think of on top of the raised alpha fetoprotein. The possibility of her child having both genetic disorders might have been enough to make her reconsider going ahead. And if she hadn't? She felt ill.

'So you can see why I was horrified to discover that I had fathered a child. But once I knew, of course there was no option but for me to take the test.'

'You should have told me, Jamie. Why couldn't you have trusted me? Did you think my feelings were so shallow that I would run at the first sign of trouble?' she said sadly.

'It's because I knew you wouldn't run that I couldn't tell you. You would have stayed with me regardless. You are that type of woman and I couldn't have borne your pity.'

'Did you pity your father? Is that how your mother felt about him?'

'No, my mother loved my father. But it wasn't easy on her, watching him deteriorate in front of her, knowing she was helpless to prevent the illness from claiming him. She spent the last couple of years of his life as his full-time carer. She wouldn't let me employ nurses to help. Said my father's care was her responsibility. That she needed to be the one to look after him. But looking after him took its toil on her health, mental and physical.' Jamie took a ragged breath, remembering how his arguments and entreaties had fallen on deaf ears.

'Isn't that what love is about, Jamie?' Sarah said quietly.

'Isn't that what people promise when they take their vows—"in sickness and in health"?'

'That's just it. You would have made those vows. And stuck by them. No matter how trapped you felt. My mother had no life of her own. And, no, I didn't pity my father. I just felt helpless. What was the point of all those years of medical training if there was nothing I could do to help? So you see, I couldn't have a child. Not knowing if I'd end up a burden on them. Never mind the chances of them inheriting the disease. Rightly or wrongly, I made up my mind.'

'Did you think of your father as a burden?'

'It would have been a privilege to do anything for him. But he would never let me. He was a proud man. He would only let my mother look after him,' Jamie said, unable to disguise the pain in his voice.

'And you've found out that you're OK. What now?'

'Now we can be a family. A real family. You, me and Calum. Isn't that what you have always wanted?'

'Is it?' she said quietly. Jamie seemed oblivious to the ice in her tone.

'You and Calum can come back to Africa with me. You can give up work or work part time. You'll love it there. It'll give you all the time you want to spend with Calum.'

'And why would I do that? What about my life here? My work, my friends, my mother?'

'It'll only be for a couple of years at first. Your mother and friends can come and visit. And as for your work—you'll find the work in Africa just as, if not more, rewarding.'

'I think you should leave now, Jamie,' Sarah said softly.

He looked at her in surprise. Clearly this wasn't the

reaction he had been expecting. Suddenly she couldn't hold back the anger any longer.

'You waltz in here, telling me that you have decided that my son and I should give up our lives and go back with you to Africa. You disappear from my life without any real explanation, leaving me to deal with pregnancy, birth and looking after a small child on my own. OK, OK.' She held up her hands to stop his response. 'I know you didn't know I was pregnant, but that's hardly the point, is it? You could have made enquiries about me. We have colleagues in common. Weren't you the slightest bit interested in how I was coping? In my life—my career? Then you saunter back into my life and nearly make love to me before rejecting me—again.' She stopped his words again. 'OK, so I did give you some encouragement. But you caught me at a weak moment. Then, after showing little interest in your son, you find out that he is hale and hearty after all. So it now suits you to have him in your life. But worst of all, instead of coming here, grovelling for forgiveness, you come in, demanding that I give up *my* life and follow you to Africa like some kind of…' She paused to draw breath. 'Some kind of groupie!' she spat finally. She stood, indicating the door. 'Now, before I say anything I might regret, I think you should leave, don't you?'

Well, Jamie thought as he walked back to his flat, that hadn't gone exactly as planned. He had to admit he had been so delighted that he didn't have the gene that he hadn't really stopped to think about Sarah's reaction. Of course it was bound to be a shock to her. He had been a blundering, insensitive fool. He should have broken the news more gently.

Taken his time. Waited for the right moment. Considered his words. But, dammit, Sarah and his son were going to be a part of his future—his future in Africa. Once more he mulled over what she had said, that she had made a life and a career for herself in Glasgow. Was he being fair to ask her to leave everything she had worked so hard to achieve? But there wasn't really an option. He was committed to at least another year of his contract and he couldn't leave Sibongele just yet—not until he knew that the boy's future was secure. There was so much Sarah could do in Africa. She would love it there—he was sure of it—if only she would give it and him a chance.

Jamie sighed. He would just have to use what little time he had left to convince her. He had forgotten what a prickly and stubborn soul she was. But he would be patient. He was pretty sure she still had feelings for him, although, he admitted ruefully, tonight she had kept them pretty well hidden if she still did. He gave a wry smile as he thought back to the image of Sarah standing in front of him, cheeks blazing. She had always been a passionate woman. Not least in bed. And he was determined that shortly she'd be back where she belonged. Back in his bed and his life. But this time for good.

CHAPTER SEVEN

THE day of Lizzie's wedding dawned cool but clear. Autumn was turning into winter, the trees scattering carpets of gold, bronze and red everywhere. The sun shone on one of those perfect crisp days that drew visitors to Scotland from all over the world.

Sarah had spent the last couple of days mulling over what Jamie had told her. Once she had cooled down, she allowed herself to feel a little sympathy for Jamie's predicament. It must have been terrible to live your life not knowing what the future held in store. And to watch the deterioration of the health, physical and mental, of someone you loved, knowing that despite your medical training you were powerless to do anything, must have been awful for a man like Jamie.

If he had told her, what would she have done? He was right in one respect. She would never have left him. She would have tried to persuade him to have the test, and if it had been positive she would have given up her dream of having children. She had loved him that much. But had he loved her? Surely if he had, he would have fought for a life together. He could never have simply have walked away from her without at least having the courage to find out whether they could have a future.

But to be fair, she could understand why Jamie had kept the truth from her. He wasn't the kind of man who would have allowed anyone to sacrifice their life. Still, it hadn't been only his decision to make. He should have trusted her. If he had loved her enough, surely he would have? At least found out whether he had the gene before deciding to give her up.

And now—did he really want to be part of her life, or was it just Calum he was interested in? And should that not be enough? Did she have the right to deny her son the chance to know his father? But Jamie hadn't said anything about staying. From what she could gather, he still intended to go back to Africa. With or without her and Calum.

Jamie hadn't sought her out over the last couple of days. The department had been busy and there were always other staff about. But surely he could have tried harder to see her and Calum in the evenings? Or was he waiting, respecting her need for time before he put any more pressure on her?

She didn't know the answer to any of her questions. She felt exhausted from the sleepless nights where she had lain tossing and turning, trying to decide what to do.

Reluctantly Sarah had allowed her mother to persuade her to go to Lizzie's wedding reception.

'You need some fun, darling,' she had coaxed. 'Some time to enjoy yourself. You're not doing yourself or Calum any good by working so hard.'

Most days, it had been all Sarah could do to get herself home in time to play with Calum before feeding him, bathing him and putting him to bed. Once he was in bed, Sarah usually had energy only for a light snack, before stumbling off to bed herself. No wonder she was losing weight.

Lizzie had added her entreaties to those of Sarah's mum. 'I've spoken to Jean and invited her, too. She's suggested that she come for a couple of hours and then take Calum home with her so that you can relax and enjoy the rest of the evening. All you'll be missing of Calum is the time he's usually asleep.' She had peered into Sarah's face, noting the dark circles under her eyes. 'You've been working too hard, girl. You deserve a break.' She had searched Sarah's eyes. 'Or is there something else? Something bothering you? Do you need to talk? You know, Sarah, I've been so caught up in wedding arrangements I haven't being paying attention to anyone else.'

Sarah had grown increasingly fond of Lizzie in the time she had known her. Since she had decided to confide in her, the young nurse and Sarah had become firm friends, finding that they shared the same sense of humour as well as a work ethic. She hadn't told her about Jamie and the reason he had given her for leaving. There hadn't really been the opportunity.

'I know I can talk to you. And I will when the time is right. But not now, Lizzie. If you don't mind?'

Lizzie hadn't pressed her further. Sarah had known it was important to Lizzie that she be there on her special day and so finally had agreed with her mother's suggestion.

She had been unsure of what to wear, finally settling on a knee-length red silk evening dress, the soft fabric draping her curves, crossing sexily at the back. It was trimmed with contrasting velvet ribbon that tied under the bust and emphasised the gentle swell of her breasts. She added a small cashmere bolero with long sleeves that would protect her against the cool evening air. After further thought she had decided to wear her designer sandals with the impossibly high heels. She could always kick them off for dancing if need be, but she had sacrificed enough by wearing flat shoes at work. The shoes deserved an outing and she deserved a glamorous look after the months of casual attire and conservative workwear. Sarah had every intention of getting at least a couple of dances in. How long had it been since she had danced?

She left her hair loose with a parting to the side. A rare visit to the hairdresser ensured that it lay perfectly straight and glossy. She had gone for the glam look with her make-up, too. Instead of the usual quick slick of lipstick, she coated her already long lashes with mascara and added just a touch of eye-shadow that brought out the green of her eyes.

'If I could wolf whistle, I would,' her mother said appreciatively when Sarah emerged from her bedroom. 'You look stunning. Can I ask,' she added with a twinkle, 'if all this is for the benefit of anyone in particular?'

Sarah had told her mother about Jamie. Jean had surprised her by supporting Jamie's decision. 'It explains a lot about his behaviour. Perhaps it wasn't the right decision but, knowing the kind of man he is, I can see why it was the one he made.'

'Getting dressed up is for *my* benefit, Mum. To be honest, I've forgotten what it feels like to be a woman again. I love being a mother, but for once it feels good to be me again.' But, Sarah had to admit, there was a part of her that wanted Jamie to see her looking her best. He, too, was going to the wedding. Although in theory it was his weekend on, management had agreed to employ one of the retired consultants to cover two weekends in four. It had long been agreed that there was too much work in the department for two consultants and, apart from old Dr MacDonald's replacement, the hospital was actively seeking to recruit a third.

Calum had had his afternoon nap and was buttoned up in his padded suit and hat in his car seat. They would be taking two cars so that Jean could take Calum home with her. His cheeks were still rosy from his nap and when he saw his mother, he squirmed and smiled, blowing bubbles. She knew how lucky she was to have such a contented baby. She had heard so many horror stories about babies who never slept or never stopped crying.

'Come on, then, darling,' she said to her son, picking him up in his car seat. 'Let's get this show on the road. Do you want to follow me, Mum?'

'Don't worry. I know my way there,' Jean replied. 'You get going and I'll be along in a bit.'

Sarah enjoyed the half-hour car journey out to the hotel, which was situated on the shores of Loch Lomond. Within a few minutes they had left the city behind and were in the countryside. The sun was just sinking in the sky, bathing everything in a dusky pink light. The wind had dropped and on her left Sarah could see the water of Loch Lomond reflecting the trees that protected its banks. In the distance, the hills of the Highlands already had a dusting of snow on their tops and Sarah looked forward to a time when she could take her son hill walking. As she sang to keep Calum amused, she remembered the many weekends she and Jamie had spent climbing and hill walking. She thought of exhilarating excursions followed by early nights in cosy hotels with log fires in the winter and stunning views in the summer. She had enjoyed hunting down the best places to stay. Neither of them had cared for the anonymity of the large hotel chains. After dinner and a couple of drinks, she and Jamie would beat a hasty retreat to their room where they had expended any leftover energy making love until finally, exhausted, they'd fallen asleep…

When they drew up at the impressive grounds of the hotel, night was beginning to fall and the hotel was lit up like a fairy castle. Calum looked at the lights, his eyes stretched in awe. As she carried him over, Elspeth rushed over to greet her and fuss over the baby.

Sarah relinquished Calum to the older woman. 'Aren't you just the most darling baby?' she crooned.

'Most of the time he is,' Sarah agreed, 'but he does have his moments. Were you at the ceremony, Elspeth? Did all go well?'

'Without a hitch. Lizzie looks absolutely breathtaking, as you'll see for yourself. She loves her wedding dress so much she's going to keep it on for the whole evening. And Stewart looked very handsome, too. As he requested, all the men are in kilts—including our own Dr Campbell. Most of the folk who have been invited for the reception are here already. They're in the bar, if you want to catch up with them.'

'I think I'll just take Calum for a look around the grounds before the light fades completely. I've never been here before. Could you let my mother know where we are when she arrives? We won't be long.'

Sarah was forced to keep to the paths, her high heels preventing her from cutting across the lawn. Calum was getting heavy in her arms and she looked forward to the time when he'd be able to toddle. She breathed in the air, filled with the scent of roses. It felt so good to be outside away from the smog and the confines of the city, even for a short time. Until tonight, she hadn't realised how much she missed spending time in the country. She looked up as she heard footsteps crunching the gravel behind her. Jamie, dressed in his kilt—Sarah recognised the Campbell tartan—was making his way towards them. He wore a dress shirt and tweed jacket with a *skean dubh* tucked in his dress socks. On anyone else the frilly shirt might have looked effeminate but on Jamie's muscular frame and with his dark eyes and hair, Sarah could only think of William Wallace, the famous Scottish hero. For one moment she let herself imagine being swept up in Jamie's arms and being carried away to some Highland bothy, where he would ravish her. Or she him, she admitted to herself as she felt a hot wave of desire wash over her.

'Here, let me take Calum,' her Highland hero said instead.

'I-I've never s-seen you in a kilt before,' Sarah stammered, not wanting him to see how affected she was by her fantasies.

'I've resisted up until tonight. But Lizzie insisted and I couldn't let her down on her big day, could I?' He tossed Calum into the air, making him squeal with delight. 'And how are you, young man?'

'I thought you didn't approve of babies at weddings,' Sarah reminded him.

Jamie had the grace to look a little shamefaced. 'I'm sorry. You were right. I had no right to tell you how to bring up your son. Not after you had the burden of bringing him up on your own. So, Sarah, have you had to think about things? Are you going to let me shoulder at least some of the responsibility?'

'He's never been a burden,' Sarah retorted, more sharply than she'd intended. 'Hard work perhaps, but never a burden. And if that's how you see him then—'

'Hey. Cool it. I didn't mean it like that. It's just that it must be hard going. Working all the hours that God sends and then caring for this little chap on top of everything.'

It was Sarah's turn to look a little shamefaced. 'I'm sorry. But, no, I haven't decided yet. That all rather depends on you.' The evening was turning cool and whether it was the night air or some premonition that made Sarah shiver, she couldn't be sure.

'Let's go inside—you look frozen. Here, take this,' Jamie said. Juggling Calum in one arm, he removed his jacket and wrapped it around Sarah's shoulders.

'Sarah, I need to go back to Africa. They depend on me. If you could only see it for yourself, you'd understand. Why don't you and Calum come for a couple of weeks?'

'It won't make any difference, Jamie. Don't you understand? I can't—won't—give up everything I've worked for, my career, my family, to go with you. It's too early for us to know whether we have a future. I thought I knew you and I was wrong. I'm just not prepared to take a chance.'

Jamie looked at her intently. 'But I can't stay here—can't you see that? I'm under contract and they are so short-staffed it would be almost negligent to resign anyway. And there's someone—a young boy—I promised I would look after.' He tilted her chin and gazed down at her. 'Give us a chance, SJ,' he said quietly, his voice thick with emotion. 'I know I was a fool, a coward even, to leave you without telling you my reasons, but I thought it was for the best. Can't you see I was just trying to protect you?'

Sarah shook her head sadly. 'That's just the problem, Jamie. You treated me as if I were a child. Not a grown woman who had the right to make her own decisions. And now you are asking me to trust *you* enough to risk everything I've worked so hard for?'

Jamie looked into the distance. 'I guess, then, that I have no option but to try and work something out. I'll do whatever it takes to be with you and Calum.'

At his words Sarah felt as if a weight had been lifted from her shoulders. For a moment she allowed herself to feel a surge of happiness.

She looked into the face knew almost as well as her own. She longed to reach out and trace the lines around his mouth, creases that she knew were caused by laughter. But she didn't trust herself to touch him. 'How can I be sure you don't want me just because of Calum?'

'Good grief, woman. I know you'd never stop me seeing Calum whenever I like. Obviously I'd rather be with him all the time, but in the meantime I'll take what I can. But make no mistake, SJ. I want you, too. And not simply because you're the mother of my child. We had something once, and could have it again if only you'll give us another try.'

Sarah desperately wanted to believe him. Could she trust him again? Take a risk that he meant what he said? That he wasn't staying just because of Calum? If only she could be sure.

'Can we take one day at a time? See what happens?'

'I'll do whatever it takes. I don't intend to lose you again. Come on, let's go and join the party.'

Inside, the dancing had started. The band, which consisted of a couple of fiddlers, an accordion player, a drummer and a singer, was playing the wedding waltz and Lizzie and her new husband were dancing to it, cheek to cheek.

Elspeth hadn't exaggerated. Lizzie looked radiant in her ivory silk dress with sweetheart neckline and antique pearl buttons. Her rich auburn hair, swept up into a flattering chignon, was the perfect foil for the coronet of miniature roses.

The room in which the reception was being held had high ceilings with ornate cornicing and ceiling roses. Long velvet curtains graced the enormous windows that stretched from floor to ceiling. Tables to accommodate the buffet and chairs were set out, while comfy sofas were stationed in strategic positions to allow revellers the opportunity to rest their feet. Beyond the opened French doors, a patio overlooked the loch. Sarah could make out the distant lights of small boats as they berthed for the night.

Taking advantage of a break in the dancing, Sarah went over to congratulate the happy couple.

'I just wish everyone could experience the happiness that I feel today.' Lizzie looked pointedly at Sarah and then looked over at Jamie, who was moving towards them, making her meaning clear. 'Make the most of your time out, Sarah, and enjoy the dancing.' As Lizzie and Stewart rushed off to greet some late arrivals, Jamie walked up to Sarah.

'May I have the pleasure of this dance?' he asked formally, then, noticing her gaze sweeping the room for her son, he added, 'Don't worry about Calum. He's having a great time being fussed over by the staff. And your mum has found a kindred spirit in Elspeth.'

What the hell, thought Sarah. Now she was here she was determined to have a good time. 'I'd be delighted,' she said with a small curtsy, equalling his formality. 'Just let me kick off these heels first.'

They joined several others who had lined up for Strip the Willow. As the dancers swirled to the music, Sarah began to relax and enjoy herself. Jamie was surprisingly light on his feet for someone so tall and muscular. But climbers had to be agile as well as strong. Every time they met in the middle Sarah was acutely aware of his powerful arms clasping hers.

'Whew!' Sarah laughed as the dance came to an end. 'I had forgotten how much energy Scottish country dancing takes. I need to cool down.'

'So do I, 'said Jamie, a mischievous glint in his eye. 'Let's go out on the patio for a while.'

As he led her out, Sarah continued, 'I'm seriously unfit. I desperately need to make time for some exercise.'

'I'm going climbing tomorrow. Why don't you come with me?'

For a moment Sarah was tempted. The drive up had made her realise how desperately she had missed the mountains. 'Who else is going?'

'I'm going on my own. None of my old climbing buddies were free so I decided to go anyway.'

Sarah looked at him. 'You shouldn't be going on your own. What if something happens? Who is going to belay for you?'

'I don't need anyone. You know I've climbed on my own a hundred times. Besides, if you come with me I won't be on my own, will I?'

'I'm afraid emotional blackmail isn't going to work. And, besides, haven't you forgotten something?'

'Calum. Actually, I've already spoken to your mum. She thinks it's a great idea for you to have a day off. She and Elspeth are busy hatching a plan for Calum tomorrow.'

'Does Elspeth know..?'

'That I'm Calum's father? I'm not sure. I certainly haven't told anyone—although you know I'd be proud to acknowledge him as my son, I rather think that's your decision, don't you?'

'Yes, it is. I'm not sure at this stage whether there is any need for anyone to know.'

Jamie left the unspoken question hang in the air. 'Think about it at least. It will give us some uninterrupted time together for once,' he said as a group of guests spilled onto the patio.

The rest of the evening passed all too quickly. Jean had told Sarah she was taking a sleepy Calum home after a couple of hours. 'I don't know about him, but I'm ready for my bed.' Sarah had cast a worried look at her mother.

'If you're feeling tired, Mum, I'll come, too. I'm quite happy to leave. After all, I've managed a couple of dances.'

'And spoil your first night out in months? No, I don't think so.'

'I don't want you driving back on your own if you're tired.'

Jamie came up just in time to hear the last of the conversation. 'Look, I have a room booked here for the night. I thought it would be more convenient for an early start on the hills in the morning. Jean and Calum could take it for the night.'

'It's very kind of you, Jamie,' Jean replied, 'but we couldn't possibly put you out.'

'I think its easier all round if I just take Mum and Calum home. Calum needs his routine,' Sarah interjected. 'Especially in the morning. Besides, I didn't bring enough nappies and bottles for overnight. Thanks for the offer, Jamie, but I'll just go and fetch my coat.'

'Stop right there,' Jamie said in a voice that Sarah knew well. 'Your mother is quite right. You need a night off. You stay and enjoy yourself. I'll take your mother and Calum home. It's the least I can do,' he finished with a pointed look at Sarah. But his look held something else. Almost supplication. Sarah knew what he was really demanding. That she let him help. 'It'll only take me forty minutes to get there and back,' Jamie continued. 'I'll be back before the band finishes, so don't give away the last dance to anyone else.'

'All right,' she agreed reluctantly, wondering if she was making the right decision. 'We can collect your car in the morning, Mum. If you want to sleep in my room, I'll take the sofa so I won't disturb you when I come in.'

'I'll just take Calum through to mine,' Jean said. 'I've got everything there he needs, including a travel cot. It will give you a chance for a lie-in. Unless you're going climbing with Jamie in the morning?'

Sarah caught the conspiratorial look that passed between Jamie and her mother. If they thought they were going to outmanoeuvre her they were very much mistaken.

'I'm not going climbing tomorrow. I simply don't want to leave Calum for a whole day when I can help it—not yet. Maybe another time, though,' she conceded.

'Perhaps the three of us could do something together tomorrow instead. I can leave the climb for another time,' Jamie suggested.

This was different. If Jamie was prepared to put his child's needs before his own, it was a start.

'I'll think about it. Let you know before the end of the night?'

'OK, you two,' Jamie said 'Let's get going. Can we take

your car, Jean? I somehow don't think I can manage two adults and a baby seat in a sports car.'

Another change Jamie was going to have to make if he was to take up his paternal responsibilities—the sports car would have to go. Sarah couldn't help a smile of satisfaction. Jamie was going to find out pretty soon what being a parent was really like.

On the way back from dropping off Jean and Calum, Jamie knew he had one thing left to do. He pulled over into a layby, and picking up his mobile, dialled the international number he knew from memory. After a pause filled with clicks and whirs, a distorted voice answered the phone.

'Lebowa Hospital. How may I direct your call?'

'Dr Lawson, please.' Jamie had to wait another couple of minutes before Greg, his friend and colleague, answered.

'Jamie. Delighted to hear your voice. I hope you're ringing to tell us you're coming back sooner than expected.'

'Actually, Greg, I'm sorry to disappoint you, but I was calling to let you know that I've decided to apply for a permanent position here. I'll be coming back for a week or two, at least until you find someone to replace me and to see Sibongele settled, but after that I'm afraid you're on your own. I'll explain everything when I see you.'

There was a short silence on the other end of the phone.

'I'm sorry to hear that, James. But I'm sure you've got your reasons. I don't have to tell you how disappointed we will be to lose you. We need all the doctors of your calibre and experience we can get.'

'I know, Greg. If there was any other way… If you like, I can try and recruit someone for you this side.'

'That would be a help. The sooner the better, and at least we'll have you back for a short while, but, James, I was just about to phone you. There's something else…'

'What is it? Is Sibongele all right?'

Jamie could hear Greg's deep sigh over the crackling of the phone.

'Actually, he's not. We finally traced his aunt and she won't take him. Says she has too many other mouths to feed, and I can't say I blame her. The trouble is, when we told Sibongele that he'd have to go into care, he became very distressed. Said he wanted to stay with you. We explained that that wasn't possible, and he'd have to go. So he ran away. We found him eventually, poor boy, frozen and frightened, and took him back to the hospital, but he says he'll run away from the home if we make him go. There's no talking to him. He just keeps asking for you. Says you'll make everything all right.'

Jamie rubbed a weary hand across his face. Poor Sibongele. He'd known so many losses in his short life—first his mother from the tuberculosis that had kept the child in hospital for the past six months, and now his aunt. And although he didn't know it yet, he was about to lose *him,* too. Jamie had promised the young boy he'd stay in touch if he went to live with his aunt. But how could he keep his promise now? Sibongele would never understand why he, too, appeared to be deserting him.

'How is he now?'

'He's not saying much, except to ask when you'll be back.'

'Look, don't say anything to him about me leaving until I have time to think. I need to be the one to tell him.'

Jamie thought for a moment. 'My locum here finishes at the end of next week. I'll try and get a flight out after that.

Keep trying to find someone to replace me in the meantime, and I'll do my best to find someone this end.'

'Any help or time you could give us would be gratefully received. Thank you.'

The two men spent the next few minutes talking about the hospital before saying their goodbyes. At Jamie's request, Greg put Sibongele on the phone for a couple of minutes.

'Hello,' Sibongele greeted him. 'When are you coming home?'

'I'll be coming soon, Sibongele. We'll talk then. But in the meantime you must promise me that you won't run away again.'

'Only if I can stay with you.'

Jamie's heart sunk. How could he make a promise that he couldn't possibly keep? Jamie knew, despite the stoicism that Sibongele had always shown through his long recovery, the fourteen-year-old would be devastated to lose him too..

'Just promise me, Sibongele. No more running away.'

'OK. Until you come back. I like it here at the hospital. They are teaching me at the school. If I learn, maybe I, too, can become a doctor. Dr Greg and the others are letting me help and they say I am quick to learn.'

'I know you are a good worker and a good student.' Jamie thought for a moment. Was there a chance he could arrange for Sibongele to study in the UK? He would need to find out before he raised the boy's hopes.

As Jamie ended the call, he felt torn. He'd have to go back, at least until they'd found someone to replace him and he knew that Sibongele was all right. Sarah would understand when he explained, and it wouldn't be for ever, a couple of months perhaps, maybe a little longer, and then he could return to be with them both for good.

Before Sarah knew it, Jamie had arrived back. She had danced non-stop in the hour he had been away and her feet were beginning to ache. She had noticed that Karen and Keith were dancing a lot together and wondered if she was witnessing the beginnings of a new romance. Or had it being going on for some time and she had been too preoccupied to notice? Whatever, she was pleased for them. They suited each other, the vivacious Karen acting as a foil to Keith's more serious nature. She hoped that if they were involved with one another, their romance would run more smoothly than hers and Jamie's had.

'Is this dance taken?' a deep voice said in her ear. She looked up to find Jamie looking down at her, his eyes glinting. Without waiting for a reply, he led her onto the dance floor, where the band were playing a waltz to slow down the tempo and bring the evening to a close.

Jamie held Sarah close to his chest as they moved to the music. She could feel the steady beat of his heart and the hard muscle beneath her hands as she slid her arms around his back. He pulled her nearer.

'Did I tell you how beautiful you look tonight?' he said huskily, sliding his hands down her bare back to the point where her bottom curved.

She felt the flames of desire course through her body. She could smell the faint whiff of aftershave and the familiar scent was intoxicating her senses. He bent his head to hers and for a moment she thought he was going to kiss her. Right there in front of their colleagues.

'Let's get out of here,' he growled instead, and, taking her hand, led her out of the door into the grounds. He found a secluded spot underneath a sweeping oak tree, before pulling her once again into his arms.

'God, I've missed you,' he murmured before claiming her mouth.

She kissed him back hungrily, allowing the months of anger and hurt to disappear. What did it matter if he left her again? Her need for him right now was too strong. Tomorrow could wait.

He caressed her face, her breasts with urgent hands. 'Stay with me tonight, SJ. Please. Stay.'

She felt helpless to resist him. She nodded imperceptibly and he led her back inside. She was barely aware of the other guests as they passed through the foyer. He led her up the stairs, too impatient to wait for a lift to take them up the couple of flights. He had barely time to close the door behind them before they were once more in each other's arms, tearing at each others clothes in their desperate need.

Within seconds she stood before him in her bra and panties. She had giggled as he had struggled out of his kilt, the unfamiliar garment becoming entangled in his feet in his haste. He had looked wounded at her laughter before pulling her onto the bed. 'Hell, don't look at me like that, woman,' he said hoarsely before finishing the removal of her silk underwear with a proficiency that left her breathless.

Naked before him, she was suddenly shy. His eyes raked her body and she felt herself tingle with the blatant desire she could see there. He placed his hands gently on her hips, circling her hip bones with his thumb. She shuddered as he raised a hand and cupped her breast. Hot flames of desire licked her body and she groaned, leaning into his touch. He let his hands travel downwards towards, stroking the soft flesh at the tops of her legs. She moaned with her need for him. She wanted him inside her, filling the void that was within her. Now! She couldn't wait any longer. It was his turn to gasp as she reached for him and guided him into her, sitting on his lap, her legs astride his. As he filled her she stopped for a moment. He took her face in his hands and they stared into each other's eyes. Then, involuntarily, she began to move her hips against him. He grasped her buttocks, supporting her until finally they both allowed their release to claim them. As they lay in each other's arms, spent, Sarah cuddled into his shoulder.

She didn't want to talk about the future or the past. All she wanted was to remain there with him and pretend the night would never end.

'Do you think anyone noticed our hasty departure?' she said, a smile in her voice.

'Don't give a damn if they did,' was the reply.

'We'll be a source of gossip throughout the hospital by Monday if anyone did.' Sarah said with a sigh.

'You don't mind too much, do you?' said Jamie lazily, allowing his hands to travel over her body, refamiliarising himself with its contours.

Sarah felt herself grow warm as his hands travelled over her, feeling the new curves that motherhood had left. Self-consciously she pulled her stomach in, aware that it was no longer the flat one that he had known.

'Hey, I like the new curves,' Jamie protested, aware of her reaction. 'They suit you.' She felt his hand travel lower still and this time her intake of breath was in case he stopped. She couldn't bear it if he stopped.

After they'd had their fill of each other once more, Sarah climbed out of bed and began to get dressed.

'Where are you going?' Jamie asked, reaching to pull her back down next to him.

'I've got to get home,' Sarah said, pulling her dress on over her underwear. 'I know Calum is safe with my mother but I need to be at home just in case he wakes up and wants me. I'll creep in and put him back in his own cot. I know Mum said she'd keep him till morning but she already does enough. She looked tired tonight. I worry it's all too much for her.' She bent down to slip on her shoes.

Jamie started to get out of bed. 'I'll drive you home.'

'Don't be silly. How will you get your car?'

'I could stay the night with you and we could pick it up on our way out tomorrow,' Jamie suggested.

'I don't think so. I think we should take things slowly for a while,' Sarah said softly, pressing him back down and laughing as she avoided his reaching arms. She picked up her bag, and looked at Jamie once more. He was lying on his back, arms behind his head, grinning at her. She wanted nothing more at that moment than to crawl back next to him

'After all, we have all the time in the world now,' she added.

'SJ, there is something I want to talk to you about,' Jamie replied.

Something in his tone stopped her in her tracks. Somehow she knew immediately that she didn't want to hear what he had to say.

'Sarah,' he said quietly. 'I'm sorry, but I have to go back…'

CHAPTER EIGHT

'GO BACK?' Sarah echoed, stunned.

'I made a phone call to Africa on my mobile while I was on my way back and—'

'But you said that you would do anything to be with Calum and me,' Sarah interrupted.

'And I meant it. But they need me—'

But Sarah was in no mood to let him finish. 'So what was all this, then?' She indicated the rumpled bed with a sweep of her hand. Suddenly she was furious. How could she have been so stupid? She should have known that Jamie would do anything in his power to achieve the result he wanted. He had clearly never intended to stay. What was it he had actually said? *I'll do anything to be with you and Calum.* Stupidly she had assumed that he'd meant he would be staying. But obviously he had never had any intention of not going back to Africa. Did he really think that all he had to do was seduce her and she'd give up everything, uproot her son and go with him to Africa?

'I want you and Calum to come with me.'

'And you thought that seducing me was the best way to persuade me to throw everything I've worked for away? That once I'd been back in your bed, I couldn't resist following you? Where was the discussion? When were my needs to be considered? Or Calum's, for that matter?

'Hey, I haven't finished,' Jamie protested.

Incandescent with anger and something else—hurt and disappointment, not just for herself but for Calum—Sarah's eyes fell on Jamie's walking boots lying in a corner. Before she could stop herself she had grabbed one and flung it at him, narrowly missing his head.

'Oh, but I think you—we—are finished,' she said, turning on her heel. 'Don't even think about turning up at my place tomorrow. You can forget any *family* walks. From now on, if you want to see Calum you can arrange it through your solicitor, although how you are going to manage access from Africa is beyond me.'

And with a last final glare at Jamie, who was regarding her with disbelief, she closed the door behind her.

Sarah used her key to creep into her mother's flat. Calum lay on his back in the travel cot, arms flung above his head, abandoned in sleep. Her heart twisted as she looked down at her son while bending to smooth a lock of hair from his brow. What had he done to deserve a father who seemed as disinterested in him as hers had been in her?

Calum seemed a little warm to her so she removed a blanket. She was reluctant to disturb him by picking him up to take him back to her flat so she switched on the baby monitor beside his bed instead. That way, if he woke during the night, or in the early hours of the morning, she'd hear him and with a bit of luck would get to him before he woke her mother. She spent a few more minutes with Calum before returning to her flat.

Her heart thudded as she made out a tall figure standing by the front door. Instead of the kilt of the evening, Jamie was now dressed in faded jeans and a grey, thin, knit sweater.

'I'm tired, Jamie. Whatever it is you've come to say, it can wait till morning.'

'I wanted to make sure you got home OK. Besides, you didn't let me finish what I was saying back there. Thank God my reflexes are still good.' He smiled ruefully. 'You nearly got me a cracker.'

'Please, go, Jamie.' She felt her throat close. 'If you have any respect or regard for me at all, please, go.'

'Not until I finish telling you what you wouldn't let me back at the hotel.'

'I don't know what you could possibly have to say that will make any difference at all, but go on.'

'I thought I could stay. I really did, SJ, but I spoke to Greg, my colleague at the hospital tonight, and they are really desperate. But it's not just that. Something else has happened.'

As succinctly as possible Jamie told Sarah about the conversation he'd had with Greg.

'Don't you see, SJ? Sibongele really needs me right now. If I tell him I'm leaving for good, there is no telling what he'll do.'

'And Calum. Doesn't he need his father? I thought you promised, just a few hours ago, that you would never abandon him.'

Jamie pulled his hand through his hair. Sarah felt a pang of sympathy as she took in the lines of tiredness and regret.

'I meant what I said. I won't leave him. That's why you

have to change your mind and come with me. Both of you. Please, SJ. Can't you see it's the only solution?'

Sarah looked at him in despair.

'Oh, Jamie, I wish I could. But I just can't. Can't you see what you are asking me is impossible? I understand about the boy. Really I do. And I do understand why you need to go back to see him and make sure he's all right.' Opening the door to her flat, she moved past him.

'It's up to you, Jamie. You have to choose. But it sounds to me as if you have made up your mind. And what's worse, if you stay I'll always feel guilty for forcing your hand. I don't want you to come to resent me for making you do something you didn't want to.'

'Why can't you trust me? What can't you trust the feelings we have for one another? Come with me. Please.' Jamie reached out and took Sarah by the arms. She could feel his fingers biting into her flesh. She looked at him, until at last he dropped his hands to his sides.

'That's always going to be the problem between us,' she said sadly, moving away from him. 'I don't trust you. Not as far as loving me is concerned, and maybe not as far as Calum is concerned. Once trust is broken, that's what happens. I realise that now. It's too late. Without that trust, there can never be a future for us.'

Jamie caught her by the arm. 'I won't accept that. I'm not going to allow you to throw away our chance for happiness. And you can't tell me that back there in the hotel meant nothing to you.'

'I'm only human, Jamie, as you're finding out. And there's a big difference between love and sex.'

'I don't believe you,' Jamie ground out between clenched teeth.

'Right now I don't care whether you believe me or not. And I'm too tired to discuss this right now. Accept it, Jamie. It's over between us. We can be friends and colleagues—after all, we will always share Calum—but we will never be anything more.'

Jamie dropped his hand, his mouth set in a stubborn line.

'OK, I'll go, but you and I will talk about this,' he said firmly. 'I'm not going to give up. Tomorrow evening when I get back from my climb. We are going to go somewhere where we can be alone and uninterrupted. I'll pick you up around seven.' And before Sarah had a chance to protest he had disappeared back into the night.

The next day, Sarah thought that Calum still felt a little warm and her usually placid baby was fractious and out of sorts.

'Perhaps I shouldn't have taken him to the wedding,' Sarah said to her mother.

'He's probably just teething,' her mother replied reassuringly.

'Perhaps,' Sarah said thoughtfully, 'but I'm just going to check his temperature anyway.'

Sarah took his temperature with a child thermometer. It was slightly raised, but not enough to cause concern. Maybe it was just teething or a mild bug. Somehow it was different when it was your own child. It was difficult to be objective. Much easier to tell whether it was something serious when it was somebody else's baby.

She decided to keep him indoors instead of the walk she had planned.

But as the day wore on, Calum became increasingly irritable. He didn't seem interested in his bottle and spent most of the day dozing in his mother's arms. It's just a mild bug, Sarah tried to reassure herself. If only she could ask Jamie. Not because he was Calum's father but because she trusted him as a doctor, despite everything.

Finally, mid-afternoon, she tried Jamie's mobile. The message came back that the caller was unavailable. He was probably up a mountain where the signal couldn't reach. Why was the man never around when she needed him? Instead, she sent him a text, asking him to call her when he returned home. If he was planning to pick her up at seven, he had obviously intended to be home before then.

But by six-thirty Jamie still hadn't called. Looking at Calum, she made a decision. Something was definitely wrong with her child. She phoned the hospital and asked them to page Dr Carty, the senior paediatrician at the hospital, and request that he call her at home.

She had met him when he had attended the department for a specialist paediatric opinion. She had found him thorough and caring and had trusted his opinion implicitly. When Dr Carty returned her call a few minutes later, she explained Calum's symptoms, trying to keep her voice calm and factual.

'I think we should see him at the hospital straight away. Can you bring him or would you like me to send an ambulance?'

Sarah was panic-stricken at his words. Had she waited too long? Had she put her child's health at risk? Dr Carty obviously thought that there could be a serious problem.

'I'm only a short distance away. I'll take him in my car. I can be there in ten minutes.'

'I'll meet you in A and E,' was the brisk reply.

Sarah bundled Calum into his outdoor suit. On her way out she stopped at her mother's to tell her that she was taking Calum to the hospital. Jean had just come out of the shower and was still in her dressing-gown.

'If you give me a minute, I'll get dressed and come with you.'

'I can't wait, Mum. Follow me when you're ready,' Sarah flung over her shoulder, already heading for the car.

Calum had stopped crying and had gone eerily quiet. As Sarah strapped him into his car seat, she knew for certain that there was something seriously wrong with her baby. She forced back tears of fear. It wouldn't do her child any good if she were to panic. For his sake, she needed to keep calm and think rationally.

As she was getting into the driver's seat, Jamie appeared at the window.

'Running away? Is the thought of dinner with me really that bad?' he said, a smile curling his mouth. Then he peered closer. 'Good God, Sarah, what is it?'

'It's Calum. He's sick. I'm taking him to A and E. Dr Carty's meeting us there.'

'Get in the back with Calum. You're in no state to drive,' Jamie said, taking control. Sarah knew it was useless to protest. Besides, now Jamie was there, all she felt was an overwhelming sense of relief.

As Jamie drove the short distance to the hospital, Sarah explained Calum's symptoms.

'It could be anything, Sarah,' he said, but she could tell from his grim voice that he, too, was thinking the same as her. Meningitis. Almost unable to look, Sarah pulled up Calum's outfit, searching for the tell-tale signs. She couldn't be sure in the dim light cast by the streetlights, but she thought she could just make out the faintest of rashes. She felt terror grip her.

'I think he's developing a rash, Jamie.' She could barely speak. Her jaw felt rigid with the effort of holding things together.

'Hold on, Sarah. Everything's going to be all right.' But they both knew that if their diagnosis was correct, everything was far from all right.

Jamie drew up in front of the A and E entrance. He leapt out of the car tossing the keys to a porter who was outside, having a break. 'Park this somewhere,' he ordered, lifting Calum out of his seat.

There was something surreal about the evening, Sarah was thinking. Here she was back in her department, but instead of the usual familiarity it felt alien, frightening. Recognising Sarah and Jamie, one of the nursing staff, an experienced nurse called Mary, came over and held out her arms for Calum.

'Dr Carty told us to expect you. He's waiting in Resus. We'll take Calum through for you. If you'd just take a seat?'

Jamie ignored the nurses and strode towards Resus, Calum still in his arms and Sarah at his heels.

'You'd be better waiting outside,' Jamie said. 'I'll make sure he's OK.'

'I'm not leaving my son,' Sarah retorted. 'I know I can't be involved in his care, but I'm not letting him out of my sight.' She lifted her chin, praying that Jamie wouldn't argue with her. She simply didn't have the strength to fight him, too.

'Fine, but you stay in the background.' He turned to her, his dark eyes sombre. 'I promise you, Sarah, I won't let anything happen to our son.'

Jamie reluctantly handed over his son to Mary, who placed

Calum's tiny body gently on a gurney. He was barely conscious and made no protest as Mary undressed his unresisting form.

Sarah reached for Jamie's hand and felt her fingernails dig into his palm. Jamie returned her squeeze reassuringly. 'He's in the best possible hands, SJ,' he said, but she could see the worry in his eyes.

Swiftly, one of the other nurses, who had introduced herself to the worried parents as Rosemary, attached the leads of the ECG monitor to Calum's small chest and a pulse oximeter to his finger.

'He's tachycardic,' Mary told Sarah, 'but at least his oxygen saturation is normal.'

It only took a couple of minutes for Dr Carty to arrive and carry out a thorough examination, but to Sarah it seemed like an eternity. The paediatrician lifted Calum's head and Sarah knew that he, too, suspected meningitis. He shifted his attention to the rash covering the infant's body. To Sarah's frantic gaze it seemed as if the rash had become more prominent even since she had first noticed it in the car.

Dr Carty turned to Jamie and Sarah. 'I know you are worried that this might be meningitis, but we won't know until we have carried out more tests. We'll need to do a lumbar puncture, Paul,' he ordered the junior doctor, who had joined the group in Resus. 'Start IV antibiotics immediately. Could you also send off bloods for haematology, U and Es and do blood cultures? Mary, could you set up for an LP? And, Rosemary, could you get a urine specimen for culture?'

The next couple of hours passed in a haze. Sarah could hardly bear it as the paediatrician inserted the needle into the space between her son's vertebrae to draw fluid. It was such a small spine. Such a small space. What if the needle slipped? Although Sarah had carried out the same procedure a hundred times herself without incident, she knew that occasionally things did go wrong. It was the worst part of being a doctor, knowing what could go wrong. All the complications of meningitis—septicaemia, amputation, brain damage, death—whirled around her mind.

'He's a bit young for bacterial meningitis,' Jamie tried to reassure Sarah. 'And even if he does have it, many, many pull through and lead perfectly healthy lives. We have to stay positive.'

'We won't know whether he has meningitis, or which form until we get the results,' Dr Carty agreed. 'Let's keep our fingers crossed, but even if it is viral meningitis, he's still pretty poorly.'

Sarah felt utterly wretched. Why had she waited so long? She should have acted sooner.

Jamie was clearly reading her thoughts. 'You couldn't have known, SJ. Think. You know this illness comes on very rapidly. You brought him in as soon as you could.'

'He's started on IV antibiotics. I think we've caught it in time. But we are going to have to admit him to the paediatric intensive care unit for observation. The next twenty-four hours will be critical,' Dr Carty informed Sarah. 'You know that there are lots of viral illnesses that can cause rashes, although I'm afraid it almost certainly is meningitis. But I won't be sure until we get the results of all his tests some time tomorrow.'

As Calum was being taken up to Intensive Care, Sarah turned to Jean, who had arrived while Calum had been in Resus. Seeing the stricken look on her mother's face, Sarah almost broke down.

'Could you go home and collect some stuff for me, please, Mum?' she said, tears close to the surface.

'Of course, darling,' her mother replied, clearly struggling to keep her own emotions under control. 'But I don't want to leave you on your own.'

Jamie stepped up, lines of worry evident on his face. 'Don't worry, Jean, she won't be. I'll stay with them both.'

'Go home, Jamie,' Sarah said wearily. 'I can manage. Besides, one of us has to be fit to work tomorrow.'

'You can stop worrying about work. I'll see to everything. As for going home, not a chance—he's my son, too.'

Sarah looked at his face. She was surprised to see that how much he was also suffering. He was right. Whatever happened between them in the future, it would be too cruel to stop him being with his son when he so obviously needed to be.

She reached out for his hand and felt his strength flow from him to her. For now she needed him, too. Right now nothing else mattered.

The nurses in the intensive care ward had offered to make up a bed in the relatives' room for Sarah or Jamie should they wish to catnap.

'We've sedated Calum and he seems peaceful. Why don't you try and get some sleep?' they had suggested. But both Jamie and Sarah had refused. Sarah didn't want to leave her son for a moment in case he woke up and wanted her. Instead, they found a couple of armchairs and made themselves as comfortable as they could by the bedside without getting in the nurses' way.

The night wore on. Jamie and Sarah watched over their son as he lay in the cot. More than anything Sarah wanted to hold her son in her arms, but the leads and drips that fed him and monitored his condition prevented her from doing anything except stroke his face with her finger.

She was barely conscious of Jamie standing behind her, massaging her shoulders and stroking her hair, but she was glad of his presence.

'God, what's taking so long? Why haven't they brought us some news?' The words sounded as they had been ripped from Jamie's body. 'Sorry. I know these things take time. But not being able to do anything makes me think of my father. It reminds me of how helpless I felt then, too. What is the point of all our medical training if we can't help those we love?'

'At least your father loved you,' Sarah said quietly. 'Mine didn't seem to care whether I lived or died.' Memories of her father's betrayal came rushing back. 'He left Mum and me when I was about Calum's age,' she went on, almost as if she was talking to herself. 'He came back to see me once or twice, but then his visits fizzled out and I never saw him again.' As always, the memory of sitting waiting for a father who had never come caused her almost unbearable pain. She was determined her son would never suffer the same feelings of abandonment and rejection.

'I'm sorry, SJ, I didn't know about your father. You never told me.'

'It turns out there was quite a lot we never told one another,' Sarah replied with a small smile. 'I guess somehow we were too wrapped up in just being together to ever really talk. I always thought there would be plenty of time for us to really get to know one another.'

The time they had been together had been spent in a flurry of activity. There had never seemed to be a right time to tell him about her father.

'And then I left,' Jamie said flatly.

'Yes. I thought you were different. I never believed that you would do to me what my father did to my mother. Against my better judgement, I allowed myself to trust you and what we had.'

'I had my reasons,' Jamie reminded her. 'I know now I was wrong, but I did what I did to protect you. I knew I was falling in love with you, and I guess I panicked.' He turned her towards him. 'You have to believe me when I tell you that I will never abandon my child.'

'What if there's no choice?' Sarah's voice broke. 'What if we lose him, Jamie? I couldn't bear it.'

'Sarah, listen to me,' Jamie said urgently. 'That is not going to happen. I won't let it.'

In the early hours of the morning Dr Carty came in to see them.

Sarah held her breath as she waited for him to bring them up to date.

'The initial results are back. It is meningitis, but it looks like it's most likely to be the viral strain. We'll know for sure when we get the rest of the results later in the day.' When she heard the news, Sarah was powerless to stop the tears. Although it was a less deadly strain than bacterial meningitis, Sarah knew that Calum was far from out of the woods. They couldn't be sure he'd recover. Not yet.

Oblivious of the staff around them, Jamie pulled her into his arms and held her as sobs racked her body. 'Shh.' He stroked her hair. 'It's going to be all right, I promise you.'

Sarah looked into his eyes. He returned the look, his eyes grim, but whatever she saw there calmed her.

For the rest of the long night, Jamie and Sarah sat in silence, each preoccupied with their own thoughts. Neither could bring themselves to discuss what could happen to Calum. Every now and then Jamie would get up and fetch them both a coffee from the vending machine. Nurses recorded Calum's vital signs at regular intervals. 'He seems to be holding his own,' they kept reassuring the worried parents. 'And so far there doesn't seem to be any signs that he's developed septicaemia.' Sarah shuddered at the thought of her tiny son battling the deadly blood infection. But if Calum survived, it would be the next big worry. With septicaemia there was always the possibility that amputation would be required. Sarah pushed the negative thoughts to the back of her mind. *Calum was going to be all right—he had to be!*

As dawn was breaking, Jamie left the ward. 'I'll be back as soon as I can,' he whispered. 'Any change—even the slightest—get the ward to page me.'

Calum was still sleeping when Jamie arrived back a couple of hours later. He had changed into theatre greens and had shaved, but he still looked tired and drawn. Sarah couldn't remember ever seeing him look so vulnerable.

'I've arranged for the locum who was covering at the weekend to stay on and cover nights. I'll manage the day shift on my own. The ward can easily page me here if I'm needed. In the meantime, management is trying to find us some extra cover.'

Sarah simply nodded. She couldn't bring herself to care. All that mattered was her son.

As the hours wore on staff from the all over the hospital popped their heads in, asking about Calum, how he was, was there anything they could do? Although Sarah appreciated their concern, anything that took her attention away from Calum was a distraction she didn't need.

Jamie was there most of the time, occasionally leaving the room to answer the phone or go to the ward. Jean had come and gone. Sarah had insisted she get some rest. Her mother couldn't survive on no sleep. Sarah was used to it and while Calum's life was still in danger, she couldn't bear to close her eyes for a moment.

By late afternoon the next day, Calum's condition was beginning to improve. 'He's responding well to treatment and you picked it up so quickly that, although it's early days yet, I think he's going to make a full recovery. He's a tough little mite. Takes after his mother, obviously.' Dr Carty smiled at Sarah's relief. 'We're going to start reducing the sedation. He should wake up soon.'

Again Sarah broke down in tears. But this time, as she found comfort in Jamie's arms once more, her tears were of relief. Calum had survived the first twenty-four hours without developing septicaemia. This was the news they had prayed for.

'Thank God,' Jamie whispered into her hair. His voice shook with suppressed emotion. Clearly the last hours had taken their toll on him too.

Although still poorly, Sarah knew that her baby was well on his way to recovery. She pulled free of Jamie's arms and made a feeble attempt to smooth her ruffled hair.

'The department's quiet just now, SJ. Why don't you go home and try and catch a couple of hours' sleep? You look exhausted.'

'You don't look so hot yourself,' Sarah teased wearily. But she felt a pang of sympathy for him. The lines around his eyes and brows seemed to have deepened overnight, and his eyes looked even darker with fatigue. After all, he had been running the department in between spending every spare moment at Calum's bedside.

'I'm all right. I'm more used to staying up all night than most. But you need to get some rest.'

'I'll have a shower in the department and maybe snatch a couple of hours in the side ward,' Sarah compromised. 'I'll come and relieve you after that. But—'

'I know, I know. If there's any change, I'll call you immediately. Now, shoo, woman, before I carry you out of here.' Seeing Jamie taking a step towards her as if he had every intention of carrying out his threat, Sarah beat a hasty retreat.

When she returned a couple of hours, later feeling a whole lot better for her shower and nap, she found Jamie asleep with a sleeping Calum in his arms. As she looked at the two figures she felt her heart twist. Whatever she tried to tell herself, these were the two most important people in her world. She shivered at the thought that she had almost lost one permanently and would never truly have the other. As if conscious of her scrutiny, Jamie's eyes flickered open.

'Hi, there,' he said softly. 'Feeling better?'

'Much,' she said, her throat tight with emotion. 'Why don't I take over here and you get some rest?'

'Perhaps in a little while,' Jamie stalled.

Sarah sat down in the chair beside Jamie and Calum. Her son seemed so settled in his father's embrace. She reached over and tenderly stroked his fine baby hair.

'I'm going to miss him so much. The thought of being on the other side of the world from him doesn't bear thinking about,' Jamie said hoarsely.

Sarah felt tears well up as she watched him gaze, mesmerised, at his sleeping child.

'Then stay,' she said quietly

'Don't you know that's what I want to do more than anything else in this world? But I have to go back. See Sibongele, work at the hospital at least until they find someone to replace me.'

'And then? Will you come back?'

'You leave me no choice, SJ.' He looked down at his sleeping child. 'I don't want him to grow up not knowing his father.'

'What about the hospital in Africa? Won't you miss it? Won't they miss you?'

For a moment she could see the sadness that clouded Jamie's eyes.

'Yes,' he said heavily. 'I'll miss them and I know they will miss having an experienced doctor around. But…' He hesitated, as if unsure whether to go on. 'But it's not just the work and the feeling that I'm letting the hospital down. It's Sibongele. I feel as if I'm letting him down, too. I don't know how he'll feel when I tell him I'm leaving. I just know he's going to think I've abandoned him as well.' Jamie stood up with his son in his arms and strode towards the window. He looked out without saying anything.

'But,' he continued, his back still facing her, 'if you and Calum won't come back with me, and it's the only way to be with you both, then I have no choice.' He turned and smiled briefly at her, as if to reassure her he felt no bitterness towards her.

He must love Calum, Sarah thought, if he was prepared to make such a sacrifice to be with his child. But where did that leave her? Why couldn't she believe that he cared for her? But how could she when he was prepared to leave them both? Surely, if he meant what he said, if he *really* cared about her and Calum, he would put them first—no matter how he felt about his responsibilities in Africa. And perhaps if he had, she would have started to believe in him again. But this way, his insistence that he had to go back made her think that he only truly cared about those he had left in Africa, and his son, of course. She had no doubts that he loved his son and wanted to be with him. Her head was beginning to ache from asking herself questions that didn't appear to have any answers.

'When will you go?'

'I've provisionally booked my flight for next Monday. They expect to discharge Calum home in a day or two and I want to make absolutely sure he's well before I go. That will give you the rest of the week off to be at home with him.'

'And when will you be back?' Suddenly Sarah couldn't bear the thought of not seeing him every day.

'Why? Will you miss me?' he teased, a wicked glint in his brown eyes. 'I'll be back as soon as I can, but it may some time—several weeks, even a few months.'

A few months? Sarah was aghast. She had been thinking a couple of weeks, three at the most.

'Calum will miss you. And, besides, we'll be a doctor down before you come back.' Sarah wasn't prepared to admit just how much she was going to miss him.

'I know. I'm sorry about that. But the other locum will

continue to cover while I'm away. And the interviews for the third post are next week. Apparently they've got a couple of outstanding candidates lined up who are ready to start straight away.'

Sarah couldn't tell him that she didn't care how outstanding the potential appointees were, it was Jamie she wanted working beside her. More than just working beside her.

'I'll be back for a visit in two, maximum three weeks. I don't want to be away from this little lad any longer than I have to. I've missed enough of his life already and if I have my way, once I return for good, he and I will have a lot of catching up to do.' He looked at Sarah, his dark eyes serious. 'And you and I have some unfinished business, too.'

As Jamie had predicted, Calum was pronounced fit and healthy and discharged home a couple of days later. Jamie was a frequent visitor to the flat in the days leading up to his departure for Africa, but Sarah rarely found herself alone with him. And when she did, he talked about work, keeping her informed about the department, the type of cases they had been dealing with and gossip about the staff.

They had appointed the new consultant. Sarah had left Calum with her mother and attended the interviews. Two of the three candidates had been a husband-and-wife team who were on a two-year working visa from Australia. They had been keen to get jobs in the same hospital. The wife, a pretty woman with an outgoing manner, had indicated that she would prefer part-time hours in the future, if possible, as they were trying for their first child. 'And I'd love to be at home at least for the first year or two.' she had confided to Sarah.

At her words a germ of an idea was beginning to form in Sarah's mind. Calum's illness had shaken her badly. Part of her still felt guilty, although she knew there was nothing more she could have done to prevent Calum becoming unwell. Perhaps she could reduce her hours and do a job share? Spend more time being a mother yet still have a career? She made up her mind to give the thought some serious consideration before discussing it with the personnel department. The hospital had appointed the husband, and the wife had another interview lined up at one of the smaller hospitals on the outskirts of the city in a couple of weeks' time, so she'd have to make a decision soon.

Shortly before Jamie left for Africa, Lizzie returned from honeymoon. She was horrified and sympathetic to learn about Calum's illness.

'Poor you,' she sympathised. 'You must have got a terrible fright.'

Sarah could feel a lump come to her throat at the memory.

'I really thought I was going to lose him, Lizzie,' she confided, a break in her voice.

'But you didn't,' Lizzie said firmly. 'I heard that Jamie was distraught. Obviously everyone knows now.'

'Funny how little it matters. It probably caused some gossip at the time, but everyone was fantastic, really concerned and offering help any chance they got.'

'And you and Jamie?' Lizzie's hazel eyes were lit up with curiosity. 'I gather he's thinking of applying for a permanent consultant post. The staff are over the moon. Absolutely delighted that he's planning to be a permanent feature in the department. And,' she added impishly, 'there is probably more than one who is working out how they can become a permanent feature in his life. Although I suspect that slot is already taken.' She arched an eye brow at Sarah, making her meaning clear.

Sarah chewed her lip. 'He's going back to Africa and it could be some time before he returns…if he ever does come back.' She swallowed hard against the lump that had formed in her throat. 'And there is no Jamie and me. There never will be. Oh, I think Jamie *will* be back…to see his son, if for no other reason. But how long for?' She shook her head sadly. 'I can't deny Calum his father, just because we couldn't work things out. I know only too well the heartache of not knowing your own dad…' Sarah trailed off.

So that's the way the land lay, thought Lizzie, but she was wise enough to keep her own counsel. From what she had gathered from the nursing staff, Jamie was besotted not only with his son but the son's very beautiful mother. Was Sarah the only one in the department who didn't know how Jamie felt?

CHAPTER NINE

'OF COURSE I can't go. How can you possibly manage without me?' Jean said.

'I'll try and change my weekend on call,' said Sarah. 'Although I've already had so much time off.' Sarah let her words tail off. Since Calum had been discharged from hospital she had been at home with him. But now that he had made a full recovery, she needed to get back to work and share some of the load. She knew from Lizzie that every moment that Jamie hadn't being spending with Calum had been spent in the department, picking up the extra work that her enforced absence had left. Sarah's mother had won a weekend break at an exclusive new health spa that had opened just south of the border. It was a once-in-a-lifetime opportunity and sharing the worry of Calum's illness had tired her mother. She deserved—no, needed—some time off to relax.

When the phone rang she picked it up, still thinking of what to do.

'Oh, hello, Jamie,' she said, recognising his deep voice immediately. 'Calum's fine. He's just about to have his lunch.' Jamie phoned regularly to check up on his son.

'What's up? Are you sure Calum's fine?' he asked, as usual immediately picking up when something was bothering her.

'Honestly, he's perfectly all right. It's just…' She hesitated, then decided to share her problem After all, it did concern him, too, both as Calum's father and as a fellow colleague. 'Mum's had this opportunity to go on a weekend break to a spa, but I'm supposed to be on call this weekend. Normally she'd move into my flat so she can be here for Calum if I'm called out. She's said she won't go but I really think she should,' she said, ignoring her mother's frantic gestures.

'Of course she should go.' Jamie agreed at once. 'I'll do your weekend on call. It's no problem.'

'I really don't want to take more time off work. Besides, you've done more than your fair share of being on call. You're not superhuman, Jamie.' Although, as she said this, she wondered if he was. Over the last week it had definitely seemed as if Jamie was superhuman. Heaven only knew when he had found the time to sleep. Slowly an idea was beginning to formulate in her mind.

'Unless…' she said slowly.

'Unless?' Jamie prompted.

'Unless you move in here for the weekend. You could look after Calum if I get called out. You can have the spare bedroom. It'll give you a chance to spend some time with your son before you leave, and an opportunity to get a break from work.'

There was a brief silence at the other end of the phone.

'Perhaps you don't think you are up to it? After all, a young baby can be hard work,' she added.

'Of course I can manage,' Jamie said briskly. 'How hard can it be? If that's what you'd rather do, SJ, it's no problem. I'll bring some stuff over tonight. You can take me through his routine and I can be there when you go to work in the morning.'

As she put down the phone, Sarah felt a small smile tugging at the corner of her mouth. She rather thought that Jamie Campbell was going to get a bit of a shock. She ignored the little tingle of pleasure that accompanied the thought of Jamie being in her flat for the weekend. She was doing this for Calum, she told herself firmly. Father and son needed some time together before Jamie went away. As for her, it was nothing to do with storing up memories for the future—it was simply that she and Jamie needed to stay on friendly terms, for Calum's sake. She turned to her mother who was looking at her enquiringly.

'That's settled, Mum. You can go for your weekend. You'll have gathered that Jamie is going to come and stay while you're away.'

Sarah's mother looked thoughtful. 'Are you sure he can manage?'

'He'll have to. If he wants to be a father to Calum, he's going to have to learn how.'

The next morning, as Sarah closed the door behind her, Jamie looked at his son. Calum was sitting in his high chair, waving his spoon around. Drops of what Jamie could only think of as gunk was flying from the spoon, spreading around the kitchen.

'Hey,' he said in surprise as a splodge landed on his face. 'Good aim.' Maybe Calum was destined to be a cricket player rather than a climber with that kind of throwing technique. But how had he managed to get so much in his hair? And all over his night things?

Sarah had left Jamie a list of instructions, starting with feeding Calum his breakfast, followed by a bath, getting him dressed and then a trip to the supermarket to pick up some nappies.

As Jamie took in the chaos around him, he was beginning to get the feeling that this wasn't going to be such a piece of cake after all. Still, he had a point to prove to Sarah. And surely a man of his resourcefulness could get through the next few hours without disaster?

Two hours later, he had finally bathed and dressed Calum. That wasn't too difficult, he thought smugly. There only remained the problem of how to get himself showered. He couldn't go anywhere, not even to the supermarket, until he had cleaned off the encrusted food that seemed to cling to every part of his head. Finally he had the answer. He strapped a protesting Calum into his high chair and lifted the chair with Calum into it and set it down in front of the shower. Calum clearly thought the novel situation deserved his full attention and watched quietly as Jamie took his shower. Jamie decided against shaving. He still had the shopping to do.

Sarah and Jamie had swapped cars for the day. Jamie was just about to turn the key in the ignition when he paused. Something was missing. What had he forgotten? Calum! With a mumbled curse he shot out of the car, taking the steps to Sarah's front door two at a time. He had left Calum in the house! Luckily his son was still mesmerised by the activity bar on his cot and hadn't noticed his father's two-minute absence. The workings of the car seat was another challenge, but eventually the infant was strapped in and Jamie could set off for the shops. Hell, that was a close call, he thought as he pulled up in the car park. What on earth would Sarah have thought had he actually left without Calum? She wouldn't trust him ever again.

As Jamie shopped with Calum in the cart—it had taken him several goes until an assistant had taken pity on him and shown him which cart to use and how to place Calum in it—one or two of the female customers came up to them and, under the pretext of admiring the child, attempted to flirt with Jamie. One even went as far to ask him out. 'Sorry, I'm committed,' he told her. And as he said the words they felt good. He *was* committed to Sarah. Whatever she felt about him, he was still determined to be part of her life.

It was after six in the evening by the time Sarah arrived back from work. Jamie felt pleased with himself. He had bought the nappies and hadn't forgotten to bring Calum back with him. He had played with him and they had both managed a nap after lunch. Calum had cried when Jamie had tried to put him in his cot for his sleep so Jamie had simply stretched out on the sofa with Calum wrapped in his arms, and that had seemed to work perfectly well. The nappy-changing hadn't been an unmitigated success, he had to admit. He couldn't quite seem to get the sticky bits to go where they should but he had managed to get the nappies to stay on after a fashion and Calum hadn't seem to mind that they hadn't fitted terribly snugly. He had fed him his evening meal—a mashed-up concoction of red and white that Sarah had left—so altogether he was feeling pretty pleased with the way the day had gone.

However, when he saw the expression in Sarah's eyes as she took in the chaos that surrounded her, he realised that she wasn't entirely of the same opinion.

'What on earth happened here?' she gasped, as she removed her coat and held out her arms for her son.

Jamie followed her gaze. Food debris littered the kitchen table. Calum's clothes were scattered around the usually immaculate sitting room. He had meant to tidy up a little before she returned, but somehow he hadn't seemed to find the time. How on earth did she do it?

'I didn't notice till now,' he said with a sheepish smile, peeling himself out of the chair he'd slumped into. 'You relax there for a moment while I tidy up a bit.'

Sarah smiled. 'Don't worry, it can wait. I'm sorry I was back so late. We had a few difficult cases. Stuff that I couldn't leave. I didn't even manage lunch. That reminds me,' she said with a mischievous look at Jamie, 'what's for supper?'

Jamie hit his head with his hand. 'Supper,' he groaned, 'I'd completely forgotten. How on earth do you find the time to cook, as well as everything else?'

'Practice. But there have been days…' She let the words hang in the air.

'Right,' Jamie said, 'I'll cook, or at least order us a take-away. I think there is enough mayhem in here without adding to it. What do you fancy? Pizza? Chinese?'

'Chinese will be lovely. There's a great take-away just a short walk away. Why don't you go down and get us something while I sort things out here?'

Jamie knew better than to argue. Besides, he could do with a walk in the fresh air. By the time he returned, Sarah had restored the flat to some kind of order and Calum was ready for bed. She put him on the floor while they ate. He was just beginning to make crawling movements and they watched his attempts, fascinated.

'He'll be walking before long,' Jamie said proudly.

'In a couple of months perhaps,' Sarah said, amused. 'Gosh, I'm tired. I think I'll have a long bath once Calum goes down and then have an early night. I hope it's quiet tonight.'

'Anyone in at the moment causing concern? 'Jamie asked, and they chatted about work while Calum had his last bottle of the day.

When Sarah returned from putting Calum in his cot, Jamie had started running a bath for her. He lit a fire while she soaked and put some soft music on the stereo. He hoped the evening would provide an opportunity for him to begin wooing Sarah in earnest. And as he thought of her lying in the bath, images of her naked body filled his thoughts. But as much as he wanted her, he was determined to take it slowly. He had to convince her that his feelings were sincere.

When she eventually appeared from the bathroom with her hair wrapped up in a towel, her bathrobe pulled around her and her cheeks flushed from the heat, he almost forgot his resolve. It was all he could do to stop from striding over to her, picking her up and carrying her over to the bed.

'Would you like some coffee before bed?' he said instead.

'Not coffee. I've had too much as it is. But a hot chocolate would be lovely.'

By the time Jamie returned with the hot drink Sarah had fallen asleep on the sofa, her long legs curled up and tucked under her. Just as well, Jamie thought as he fetched a blanket from the spare room to put over her. He didn't know if he really did have the strength to resist her.

When Sarah woke up the next morning she felt a little disoriented. The last she remembered was sitting in front of the fire while she waited for Jamie to bring her the hot chocolate she had requested. But here she was in her own bed. Her cheeks flamed as she realised that Jamie must have carried her. She hadn't been wearing anything under her bathrobe and now she was completely naked under the covers.

She followed the smell of coffee into the kitchen, where Jamie was feeding a laughing Calum his breakfast. He was only wearing a pair of jeans low on his hips and his muscular chest was bare. His hair was still damp from his shower and he smelt of soap and shaving cream. He had nicked himself while shaving and she suppressed the impulse to reach out and touch his face. She averted her eyes hoping that by doing so she could banish the effect his half-naked body was having on her.

'After yesterday I thought it would be a good idea to have my shower before this little fellow woke up. Unfortunately I didn't have time to finish getting dressed when I heard him stirring.'

'Good grief. What time is it?' She glanced at her watch and was horrified to find it was almost nine. 'I should have been at work half an hour ago. Why didn't you wake me?' she accused Jamie, stopping just long enough to grab the coffee-cup out of his hand and to plant several kisses on Calum's upturned face, before heading back to the bedroom.

'Hey, no need to rush,' Jamie called after her. 'You needed to sleep. I phoned the department an hour ago, and everything's under control. You can take your time.'

Sarah didn't know whether to be grateful to Jamie or

furious with him. He had to realise that he couldn't make decisions for her. Even though he was trying to help, it wasn't up to him to decide when she should go into work. But, she admitted to herself, perhaps the real reason for her feelings of discomfort was caused by having Jamie in such close proximity. She was glad he was spending time with Calum, but having him so near, sharing the flat, was doing her own resolve to keep him at a distance no good at all. Thank goodness her mother was returning that evening and Jamie would be going back to his own place. She didn't know if she could keep her hormones under control for very much longer.

When Sarah arrived back that evening she found a completely different scenario to the one of the day before. The flat was spotless and Calum was dressed in his nightwear. The fire had been lit and delicious smells of a lamb curry were floating from the kitchen. Jamie was stirring a pot as he balanced Calum in his spare arm. Both males were looking into the pot with great interest. Calum was babbling away as if discussing the ingredients with his father.

What on earth happened here? Sarah thought immediately suspicious, shrugging off her coat. Had her mother returned early and been drafted in to help? That would be cheating. Jamie had to learn to cope on his own.

'Is my mother back?' she asked.

'Jean? Yes, she returned a short while ago. Popped in to say hello and that she'll come to see you later,' Jamie replied, handing Calum over to Sarah. 'Here, you take Calum while I take your coat and fix you a drink. You *are* finished for the evening?'

'Yes, Dr Holden has taken over. A small white wine would be lovely. If there is any?'

'There's white and red actually.'

'Have you been shopping as well as all this?' Sarah couldn't believe what she was seeing. 'Has my mother been helping?'

'Of course not.' Jamie hesitated for a moment. 'Actually, I phoned up an agency and arranged for someone to come over for a couple of hours to do some housework and shopping,' he admitted. 'Cost me an arm and a leg, what with it being Sunday and short notice, but I just don't see how it would have been possible otherwise.'

Sarah had to laugh. 'I do think that's cheating, Jamie, but what the heck—it's your money.'

'I'm sure I'll get better with practice,' he said, handing her a chilled glass of Chablis, 'but at the moment I'll take all the help I can get. Your mother did suggest she take Calum over to her for the night. She says she's missed him and would really like some time with him on her own. Do you mind?'

Sarah didn't know if she minded or not. On the one hand she hadn't seen her son for the best part of the day, on the other an occasional night off wouldn't do either of them any harm.

'Is she coming for supper?' Sarah asked. 'What is it anyway? Did you cook that yourself or has it been sent over from a deli that does outside catering?'

'I'm not completely hopeless!' Jamie protested. 'I was hoping that this needn't be for tonight, but could go in the freezer for another time. Actually, I have also taken the liberty of booking us a table at a restaurant in town.' He named a place that Sarah had heard about and had been dying to try. 'Unless you're too tired to go out?'

Making her mind up, Sarah smiled up at Jamie. 'I'd love to go out for something to eat.' She didn't tell him that she didn't know whether she could trust herself alone with him in the flat. Not without the limiting presence of Calum. Besides since the night of the wedding she hadn't left the house, apart from trips to the supermarket and the hospital. A change of scenery was needed, and time with Jamie on neutral ground would be safest.

Sarah's mother arrived a little later and, after bringing Sarah up to date with the news of her weekend, took a sleepy Calum back with her to her flat.

Jamie returned to his hospital digs to have a shave and change, while Sarah had a quick shower and applied some make-up. She knew the restaurant was quite formal and had slipped on a simple black knee-length dress that she thought would be sufficiently formal without going overboard. She twisted her hair into a French plait that emphasised the fine features of her face, and added her favourite green earrings and high heels. When the doorbell rang, signalling Jamie's return, she opened the door to his admiring wolf whistle.

Sarah resisted the impulse to wolf whistle back. He looked jaw-droppingly gorgeous, she thought. He was wearing a dark, well-tailored suit, which emphasised his lean frame, with a shirt in the palest pink and a navy tie. He looked incredibly handsome and suave. Sarah felt her heart turn over.

'You look amazing,' he said softly, his eyes gleaming. 'Are you sure you still want to go out?'

Sarah chose to ignore the meaning in his words and the look in his eyes. 'Let's go,' she said quickly.

Jamie opened the door of his sports car and Sarah sank into the soft leather seats. The car smelt of the leather and the faint tang of aftershave. Like Jamie, it was very masculine.

Jamie drove quickly and expertly and it was barely twenty minutes before they were being seated by the maître d'. Sarah took in the plush surroundings. The floor-to-ceiling windows looked over the city, its lights a diamanté bracelet of twinkling colour. The tables were laid with crisp white tablecloths and silver knives and forks. Candles cast a soft light. The restaurant was filled to capacity and the soft murmur of the other diners filled the air. Delicious smells drifted in from the kitchen. Suddenly Sarah was starving.

Jamie was an attentive and amusing dinner companion. They kept to neutral subjects, mainly about the work they shared. Jamie spoke about his work in Africa and as he spoke about the hospital, telling Sarah about the types of cases they dealt with, how children still died from malnutrition and mothers in childbirth, Sarah began to appreciate the depth of his passion for his work. He told her about Sibongele, the orphan who'd had been in the children's ward for several months. He spoke again of how the boy had developed a strong attachment to him.

'And I've grown fond of him, too. He's very bright and the mission school has offered him a scholarship. One day, with luck and hard work, he'll be working at the hospital as a doctor. All he needs right now is a little stability in his life.'

'You miss it all, don't you?' said Sarah

'Yes.' For a moment there was a far-away look in Jamie's eyes. 'It's such a beautiful country—and the people. They really appreciate the smallest thing you can do for them. It's just frustrating not to be able to do more.'

'You must be keen to get back,' Sarah prompted

'Yes, I am, although I'll miss you and Calum. Still, it won't be for ever. Anyway, let's talk about something more cheerful.'

The rest of the evening passed quickly. Jamie told her more about the places he had visited in Africa and some stories that had her laughing out loud. She couldn't remember the last time she had enjoyed herself so much. She was so busy listening to Jamie she was unaware of the waiter topping up her glass. It wasn't until they stood up that she realised the wine she had drunk had made her head swim. It had been so long since she had drunk more than a glass of wine that the extra glass or two was having the strangest effect on her. Jamie, on the other hand, had kept to mineral water as he was driving.

She was still feeling a little light-headed by the time they pulled up outside her flat. She chose to believe it was the extra alcohol that was giving her the warm glow rather than Jamie's company.

'Would you like to come up for a coffee?' she asked Jamie, not wanting the evening to come to an end just yet.

Jamie looked at her speculatively. 'Just for a moment. Just to make sure you get in OK.'

Sarah felt herself bristle. He was doing it again. Treating her as if she were some helpless female who needed looking after.

'I am perfectly able to see myself in,' she replied tartly

'Nevertheless, I'll come up for a moment.' As Sarah eased herself out of the low-slung sports car, she stumbled slightly in her high heels.

'Bloody shoes.' She grimaced, hoping she hadn't twisted her ankle.

'Come on.' Jamie laughed, getting out of the car and going to her side. 'I could always carry you up the stairs.'

'You put a hand on me, Jamie Campbell, and I'll…'

But before she could finish her threat, Jamie was advancing

towards her, a wicked glint in his eyes. 'You know I never could resist a challenge,' he said, picking her up and throwing her over his shoulder in a fireman's lift. Ignoring Sarah's beating fists, he carried her up the short flight of steps to the front door. He took the key that Sarah had given him in case of emergencies from his pocket and opened the door. Still ignoring her cries and threats, he deposited her gently on the sofa.

Sarah looked at him, eyes blazing, 'You, you Neanderthal, you!' she spat finally.

'I was only trying to help a damsel in distress!' Jamie replied, grinning broadly.

'I'm more distressed now! You could have picked me up in a more elegant fashion!' Sarah retorted, before seeing the funny side and beginning to laugh. 'Not exactly a bride being carried over the threshold, was it?' As soon as the words were out, she could have bitten her tongue.

'I mean,' she added hastily 'not really romantic.' Oh, dear, she thought, this was going from bad to worse.

'If it's romance you want…' Jamie said, pulling her up gently by her arms before finding her lips. He held her in his arms while he dropped kisses light as raindrops on her hair. Sarah took a deep breath. She knew she should pull away, but she couldn't quite bring herself to remove herself from the comfort of his arms. Just a few more minutes, she thought. He's going to be away for a while.

Jamie groaned before finding her mouth. His kisses sent sparks of desire through her body. She knew if she didn't stop him soon, she would never be able to stop. And this wasn't what she needed.

With an almost unbearable effort she pulled herself out of

his embrace and stepped back. She couldn't think coherently when she was in his arms. She needed space.

'No, Jamie,' she said, her voice tinged with regret. 'I am not going to sleep with you again—however much I want to,' she admitted. 'Good sex—OK, fantastic sex,' she conceded when he cocked his eyebrow at her, 'just isn't enough for me.'

Jamie dropped his hands to his sides. He looked at her, his brown eyes serious.

'Do you think that's all I want from you? Sex? Good God, woman, don't you know me better than that?'

'What is it you want from me, Jamie?'

'I want to be with you. Share your life. Go to sleep with you. Wake up in the morning with you. I want us to bring up our son together. Don't you know that I love you?' The last words were ground out as if ripped from his body. 'I never thought I'd ever say that to a woman. But I'm saying it now.'

For a long moment Sarah let his words sing through her body. How long had she waited to hear him say those words? But now it was too late. She still couldn't bring herself to trust him. He wanted Calum. There was no doubt in her mind about that. But she couldn't shake the thought that he would tell her he loved her, marry her even, do and say anything to achieve his own ends—to have Calum in Africa with him. She didn't doubt that he found her attractive, wanted her sexually, enough to marry her and have her with him, but lust and a need to be with his son wasn't enough for her.

'I wish I could believe you, Jamie,' she said sadly. 'But you've hurt me too much. I just can't trust you to be honest with me. You left me once. I couldn't bear for that to happen again.'

'God dammit, SJ. I've promised to come back. What else can I do to prove that I love you?'

'You're still leaving me now.'

'But only for a short while. You know I have to go back right now. But I've told you I am prepared to give it all up for you and Calum as soon as I have honoured my responsibilities. Isn't that enough?'

'And how will I know that you won't eventually resent me for that? That eventually you'll feel trapped. Come to hate me. And leave again. It's not just me. I have to think about my son.'

'*Our* son, Sarah,' Jamie reminded her. He looked at her calmly. 'OK, you win for now, but when I come back I'm going to do whatever it takes to convince you that you and I belong together. You can't hold out on me for ever. I won't let you. That's one thing you can count on.' He kissed her lightly on the lips. 'Look after yourself and our child until I get back.'

When he had gone Sarah stood for a while. Thoughts rushed through her mind. He had said he loved her, wanted to spend his life with her. What was wrong with her that she couldn't believe him when every nerve in her body was straining towards him? And how was she going to live without him?

CHAPTER TEN

SARAH missed Jamie in the weeks that he was away. Dr Shepherd was an excellent colleague, but Sarah had to admit it just wasn't the same as having Jamie around.

He phoned a few times to enquire after Calum, but he had warned Sarah that getting access to international calls was difficult with the rather antiquated phone system that the hospital used. He sounded exhilarated when he spoke briefly about his work at the hospital. The way he described it made Sarah want to see the place for herself.

She knew that Jamie was due back for a short visit at the weekend, but he was unsure how soon he'd be able to catch a flight from London. His mother had moved to the South of England to be closer to her sister and Jamie planned to spend a night with her *en route* to Scotland.

So she was surprised and secretly delighted on a Sunday evening to answer the door and find Jamie there. He looked lean and fit and she felt her heart turn over.

'Hi,' he said, grinning down at her.

He had caught the sun in the last few weeks and his teeth flashed white against the light tan on his face. Sarah could feel the energy and vitality emanating from him. It was as if his time in Africa had recharged him.

'I hope you don't mind, I just wanted to look in on Calum before I went home. I know he's probably asleep, but just a few minutes?'

Sarah stood back from the door to let him come in. Her legs felt shaky at the sight of him. How she had missed him. She hadn't realised how much until she'd seen him standing before her.

They stole into the nursery. Jamie looked down at his sleeping son and bent slightly to touch his cheek with a gentle finger.

'He's grown since I've been away,' he said, regret tinging his voice. 'SJ, I really don't want to miss another minute of his life. I've missed too much already.' He turned towards Sarah, a wicked glint in his eyes. 'And I missed you, too. Did you miss me? Even a little?'

'We missed you at work. The new consultant is excellent but…' Jamie cocked an eyebrow, encouraging a reluctant Sarah to finish. 'But he's not you,' she admitted finally. 'I kind of got used to working with you again.'

'You only missed me at work?' Jamie raised a disbelieving eyebrow. 'Are you sure? Well, I'm back for a week and I plan spend as much time with Calum as I can. Would it be all right if I came over in the evenings to see him before bedtime? And perhaps we could have some time as a family next weekend? We can take Calum to the zoo or wherever kids like to go when they're his age?'

Sarah couldn't help the pang of disappointment she felt at his words. It was good, of course it was, that he wanted to spend time with her *and* Calum, but if she was honest she'd thought he'd be keen to spend time with her alone.

When he saw Sarah's crestfallen expression Jamie felt a flicker of triumph. She wasn't as good at hiding her feelings as she'd thought. But he wasn't going to play games with her. He knew he had to be straight with her if she was ever going to trust him.

'Perhaps we could get a babysitter at the weekend? So you and I can have some grown-up time together?' Noting her small smile, he added, 'But not too grown-up, eh?'

Sarah blushed. Damn him! How was he able to read her mind so easily?

'How do you fancy a climb? It'll be like old times. I'm sure Jean won't mind looking after Calum for the day.' Sarah couldn't help the treacherous leap her heart gave at the thought of spending the day with Jamie. They needed to remain friends, she told herself. After all, he was the father of her child and it was important that they got on, even if they didn't live together. However, she suspected she was kidding herself.

True to his word, Jamie came around every evening and most of the days to spend time with Calum. He also arranged for he and Sarah to spend the next Saturday climbing one of the Munros outside Fort William. The day dawned cool but crisp. The sun shone weakly. It was perfect weather for their climb.

Sarah had rescued her box of climbing gear from the attic the night before, brushing dust off her boots, which hadn't been worn since she and Jamie had last climbed together.

Getting ready that morning, she shook the creases out of her red down-filled jacket and packed the rest of her gear into a small back pack, along with a Thermos of coffee and emergency provisions. When Jamie arrived to collect her, looking ruggedly handsome in his navy mountaineer gear, he insisted on rechecking her harness and ropes.

Satisfied that they had everything necessary, Jamie stood up. 'I don't anticipate that we'll be needing all this gear, but rather safe than sorry,' he said, turning his scrutiny to Sarah. Gently he tucked her fringe under her thermal hat and nodded his approval.

Ignoring the frisson of desire she felt at his touch, she said warningly, 'Jamie—you're doing it again!'

Raising an eyebrow and smiling broadly, Jamie asked with feigned innocence, 'Doing what again, SJ?'

'You know damn well. Treating me like a child. Don't you have any faith in my ability to prepare adequately?'

Jamie held up his hands in mock submission, before turning serious. 'Sorry. But I can't help it—you know how precious you are to me.'

Suppressing the warmth his words gave her, Sarah said briskly. 'Right, let's get going.'

'The weather is forecast to break later today, 'Jamie cautioned as they drove. 'So I want to be off the hill well before it gets dark. We're turning back early this afternoon, whether we've made the summit or not.'

'Fine by me,' Sarah acquiesced. 'I've no plans to spend the night freezing on a mountain.'

Although they chatted comfortably on the way up to Glencoe, there was a sexual tension between them that was palpable. Sarah sneaked glances at Jamie's profile, all too aware of his nearness in the small space of the sports car. When his hand brushed against her leg as he changed gear,

Sarah felt charges of electricity course through her body. It was almost a relief to her when they made good time and arrived at the base of the mountain before ten o'clock.

When they got to the top, they ate a picnic of pitta bread sandwiches and hot coffee that Sarah had brought. Jamie found a flat stone near the cairn that marked the summit for them to sit on. The air was a lot colder at the unprotected top, and already clouds were beginning to scud across the sky. Sarah snuggled deeper into her jacket.

Jamie, noticing her shiver, sat behind her and stretched his long legs on either side of hers. He wrapped strong arms around her frame and pulled her close into the embrace of his body. For a moment she resisted before she let herself sink against him, her body absorbing the heat that radiated from him. She felt safe and protected in his arms. She felt his lips brush the top of her head like a whisper.

'I missed you,' Jamie said, his voice deep with emotion. 'Are you sure you didn't miss me? Even the teeniest bit?' he teased.

'I missed you at work.' Sarah repeated the words she had used before. She wasn't ready yet to trust him. Not while there was the slightest chance he was using her to get to Calum.

'Just at work?' Jamie mocked her. 'I see I'll have to do a little bit better.' Gently he turned her face towards him before bringing his lips down hard on hers. She shifted her body to kiss him back. All the weeks and months of missing him were in the kiss. When they eventually broke apart, they were both breathing heavily.

'If it weren't so cold up here, I would—'

'Just as well,' Sarah said primly, a small smile belying her words.

'Let's get you home, then,' Jamie said, his voice heavy with meaning. 'But first I have something to ask you.' He pulled her gently to her feet. He tipped her chin with a long finger so that she was forced to look into his eyes. 'Sarah Jane Carruthers, will you do me the honour of becoming my wife?'

Sarah looked at him, her eyes luminous with unshed tears. Was she about to make the biggest mistake of her life? She thought she probably was, but was powerless to prevent herself. It was as if there were a little demon inside her head, shouting, *Don't do it. You know he's just the same as all men. Remember your father. He told you he loved you, that he'd always be there for you. And he never was—no matter how many times you believed him.* 'I'm sorry, Jamie. I can't say yes. Not yet.'

He let his hands fall to her shoulders. He shook her gently. 'What is it, SJ? Do you need more time?'

She bowed her head in her misery. 'When you left that first time I felt as if something inside me had broken. Something that could never be fixed. The terrible aching loss I felt reminded me of all the times that my father had left me, promising to return. And, of course, he never did—even though he promised. So I built up a shield to protect the child that I was. And when you left, I found that I needed that shield again.'

Jamie listened intently.

'And then when I found out I was pregnant, at first I was terrified.' She raised bleak eyes to his. 'How would I cope? Would I be enough for my child? Didn't every child deserve two loving parents?'

Jamie cursed savagely under his breath and she knew she had hit a nerve. He pulled her into his arms and she let her head rest against his chest.

'Go on,' he encouraged gently.

'Then when I thought there might be something wrong with the baby… I had a raised Down's risk when I was sixteen weeks pregnant, you know?'

'I didn't. At least, not until I overheard you telling the lady with the Down's syndrome child. My God, SJ, I wish I had been there for you.' Jamie's voice was deep with regret.

'It was so hard.' The words began to spill out from Sarah as she remembered the loneliness of having to make those decisions on her own. Of course, her mother had been there and had been a tremendous support, but it hadn't been the same as having the father of her child there beside her. 'I knew that whatever might be wrong, whatever the future might bring, I wanted my child. And at least there would be a part of you that would always belong to me, that no one could take away from me. So I made up my mind to continue the pregnancy. But I also decided that I would never love another man. That from then on, my child would be my life and, apart from my work, my world. We wouldn't rely on anyone else. I had all I needed.'

'I'll never forgive myself for leaving you. I was stupid, selfish, I can see that now, but can't we put the past behind us and start again? I promise you that I will never let you or Calum down again.' His voice was raw with his need to convince her.

Sarah shook her head. 'I don't think so. I wish I could say differently, but I can't. It wouldn't be fair to pretend otherwise.'

He shook her again. 'Won't you at least take a chance? Give me the chance to prove that I love you, that I want you with me? And not just because I want my son?'

'I can't. I'm sorry.' Her voice trembled with the pain. Pain she knew she was inflicting on both of them. But somehow the thought of more pain in the future was worse.

'Damn it, Sarah. I'm only human. Nothing in this life is certain. You and I both know that. Where is the Sarah I used to know? The woman who took risks? Who loved life enough never to hide from it?'

'I don't know. I think she disappeared when you left her that first time.'

'Then I'm sorry, SJ. You're not the woman I thought you were. I can't keep pursuing you if you are never going to change your mind. I'll be back as soon as I can to be with Calum and obviously we'll have to stay in contact as his parents, but apart from that…' He let the words hang in the air. Sarah knew she couldn't blame him. If she couldn't give him what he wanted then she had to set him free to get on with his own life. She supposed she owed him that at least.

'I won't stop you from seeing Calum,' she said through lips that were numb from the effort of holding back the tears.

'I won't let you,' he said. 'I can't make you be with me, but neither can you prevent me from being with my child. Or him being with me.' His voice was flat. Sarah knew she had hurt him, but she also knew that he was angry and confused. Soft flakes of snow began to fall and the sun disappeared behind a cloud. The snow seemed to muffle the outside world until it felt as if nothing else existed except the two of them. The light began to leak from the sky.

'We'd better get back down,' Jamie said.

It was still snowing gently when they reached the bottom of the hill. They had been silent on their journey down, each preoccupied with their own thoughts. There were several other climbers in the car park who had come down from other hills. They exchanged comments about the weather with them as they changed out of their boots in preparation for the journey home.

The snow began to fall in earnest as they drove along the steep and winding road that passed through Glencoe. The snow and clouds made visibility poor and Jamie concentrated on his driving. Sarah knew there was nothing left to say.

Suddenly and without warning the car in front of them skidded on one of the sharp bends. It bounced into the crash barrier before hitting the car in front of it, sending the vehicle straight towards the steep drop at the side of the road.

As Jamie brought his car to a controlled stop, the car that had been hit slammed into the damaged bit of the crash barrier. Sarah and Jamie held their breaths as they hoped the barrier would hold the car. They could make out the shapes of the two passengers—the driver, a young man whose face was stretched in horror, and a child, strapped into a car seat in the back. Jamie pulled his car to the side of the road just as, with a sickening screech of metal, the car tore through the barrier and slid over the side of the road, disappearing from view.

Jamie and Sarah were out of the car almost before it had come to a complete stop.

The car that had caused the accident also pulled over and two young men jumped out, the driver clearly in shock.

'I couldn't stop from hitting them,' he kept repeating. 'Can you see the car? Are they all right?'

'Here,' said Jamie, opening his car boot and removing a couple of triangular warning signs. He shoved them into the hands of the driver. 'Take these and put them a little way up the road to warn oncoming cars that there's been an accident.' He turned to the passenger. 'Phone for an ambulance and the fire brigade.' And then, as the men stood rooted the spot, he ordered, 'Move it!'

His tone was enough to galvanise them into action. Sarah and Jamie ran to the side of the road. Sarah felt dread close her throat as she peered over the edge. She thought it was unlikely that anyone could have survived the drop. But as they looked, they could see that by some miracle the car had been stopped by an overhang about a third of the way down the slope. In the fading light they could just make out the faint line of a body lying a few metres away from the wrecked vehicle.

'It looks like the driver has been thrown out. That means the child is still in the car,' Sarah told Jamie.

'We need to get down to them,' Jamie said tersely.

'It's too dangerous,' Sarah protested. The slope was too steep to scramble down. The only way the occupants of the car could be reached was by someone climbing up towards them from the bottom. But that would take time. 'The rescue services should be here shortly.'

But Jamie was already emptying his car boot of the climbing ropes he had brought with him. 'I'm going down.' He said. 'We don't know how long the emergency services will take. I need to assess their injuries. We don't know how badly they are hurt. If we wait, it could be too late.'

As Jamie spoke, one of the men called out. 'There's smoke coming from the car!'

Sarah felt fear close her throat. If the car was on fire, it could explode.

'I'm coming with you,' she said, already beginning to slip on her harness.

'No, you're not! It's too dangerous. The car could go at any time.'

'For the last time, Jamie Campbell, stop telling me what to do.' But Sarah smiled wanly to take the sting out of her words.

Jamie gripped her by the shoulders. 'Good God, woman, think of Calum. He needs his mother.' For a moment a look of anguish crossed his face. 'And I need his mother.' For a moment he brushed her ear with his lips. 'I love you, SJ. I couldn't bear it if anything happened to you.' Jamie looked at her steadily for a long moment. Then, reading the determination in her expression, he made a decision.

'You always were the most stubborn woman. OK, we don't have time to argue. You head for the driver and I'll head for the car. Here, let me check your gear.'

Despite everything, Sarah felt her heart soar. There was no mistaking the expression in those eyes. He did love her. Of course he did. She knew it now—there was no more doubt in her mind!

Sarah tried to open her mouth to tell him that she loved him, too. So very, very much. But as she tried to form the words, Jamie began issuing instructions to her, pointing out the best route for her to take to get to the injured man.

Sarah slipped over the side as Jamie held the rope for her. Within a minute or two she was beside the driver of the car. The man was conscious, though clearly in a lot of pain.

'My daughter. Is she all right?'

'How many of you were in the car?' Sarah asked, dimly aware of Jamie passing her on the way to the car.

'Just me and Ruth. My three-year-old. Where is she? I couldn't control the car.' The man started to moan with pain and fear.

'Jamie—just one other occupant in the car. A little girl.' Sarah called out. Jamie acknowledged her with a lift of his hand. Sarah could see that the smoke from the car was getting thicker. Red flames licked at the car bonnet. The sound of a child's terror and rage filled the air.

'Everything is going to be just fine,' Sarah soothed, checking her patient. Apart from a fractured femur and a few cuts and bruises, he appeared remarkably unharmed. Trying to ignore the burning wreck below her, she strapped his legs together and made him as comfortable as possible. All she could do now was wait for the emergency services to remove the man safely.

She glanced up to see the anxious faces of the bystanders looking towards the car.

Jamie was half in and half out of the back door. The flames were getting bigger by the minute. What on earth was taking him so long? He seemed to be struggling to remove something from the back seat. Was the child pinned in the seat? Sarah felt her blood run cold. Surely there was only a minute or two before it exploded. She knew with a dread that froze her blood that Jamie would never leave the child.

If anything happened to Jamie, she couldn't bear it. How could she have been so stupid? Why had she wasted so much time? Time that they could have been together. Whatever the future brought, she needed to be with Jamie. She, Jamie and Calum together. That was her life, her future, her destiny. She knew now with absolute certainty that Jamie loved her, and not just because she was the mother of his child. He had been prepared to give up everything for her and Calum—to be a permanent part of their lives. He had put his own needs and dreams to one side. And still she hadn't trusted him. What if she lost him now? Before she told him how she felt about him? She closed her eyes and took a couple of deep breaths. She couldn't let herself think like that. She needed to concentrate. Work out how to help him.

He was still struggling to pull the child from the wreckage. Sarah knew she had to go to him. She couldn't stand by and do nothing.

'I'll be back as soon as I can,' she told the driver. 'Just a little longer and we'll have you out of here.'

It only took a few seconds until she was almost down by the car. She could hear the crackle of flames and smell the acrid smoke. In the distance she could hear the sounds of sirens.

Jamie must have sensed her approach. 'Sarah, get out of here!'

'What's wrong? What's taking so long? Why aren't you getting the hell out of there?' she yelled.

'The seat belt's jammed. I can't get the child or its seat out of the car. Don't come any closer.'

Sarah ignored him and slithered the few inches towards him. 'Here.' She handed him her climbing knife. 'Try this.'

'Thanks!' Jamie said 'Now, get going.'

Reluctantly Sarah moved to a safe distance. There was nothing more she could do. She sent a prayer heavenwards.

She heard Jamie's yell of triumph as the girl came loose. Cocooning the child in his arms, he turned away from the car and edged along sideways. As Sarah watched him make his painstakingly slow way, there was a sudden whoosh and the car exploded, rocking the surroundings with the blast. Sarah's heart stopped as she cried out his name.

'Jamie!'

As the smoke cleared she could make out the still form of Jamie lying on the ground. There was no sign of the child. Tears running down her cheeks, Sarah scrambled her way back down the slope, loose gravel causing sharp spasms of pain through her trousers like the sharp bites of tiny predators. She was barely aware of voices calling to her, telling her to stay where she was. She ignored them. She had to get to Jamie. He needed her. One of the rescue team arrived just as she got to Jamie, whose still body showed no sign of life. He had sheltered the child from the worst of the blast with his body. Judging by her loud wails, she seemed to be in one piece.

She shook him roughly. 'Jamie, wake up. Please—I need you. For God's sake don't leave me—I love you.'

Jamie came to slowly. The noise of the blast still rang in his ears. He couldn't hear anything else. Dimly aware of being shaken, he struggled to open his eyes. He saw Sarah bending over him. She was shouting at him. *Typical* he thought. *I'm half-dead and she's still finding something to complain about.*

He looked at her. He saw her lips moving. Tears were cascading down her face. Could he be hearing things? Had the blast addled his brains on top of everything else, or was she really telling him she loved him, would never leave him?

Twenty long minutes later Jamie was being stretchered into the ambulance along with the driver and his daughter. The ambulance would be taking them to the local hospital, from where Jamie would be airlifted to Glasgow if necessary.

He opened his eyes as the paramedics were securing his stretcher.

'Is the child all right?' he asked Sarah.

'She's fine. Frightened but fine. How are you?'

'I'll live.' He smiled painfully. He reached out a hand to Sarah and clasped hers in a surprisingly strong grip. 'You'll have to marry me now.'

'I suppose I will.' Sarah smiled down at him, her eyes awash with tears. 'I guess it's the only way I can keep you from doing crazy things.'

'At least life will never be boring for us,' Jamie murmured, before he lapsed once more into unconsciousness.

Sarah stood at the side of the ship, holding Calum's hand. A few more hours and they'd be docking in Cape Town. From there they would be taking a flight to Johannesburg, before completing the rest of their journey by car. Although she felt a little apprehensive when she thought about the future, she knew with absolute certainty she had made the right decision. The hospital had been sympathetic to her request to take an eighteen-month sabbatical. Especially when she'd been able to convince them that the husband-and-wife team would be perfect locums for the time that she and Jamie would be away. Just thinking of Jamie brought a smile to her lips. While he had recovered in hospital, they had talked for hours, discussing their hopes and dreams. She had realised that Jamie needed to be back in Africa, that he still had work to do there, and had decided that she and Calum would go with him. Her job would be kept open for her.

She felt warm arms enfold her.

'No regrets?' Jamie asked, nibbling her ear.

'None. There's plenty of time for me to be a consultant. This way I can spend more time with Calum. And anyway…' she laughed '…how could I possibly not go to Africa? I have to see this place you love so much for myself.'

'And you're sure you don't mind Sibongele living with us?'

'How could I? I know that Calum and I are always going to have to share you. But somehow I think there is enough love in this family to have some to spare.'

Jamie bent down and scooped his son into his arms before he made his escape. He had just started to toddle in the months leading up to their departure and was constantly trying out his new-found freedom.

'They'll be no more running away, Calum,' Jamie said with mock severity. He looked at Sarah, locking her eyes with his. 'For any of us. Ever again.'

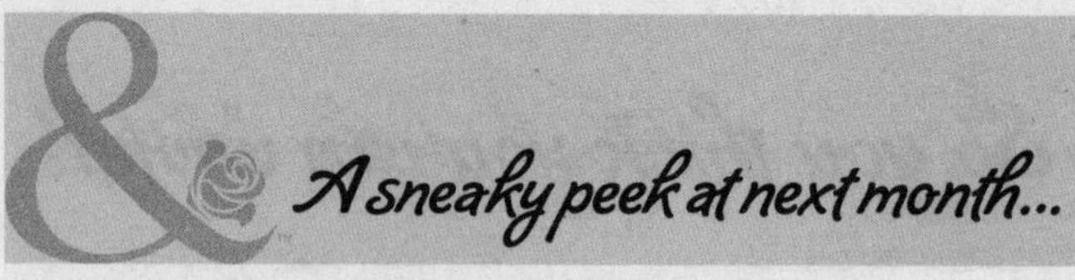
A sneaky peek at next month...

By Request

RELIVE THE ROMANCE WITH THE BEST OF THE BEST

My wish list for next month's titles...

In stores from 21st September 2012:

- ❑ Mistress to the Mediterranean Male – Carole Mortimer, Diana Hamilton & Kathryn Ross
- ❑ The Equalisers – Debra Webb

3 stories in each book - only £5.99!

In stores from 5th October 2012:

- ❑ The Garrisons: Parker, Brittany & Stephen – Roxanne St. Claire, Sara Orwig & Anna DePalo

Available at WHSmith, Tesco, Asda, Eason, Amazon and Apple

Just can't wait?

Visit us Online

You can buy our books online a month before they hit the shops! **www.millsandboon.co.uk**

0912/05